12 years

12 years
my messed-up love story

CHETAN BHAGAT

HARPER FICTION

An Imprint of HarperCollins Publishers

First published in India by Harper Fiction 2025
An imprint of HarperCollins *Publishers*
HarperCollins *Publishers* India, Cyber City,
Building 10-A, Gurugram, Haryana – 122002, India
www.harpercollins.co.in

2 4 6 8 10 9 7 5 3 1

Copyright © Chetan Bhagat 2025

P-ISBN: 978-93-6989-687-5
E-ISBN: 978-93-6989-544-1

This is a work of fiction, contains mature themes, and is intended for mature readers. There are brief references of mental health struggles including suicide, as part of the narrative. The book does not endorse such actions. Reader discretion is advised. The narrative context provides sufficient literary or thematic justification for such content. All characters and incidents described in this book are the product of the author's imagination. Any resemblance to actual persons, living or dead, is entirely coincidental. The characters, situations, and community references are created in a light, humorous vein and are not intended to offend or disrespect any individual, group, or religious community.

Chetan Bhagat asserts the moral right
to be identified as the author of this work.

All rights reserved. No part of this publication may be reproduced, stored in a retrieval system, or transmitted, in any form or by any means, electronic, mechanical, photocopying, recording or otherwise, without the prior permission of the publishers.

Without limiting the exclusive rights of any author, contributor or the publisher of this publication, any unauthorized use of this publication to train generative artificial intelligence (AI) technologies is expressly prohibited. HarperCollins also exercise their rights under Article 4(3) of the Digital Single Market Directive 2019/790 and expressly reserve this publication from the text and data-mining exception.

Typeset in 11/14.5 Minion Pro
by HarperCollins *Publishers* India Pvt. Ltd

Printed and bound at
Replika Press Pvt. Ltd.

This book is produced from independently certified FSC® paper to ensure responsible forest management.

HarperCollins Publishers, Macken House, 39/40 Mayor Street Upper, Dublin 1, D01 C9W8, Ireland

To those who I might have hurt or disappointed unintentionally.

Micchami Dukkadam.

I seek your forgiveness.

Also by Chetan Bhagat

FICTION

400 Days
The Girl in Room 105
One Arranged Murder

NON-FICTION

India Positive: Simple Takes on India's Burning Issues
11 Rules for Life: Secrets to Level Up

PROLOGUE

*M*umbai *is a vibrant city full of options. However, it offers limited choices when it comes to committing suicide. You can do the usual—slit your wrists, hang from a ceiling fan or pop a handful of sleeping pills—but none of these have the essence of Mumbai in them. These options are also somewhat lame. Nobody would even notice. She wouldn't notice. And neither would her parents.*

I wanted to go out with a bang, literally. I wanted her to see how she had wrecked, shredded, ground and crushed my heart when she left.

Maybe the Bandra–Worli Sea Link? That's dramatic enough to make the headlines: 'Saket Khurana, thirty-four-year-old struggling stand-up comedian jumps off the Bandra–Worli Sea Link after getting dumped.'

She will care then, won't she?

Except that the stupid Sea Link isn't high enough. What if I don't die? What if I fall those fifty-odd feet into the sea, and the Koli fishermen who live nearby rescue me? Then they would become the heroes of the story instead: 'Koli fishermen save failed stand-up comedian, unsuccessful in his marriage, career, love and suicide attempt.'

No, that wouldn't work. She'd probably become even more convinced that dumping me was the right decision.

PART I
MUMBAI

'No, Mudit, my brother, please. Next weekend. I promise,' I said, folding my hands.

We were backstage at the Crayon Club, and I had three minutes left before going on stage.

Mudit, my best friend and the owner of the club, remained unmoved. His thin, wiry frame belied his strong, authoritative tone. 'No, Saket. Listen to me. You go on stage. Now,' he said.

'Bro, listen—' I said, sweat breaking out from every pore of my body.

'Go!' Mudit said, cutting me off and pointing at the stage.

I froze.

'You've told me a million times that this is your passion. You left everything for this,' Mudit said.

I looked at him, still unable to move.

'Come on, Saket. You're nearly six feet tall. Look at these biceps and these abs. And *you* are scared to crack a few jokes?'

'Our next act, ladies and gentlemen'—I heard the emcee's voice from the stage—'is someone new. Well, he's not exactly new on this planet. He's thirty-three. This means, in the normal world, he's middle-aged. But in the world of stand-up comics, he's a senior citizen. So let's all pay our respects with a big round of applause for our newest and oldest comic today, Saket Khurana.'

I whispered a silent prayer and slow-jogged to the stage. The Crayon Club has a small, intimate auditorium, no larger than a college lecture hall, meant for shows like mine. An audience of about seventy people had their eyes on me. I took a deep breath.

Come on, Saket, you got this.

'Hello, Mumbai.' I opened my act.

Nothing in response. An eerie silence, equivalent to death for a stand-up comedian.

'I know what you all are thinking. When did bouncers become stand-up comics, huh?' I said, pointing to my muscular biceps. 'Well, the management here is cool. The club owner said he no longer needed a bodyguard, so I could take a shot at the stage here.'

A few chuckles in the room. Okay, okay, not bad, keep going.

'You know, talking of the stage, I was that guy in school who always got picked for the same role in the school plays: Bheem.'

A few laughs. Good, go on.

'Did you guys ever take part in school plays?'

Some nods in the audience.

'There are only two or three plays that are performed in our schools every year. One is the Independence Day type of play. There's always one fixed Gandhiji—the same poor kid who's chosen every year. Someone thin and scrawny, with a bald wig pulled over his head. He has to bend and walk and recite the same dialogues year after year: "Ahimsa is the best way. Non-violence is the right path." They play patriotic music in the background—"Vande Mataram" mostly. It's all awesome, India is achieving freedom, and it's all happening on stage. But bro, behind the stage there is pandemonium. A teacher is going crazy. She has lost her freedom. She's trying to coordinate all the kids and time their entry on stage. She's screaming. I remember our dramatics teacher, Mrs Dutta, shouting, "Oye, Gandhiji kahan hai? Bathroom? Yeh time hai bathroom jaane ka?"'

Laughter in the audience. Phew.

'Gandhiji arrives, Class III-B student Manish Verma, tackling a dhoti he's clearly not comfortable with. Mrs Dutta pulls his ear. Slaps him. "Where did you vanish? Now go on stage or you'll get one more thappad."'

More laughter.

'Clearly, nobody backstage cares about ahimsa or non-violence. Gandhiji, scared of Mrs Dutta, runs out onto the stage to show his fearlessness against the British. "Now where is Subhas Chandra Bose?" Mrs Dutta screams behind the curtains. "Arrey, button up your shirt quickly and wear your cap. And go."'

And there it is, my first full-blown audience-bursting-into-laughter moment. Roll with it, Saket.

'The other play we often did was the Mahabharata. And, like I said earlier, there's that one giant kid in every grade'—I held the mic in one hand and, rolling up the sleeve of my T-shirt, flexed my biceps—'who's perfect for one and only one part: Bheem. That's me, people. I am Bheem.'

Ha ha ha. Some of the laughs were louder than the rest.

'You just know the batch Bheem. He's an outlier in height and weight. Big and born for the role. No matter how sensitive he is, how funny he is, or how deep and emotional he is. Nobody cares about his acting skills. Nobody even cares if he wants to do the part in the first place—he simply has to do it. Because given his frame, he is Bheem. This year, next year and every other year until he leaves school. I was Bheem for six years. It was my entire childhood. This one time, I went up to Mrs Dutta and said, "Ma'am, next year we're doing *Cinderella*. May I take part in it?" And Mrs Dutta was like, "As what? The prince? Have you gone mad? You are Bheem. There's no Bheem in *Cinderella*. Saket, you can take part in any play as long as you do the role of Bheem." I protested. I yelled. I fought. But like all Bheems when upset, I was handed this universal line: "Shaant, gadadhaari Bheem, shaant.'"

The audience burst into laughter again. I had momentum now. I shifted acts.

'You guys take flights, right?'

Many in the audience nodded and said yes.

'Which class? Business or economy?' I said.

'Economy,' most of the audience said in unison.

'Business,' a female voice came from somewhere in the first row.

'Wow, who's this rich princess over here?' I said, my eyes searching for her in the dim light.

Giggles from the audience.

She sat in the front row, fourth seat from the left. A young, attractive woman in her early twenties. Long hair, glowing complexion and deep-brown eyes that gleamed even in the low light. Her beauty distracted me.

Crowd-work time. Focus, Saket.

'So, madam, you travel business class?'

'Sometimes,' she said.

'You're a princess then. Let me guess, daddy's princess? Papa ki pari?'

Everyone laughed, except her. She looked annoyed.

'No, I travel business class for work,' she said, tucking a strand of hair behind her ear.

'Oh, work. Okay, well, someone has a real job here. What work do you do, young lady?'

'I'm in private equity,' she said.

Collective sighs of admiration.

'What?' I laughed. 'I used to work in private equity earlier. I ran away to do comedy to avoid meeting private-equity people. And here we go.'

The sweet sound of laughter from the crowd.

She shrugged and half-smiled.

I turned to speak to the entire audience. 'Apart from a few special people, we all fly economy, right? Yes, I do too. I'm a cheap bastard. Plus, my soon-to-be ex-wife bankrupted me, so I have no choice.'

Chuckles in the audience.

'Here's the weird thing—if you're flying economy, they make you walk through business class, and even first class, before you get to your seat. And when you reach your seat, you know it sucks. Because you've already seen the fully reclining seats and the pomegranate juice and the champagne. You imagine the business-class people doing their hot-towel facials. Meanwhile, you're struggling to put your backpack in the overhead bin, fighting for space with aunties carrying ten-kilo atta packets to their destination. I mean, why make us, the poor economy-class types, walk through first and business class? It's like living in Dharavi and having to pass through Antilia to get to your house. "Hello, rich people. Nice fluffy blanket, people. Amazing champagne, people. Enjoy. Now bye-bye since I can't afford this. And yes, I'm poor." I mean, what the hell. Can't it be the opposite? Make the business-class folks walk through that narrow aisle, past those cramped seats, so when they reach their own seats, they find them extra amazing? Right now, it's like walking through a five-star hotel to get to your Oyo room, bro.'

Audience laughter.

Mudit, standing in the corner, gave me a thumbs-up.

I proceeded to the concluding part of my act.

'Now, what's the deal with Jain food? Any Jains in the audience here?'

A man in the fifth row and the same private-equity girl raised their hands.

'You? Again?' I said, turning to her.

Scattered titters in the crowd.

'They're going to think I planted you,' I said.

'What to do? I'm Jain,' she said.

'Me Tarzan, you Jane?' I said. Okay, that was a bad recycled joke.

Nobody laughed. I deserved that deathly silence.

'What's your name again?' I asked.

'Payal. Payal Jain,' she said.

'Like James Bond. Imagine if *he* was Jain,' I said, and switched to a James Bond impersonation. 'Hi, I am Jain. James Jain. One Martini, shaken not stirred, with no onion and garlic, please.'

This unscripted line wasn't the best joke. However, the audience still laughed.

'Jains definitely go to heaven, by the way. Yes, they do. Just hear me out on this,' I said. 'See, we Punjabis eat non-veg. We're surely going to hell. Then there are the vegetarians, who get the lower levels of heaven. The vegans are above that. And then there are the purest of the entire lot—the Jains—who get the best spots in heaven. Like sea-view apartments, with the top heaven contenders as neighbours. Maybe like right next to Anna Hazare and Mother Teresa.'

Payal giggled. The audience did as well.

'So, Payal, congrats on getting prime heaven real estate. However, you do realize that most of the fun people will not be in heaven, right? The party people will be down in hell. Drinkers, gamblers and the gossips. All us fun people will be hanging out in hell. Sure, we won't have air conditioning. The food and the booze will be low-quality and awful. But boy, we will party. The Jains, meanwhile, they will have to hang out with Anna Hazare. He'll be like, "Come, beta, it's pravachan and satsang time again." Dude, hell sounds way better.'

Someone in the audience clapped. I proceeded to my closing.

'I'm definitely going to hell for tonight, and so are many of you for laughing at my jokes. Okay, that's it from me tonight. This is Saket Khurana, and I love you all for being a wonderful audience and encouraging me in my first show.'

Applause and cheers erupted as I left the stage.

Mudit high-fived me as I reached backstage. 'Let's go to the bar and celebrate this,' he said.

~

'You did it,' Mudit said, handing me a glass of tequila and soda.

The Crayon Bar is located right outside the auditorium, for the audience to hang out in after a show. According to Mudit, the bar brings in more revenue than the actual gigs do.

'Was I good?' I asked Mudit as I took a sip of the tequila. 'I thought I could've done better.'

'We all think that way. But not bad at all for your first show.'

'That girl,' I said, 'I tried crowd work there. Not sure if I should've.'

'That was good,' Mudit said. 'You got lucky. She was sporting enough. And the audience liked your spontaneous banter. The James Jain bit was made up on the spot, right?'

I nodded. 'I hope she's not too upset.'

'It's okay. She's come to a comedy club. She can't be that thin-skinned,' Mudit said. 'Oh, there she is.'

Mudit pointed to the other end of the bar. Payal stood there, three or four inches over five feet, petite and gorgeous in a black dress. Two guys in formal suits stood with her.

'She didn't like the daddy's-princess comment, I think,' I said.

'Let's ask her. Never hurts to check on the customers,' Mudit said.

Before I could respond, he pulled me by my hand and made his way to the trio. I followed him along.

'Did you guys enjoy the show?' Mudit said, walking up to Payal and her companions.

The three of them turned around to look at us.

'Hi, I'm Mudit. This is my club. And this is Saket; you just saw him on stage,' Mudit said.

'Hi Mudit. And hi Saket,' one of the men said. 'We had a great time.'

I tilted my head, keeping it cool.

They introduced themselves. The younger-looking one was Nimit, and the older one Jagdish. All three of them worked at Blackwater, a major global private equity firm.

'You sure made Payal famous today,' Nimit said, smiling.

I turned to Payal. 'Hi Payal. I came over to say thanks,' I said.

'For what?' Payal's pleasant voice was neither too high nor too low.

'For being a sport. And for not getting offended,' I said.

'I've come here before, and I've seen audience roasts. This was tame,' Payal said.

'Ouch,' I said. 'Clearly, am not that good.'

'You were pretty good,' Mudit said, slapping my back. 'So, Nimit, any investing interest in comedy clubs with an F&B angle?'

'Ooh, business time,' I said, pretending to look at my watch.

'Always,' Mudit said.

Everyone laughed. As Mudit ushered everyone towards an empty table, I saw Payal clearly for the first time. Could a person's skin be made of jasmine petals? I tried not to stare.

'Scalable?' Nimit was saying to Mudit.

'Definitely. And scalable to various cities. Would you guys like me to show you the club? I'm planning a restaurant too,' Mudit said.

'I have to leave, actually,' Jagdish said. 'Nimit can have a look. Bye, guys, see you in office tomorrow.'

After Jagdish left, Mudit turned to Payal and me and said, 'We'll return in just ten minutes, okay? Come, Nimit, this way.'

Without waiting for a reply, Mudit whisked Nimit away, leaving Payal and me alone at the table. In the silence that followed, Payal took a sip of her white wine. I smiled.

'What? Some joke about Jains not drinking or something?' Payal said.

I shook my head. 'Wine is veg. No onion, no garlic either, so it should be okay,' I said.

'True that,' she said. We lifted our glasses and did a 'cheers'.

'I used to work in private equity too,' I said.

'Which firm?'

'Yellowstone Capital.'

'Oh, they have an office in Mumbai?'

'In San Francisco. I moved to Mumbai only recently.'

'How come?'

'Personal issues,' I said after a pause. 'My marriage ended. I wanted a fresh start. Live my own life, finally.'

'Hence stand-up?'

'Yes, stand-up is my passion. I'm not that great though.'

'Why do you say that? The audience laughed quite a few times. Just build on that. You'll only get better.'

'That's supportive of you. Thank you.'

'Even though I was the scapegoat of the show today.'

'Sorry about the daddy's-princess comment. Unnecessary.'

'It's okay. It's comedy. One can't get offended over little things.'

'Thank you.'

We took a few sips of our drinks in silence.

'How long did you work in private equity?' she said after a while.

'Too long. Around ten years. How about you?'

'Ten months.'

'Ah. You're a baby.'

'Here we go again.'

'What?'

'I get that a lot. I finished undergrad and they hired me right off. What can I do if I'm young? Everyone at work calls me the office baby. But I'm not a baby.'

'How old are you?'

'I'm twenty-one. Nearly twenty-two.'

'Well, I'm thirty-three. Compared to that, you're a little kid.'

'Am I?'

'Yes, you're twelve years younger than me. What's incredible, though, is that you had an offer from Blackwater straight after college. Where did you study?'

'Stanford.'

'Oh,' I said. 'California ... I used to live in California too.'

'Ah, I see. And you're right, by the way. I'm a bit of a daddy's princess. He paid my college tuition fee.'

'But you cracked Stanford. And now Blackwater. He must be so proud.'

'I don't know. He doesn't even know Blackwater. Most people don't, actually.'

'Only three hundred employees worldwide. But Blackwater manages a hundred-billion-dollar-strong portfolio.'

'One hundred and twenty billion now,' Payal said, 'but I'm a rookie. And the problem with there being so few employees is that nobody's got the time to teach you anything. They expect you to hit the ground running, be an expert in private equity and evaluating companies from day one. It's crazy.'

Here was my chance. And I was going to take it.

'If you ever have any doubts or questions about private equity, no matter how stupid they might seem to you, feel free to ask. I do stand-up comedy now, so I may not know the latest stuff, but I can try to help.'

'You worked at Yellowstone for a decade—'

Before she could finish her sentence, Mudit and Nimit came back to our table.

'Nice set-up,' Nimit said. 'Definitely has potential.'

Translation: You're too small for us to invest in right now.

'If you guys come in—' Mudit said but Nimit interrupted him.

'Not now. It needs critical mass for Blackwater to consider it,' he said.

There you go. Too small.

I looked at Payal again. Our eyes met, as if we were thinking the same thing—that Nimit was just politely turning Mudit down.

She had a cute round face and, now that I knew about her education, a super-sharp brain as well. After how my marriage had ended, I had sworn to never ever fall for a woman again. No, wait, I wasn't falling for Payal.

'Bro, he's talking to you,' Mudit said, waving his hand in front of my face.

'What?' I said in a bit of a daze.

'Nimit asked you a question,' Mudit said.

'Sorry,' I said. 'What?'

'I said, how did you end up at Yellowstone?'

'Ages ago, I had a small tech start-up. After a few years, I sold my company to a bigger tech company, where Yellowstone was an investor. During the negotiations, Yellowstone asked me what I was going to do after selling the company. I had no plans. They offered me a job, and I took it.'

'Oh, so you've been a founder too?' Nimit said. 'From founder to private equity investor. Impressive.'

'Yes. It was a tiny company though. I'm not one of those unicorn founders.'

'Still a founder,' Payal said.

Why was I experiencing this strong urge to be alone with Payal and talk to her again?

'You built and sold a company. I can see why Yellowstone took you in,' Nimit said.

'He's a bright fucker,' Mudit said. 'We're buddies from IIT Bombay. Roommates for four years.'

'Oh, you mean you're also—' Nimit said, but Mudit interrupted him.

'Yes, I'm also a wasted engineer. Like Saket. No wonder we're best friends. Misfits in this world of corporates and big deals. Engineers wasting their degrees and doing comedy. That itself is a comedy.'

Everyone laughed.

'We better leave. Have work tomorrow,' Nimit said.

'But tomorrow is Sunday,' Mudit said.

'Doesn't matter. We have a new IM due on Monday,' Nimit said.

'IM?' Mudit said.

'Investment memorandum,' I said. 'We make those to evaluate any new opportunity.'

'You guys are too smart,' Mudit said.

'Not really,' Nimit said. 'Anyway, see you guys. Our driver is waiting. Come, Payal.'

'See you guys,' Payal said.

I realized then that I did not have her number, and that I had ten seconds to come up with something. Else, she would be history. And none of the craziness that transpired later would happen either. But, as luck would have it, destiny had other plans in store for us.

'I don't have your contact details, guys. I could add you both to our broadcast list,' I said, 'in case you want to attend any of my future shows. Bad comedy can be contagious.'

'Sure,' Payal said, laughing. She opened her black Tumi laptop bag, took out her business card and handed it to me. Nimit gave me his card as well.

'We won't get spammed, right?' Payal said.

'Never,' I said.

Mudit and I stayed back at the bar after Payal and Nimit left. Mudit kept staring at me.

'What?' I said.

'You like her,' Mudit said.

'Who?'

'Stop the bullshit. You know who.'

'It's nothing like that, bro. She was just a guest at our show.'

'She's pretty. Round face, long hair, delicate-looking. Your type completely. And same industry too.'

'She's twenty-one, Mudit. Too young.'

'That's what's stopping you? Really?'

'Yes, really. Firstly, you know what happened with my marriage. I'm out of the relationship world. For the next five years at least. Or fifty. Secondly, I don't know if she's keen.'

'She's keen.'

'What? No.'

'She gave you her card. Message her.'

'I *asked* for her card.'

'Fine. So, you're keen. That was my original point anyway. You like her.'

'I just wanted to add her to the broadcast list. The bigger our list, the better.'

'Really? Why don't you go up to all these other men in the bar right now and add them to the mailing list?'

I threw up my hands in frustration. 'Bro, I just had my first show. Let me enjoy that? And you're right. I did ask for her card. That was a weak moment. She's history. Fuck it,' I said. I took Payal's card and put it in Mudit's shirt pocket. 'Here, you keep it,' I said. 'Or better still, just throw it.'

'Shh,' Mudit said, placing Payal's card back in my hand. 'Keep it. Don't be so hard on yourself. Not everyone is Raashi.'

I covered my ears. 'Don't take her name. Please.'

'Fine. Anyway, let me check on some of the other guests. You enjoy the success of your first show. Okay?'

I stood at the bar, holding my tequila glass in one hand and Payal's card in the other.

Payal Jain

Analyst

Blackwater Capital

I ran my finger over her embossed name a few times. The card had her Nariman Point office address. It also had her email, office landline number and mobile number.

Should I message her?

'No, absolutely not,' a stern voice screamed inside my head.

'You were great,' a girl's voice interrupted my thoughts.

I turned around to see a young couple standing in front of me.

'That bit about the school plays was good. I was also Bheem in all the plays in school,' the guy said. He was well-built, six feet two and many more inches wider than normal people.

'Welcome to the Bheem club.' I laughed.

'Can I take a selfie with you?' the girl said.

Wow, my first-ever selfie request.

Mudit sat a few tables away from me with some of his regular customers. He looked at me and smiled, lifting his glass to show his support for me.

Maybe, just maybe, a tiny bit of my life was working out after all.

∼

'Listen, Kushal. She needs to sign the final agreement now. I've agreed to everything,' I said.

My lawyer, Kushal Devraj, sat in his drab office in San Francisco, with a virtual background of a beach on our late-night Zoom call. He wore a suit, making him look totally out of place compared to the fake tropical paradise behind him. Despite my terrible mood, I wondered if I could put together a comedy set on Zoom calls. On workaholics like Kushal whose idea of a vacation was changing their virtual background on Zoom.

'She's refusing to sign it. She wants more. Eighty per cent of all your assets if you want to forgo the monthly alimony.'

'Eighty? Has she gone mad? We already agreed to sixty-six. We had a verbally locked deal.'

I sat on the ledge of my living-room window, in my one-bedroom apartment in Pali Hill, Bandra. I took a sip of my black coffee, which I shouldn't have, not at midnight. The caffeine and this high-stress divorce-settlement call would surely keep me up all night.

'Let's discuss what happened,' Kushal said.

'What? Nothing happened. She's being a greedy bitch. She's squeezing me because she knows I want to get this over with as soon as possible.'

'Really? Nothing happened? Try to remember, Saket,' Kushal said. Even through his 480p laptop webcam, I could see his judgemental looks.

'I have no clue what happened. You told me she's entitled to fifty per cent of all my assets, plus a monthly alimony.'

'Yes, that's Californian law.'

'We decided to give her sixty-six per cent of the assets, in lieu of a monthly alimony. Because I don't want to deal with her ever again. That's the deal we agreed to sign and submit in court. I'll get my divorce without going to trial. I'll be poor, but free.'

'Yes.'

'And now she suddenly wants eighty per cent? After we agreed to a sixty-six per cent deal? Tell me, is she a greedy bitch or not?'

'I cannot comment on a statement like that, Saket. However, I understand from Ms Raashi's attorney that there has been some provocation and a breach of the agreed-upon conduct from your side.'

'What is that supposed to mean? Oh, fuck,' I said as I spilled some coffee on my laptop.

'Language, Saket.'

'Bro, my coffee just spilled all over my keyboard. If this laptop conks off, I can't work. I don't have the money to get a new one. Because you're ensuring we give everything to her. So, pardon my language, and wait a minute.'

I placed my laptop on its side on the window ledge to make the coffee drip off the keyboard without any of it going into the circuit inside. Then I ran to the kitchen and came back with a washcloth. I wiped the laptop and resumed talking to Kushal.

'What provocation?' I said.

'Did you communicate with Ms Raashi last week?' Kushal said, tilting his head. 'And why am I seeing you sideways?'

'I am draining the coffee out of my laptop. Anyway, I had a brief WhatsApp chat with her. She wanted to know if I had paid the property tax for our, sorry, now *her*, her California house. She'll get the house. She'll live there. But I need to keep paying the property tax.'

'Until the settlement is done, yes. Did you converse with her about anything else?'

'I asked her why she hadn't signed the settlement agreement yet.'

'Why? Didn't we agree to speak about the settlement only through each other's attorneys?' Kushal said.

'I know, Kushal,' I said, wiping the keyboard one final time before straightening the laptop. 'But I'm getting impatient.'

'Did you, at any point, use abusive language during said chat?'

'No.'

'Are you sure, Saket?'

I opened my phone and scrolled through my chats with Raashi.

'Okay, at one point, I did use some strong words,' I said.

'Strong as in?'

'I said, "Go fuck yourself, Raashi."'

'Come on, Saket,' Kushal said, raising his voice, unusual for his perennially calm personality.

'Sorry, Kushal. I got carried away. She said I could not bully her into signing the agreement. I wasn't bullying her. I was just urging her.'

'Well, she has the right to interpret it as threat and intimidation. With use of abusive language suggesting harm.'

'Harm? What harm?'

'The term you used can be seen as a suggestion of physical harm.'

'Are you fucking kidding me? It's hardly even abuse. Ever been in an engineering college, Kushal? Or any Indian college?'

'No. I went to Harvard. Anyway, that's not the point. The point is, if she refuses to sign, forces you to take this to trial and presents this chat as evidence of threat and abuse, it won't end well for you.'

'It's not ending well for me anyway.'

'Saket, if you want this done, stay away from her.'

'She messaged me first.'

'Yes. But the law protects her. Not you. Not as much at least.'

'That's unfair.'

'We can discuss the fairness of gender-specific laws another time. For now, what do you suggest we do?'

'Meaning?'

'She wants eighty per cent. And her attorney knows they've got us.'

'By the balls?'

'I will ignore that comment. Are you okay with eighty per cent? I can negotiate a bit, bring it down maybe to seventy-five, but not beyond that.'

'Let's go to trial. This is just wrong.'

'No, Saket. A trial's not going to be good for you. I'll bill you more and make more money in a trial. But, no, let's not do that.'

'Then?'

'I suggest you let her have it. I'll try for seventy-five.'

'Whatever.'

'Is that a yes? I can go back to them?'

'Yes.'

'Okay, anything else you want me to convey? To her attorney or Ms Raashi?'

'Yeah.'

'What?'

'Tell them to go fuck themselves.'

I cut the Zoom call and slammed my laptop shut.

I stared outside my window. The trees below my fifth-floor apartment glowed in the fluorescent light of the streetlamps. I could hear a few cars and autos rumble past on Nargis Dutt Road below. Bandra was where the movie stars lived, the more famous ones in mansions with staff rooms bigger than my entire apartment. Technically, I couldn't afford to stay in this neighbourhood. Raashi had gouged out most of my savings, and my comedy career barely covered auto fares around Bandra, let alone allow me to breathe the same air as Aamir Khan and Ranbir Kapoor. But I needed a tiny haven in this otherwise-crazy, cramped city. And when I found this five-hundred-square-foot apartment in this thirty-year-old building with a crumbling exterior, it became my home, office and pity-party pad. It was less than one-tenth the size of my Bay Area house—sorry, Raashi's Bay Area house. But the best part about my Bandra place was the cover of the trees below, visible from my living-room window. It hid the traffic and the concrete jungle beneath and, sometimes, even my pain and sorrow.

Hi, I'm Saket Khurana, I'm thirty-three and my life is going nowhere. I'm a failed husband, a career quitter and a not-so-great stand-up comic. I spend my days either working on my jokes or my divorce settlement—which is also a kind of joke, anyway.

I could take you into a full flashback. I could tell you what happened between Raashi and me, how our marriage broke down. But it would be my biased version of things, so there's no point in doing all that.

Our marriage fell apart four years ago after I discovered she was having an affair with her so-called family friend and 'rakhi brother'—the latter being a term so abused in India that it should be banned. The rakhi brother and rakhi sister had apparently started their antics even before our marriage. And as it turns out, they never really stopped even after Raashi married me.

Again, this is my version of things. If you ask Raashi, she'll tell you that her affair with the rakhi brother was 'not what I think it was'. It was more about 'her finding herself'. I've never really understood how some people 'find themselves' by fucking another person, but let's leave that aside for now.

When I confronted Raashi about the affair, she claimed that she felt lonely and alienated in San Francisco and couldn't fit into its NRI culture. She felt that I neglected her since I was always busy with work. Several thousand dollars' worth of marriage therapy later, we agreed to give the marriage another shot. But Raashi continued to keep in contact with the rakhi brother—in more ways than one. Meanwhile, I sank deeper into depression. Alcohol became my best friend.

On a boys' trip to Vegas, I got smashed. I woke up in a hotel room with hookers that I may or may not have called. Anyway, someone in our boys' gang snitched and Raashi found out about the hookers. Another round of hell ensued. I tried the same I-was-finding-myself argument to justify why I had hired a Colombian whore who didn't speak English. Somehow, though, this line doesn't work as well for guys as it does for girls. I apologized multiple times, but it made no difference. Raashi hired lawyers to get a good divorce settlement and squeeze the last red blood cell out of me.

California law worked in her favour anyway.

Long story short, here we are. She gets eighty per cent of everything. The total wealth I had was three million dollars. Raashi will get 2.4 million. I get six hundred thousand dollars. Net of legal and other fees, I'll be left with half a million. It's still decent money, especially in India, where it translated to about two and a half crore rupees at current exchange rates. I could rent a small place, invest what I had and then make some money from comedy. It would be enough. That was the rough plan in my head.

'You know what, Saket?' I said out loud to myself. 'It's okay. You have less money, but you're free.'

Yes, I'm finally free. To do stand-up comedy, to walk away from a bad marriage—free to do whatever I wanted to.

All my life, I've done what people expected me to do. Parents, relatives (maasis and buas and chachis who have an opinion on everything), friends and neighbours. I've wanted their approval all my life.

You're smart? Try for IIT.

You're in IIT? Go to Silicon Valley.

You're in Silicon Valley? Open a start-up. Or get a job in a prestigious tech company.

Get married.

I did all these things.

Tick marks—that's what we need from people. We live our lives collecting all these damn tick marks.

College, tick.

Job, tick.

Money, tick.

American dream, tick.

Marriage, tick.

Yet, life fucked me over. And my wife fucked somebody else.

Maybe that's the expected outcome when you live your life trying to please others and conform to social norms.

Raashi seemed sweet when I had first met her. I had even found her stubborn nature cute. But I suppose that's what happens when you take a female-deprived guy from an Indian engineering college and put him out in the world—the first girl he meets becomes a living goddess.

In retrospect, I deserved my fate. Raashi had red flags that I never even spotted. She never opened up to me emotionally. She never laughed at my jokes. She liked spending money, particularly on designer handbags, watches, clothes and shoes. It was the only time I would see her smile. She was on her phone all the time. She never initiated physical intimacy. Damn, Raashi had more red flags than a Chinese Communist Party parade. I should note that down. Decent joke for a show.

I discovered comedy during my marital crisis. Comedy club bars became my escape in San Francisco. They give you alcohol and make you laugh. What better way to run away from your problems, even if for a few hours?

Right around the same time, Mudit quit the traditional corporate path in Mumbai to make a career in live events, eventually specializing in comedy. We connected while I was still in San Francisco. He saw my interest in comedy and told me to give it a shot someday.

I tried a few jokes at some NRI parties, one of the most boring gatherings of human beings on earth. Each NRI party, no matter where in the world it takes place, follows a predictable pattern. First, the men and the women segregate. Then the men discuss cricket, the stock market and whisky. If it's Silicon Valley, they also discuss who sold their start-up and got rich. The women, meanwhile, discuss part-time-helper woes and where to get cheap waxing done and source the best idli batter from.

Finally, I unplugged the computer of my US life. I did a full shutdown to end it all—my job, my marriage, my life in San Francisco, everything. Now, here I am, drinking bad instant black coffee and staring out of my window at one in the morning. Alone, broken, jobless and directionless, but free.

I got up from the window ledge and walked to my bedroom. I turned off the lights and lay down on the bed. But the coffee and all the memories of San Francisco made it difficult to sleep. The problem with the brain is that it stores the past in its entirety, especially the painful bits.

No, you've got to move past this. San Francisco is history. You are here now. Think about what you're going to do tomorrow. Think about the big show next weekend.

I checked my phone. I had a message from Mudit: 'Up?'

'Sort of,' I replied.

Mudit immediately gave me a call.

'Bro, it's one-thirty in the morning. I'm trying to sleep,' I said.

'But you replied. What's up?'

'Nothing. Just spent five hundred dollars on a video call.'

'Wow, some sex show that must've been. Which porn site?'

'Not a porn site, you ass. Zoom call with my lawyer. Paid him only to find out that I need to pay my ex-wife even more money.'

'That crap isn't settled yet?'

'Almost. Anyway, why did you call?'

'I'm nervous about the show next weekend.'

'Why?'

'It's our biggest show, man. Two star comics are coming. And there are five more acts, including yours.'

'You're making me more nervous now.'

'No, no. Don't worry. You'll be great.'

'I hope so.'

'But Saket, the media is coming. We need to have a full house, okay? Like packed. Barely any standing room only. People-sitting-on-the-floor types.'

'Yeah. How can I help?'

'Can you send a broadcast invite to your entire contact list? Like everyone you know.'

'Okay, I will.'

'Please. Right now.'

'Now? Dude, it's pretty late.'

'Doesn't matter. They'll see it in the morning. Every person who's given you their contact or their business card, invite them, please. We have to crack this.'

'We will, Mudit, relax.'

'Anyway, I need to work on a new poster. See you soon. Good night,' Mudit said and ended the call.

I opened the comedy broadcast group on my WhatsApp. It had over one hundred members. I quickly composed a message: 'Hi guys, Saket Khurana here. I want to invite you to Crayon Comedy Club's biggest night ever. Seven comics, including yours truly, and two all-star acts. This Saturday. Click on the link for tickets. Drinks and food included in the ticket price.'

I pressed send, kept the phone on my bedside table and lay down again.

A second later, my phone pinged. I picked it up.

'You need me for the Jain jokes again?' Payal Jain had messaged.

I had, needless to say, added her number to the broadcast list.

'Hey,' I replied.

'Thanks for the invite.'

'You'll come?'

'I'll try my best to be there. I do need a break.'

'That's great. Up so late?' I responded.

'Yeah, still in office. Can you believe it?'

'Now?'

'Working on an investment memo. You're lucky. You quit the rat race.'

'Quitting has its own challenges though.'

'Like what?'

'Big event this Saturday. With star comics. I'm nervous.'

'But good nervous, right?'

'Good nervous?'

'Many things can make us nervous. But some are "good nervous". The good problems to have in life.'

'As in?'

'As in, you're doing comedy. Think about it. This was your dream, and now you get to live it. That too, a show with other big names.'

'Are you always this upbeat and supportive?'

'Ha ha. For others, yes. Not for myself.'

'Meaning?'

'I'm hard on myself.'

'Explain?'

'Umm ... like I feel I'm wasting my time chatting with you. I should get back to my proposal.'

'Oh, I'm sorry. Yes, please do get back to work.'

'Don't be. It's fine.'

'Anyway, I'll hopefully see you on Saturday. Good night.'

I kept my phone aside and closed my eyes. Thoughts of Payal floated around in my head. Did I have a chance with her? I continued to wonder as I drifted off to sleep.

~

'Speak louder, Mummy,' I said. 'I'm on a train.'

I struggled to stand in the crowded compartment of the local train, using one hand to hold on to the handrail above me and the other to press the phone against my ear.

'Train? Where are you going?'

'Local train. It's how people travel here. And I'm going to the comedy club in Parel. Ouch,' I said as the man in front elbowed me.

'What happened?'

'Nothing, Mummy. Can we speak later? It's hard to balance in a moving train with the phone in one hand.'

'Can't you take a taxi to Parel?'

'I have a train pass. Why waste so much money?'

'You gave Raashi a palace in America. And now you have to take the local train?'

'I can take a taxi, Mummy. But trains are faster. Besides, I want to live like a struggler. Which I am, in comedy.'

'I can't bear this. Come home, Saket. If you want to live in India, that's okay. But come here. Do this comedy-vomedy here. All your uncles are here. They're all so funny.'

'There is no comedy scene in Chandigarh.'

'At least move closer to us. Delhi?'

'No. Mumbai is where the comedy action is. Mudit is also here; he's a huge support.'

'What comedy-comedy you keep doing? We never had all this in our time. We had Johnny Walker, Keshto Mukherjee, Mehmood—'

I cut her off mid-sentence. 'They were all comedians in movies. I'm a stand-up comic.'

'You can get a good job in India also.'

'I'm fine, Mummy,' I said. I gasped as a man stamped on my foot while getting off at the Mahim station.

'Raashi signed the papers?'

'Not yet. She'll do it soon.'

'See, she still wants to save her marriage. No woman wants to break her house, beta. You should reconsider. I've always thought of her like a daughter.'

'Mummy!' I shouted. 'Stop it. Do you even know what's going on?'

'What?'

'She's not signing the papers because she wants more money.'

'How much?'

'Eighty per cent of everything.'

'Eighty per cent? Has she gone mad? I knew she's a complete evil witch. Chudail.'

'I have to go. My station is coming up.'

'I feel really bad, beta. I pushed you to agree to this match. I thought they were simple people. They live in the next sector …'

'It's okay. I agreed to the wedding. It's my fault. I messed up. I'm paying for it now.'

The train entered the Lower Parel station.

'At least don't be angry, beta.'

'I'm not angry, Mummy. Did I say anything to you?'

'Do you need anything? Money?'

'No, I'm fine. Have to go, Mummy. Bye.'

The train screeched to its fifteen-second halt at Lower Parel. A sea of humanity rushed out of the train doors like toothpaste extruding out of a tube, extracting me along with it.

∼

When I entered the Crayon Club, it was mostly empty. Only Mudit was there, giving instructions to some workers placing plastic seats behind the last row.

Mudit high-fived me when I walked up to him.

'We're sold out,' he said. 'Oversold, rather. It's not allowed, but I'm adding a temporary row at the back and mattresses on the floor in front of the first row.'

'Amazing,' I said.

'All set for your act?' Mudit said.

'Freaking out on the inside. There are big, established comedy stars performing today. And I'm in the same show.'

'Exactly. My brother is getting into the big league,' Mudit said, slapping my back. 'Wow, those are some serious back muscles, dude. That gym membership is paying off, huh?'

'Trying my best,' I said.

'Do the same here,' Mudit said, fist-bumping me. 'Stay calm, okay? And kill it.'

∽

'Anyone married here?' I said, scanning the crowd.

Around half of the hundred-and-twenty-plus audience in the packed auditorium raised their hands.

'Damn, no wonder all of you are here to cure your depression,' I said.

Titters ran through the crowd.

'Who got married the north Indian way?' I said.

Some twenty people raised their hands.

'And who had a south Indian wedding? Also known as the six-in-the-morning, no-fun torture wedding?'

Laughter rippled through the crowd. Five people raised their hands.

'Okay, I had a north Indian wedding. And now I'm going through a north Indian divorce too, but that's a different story.'

The audience laughed heartily.

'No, seriously, north Indian divorces have their own drama, just like north Indian weddings do. I don't know about other moms, but Punjabi moms have their own unique style when it comes to dealing with their sons' divorces. Today, my mother actually apologized to me for finding my wife for me.'

A few in the audience went 'aww'.

'Then she said, "I thought they were simple people." What's this Indian obsession with simple people, really? Who exactly are these "simple people"? More importantly, who are the "complex people"?'

Laughter in the audience. I kept going with the improvised set.

'Punjabi moms are also great at switching their affection. At the start of the same call, when my mother still had hopes that my marriage could survive, she said my wife was "just like her daughter". Then, when I told her that her supposed daughter wants a huge settlement, my mom said, "I knew she was an evil witch. Chudail." Punjabi moms can go from "like my daughter" to "chudail" in a few seconds, I tell you.'

A loud burst of laughter.

In the far-left corner of the club, I saw a door open and a girl enter. It was Payal. She sat on one of the plastic chairs in the last row.

'Anyway, I'm getting screwed in my divorce settlement. I had to get screwed. You see, I'm an extra-trusting sort of a guy. Like I even believe all the ads on TV. You guys have heard of Axe deodorants?'

Many in the audience nodded and said yes.

'Yeah, well, I'm so trusting that when I first saw the ad—the one that showed girls running after you if you sprayed the deodorant on yourself because it made you irresistible—I actually believed it.'

Giggles from the crowd.

'No, really. I sprayed like half a can on myself, and then went out to the shopping mall. I went inside some women's clothing stores. But nobody moved even an inch closer to me. I sprayed the whole damn can all over myself. Even then, nothing.'

The laughs I got felt like a rain shower.

'That's when I figured that they were lying. If their deo spray actually made women go that crazy and made them run after you, imagine what the situation would be like in the Axe factory? Things would be out of control, with mobs of women at the gates every morning.'

Loud chuckles.

'All that aside, while testing the deodorant, I even ended up in a lingerie store. No Axe effect there either. But I learnt that there's something called the push-up bra,' I said.

Many women in the audience nodded.

'Now, some names just don't translate well from English to Hindi. Take the push-up bra, for example. What would you call a push-up bra in Hindi? Dhakka-maar bra?'

Giggles ran through the crowd.

'Anyway, let's leave the push-up bras aside, which, some may argue, are a form of deceptive advertising.'

A few scattered laughs. I saw Payal smile but shake her head in disagreement.

'Moving on, any food lovers out here?' I said.

Up went some hands.

'They say food can also become an addiction. You heard that?'

The audience nodded.

'I sort of get what they're trying to say, but addiction is a strong term, don't you think? Because it isn't like a drug addiction or even an alcohol addiction. Drug addicts and alcohol addicts have been known to shoot and stab people to get money for their fix. Food addicts don't do that. Like have you ever heard of someone holding a person at gunpoint for some jalebis? Or that a Punjabi mom stabbed someone over a plate of gulab jamuns? Though that may have actually happened somewhere. Probably in Chandigarh, Sector 17. "Give me that gulab jamun, you chudail,"' I said, stabbing at the air.

Loud laughter in the entire auditorium this time. Payal laughed as well, this time hysterically.

I cracked a few more jokes before ending my act. Mudit, the emcee for the night, came on stage.

'That was Crayon Club's homegrown rising star, Saket Khurana, everyone. Let's hear it for my childhood chaddi buddy.'

The gracious crowd sent me off with a huge round of applause. As I exited the stage, a man came up to me.

'Do you do corporate shows as well?' he said.

'Huh … Yes, I guess. Why not?' I said.

We exchanged numbers. I looked up to the heavens above. Thank you, God, for looking out for me, I said, and mumbled a silent prayer.

~

'I hope you haven't paid for that drink yet,' I said, walking up to Payal.

She sat on one of the high stools at the club bar, a glass of white wine in one hand and her phone in the other.

'Oh hi,' she said, her eyes shining as she turned around. 'Good show.'

'You think so?'

'Yes. You're getting better. The jokes, the delivery, your gestures and voice modulation.'

'In other words, last time I sucked,' I said, laughing.

'I did not say that,' Payal said. 'Anyway, can I get you a drink?'

'No, I'll get one myself. You're my guest after all.'

I took out some staff vouchers from my pocket and gave one to the bartender. 'Gin and tonic, please,' I said. A minute later, the bartender passed me my drink.

'Cheers,' Payal and I said in unison as we clinked our glasses.

'Thank you for coming,' I said.

'I had fun.'

'You came alone?'

'I wasn't supposed to. My best friend, Akanksha, was going to come along. But she bailed on me at the last minute.'

'But you came anyway ...' I said.

'Well, you'd personally invited me. And I'd accepted as well, remember?' she said.

Our eyes met.

'Wow, thank you.' I smiled.

'You don't have to keep me company. You just wrapped up a show—go move around. Meet whoever you have to,' Payal said.

'I don't need to be anywhere,' I said.

'You sure?' she asked. 'Mudit doesn't want you out there, mingling with the guests?'

'No. It's fine. Another drink?' I said, noticing her empty glass.

'Okay, but just one more,' she said. 'I'm going to my parents' place today.'

I gave two more vouchers to the bartender and asked him to repeat our respective drinks.

'They don't even know that I drink. I'll need a lot of mints before I get there.'

I looked at her, surprised.

'They're somewhat conservative,' she said.

'And you?'

Payal looked at me incredulously. 'I'm not. I drink. I love comedy. I do a few other rebellious things as well. However, I still try to do what they expect me to do.'

'And what do they expect you to do?'

'Work hard. Be a good Jain. Listen to them. Not have a boyfriend.'

'And you do all that?'

'I try to.'

Okay, so she probably didn't have a boyfriend. That was the good news. But she wasn't allowed to have one either. And that was the bad news.

'So, you're a good Jain,' I said.

'Except for the wine.'

'We've already established that wine is Jain-friendly.'

'It's still alcohol though. My parents don't drink. Like, at all.'

'Who else is there at home?'

'I have an elder brother. He works in the family business, supposedly. Dad still does most of the work.'

'What business?'

'We manufacture electrical cables. There's a factory we have in Thane. Basically, boring stuff. Nothing like the exciting work you do.'

'Bet cables make a lot more money than comedy does.'

'Bet comedy is a lot more fun than making cables though.'

Both of us smiled.

'Money can be fun too,' I said. 'For now, though, I have these staff vouchers for fun. More drinks? Or I could get us some food.'

'No more drinks. But, yes, I'm starving,' Payal said.

'Jain-friendly food, right? Will nachos and French fries do?'

Payal told me that French fries could be considered non-Jain if one applied the more orthodox Jain rules, which meant no root vegetables. However, she and her family ate potatoes, so I could order the French fries and the nachos, without onion and garlic, of course.

When the food arrived, I took a single French fry and nibbled on it.

'You don't eat French fries?' Payal said.

'I do,' I said. 'But I'm on this high-protein diet right now. Boring bodybuilder gym stuff.'

'Bodybuilding is your religion then? I don't eat some things because I'm Jain. You don't eat some things because you're a bodybuilder.'

'Sort of. There's a lot of meat in my diet though. Jains go to heaven. Bodybuilders probably won't.'

'But like you said, all the fun people will be in hell. Who wants to hang out in heaven all day with Mother Teresa and Anna Hazare?'

'Oh, you remember,' I said. Both of us laughed.

Just then, she received a notification on her phone. 'Sorry, I need to reply to this. It's a work thing,' she said.

'Sure, go ahead,' I said.

She furiously typed an email on her phone, silently mouthing the words as she hit the keys, unaware of the tenderness welling up inside me. How were her fingers so delicate? With nails of pale rose. Her floral-print yellow chiffon top billowed like cotton candy. Gold dolphins danced down her ears. Her hair, tied in a long ponytail, made her look younger than her age.

She looked up at me and softly mouthed 'sorry' for taking too much time. I smiled and gestured that it was okay.

Should I ask her out? But then what about my no-more-women-in-my-life rule? And what about her no-boyfriends-allowed rule? And what about the age-difference rule, if there was indeed such a rule?

The problem is that when you actually like someone, all the rules go for a toss.

'Sorry, I had to respond to this,' Payal said, finishing her email. 'They obviously don't care that it's a Saturday night.' She kept her phone aside.

'How is work anyway?' I said.

'Busy. I'm stuck on this one particular problem while valuing a company. But I'm afraid that if I ask my seniors, they'll think I'm a total idiot, which I am.'

'No, you are not. What are you stuck on?' I asked.

'This company that I'm valuing has issued a lot of stock options to its employees. ESOPs, you know?'

'Yeah, I do.'

She shook her head; the ponytail swayed in tandem. 'There are multiple layers and tranches of ESOPs, all of which we need to account for.'

'Yes. If the company has issued too many stock options, you'll have massive dilution,' I said.

'Exactly. However, these particular ESOPs are complicated. It involves valuing complex options.'

'Beyond the Black–Scholes formula?'

She nodded.

'I can help,' I said after a pause.

'What?'

'I've valued complex stock options during my Yellowstone years. We can discuss the ESOPs you're dealing with. Just don't give me any names or other confidential details about the company.'

'Yeah? We can do that?'

'Why not? You have the ESOP details? I can look at it now.'

'Not today. It's your big night.'

'When do you want to do it then?'

'I can do it tomorrow. I'm going to my parents' place in Ghatkopar tonight. But I'll return to my own place in Parel tomorrow. I can stop in Bandra on the way back,' she said. 'Will that be convenient for you?'

'Extremely. I live in Bandra. Okay, let's meet at Bombay Salad Co. tomorrow? That's where I go for lunch on Sundays anyway.'

'Sounds too healthy,' she said doubtfully.

'Is that a problem?'

'No.' She laughed. 'I'll see you tomorrow.'

~

'One Ironman chicken salad. Also, one Feel Good salad with tofu, Jain, no onion or garlic, not even in the dressing,' I said to the server at Bombay Salad Co.

'No tofu either, please. I hate it,' she said.

Payal wore a dark-blue salwar kameez with tiny golden polka dots all over it. A matching bindi adorned her forehead. She had removed the dupatta she was wearing and had placed it next to her large Gucci tote bag. She had worn jhumkas as well—long silver ones with peacock feathers that matched the colour of her clothes dangling from the ends.

'Are those real peacock feathers?' I said, pointing at her earrings.

'Yes. But they're Jain-friendly. No peacocks were harmed in making these.'

'How do you know that?' I smiled.

'Peacocks shed feathers naturally, that's how. Anyway, I know I'm overdressed. Totally out of place amongst these Lululemon ladies of Bandra in the restaurant here.'

Almost every other table around us had people in athleisure attire.

'I look like someone who's come to eat a Gujarati thali before garba night,' she said.

I laughed.

'It's my mother. She buys all this for me and then forces me to wear them every time I visit them.'

The waiter arrived with our food just then.

'Everyone is so fit in this restaurant. Including you,' she said.

'Thank you. Ever since I stopped working fourteen hours a day in office, I've had plenty of time to work out.'

'I wish I had your life,' she said, sighing.

'You can. Just quit your job, give up on this mega-paying career and do something impractical and pointless, like stand-up comedy.'

'Comedy isn't pointless. It makes people laugh. It makes them happy. And that's the entire point of life, isn't it? To be happy?' Payal said.

'Wow. Never saw it that way,' I said, taking a bite of my salad.

'I invest rich people's money to make them even richer. That, one can argue, is pointless,' she said.

'Thanks. I don't feel so bad anymore. You're quite the capitalist philosopher, aren't you? Evolved thoughts for such a young age.'

'Well, I've been told that I'm quite mature for my age.'

'By whom?'

'Akanksha, my best friend.'

'Ah yes, the one who ditched you at the last minute yesterday.'

'Oh, someone listens.'

'I try,' I said, smiling.

We ate in silence for the next couple of minutes.

'Speaking of making rich people richer, you want to discuss the ESOPs?' I said, pushing my plate aside.

'Yes, I do,' Payal said. She pulled out her laptop from the tote bag. Then she took out a notebook, a set of printouts and two pens. How can girls store so much in their handbags?

She opened a spreadsheet on her laptop and turned it around so the screen was visible to both of us.

'I hid the company details, but here is the ESOP structure. These printouts have more information,' she said, sliding the documents towards me.

'Okay, let's see,' I said as I scanned the spreadsheet.

I spent the next hour working with her. In between, we ordered two rounds of black coffee. I modified the spreadsheet, adding a few new rows and formulae.

'And that's it,' I said. 'This is the value of the ESOPs.' I turned the laptop screen towards her.

'This makes sense,' she said a minute later, going through the spreadsheet. 'And the ESOPs are worth almost twenty-five per cent of the total shares in the company.'

'Yes, a quarter of the company.'

She looked up. 'Thank you, Saket. This is incredibly helpful. I almost feel like calling you Saket sir.'

'Please don't. I don't need any more reminders about my age. Even this morning, some college kid at the gym said, "Uncle, are you done with the cable machine?"'

'That's all right,' Payal said, unable to suppress her laughter.

'The dude was twenty years old. And a giant. Bodybuilder type.'

'I'm also twenty-one. Maybe I should also—' she said, but I interrupted her mid-sentence.

'No, please, no. Not "sir". And definitely not "uncle". Saket is okay.'

'Okay … Saket,' she said, grinning. 'Wish me luck. I have to present this next Thursday.' She shut her laptop and put everything back inside her tote bag.

'You'll rock it,' I said. I knew she would.

We finished our coffees and came out of the restaurant. She called her driver, who arrived in a BMW.

'It's my dad's, in case you're composing,' she said.

'Composing what?'

'More papa-ki-pari jokes?'

I laughed. She was funny. Also smart, thoughtful and beautiful. *How and who was I to resist this?*

Before leaving, Payal gave me a quick side-hug. Girls have different categories of hugs. If they don't know you, there are no goodbye hugs at all. If they somewhat know you, you get a side hug. If they know you well, you get a proper full-frontal-embrace hug.

Okay, so I was now in the somewhat-know-you category.

~

'Aarrghhh!' I screamed, doing a bicep curl with twenty-kilo dumbbells while on a call with Kushal. I had him on my AirPods.

'Are you okay, Saket? I thought I gave you good news,' Kushal said.

'Yeah, sorry. In the gym.'

I kept the dumbbells back in the rack and sat down on a bench.

'I can call later. Just wanted to give you the good news.'

'Eighty per cent of my savings are gone. Still, it's good news. Fine.'

'She didn't budge. But at least she signed the papers. It didn't go to trial. You're a free man.'

'I'm officially divorced now?'

'Yes. The judge will sign the order later this week.'

'Fine.'

'And also ...' Kushal paused.

'What?'

'Our pending legal fees,' he said in a sheepish voice.

'Sure. Take whatever you want. The remaining twenty per cent?'

'No, Saket, only what is due. I'll send you an invoice. Take care.'

I ended the call. Then I walked back to the rack and picked up two thirty-kilo dumbbells.

'Too much,' one of the trainers at the gym said when he saw me struggling to do bicep curls with the massive weight.

'What?' I said, keeping the dumbbells down and turning to him.

'That's too much weight. You can get hurt.'

But what if I'm already hurt?

~

'Free?'

The one-word message from Payal popped up as a notification on my phone. I stopped writing and pushed my laptop aside.

'Yes, wasup?' I replied.

'Finishing up the investment memo. How are you?'

'Good. Preparing for a corporate-show audition.'

'Oh, that's great.'

'Yeah, let's see how it actually goes. How is the IM looking?'

'Good. I need your help. Again.'

'Sure.'

'I've finished the section on the ESOPs, with explanations. Can you take a quick look and see if it all makes sense?'

'Yes, sure. Email it to me.' I shared my email address with her.

In a few seconds, her email arrived in my inbox. I opened the attached file and spent fifteen minutes going through it before giving her a call.

'Hey,' she said, picking up. 'Is it terrible?'

'No. It's absolutely fine. Why were you even doubtful?'

'Sorry, I'm just nervous.'

'Good nervous, though, right?'

She laughed. 'Hopefully. You have that corporate audition soon, yes?'

'This Friday. For a company called Reliable Polymers. They have an annual conference coming up and need an entertainer.'

'Sounds exciting.'

'Hardly. Corporates pay well, though, that's it. Crayon Club, on the other hand, hardly pays.'

'But you're building your name at the club. Which allows you to make money through private functions like these corporate offsites.'

'That's true. I'm nervous though. I have to make a room full of HR people laugh. Does anyone ever associate HR with laughter?'

Payal laughed. 'See, now that's funny. You can use that,' she said.

'Can't use HR jokes on HR people.'

'Relax, you're naturally funny.'

'You think so?'

'I know so. Don't worry, you'll ace it.'

'Thank you, Miss Motivation.'

'You're welcome, Mister ESOP.'

Were we flirting? Did this, in some part of the universe, count as flirting? Should I take the next step and ask her to meet up again?

'If we both rock our respective presentations, let's go out and celebrate together,' I said.

'Done,' she said, and ended the call a second later.

Wait, did she just agree to go out with me? Sort of?

I opened my laptop again and resumed writing jokes about dentists, praying nobody in Reliable Polymers' HR department was related to a dentist.

~

'I feel bad for dentists. Any dentists or anyone related to dentists here?' I said, looking at the eight people from the HR department who sat in the conference room at Reliable Polymers' office. The office was just as boring and dull as the name of the company. Everything—from the furniture to the walls to the people—was grey.

I continued, 'Anyone here in HR who secretly wanted to be a dentist? Pull people's teeth out?'

Half the people in the room had a rather pained expression on their faces, as if they were getting a colonoscopy done while listening to my audition. Trying to make HR guys laugh is like trying to make a funeral procession dance. One of the senior HR guys, however, smiled. Imitating him, two junior guys smiled as well.

Okay, this was progress.

I figured the senior HR guy was the key. In the world of corporates, the juniors only laugh at the jokes their seniors laugh at.

'I think the medical education board's been unfair to dentists. It's like they said, "Okay, some of you are going to be doctors. You'll get to treat the whole body. And some of you guys will be dentists. You'll only get to fix teeth." The dentists were like, "Only teeth? Can we not treat the whole face?"

The board was like, "No!" The dentists said, "How about the head?" No. "Give us the lips or the nose at least." Nope. "You guys are dentists. Your job is to learn about teeth, and only teeth. The thirty-two teeth that humans have, that's it. And you'll do this over four years."'

I walked up and stood in front of the senior HR person. I looked directly into his eyes and said, 'Sir, tell me, what do they even do in dental colleges? Learn about thirty-two teeth? Sure. That's eight teeth a year, over a duration of four years. That's, what, like four teeth per semester?'

The senior HR guy laughed. *Jackpot.* On cue, his juniors followed and then the juniors' juniors followed. The entire room erupted into laughter.

I continued, 'Doctors are learning about the nervous system, the circulatory system, the endocrine system and so many more systems—all in one term. Meanwhile, the dentists are like, "What do we do now, sir? We've already learned about eight teeth this year. What now?" And what does the board tell them? "Why don't you guys check all the toothpastes in the market and figure out which toothpaste is to be recommended by dentists in ads?"'

Everyone laughed without waiting for any cues from their seniors this time.

I bowed as I finished my three-minute audition.

'It's fine, you're on,' the senior HR person said, offering me a handshake. 'I'm Priyansh Gupta. Head of HR here.'

'Thank you so much, sir,' I said.

Priyansh then turned to his two immediate juniors and introduced them. 'This is Akhil, he handles our offsites, and this is Rakesh, he looks after employee welfare.'

I wondered what kind of welfare activities a soul-crushing, blood-sucking corporate that made polymer resins did for its people. *Okay, resist making any HR or corporate jokes.*

Akhil walked me out of the conference room.

'We have to discuss the commercials with you,' he said.

'Mudit manages all that,' I said. 'I'll ask him to call you.'

'Sure. Would you like to do a deal for multiple events? We have four zonal offsites—Goa, Kochi, Jaipur and Siliguri.'

'I'd love to do all four. I'll ask Mudit to call you and work out the details and the commercials,' I said, mentally high-fiving myself.

∼

'Done, bro. I spoke to Akhil already. Four cities, all in a row. Sixty. Cool?' Mudit said to me over the phone. I was in a cab, on my way back from Reliable Polymers.

'That was fast. And sixty thousand? For four cities? Okay, cool,' I said. Crayon Club paid me five thousand for a night. This was fifteen thousand per show.

'No, bro. Are you mad?' Mudit said. 'This is a corporate gig. Sixty thousand per city. Travel and stay separate. Four cities mean two lakhs forty thousand. The club will keep fifteen per cent. You'll make two lakhs or so.'

'Two lakhs?' I sat up, unable to contain my excitement. I hadn't heard the word 'lakhs' in the context of my earnings ever since I became a stand-up comic.

'You're welcome,' Mudit said, laughing. 'You should've made me negotiate your divorce settlement, dude.'

'I swear. You're the best. No wonder you're the boss,' I said, ending the call.

I decided to call Payal.

'Free to talk?' I asked when she picked up on the first ring.

'Hi. Yes. I'm heading home from work. I was going to call you today as well.'

'Really?'

'Yes. Two things. First, I wanted to check how your corporate audition went.'

'You remembered? I'm just on my way back from Reliable Polymers actually.'

'And?'

'So, the thing is … I'm not doing the one event.'

'Oh,' she said in a disappointed voice.

'Because I'm doing four,' I said. 'All in different cities. And they're paying me a lot more than I expected. Turns out, HR people do laugh at dentist jokes.'

'Oh. Congrats, Saket. I want to hear the dentist jokes right now,' she said.

'Sure, sure,' I said. 'But wait, if I may ask, how did your IM presentation go?'

'That was the second thing I wanted to talk to you about.'

'Okay. And?'

'Smashed it,' she said in a soft voice.

'Really?'

'Wait. Let me read out the message that Jagdish sent me. He said, "You did an incredible job with the IM, Payal. Considering the ESOPs and valuing them properly was a great insight. Well done."'

'That's insane. Well done, you,' I said, emphasizing each word.

'Jagdish never praises anyone. And he sent this message on the office chat group.'

'You're a star, Payal.'

'All because you helped me.'

'No, no. It was all you,' I said.

'Thank you,' Payal said.

Saket Khurana, you can do it, I told myself and asked the question: 'Payal, what are you doing this weekend?'

'Nothing. I'm free only.'

'Okay, I was wondering if I could take you out for dinner?'

'Dinner?'

'Yeah ... We said we'll celebrate this, remember?'

'True. But I should be giving *you* a treat. For helping me.'

'No, I want to take you out,' I said. 'I cracked the corporate deal. And I'm older than you anyway.'

'Okay,' she said. 'Where?'

'Let's go to Aer? Tomorrow at 7.30 p.m.?'

'Aer at Four Seasons, Worli? Isn't that really high-end?'

'Don't worry about it. It's sponsored by Reliable Polymers. See you tomorrow.'

~

Aer, the rooftop lounge and bar, offers a stunning panoramic view of Mumbai and the Arabian Sea in the horizon. The bright lights of the city twinkle below it at night, while the darkness hides the less savoury bits, like all the dilapidated buildings and the slums. It has an all-white decor, with everything from the chairs and the tables to the bowl-shaped bar in the middle done up in a stark, minimalist white. Everything is high-end, as are the prices on the menu. If Reliable Polymers cancelled their deal, I would've to do shows at the Crayon Club for a month to pay for tonight's meal.

I reached Aer first, and the hostess ushered me to a table near the edge, for a better view. I'd barely been there for five minutes when Payal reached as well.

'Got stuck at the last Worli Naka signal, sorry,' she said.

When you look that stunning, you don't need to apologize for anything.

She had worn a short shimmery dress, the colour of red wine. Her lipstick matched the dress. Around her neck she wore a rose-gold chain with a tiny butterfly pendant. She had left her hair open, and it cascaded down to her waist in waves. She had a tiny mole on the left side of her neck, right where it curved up. And that was all I kept looking at for a while.

'I said hi,' she said again.

'Oh hey, hi. Sorry. Come, please sit. Umm … You look amazing.'

'Thank you,' she said, blushing a bit. 'What a view.'

She sat down across from me.

'A glass of Prosecco, please,' she said when the waiter came to take our order.

'I'll have the same,' I said and then, turning to Payal, said, 'Should we make it a bottle?'

'Really?'

'Yeah. Why not?' I turned to the waiter. 'A bottle of Prosecco, please. And some dips and pita bread. Can you make the dips without onion and garlic though? Jain-friendly?'

'Yes, sir, we can,' the waiter said.

'I'm such a pain to be out with,' Payal said after the waiter took our order and left.

'It's okay,' I said.

The waiter returned a few minutes later with the wine and two wine glasses. He placed the sealed bottle in a silver ice bucket and left.

'This is exactly like champagne. Strange that they're not allowed to call it champagne,' I said.

'Yes, only sparkling wines made in the Champagne region of France can be called champagne,' Payal said.

'It's like lassi not being allowed to be called lassi outside Punjab,' I said. 'Imagine Punjab saying, "Lassi is ours. Gujarat, you better call your Amul drink sweet dahi smoothie or something. Else we're shutting down your factory and arresting you."'

Payal laughed, hand over her mouth.

'That's what the Champagne people do in France, literally,' I said.

'It's fun to come out with a comic. I get front-row seats to a free show,' she said.

I smiled and proceeded to open the sparkling-wine bottle. The cork came out with a gentle pop. I carefully poured the wine into the two glasses and passed one to her. As we clinked our glasses, the waiter arrived with our food as well.

'Thank you again for helping me with the ESOPs,' Payal said, dipping the pita bread in some Jain hummus and taking a bite.

'You don't have to keep thanking me,' I said.

Payal nodded. She looked around Aer as both of us sipped our Prosecco.

'A lot of dating-type people here,' she said, subtly gesturing towards the other couples sitting at the tables around us. One of them was holding hands.

'Yeah, it's a popular date spot,' I said.

'Oh, really? I wouldn't know anything about all that,' Payal said.

'You've dated people before, right?' I said.

'As in? Having a proper boyfriend or something like that?'

'Well, yes.'

'Not really.'

'What does "not really" mean?'

'It means no. I've never had one. Crushes, yes. Boyfriends no.'

'Like never?'

Payal looked at me with a sheepish smile and shook her head.

'You've never been on dates, held hands or kissed anyone?'

'No and no, but I've kissed, yes. On the cheeks only, and that too my younger cousins.'

'No, like a proper kiss.'

'This is so embarrassing, but no.'

My mouth stayed open as I wondered what to say next.

'Okay, that can happen. You're still young. What about Stanford? Didn't meet anyone there?' I said.

'I had a crush.'

'You did?'

'Yes, but again, it's embarrassing. It was a professor. A young assistant professor, to be more specific, but he was still a fair bit older than me.'

'How old?'

'I was nineteen. He was thirty-one. Taught microeconomics. I aced his class, hoping to make him take notice of me.'

'And?'

'Nothing. It was just a silly crush on an older guy. Went nowhere.'

'Do you like older guys then?'

'My crushes would suggest so. Who knows though? I don't have any real dating experience.'

I nodded.

'It's probably hard for you to imagine someone like me in today's day and age,' Payal said after a while.

'It's a bit unusual, yes,' I said.

'You can't imagine the environment in my home. I told you no? The restrictions I grew up with?'

'Yes, no meat, no eggs and no onion and garlic.'

'And no boys. Having a boyfriend would rank as sinful as me eating a beef steak.'

'Why?'

'Because my mother drilled it into me—only bad girls have boyfriends.'

'What do the good girls do?'

'They study well and listen to their parents.'

'Like you. You're a good girl then.'

'Yes. It's who I am now. Even at Stanford, I had to top the class. It wasn't my parents pushing me there. I just had it imprinted in me. If I lost even one grade, I'd berate myself for months.'

'A perfectionist?'

'A toxic perfectionist, if you ask me. To top at Stanford means having no life. Guys did try, by the way. They'd ask me out for coffee, drinks, dinner.'

Of course, they did.

'And?' I said, keeping my face politely curious.

'I said no each time, what else …'

'And yet you're here tonight.'

She looked at me, somewhat surprised. 'Is this a date?' she said softly.

A trick question. If I said no, my chances would be blown forever. If I said yes, she could take it the wrong way. When there is no right answer, the best response is another question.

'What do you think?' I asked.

'We met for dinner. To celebrate our wins.'

'Correct.'

'But, like you said, this place is a date spot. It's full of couples.'

'Also true.'

'When does this become a date? I don't know,' she said.

'Are you really that innocent?' I said, and laughed.

'Fine, make fun of me,' Payal said, taking a big sip of her wine.

'I'm not making fun of you. It's just cute.'

'I'm trying to change … I'm now aware of my mother's over controlling nature. See, I'm pouring myself a second glass of alcohol. Another forbidden item.'

Payal refilled her glass and mine.

'Didn't we establish that wine is Jain-friendly?'

'It's not about it being Jain-friendly,' Payal said. 'Wine is too much fun. And as per the *Yashodha Jain Manual on Bringing Up Good Girls*, anything fun is not to be done.'

'That's your mother?' I said.

'Correct. The only fun thing we're allowed to do at home is eat unhealthy food, as long as it's Jain-friendly of course.'

'Like what?'

'Bhujia, laddoos, halwa, kaju katli. There's an unending list of Jain-friendly foods that are unhealthy. No problem in all that. But boys and alcohol, bad.'

'So, both these things, very bad,' I said, pointing first to her glass and then towards myself.

Payal laughed. 'Yeah. Pure-evil-level bad. Anyway, enough about me. Tell me about yourself.'

'What do you want to know?'

'You live in Mumbai alone?'

'Yes.'

'And your family?'

'My parents live in Chandigarh. Dad retired from the Army eight years ago.'

'Hmm ... and that whole difficult divorce thing you mentioned in the show? Is that true? Or was it just show material?'

'It's true. My divorce literally came through a few days back. Although, Raashi and I have been separated for years now.'

'Raashi, your wife?'

'Ex-wife.'

'How long were you married?'

'Six years.'

'No kids?'

I shook my head.

'What happened between you guys?'

'Long story. I'll tell you some other time,' I said.

'Sorry, I didn't mean to pry,' Payal said, looking apologetic.

'No, it's fine. I'll tell you in short: she fucked her rakhi brother before, during and after our marriage.'

'What?' she said, looking shocked.

'I'm sorry. I shouldn't have used such crude language. What should I say? Ugh ... she was intimate with her rakhi brother? Or she made love to her rakhi brother?' I said, somewhat agitated. 'Does that make it sound better?'

'Is this making you upset? Sorry ... We can change the topic.'

'It's okay. Bottomline, she had a thing with someone. We also wanted different things in life. She wanted money, assets, the high life basically. And you've seen me, doing dumb things like quitting private equity for the sake of cracking jokes.'

'It's not a dumb thing. It's a brave thing,' Payal said.

'You think so?'

'Yeah. Chasing your dream is brave, not dumb. But people continuing in jobs they hate, that's dumb.'

'Thank you. I guess I needed to hear that,' I said.

'You're welcome. Sorry you had to go through all that in your marriage.'

'Well, it's all over now,' I said. 'And I'm sure Raashi has her own version of events. As a reaction to what she did, I did some stupid things myself. I'm not proud of that.'

'There are always two sides to a story.'

I kept my glass down. 'I want to say something to you.'

'What?'

'I like you.'

'Oh, I like you as well.'

'No, I mean ... I don't want to be just friends with you. I mean, I couldn't, even if I tried.'

'What do you want to be then?'

'Perhaps one of the items on your banned list?'

'Garlic?' she said, and grinned. 'Sorry, that was a bad one. But I couldn't help it.'

I laughed. 'That was good, actually. You, too, are funny. Who's the real comic here?' I said.

'Thank you, I'm learning from the best,' she said.

'So, umm, I like you. And not just as a friend.'

'Wow.'

'Is that a good wow or a bad wow?'

'It's an I-don't-know-how-to-react wow. I've never done this before, Saket.'

'In a way, it's a first for me as well. Raashi and I had an arranged marriage.'

'Is this a date now?' Payal said.

'Depends on your response.'

'I'm not allowed to have a boyfriend, you know that,' she said.

'I also know that sometimes you like to rebel and make your own decisions, no matter what the rules are,' I said, pointing to her glass.

She smiled.

'And if you can decide whether to invest millions in a company or not, you can also decide what you want for yourself.'

Payal remained quiet. I gently placed my hand on top of hers. She didn't retract her hand.

'Do you like me?' I said.

'What? Of course, I like you. You're nice.'

'Are you attracted to me? Even a little?'

'What does "a little attracted" mean?'

'Do you think about me? Do thoughts about me randomly pop up in your head?'

'Yes ... sometimes ...'

'What kind of thoughts?'

'Oh … I feel like talking to you. Spending time with you. I wonder about what you are doing. I think about you performing at the comedy club.'

'How many times a day do you think of me?'

'I don't know. Two? Three? I haven't counted. How often do you think of me?'

'Fifty, sixty times.'

'What?'

'Relax. I'm joking,' I said, laughing. 'But I think of you a fair number of times.'

'Okay,' she said, looking uncertain and amused at the same time.

'Also, I know I'm divorced and older. So it's not an easy decision for you.'

'Well, I've never been married or even dated anybody.'

'I know.'

Payal leaned forward. 'Whatever this is, Saket, take it slow, please,' she said. 'I'm curious about things. I want to see where this goes, but I really haven't done this before.'

I removed my hand and looked into her eyes. 'Slow is good.'

'Thank you.'

'From now on, I'll be like an actor in a slow-motion movie,' I said and picked up the menu card in slow motion. Then I lifted my wine glass and sipped the Prosecco in slow motion.

She laughed.

'Shall we order some dinner?' I said, gesturing for the waiter in slow motion.

'Do you want me to get you a cab?' I said. 'Parel, right?'

We were in the lobby of the Four Seasons Hotel, having come down after finishing dinner.

Payal checked her watch. 'It's only 10 p.m. Not that late by Mumbai standards,' she said.

Okay, she wanted to spend more time with me.

'You want to go somewhere else?' I said. 'Like a nightclub or something?'

'Somewhere we can take a walk? Near the sea maybe?'

'There's the Bandstand in Bandra. Shall we go there for a bit?'

'Sure,' she said.

We took a black-and-yellow cab up to one end of Bandstand.

'That's Galaxy, Salman Khan's house,' she said, pointing to an apartment complex.

'Yes, and at the other end of Bandstand is Shah Rukh's Mannat.'

'Let's do the Salman to Shah Rukh walk, shall we?' she said.

Bandstand was full of walkers and strollers even this late in the night. Payal walked close to me, her bare arm occasionally grazing my shirt sleeve. Halfway through our walk, when we passed a bhutta seller, we stopped to buy one.

'I love this,' Payal said, taking a bite of the bhutta before passing it to me as we continued walking on the promenade. It felt more intimate than Aer. Every now and then, our fingers touched.

'You have a brother, right? You told me about him that day,' I said.

'Yes. Vansh. According to my parents, he can do no wrong,' Payal said.

'What do you mean?'

'He never did well in studies, not that my parents cared. Dad wants him to come help in the factory, but Vansh doesn't want to work hard. He prefers hanging out with his friends and playing video games. And yet ...'

'And yet what?'

'He's the son. I'm the daughter.'

We reached Shah Rukh's home, Mannat. Quite a few people stood outside, taking pictures and hoping to catch a glimpse of the superstar perhaps. I held Payal's hand in mine as we crossed the road and turned around to walk back.

'Was it hard? The divorce?' she said, edging closer.

'Changed everything. I lost my home and my life in the US. Most of my wealth too.'

'I mean, was it hard for you emotionally?'

I turned sideways to look at her. 'Nobody has ever asked me that.'

'You don't have to tell me if it's too personal.'

'No, it's okay. It was difficult emotionally,' I continued. 'Finding out that she was involved with someone else, that too since before our marriage. But she still chose to marry me. In a sense, she fooled me from the start.'

'Why did she marry you? Why not the person you said she was with?'

'The rakhi brother? That guy's family had a higher status than Raashi's. His parents said no. You know how Indian families are.'

She nodded. 'And what made you get married?'

'I didn't know any better. It was the logical next step according to the tick-markers.'

'Tick … what? Who?'

'Well, I have a theory. All the people around us, who judge us and tell us how to live, they are tick-markers. If we do what they say, they give us their approval—tick marks,' I said, making tick marks in the air.

'Interesting concept.'

'It's a trap. But like most people, I fell right into it. Tried to live up to others' expectations and lost myself in the process.'

'Are you okay now?' Payal said.

'Yes, I'm much better. Honestly, though, I've lost faith in the whole institution of marriage.'

'That's not surprising. You've really been hurt,' Payal said, looking into my eyes.

I remained quiet. She held my hand and squeezed it.

'Sorry, I didn't mean to make our outing all serious,' I said finally.

'It's fine. I'm always happy to listen to people's stories.'

'You sound so mature and sensible for your age,' I said. 'And you're a great listener.'

'Thank you,' she said and smiled.

We reached the point where we'd started our walk from. I checked the time: 11.30 p.m.

'It's late,' I said. 'But I still feel like spending more time with you.'

'It's not late for a Saturday night in Mumbai,' Payal said softly.

'How about some coffee?'

'Sure,' she said. 'Where should we go?'

'There are many cafés on Carter Road. But Saturday night means they'll all be super crowded,' I said.

'Somewhere not too crowded, please,' she said. 'Somewhere we can sit in peace, and talk.'

'I have a place in mind. We could go there, but only if you're okay with it.'

'Tell me.'

'My place is not far from here. I have everything there—coffee, tea, wine. And it's also not crowded.'

Payal stared at me for a second and then looked away, biting her lower lip, as if mulling over the idea.

'We don't have to,' I said hurriedly when she didn't respond. 'Also, it's a big mess. This wasn't the plan. I mean, it was just—'

'Okay,' Payal interrupted me. 'Let's go to your place. Why not? It'll be more relaxing than a busy, crowded café.'

~

'This is so nice. And such a cute window,' Payal said.

We stood in my living room. I switched on the table lamps, including the one next to the window ledge.

Payal walked up to the window, sat on the ledge and turned to me. 'If I lived here, I'd always sit here,' she said.

'That's exactly what I do,' I said.

Leaving her looking out of the window, I went to the small kitchen next to the living room. 'What do you want?' I said loudly so Payal could hear me outside.

'What do you have?' she said, walking into the kitchen.

I opened a wooden cabinet and showed her its contents—there was black tea, green tea and coffee.

'I also have some soft drinks and wine in the fridge,' I said.

'May I?' she said, pointing to the fridge.

'Of course,' I said, laughing. 'It's not my private safe. Not that I have a private safe.'

She opened the fridge. It was filled with whey protein shakes, pre-workout drinks and about five dozen eggs.

'Wow. You're really hard-core,' she said.

'I try.'

She dug a little deeper into the fridge. 'Is this regular white wine?' she said, pulling out a bottle.

'Yes, what else would it be?'

'I don't know. Maybe you keep some high-protein wine or something,' she said.

I laughed. She spoke like me, making smartass comments when you least expected them.

She kept the bottle on the kitchen counter.

'Are we drinking this then?' I said.

'No?' She blinked.

'I thought we were going to have coffee or green tea, but wine is fine.'

'Maybe, at your age, green tea is better …' she said.

'Ouch. Are you making fun of me?'

'No. You're supposed to be the funny guy, right?' she said with a twinkle in her eye.

I laughed and poured the wine into two wine glasses.

'Let's sit at the window …' she said.

We returned to the living room and sat on the ledge, facing each other, with our backs against the wall, our legs extended. We sipped the wine in silence, gazing out of the window. The gentle rustling of the tree leaves in the breeze and the occasional sound of vehicles passing on the road below filled the space. My right leg brushed against her left leg.

Her phone rang a little later. She ignored it. But it rang again. This time, Payal cut the call and began typing a message.

'Everything okay?' I said. 'Take the call if you want ...'

She shook her head. 'It's my mother. She called earlier when we were having dinner. She calls every night, to check if I'm okay.'

'Then take the call.'

'No. She'll ask too many questions. What did you eat for dinner? Who did you meet?'

'And you can't tell her you met me.'

'Not unless your name is Sakshi instead of Saket.'

'You can call me Sakshi. I could pass off as one.'

Both of us smiled.

'I've messaged her. I wrote that I ate dal chawal, worked and then dozed off,' Payal said.

'Listen, if you want to call her back ...'

'No, it's all right. It's Sunday tomorrow. I'll visit them anyway,' she said and kept her phone aside.

'Music?' I said.

I connected the Bluetooth speaker in my room to my phone and opened the YouTube app. A.R. Rahman's 'Piya Milenge' filled the room.

'Nice song,' she said, swaying slightly to the music.

'It's a new song, from the movie *Raanjhanaa*.'

She nodded and looked outside the window. 'These trees. It's so peaceful here ...' She sighed.

'May I sit next to you?' I said.

'Yes, sure,' she said. She slid her slender body towards the window to make space for me.

'Is it really true?' I said as I sat next to her.

'What?' she said, turning her face towards mine.

'That you've never been kissed?'

'Oh, that,' she said, making a silly face. 'Yes. It's true. Rather stupid in this day and age, isn't it?'

I looked at her, maintaining eye contact. I leaned forward, our faces mere millimetres apart. Her breath quickened. She turned her gaze away and then looked back at me.

Somewhere in the background, the song reached its crescendo.

'Okay?' I whispered.

She gave me a brief nod.

Gently, I held her chin with one hand and kissed her lower lip as softly and slowly as possible. A moment into the kiss, I increased its intensity, and felt her respond. She shifted her body closer to mine. Never in my life had I felt so much from a kiss alone. The world seemed to have receded somewhere into the background. Minutes passed. The song ended. Two YouTube ads, one for a detergent and another for an anti-dandruff shampoo followed, making the most mood-killing first-kiss background track ever. However, we didn't really care. We just continued to kiss, our lips fused together.

When we finally broke apart, Payal leaned her head against my chest and hugged me. A second or two later, I felt a wetness on my chest where her eyes touched me.

'Payal? You okay?' I said.

'Yeah. I'm fine,' came her muffled reply, her head still buried in my chest.

'Are you crying?'
'No.'
'Payal?'
'Just a bit.'
'Why?'
'I don't know ... a part of me had started to believe that something was wrong with me. That nobody would ever kiss me.'
'What? Are you crazy? Who wouldn't want to kiss you?' I said.
'Thank you,' she said softly, lifting her face from my chest to look at me. 'Also, one more thing,' she said.
'What?' I said tenderly.
'Can we skip these Surf Excel ads and put on some real music?'
Both of us burst into laughter. I selected the next song and hit play. The opening strains of 'Saajnaa', from the film *Lamhaa*, filled the room.
'Such a soulful song,' she whispered.
'So, how do you feel?'
'You mean after my first kiss?'
'Yes.'
'I'm okay, I think. A part of me was like, "Wow. This is finally happening." Another part was like, "This is it? This is what the big fuss is all about?" And then there is that nasty part, spoiling things as always.'
'What nasty part?'
She didn't look at me. 'The part that guilt-trips me. Says things like, "You're a bad girl, Payal. What are you doing? This is so wrong. You're letting your parents down."'
'Really?'
'Yeah. And that's why, more wine please.'

'I think we've had enough—'

'You're old, *you* should keep it in check. But please, I'd like some more,' she said, holding her empty glass out towards me.

'You, Payal Jain, are brutal.'

'Come on, a first kiss is momentous. A girl's allowed an extra glass of wine after that,' she said.

Shaking my head, I got up and refilled both our glasses.

'Cheers,' I said as I handed the glass back to her and took a sip of the wine.

Maybe it was all the wine we'd had, or perhaps it was the kiss that made me bold. I sat down and placed my hand on her leg. An electric current shot through me.

'I like you, Payal,' I said.

'I like you too, Saket …'

'And I trust you. After a long time, I feel like I can trust someone. And that's you.'

'I trust you too.'

'And I feel special.'

'Why?'

'Because I'm the first guy to kiss you.'

'Oh,' she looked at me, her gaze steady, and said, 'I feel special too.'

'Why?'

'Because I'm the first girl you've liked after your divorce, right?'

Before I could answer, however, she spoke again. 'Or wait, I may be wrong. Am I? I'm just assuming—'

'No, you're right,' I cut her off mid-sentence. 'I had decided to never be in a relationship again. But you, something about you …'

'What about me?'

'Initially, I thought it's just physical attraction, an infatuation perhaps.'

'And now?'

'Now ... it isn't just that. When we sat here on the ledge earlier, sipping our wine in silence, it felt right. I felt at peace. That's the best test—when you feel comfortable in the silences, and it doesn't feel awkward. There's something real there.'

Payal didn't respond. She just continued to look right into my eyes.

I stood up and gently pulled her by her hands to make her stand beside me. Then I leaned forward and kissed her again. She wrapped her arms around me and kissed me back, pouring herself into the moment.

I unbuttoned the top few buttons of my shirt and placed Payal's hand inside. Fine, I admit it—I wanted her to feel my chiselled pecs. Did she notice? I couldn't tell. She only held me tighter as we kissed again, and again and again. She had waited more than twenty years for her first kiss, but the next hundred came by in just twenty minutes.

I pulled away for a quick second to drop my shirt on the floor, and came back to kiss her.

'Is this wrong?' she said once, her hands caressing my upper body.

'What?'

'I haven't done this before, Saket. I don't know, but is this how it's supposed to happen?'

'There are no rules about how it happens.' I kissed her again. I kissed her eyes. Her neck.

She giggled. 'Sorry, that's a bit ticklish,' she said.

I whispered in her ears, 'Let's go inside? But only if you want to …'

'I want to,' she said after a pause.

'Sure?'

'Yes.'

I held her hand and led her into the bedroom. We sat on my bed, facing each other.

'You're beautiful, Payal,' I said.

'Thank you,' she said.

I put my arms around her and found the zipper at the back of her dress. She lifted her head to look at me. I gently tugged at the zipper. But I couldn't open it. She moved her hands back to assist me, and a second later, her unzipped dress fell to the side, pooling around her waist. She sat there on my bed, looking vulnerable and beautiful, her hands instinctively going up to cover her breasts. I felt my breath catch. I kissed her again, keeping it slow and easy until I felt her relax in my arms. Her hands moved up across my chest. When I made a move to unhook her bra, she didn't protest. With the tips of my fingers, I skimmed over her breasts, which were barely visible in the dark room with only the diffused streetlight coming in from outside. She shivered in immediate response, her back arching at my touch.

'I've never … I've never felt anything like this before,' she said softly.

'I'll go slow,' I said. 'Trust me?'

She closed her eyes and nodded.

I kissed her again and again, showering little pecks all over her face. I caressed her breasts, her arms, her face. I couldn't get enough of her. Overwhelmed, I sat up straighter and took a few deep steadying breaths.

'You okay?' she asked.

'It's been a long time since ...'

'I know ...' she said softly, interlacing her fingers with mine. 'Is this what people do then?' she asked a second later.

'Meaning?'

'People who date?'

'Well, yes.'

'Are we on a date then?'

'Now, definitely yes.'

'Nice,' she said, closing her eyes and smiling. 'We're definitely dating right now. Cool.'

'You are way too cute.' I pulled her to me, and her breasts touched my chest, instantly turning me on again.

'Come here,' I said, making her lie down on the bed with me, her body pressed against mine as we cuddled in our underwear.

'You're turned on?' she said after a second.

'Of course,' I said. 'What else did you expect?'

'I don't know. I ... I've never seen it before.'

'Never seen what before?'

'A man's thing. Turned on. Or even otherwise, actually.'

'Would you like to?'

'I think so. I mean I want to, out of curiosity. But I'm also feeling very shy,' she said, hiding her face in my chest.

'You've seen it in pictures, right? Or movies?'

'You mean porn? Yes, I've seen porn.'

'Have you ever done things with porn?'

'Like what?'

'Like ... you know ... touch yourself while watching porn?'

'Stop it. What kind of questions are you asking me?' she said and giggled.

'I'm only trying to understand how much you know.'

'Ugh. I tried. To do the touching thing,' she said, giggling a little.

'And? What happened?'

'It kind of felt good. But I don't think anything happened. Also, maybe it was just the movie I chose, it looked too graphic and gross. After a while, I went eww and stopped it.'

'Did you ever try it again?'

'Only a few times. But I felt nothing. Apart from the guilt, of course, the great Jain guilt.'

'Porn and masturbation are also on the Jain not-to-do list?'

'Why won't they be? Anything sinful and fun is on that list. Not just Jain, it's on every good Indian girl's not-to-do list.'

'But did your parents specifically tell you that?'

'No. But which Indian parents talk to their kids about sex?'

'True.'

'But I'm learning now,' she said, turning towards me. 'And this doesn't feel gross. It feels ... nice? Exciting?'

I kissed her again. Her breathing quickened.

'You've never had an orgasm?' I said.

'I don't think so,' she said.

'Well, since today is a day of many firsts for you'—I half rose, leaning on my elbow—'is it okay if I try to make you have one?'

Our eyes met. She nodded.

I kissed her face, and then moved down, kissing her neck, her shoulders, her breasts, stomach and navel. When I reached the waistband of her underwear, I stopped. I hooked my fingers around it and looked at her. She lifted herself up on her elbows to look at me.

'I'm nervous,' she whispered.

'Why?'

'I've never been fully naked in front of anyone. Not even a doctor.'

'I understand. But good nervous?'

She smiled. 'Yeah. But I also don't want to get pregnant or something.'

'We're not having sex.'

'We're not?'

'No. I don't even have any protection with me.'

'Oh?'

'I don't have any condoms lying around. I wasn't planning on anything happening. I didn't even know we would be coming here, to my house.'

'Do you think I shouldn't be here?' she said.

I sat up and looked into her eyes. 'I think you should always be here and never leave.'

She smiled shyly.

'Relax,' I said, and gently pushed her back down on the bed again. Then I peeled her underwear off, and slowly pushing her legs apart, I placed my mouth between her legs.

'Oh my ... ah!' She bit her lower lip to stifle her moans as I began pleasuring her.

I clasped both her hands with mine. A few minutes later, her body trembled, her back arched and she moaned loudly before collapsing limply.

'Oh my God,' she said after a few seconds, her eyes fluttering open. She let out a deep sigh. 'What just happened?'

'You tell me,' I said.

'It felt like … I don't know. It was an intense sort of a pleasure for a few seconds. My whole body shook, and I thought I'd explode. Look, I'm still shivering. I had an orgasm, isn't it? I did no?' She looked amazed.

'That's it then. You did have one,' I said, grinning.

'Wow. Thank you.'

'You don't have to thank me.'

'Why not? You made it happen. So, thank you.'

'What can I say? My pleasure.'

She smiled. 'And … how about you?' she said.

'What?'

'Won't you … you know, do your thing as well?'

I looked at her and smiled.

'Anything I can do to help?' she said.

'Just hold me and lie next to me,' I said, climbing back into the bed. She cuddled and kissed me as I pleasured myself. When I finished a few minutes later, I wiped myself with some tissues from the bedside table and then turned to hold her.

'How did it feel?' she said.

'Amazing.'

'Okay, I'm happy to hear that,' she said.

She yawned. I found that cute as well. Was I falling in love with her? Wait, was I already in love with her?

'Sorry, but I'm feeling sleepy. I'd better go,' she said, sitting up and searching for her clothes in the darkened room.

'Go where?'

'Home, where else?' she said, picking up her dress from the floor.

'It's two in the morning.'

'So? It's okay. Mumbai's pretty safe.'

'Just sleep here, Payal,' I said.

'What? How?'

'I'll give you a T-shirt to sleep in.'

'It's not that. I've to go to my parents' house in the morning. I don't have my Indian clothes here.'

'Just go to your Parel flat in the morning and then to your parents' place. It's Sunday. There won't be any traffic.'

Payal continued to hold her dress and sit. She spoke after a pause, 'Fine, but I'll leave early.'

'Sure,' I said.

I got up and went to my closet. I came back with an old T-shirt from Gold's Gym, San Francisco. On me, it looked fitted. On her, it felt massively oversized.

'Sleep now.' I stroked her hair.

'You're really nice, Saket,' she murmured, drifting off to sleep.

∼

'Good morning,' I said cheerfully.

Payal dragged her feet into the living room, rubbing her eyes and squinting as she adjusted to the bright sunlight. A small bulbul was perched on the window grill, its sweet cooing filling the room.

'Good morning,' she said in a sleepy voice. 'What time is it?'

'Eight.'

'Damn, I'm late,' she said. She noticed the spread on the dining table. 'What's all this?'

'We have toast, jam, butter, Nutella, cheese and peanut butter. I have cereal and milk. There's Greek yogurt, cut fruits and some fresh orange juice as well. I also made some poha. There's tea and coffee. And guess what? Everything is Jain-friendly,' I said with a grin.

'Wow. Why so much?'

'I didn't know what you'd like for breakfast.'

'When did you wake up?'

'Six. Couldn't sleep, so I thought I'd make us some breakfast.'

She looked at the flowers on the dining table. 'And these flowers? I didn't see them last night.'

'No, I bought them now. When I went down to get stuff for breakfast. You like them?'

'Yeah, but—' She stopped mid-sentence. 'Wait, where are my clothes?'

'Why? You look cute in my T-shirt. Come, sit. Coffee? Or tea?'

'No, I need to go home.'

'I know. But have something first. You can book an Uber later.'

'I'd rather go now. Ow, I have a headache,' she said, holding her head in her hands.

'You're hungover. Have some orange juice. It'll help.'

'Where are my clothes?' she asked, ignoring me and going back into the bedroom. 'Found them,' she called out a second later.

I followed her into the bedroom.

'Hey, I'm changing!' she said when I walked in.

'Sorry,' I said and retreated to the living room.

She came out dressed after five minutes.

'Juice?' I said, offering her a glass.

'My Uber is on its way,' she said.

'Oh, you booked one already?' I said. 'How far is it?'

'Two minutes away. I'd better go down.'

'Just have some juice before you leave, please.'

She took the glass of juice from me and gulped it all down in under ten seconds.

'Thanks,' she mumbled and quickly walked out the door.

'You really are in a rush,' I said as I took the lift with her.

'I am.'

Outside, her Uber had arrived.

'I had a great time with you yesterday. The whole thing. Aer. Bandstand. Home,' I said.

'Oh, thank you as well. Thanks for dinner,' she said, getting into the cab.

'I'll see you soon?'

'Let's see,' she said and zoomed off in her hired cab.

Let's see—the two most cryptic words a woman can say. Ever.

∽

Seven hours and forty-seven minutes. That's how long it had been since Payal had not replied to my message. She hadn't enabled the blue-tick feature on WhatsApp, so I couldn't even tell if she had seen it. Why do people turn off the blue ticks anyway?

I had messaged her, 'Was great seeing you. Hope you made it in time for lunch at your parents'?'

Innocent enough, right? So why the hell hadn't she responded? Had she 'ghosted' me, a term her generation used all the time? What was happening? She'd been cuddling with me just hours ago. Now I was waiting for her reply like a death-row convict waiting for a pardon.

Should I message her again? But that would be double-texting—something only clingy people did. Was I being clingy? Why was I, a five-foot-eleven bulked-up man with a six-pack, feeling so powerless waiting for a tiny notification to pop up on my phone? This was exactly why I'd wanted to avoid relationships. *Damn it, respond already, girl.*

I typed out 'Hey, everything okay?' while sitting at the dining table. But I didn't press send. It sounded too desperate. I deleted it.

Should I just call her? No. What if she was still at her parents' house, where boys were banned? She could get into trouble. Maybe it was better to just double-text.

'U there?' I typed and pressed send.

No reply for thirty long minutes.

'Just want to know you're okay.' Triple-text, an hour later.

'You haven't replied all day. Was getting worried.' Quadruple-text, two hours later.

This time, I saw the typing notification on her WhatsApp chat window. Okay, clearly, she was alive. And typing out a reply. But then she stopped typing. Then she started again. My eyes remained glued to my phone screen.

'Hi,' she replied.

That's it? After so many hours and quadruple-texts later, that's all she has to say?

'Hey there,' I replied instantly. 'There you are. What's up?'

'Just came back to Parel. About to go to bed.'

'How was lunch at your parents' house?'

'Good.'
'You didn't message all day.'
'Sorry, was tied up.'
Even on chat, I could sense her coldness.
'Everything okay?'
'What do you mean?'
'You didn't respond all day. And even now, you sound distant.'
'I'm fine.'
'You sure?'
She took a few minutes before responding. 'I'm not okay with what happened.'
My heart sank. 'You mean the whole evening? Aer, Bandstand, everything?'
'No, all that was fine. But whatever happened at your place.'
'What's the matter, Payal?'
'I know it happened in the heat of the moment. And it seemed okay then. But I'm not okay with all that now. The rest is fine. We can be friends.'

We can be friends?

Her words hit me like a jackhammer. One night ago, I was the first man she'd ever kissed. Less than twenty-fours later, I was being friend-zoned? What the hell happened? I couldn't figure this out over chat.

'May I call you?' I said.
'No. I'm tired. Have work tomorrow.'
'We need to talk about this.'
'There's nothing to talk about. I'm not that kind of girl, Saket.'
'What kind of girl?'

'Nothing. Good night, Saket.'

I flung my phone aside and flopped down on the bed, mentally preparing myself for a night of tossing around with no possibility of getting any sleep.

~

'Payal,' I called her. She had just come out of Express Towers, the building that housed the Blackwater office, and was waiting in the front porch for her car to arrive.

'Saket?' she said, turning around. She wore a black formal pantsuit, with a heavy laptop bag slung over her delicate shoulders.

'Why aren't you answering my calls or messages?' I said. 'I've been trying for days.'

'I had a busy week.'

'It's Friday now,' I said. 'Can we please sit somewhere and talk?'

'My dad's driver is just about to get here. I have to go home tonight.'

'Ten minutes, please.'

She leaned forward a little, craning her neck to look at the cars entering the building premises. She couldn't spot hers. 'Fine. Where do you want to go?' she said.

'Let's go to Leopold. It's close by.'

Nodding, she called her driver and told him not to come immediately and wait for a while instead.

Payal and I took a taxi to Leopold's, a short five-minute drive away. The iconic restaurant in Colaba had become even more famous after the 26/11 terror attacks in 2008 when terrorists had stormed in and blindly opened fire at the people inside. The restaurant still had a window with bullet holes from that fateful night.

We entered Leopold's, not having exchanged a single word throughout the taxi ride, and found it packed. Waiters scurried around, serving all types of customers, from backpacker firangs to investment bankers who'd just finished work in Nariman Point.

'Beer?' I said to Payal as we sat down facing each other.

'No, just water.'

I told a waiter to get us a pint of draft beer, a bottle of water and a plate of masala peanuts.

'How long had you been waiting outside my office?' Payal said.

'Two hours maybe.'

'Why?'

'Doesn't matter. What's going on, Payal?'

'Nothing is going on, Saket. I told you.'

'Told me what exactly?'

'That I'm not comfortable with whatever happened.'

'And instead of talking about it, you decided to just cut me off?'

'I needed some space,' she said.

Our eyes met for a brief second. The waiter arrived with our order. I took a sip of the chilled beer, along with a spoonful of the spicy peanuts, mixed with a generous sprinkling of raw onions, green chillies and coriander leaves.

Payal played with her glass of water.

'I thought we had an amazing evening that day,' I said.

'It was just too much.'

'I know. I admit that. We went too far, way too soon. But it just felt like we have this insane chemistry and—'

'Saket,' she interrupted me, 'please understand ... I've not done anything like this. With anyone. And then ...'

'Then what?'

'I felt so guilty the next day.'

'Why did you feel guilty? We're both single and we both like each other. That's what happens when a man and a woman like each other.'

'This stuff should ideally happen after marriage. At least that's what I've been brought up to believe.'

'Are you serious? Look at all the couples in this restaurant. Most of them are not married. You think they aren't going to do anything tonight?'

Payal looked around. Two tables ahead of us, a young twenty-something couple was kissing.

'I'm not that kind of girl,' Payal said.

'Neither is the girl at that table. She's just kissing her boyfriend.'

'But we aren't even boyfriend and girlfriend,' Payal said in a high-pitched voice.

'Calm down,' I said. 'Please. Don't be upset.' I placed my hand on hers, but she pulled her hand away.

'Did you eat dinner?' I said.

She remained quiet. After a minute, she shook her head.

'Let's eat some food. People are allowed to do that, right?'

Without waiting for her to respond, I summoned a waiter. 'Madam is Jain. What can we order?' I said.

The waiter suggested we order either a pizza or Indian vegetarian fare, made Jain-style. I chose the latter, ordering a yellow dal, paneer masala and rotis. 'Also, can you get some peanuts without the onion?' I said.

'And a glass of white wine,' Payal said.

The waiter nodded and left.

'Thanks,' she said, looking down at her hands.

'Don't be so formal,' I said. 'And may I say something?'

She looked up.

'I hear what you feel about that evening. I get it. I know how it must've come across.'

'How?'

'Me, an older man, married and then divorced. You doing things for the first time. Sort of creepy on paper.'

'I ...' Payal said after a pause, 'I wouldn't say it was creepy. But it was a bit fast.'

'I agree.'

'Thank you.'

'No need to say thanks. Would you like to know how I felt?'

A tight nod.

'Firstly, I didn't plan it. I never thought you'd come home.'

'I know,' she said.

'I loved hanging out with you, at Aer and then the walk.'

'I did too.'

The waiter came back with her glass of wine. She took a sip.

'It felt magical to have you at my place. Ever since you left, every day I imagine you sitting at the ledge.'

She smiled. I looked straight into her eyes.

'It's been years since I felt connected to someone like this. My marriage died four years ago. Not since then.'

Her eyes still guarded, she said, 'Why me?'

'I cannot explain it. We have a connection. Maybe the way you supported me when I was nervous. Maybe it's how much

I enjoy talking to you, even helping you in your work. It's how you're witty and smart and, of course …'

'Of course, what?'

'You're beautiful. I've never been as attracted to a woman as I'm to you. Maybe that's why things went so fast.'

We stared at each other in silence for a few seconds. She shifted in her seat, looking unsure about how to react.

I spoke again. 'Payal, if being boyfriend and girlfriend is what it takes, I'd love for you to be my girlfriend.'

'I'm twenty-one. You're thirty-three. We have a twelve-year age gap.'

'So what?'

'You've been married and divorced. I've never even been in a relationship. How is this ever going to work?'

'How do you know it won't?'

She stayed quiet.

'You must've felt something too,' I said, 'that you made me your first.'

'Like you said, it wasn't planned. It just happened. I also felt something, yes, but Akanksha said—'

'Akanksha?' I interrupted her. 'That girl who was supposed to come with you for the show that day?'

'Yes. Akanksha is my best friend. We tell each other everything.'

'Okay. What did she say?'

'You don't want to know.'

'I definitely want to know.'

'She told me to stay away from you. To cut off all contact.'

'Which is exactly what you did.'

'She even asked me to block your number. But I didn't do that.'

'Thank God for small mercies,' I said sarcastically.

'I freaked out. You must understand, Saket, it was all too much. We barely know each other, and yet, so much happened that night.'

'I know. But like you said, it just happened.'

She exhaled. 'Akanksha also said that this is just a crazy infatuation. Doesn't mean anything.'

'And? What else?'

'That you're just this older guy looking for some young piece of action.'

I took a deep breath to remain calm.

'And you believed her?' I said.

'She's my childhood friend. We've been together since school. I trust her.'

'What does this Akanksha do?'

'She's a housewife. She's also an Instagram influencer. Just starting out though.'

'You said childhood friend. She's your age then?'

'Yes. She married early.'

'Wow.'

The waiter arrived with our food. I quickly served both of us.

'I don't know about Akanksha,' I said, tearing a piece of roti and dipping it in the dal. 'All I know is that I've never waited outside an office building to just talk to a girl. And I probably never will.'

'I'm sorry I cut you off like that,' Payal said. 'I didn't mean to hurt you. I'm not experienced in all this and—'

'It's all right, Payal,' I said, interrupting her mid-sentence. 'And I want to say something about the physical stuff as well.'

'What?'

'It can wait.'

'Meaning?'

'Meaning, you're right. We don't know each other well. We took things too far the other night. And one more thing.'

'What?'

'You're not just some young piece of action for me,' I said.

She looked at me. Our eyes locked.

'Can you trust me?'

'I'll try,' she said in a subdued voice.

For the next few minutes, we ate our dinner in silence until Payal spoke again.

'I overreacted. I'm sorry, really. I shouldn't have cut you off. It was immature of me.'

I shrugged.

'And sorry for leaving like that the next morning. That was rude. You'd put in so much effort in arranging that nice breakfast.'

'You must've been processing a lot.'

'I've told you about my upbringing, right? Even speaking to boys is a sin. All of this, it's a complete no-no.'

'I understand.'

'Also, Akanksha said I'm making a big mistake. It's my older-men crush thing. She said I'll just end up getting used.'

'So, you have a crush on me ...' I said.

She smiled. 'You understand her point? Both of us might just be indulging in some weird fantasy,' Payal said.

'Like what?'

'I'm this innocent twenty-one-year-old you get to do things with. It makes you feel young and helps you get over your divorce. You, on the other hand, are this mature, experienced man who's giving me loads of attention and I'm drawn to it.'

'Wow, you've really been thinking about this a lot.'

'More like overthinking. Which I'm an expert at. Anyway, all of this may not be real, Saket.'

I responded after a few moments. 'Maybe you're right. Only time will tell. But so what? As long as we like spending time together, who cares?'

'Is it that simple?'

'Payal, don't live your life to please others. I did that, and I regret it.'

We finished our dinner in silence after that.

'Thanks for listening to me,' Payal said.

We had come out of Leopold's and were standing by the street.

'Thanks for listening to *me*. Do you want to call your driver?'

Payal looked at me for one long second. 'Or I can just send him back,' she said. 'If you want to hang out some more, that is.'

I looked at her for a few seconds. 'Sure,' I said.

She called her driver and asked him to go home.

'What do you feel like doing?' I said.

'I don't mind sitting on your window ledge and having green tea.'

I looked at her, taken aback. *What was this woman?*

'I love sitting on that ledge. Can we do that, please?' she said.

∼

'Green tea?' I said.

Payal sat cross-legged on my window ledge, looking somewhat uncomfortable in the pantsuit.

'Sure,' she said, looking down at the street below. 'Or actually wait, do you have some wine?'

'Really?'

'Please don't judge me. I only had that one glass at Leopold's. It's the weekend, and I had a rough week—fourteen-hour workdays.'

I went to the kitchen and returned with two glasses of white wine. Like the last time, I sat on the opposite end of the ledge, facing her.

'So, how's work?' I said, deciding to stick to neutral topics.

'Busy. We're about to close a deal, and there are thousands of pages to read.'

'Yeah. Private equity is mostly reading legal documents. I don't miss that part.'

'How's your work going?'

'I had to work on a new set last week. Couldn't.'

'Why not?'

'Too disturbed and preoccupied.'

'Oh? Why?'

'Someone ghosted me.'

'Ouch. Sorry again.'

'Don't worry about it. You're here now.'

'Can I get away with claiming that I'm too young?'

'You're old enough to sift through private equity legal documents. But I guess you're too young to know how to communicate your feelings.'

She laughed. 'Something like that,' she said, taking a sip of her wine and gazing out of the window. We sat in silence for a few minutes.

'Do you miss her?' she said eventually.

'Who?'

'Raashi.'

'No, not really. We shared some good times in the beginning. But those memories are hazy. Only memories of the divorce are fresh.'

'I'm sorry.'

I shrugged.

'I shouldn't have told Akanksha about you.'

'It's okay. She's your best friend.'

'Yes. But I'm not like her.'

'Really?'

'Akanksha is what my parents want me to be. No boyfriends. Married at twenty. Loves cooking and taking care of the house.'

'Twenty? That's early.'

'Yeah, to Suraj Chandak. A boy chosen by her parents. She's Marwari, so it had to be a Marwari boy.'

'Didn't you say she's an influencer?'

'She's trying to be one. Guess what her account is all about?'

'No idea.'

'Being a proud housewife. It's called Home Diva. It's about how she's living her best life as a housewife. She's always posting stuff about the dishes she makes, the rooms she decorates and the mangalsutra she wears.'

'Is she doing well?'

'More than you can imagine. Loads of comments from men telling her that she's really a domestic goddess, and that they want to marry a girl just like her.'

She opened Instagram on her phone. She showed me an account called 'AkankshatheHomeDiva'. It had twenty thousand followers. Akanksha resembled a moderately attractive Indian housewife from one of those TV serials where mothers-in-law plot to hurt their daughters-in-law all day long. Most of Akanksha's posts had her wearing a saree or a salwar kameez, along with gold jewellery. Her most recent post was about her observing Karva Chauth by fasting for her husband's long life all day. She had shared pictures of herself performing puja and animatedly spotting the moon. She'd also written a caption about how fulfilled she felt as a woman doing these rituals. The post had many comments, most of them praising her: 'Upholding Indian values, amazing!' 'I want my daughter to be like you.'

'She's your best friend?' I said to Payal, returning her phone.

'Yes. We've been together since primary school. She's somewhat exaggerating her traditional persona online. In real life, she's not entirely like this. She wears jeans and drinks wine sometimes.'

'She still got married at twenty,' I said. 'As per her parents' wishes, and to a boy they chose.'

'True. And now she does Karva Chauth in a red-and-gold saree and feels fulfilled. Meanwhile, I review shareholder agreements in a dark-grey suit and feel exhausted.'

'You're working for Blackwater, that's one of the hardest jobs to get in the world. You're doing so much at a young age.'

'What's the point though? Sometimes I wonder if Akanksha is on a better path.'

'Are you crazy? You're smart and talented. Don't you want to fulfil your potential?'

'But she feels fulfilled. I feel overworked.'

'Sure, she says so. On social media. But if she's truly so fulfilled, why does she feel the need to post it all on social media?'

'I don't know,' Payal said and shrugged, taking a sip of her wine.

'You have to be true to yourself,' I said, 'and be comfortable with your choices. Even if they're different from those others make.'

'What if they're crazy choices?'

'Aiming to have a good career as a young girl is not a crazy choice.'

'What about the same young girl sitting on the window ledge of a much older, recently divorced man's apartment at night? Is that a crazy choice?'

I looked at her. She stared back at me.

'We're just sitting and chatting,' I said slowly.

'Are we?' she said, shifting a little and resting her leg on mine.

'Wasn't that the plan?'

'Was it?' she said and smiled, giving me a brief nod and gesturing for me to come closer.

I started to lean forward but then stopped myself. 'Payal,' I said, 'I really want to kiss you right now. But I don't want to lose you again like I did last week.'

Payal scooted forward and rested her head on my chest. I held the back of her head and lightly ran my fingers through her hair.

'I'll try not to freak out, I promise,' she said. 'Is this what is called sending mixed signals?'

'Maybe. I don't know. I just want you to be clear about what you want.'

'I like being with you, Saket. I want this,' she said. 'I'm done living my life according to my mother's prescription.'

She brought her face close to mine. I was fast losing my ability to think straight.

'I like you, Payal,' I said, 'a lot.'

Love is what I meant, not like.

'I like you too, Saket.'

Despite all my self-control, I couldn't resist giving her a little peck on her lips. She kissed me back. I pulled myself away. 'I don't want to be ghosted tomorrow morning.'

'I'll try not to,' she said.

We kissed again. The whole week of separation and uncertainty we'd both been through gave our kisses a sharp intensity. Our tongues met. I almost bit her lower lip. This time, we had no music playing in the background—only the sound of our breaths quickening. I ran my fingers down her neck, and she shivered. We continued to kiss for a long time.

'Let's go to the bedroom,' Payal said after a while.

'Are you sure?'

'Yes.'

Without another word, I got up and led her to the bedroom. We undressed quietly and lay down on my bed, with only a sheet covering us. I kissed her again and gently touched her all over. Then I heard something a man doesn't hear every day.

'I want to have sex.'

'What?' I said, shocked.

'I do,' she said.

'Are you sure? Why?'

'I want to try it. See what it's all about. And because I trust you.'

'You don't have to do this. Don't feel obligated.'

'I'm not. I want to. Do you have the stuff?'

'What stuff?'

'The contraceptives.'

'Payal, are you sure?'

'Yes. I'm not that kind of a girl. But I'm also sick and tired of not having tried anything either. Even Akanksha has had sex. My friends in Stanford did it with multiple people.'

'Akanksha is married.'

'True. But I don't want to get married anytime soon. And I don't want to wait that long. Now, do you want to or not?'

'What?'

'Have sex?'

'You're asking a guy if he wants to have sex? Seriously?'

'Is that a yes?'

'It's a hell yes!'

'Cool, so do you have protection?'

'No. But I have a chemist's number who can deliver it fast.'

'You want to call him?'

I looked at Payal, still shocked. Then I picked up my phone and called the chemist.

'Waled bhai, I need an urgent delivery.'

'What?'

'Digene bottle, one paracetamol strip, Tiger Balm. And a Durex.'

'Okay, I don't have Tiger Balm.'

'That's fine. Just send the rest.'
'Okay, which Durex?'
'Which ones are there?'
'Pack of three or ten?'
'I don't know. Pack of three?'
'Okay. Extra thin, ribbed, dotted … which one?'
'Whichever.'
'Extra thin is in demand. Will send that.'
'Okay, thanks.' I ended the call.

'Why did you order Digene and paracetamol?' Payal said, blinking.

'It's weird to order only condoms.'

'Really?' She giggled.

'I don't know. Come here,' I said, pulling her close to me.

We were kissing passionately when the doorbell rang. I quickly wrapped a towel around my waist before answering it.

'I came in time no?' Waled bhai said, grinning as he handed me a brown paper bag.

I didn't respond, but gave him a five-hundred-rupee note instead.

'No change,' he said.

'Keep it,' I said and shut the door.

I hurried back to the bedroom.

'Show me the box,' Payal said.

'What?'

'I've never seen a condom.'

I took out the small Durex packet from the brown paper bag and handed it to her.

She opened it and took out one of the three sachets inside. 'It's squishy,' she said, squeezing the sachet.

'Yes, because of the lubrication.'

'It has lubrication?'

I smiled as I took the sachet from her and opened it. Like a diligent student, she sat up to observe how I wore the condom.

'Does it hurt when you wear it?'

I smiled and shook my head. I pushed her shoulders back and made her lie back.

'Is this going to hurt?' she said.

'It might. I'll be gentle.'

She clutched my shoulders tightly as I eased into her.

'Ow!' she screamed in pain. Her nails dug into my shoulders.

'Are you okay?'

'Yes,' she said, breathing heavily.

'Okay.' I stayed still for a second, kissing her gently to soothe her.

'I can feel you inside,' she whispered.

'I can feel you too.'

She held me tight.

And a magical few minutes later, we lay next to each other, breathing hard, totally spent.

'So, it's all done now,' she said after a while.

'Yeah.'

'I've had sex …'

'Yeah.'

'Wow. I, Payal Jain, am no longer a virgin.'

'I guess not.'

Was she going to freak out on me now?

'How are you feeling?' I said, turning on my side to look at her.

'It hurt a bit at the start, but it felt good later.'
'And?'
'Don't worry. I'm fine. How are you feeling?'
'I'm feeling too many things. A bit overwhelmed.'
'Really?' Payal said, raising herself up on an elbow and facing me.
'I want to date you, Payal.'
'Are you proposing to me? Now? Like this?'
'Yes. I feel close to you, and I can't bear the thought of losing you. So, yes, I'm proposing to you. Be my girlfriend, Payal.'
'I guess I already am, right? What we did was a girlfriend-boyfriend thing.'
'They do more. Like they sometimes eat Nutella toast together for breakfast, without anyone freaking out.'
She looked at me and smiled. 'Do you want me to stay over?' she said.
'How about staying over forever?'
'You're good with lines.'
'Thank you. I'll get you an old T-shirt.'
'Yes, please. Before that, can I ask a stupid question?'
'Yeah.'
'What does one do with the condom you were wearing after you're done?'

~

I sent Payal a message from the backstage area at the Comedy Club: 'Nervous.'
'Remember, good nervous. All the best,' she replied.
'Two minutes to go. Keep chatting with me. About anything. It helps.'

'Okay. Listen, did you order the Surf Excel? And the coffee?'

'Seriously? We're talking about groceries now? What are we, a married couple of twenty years?'

'Ha ha. Focus on the show now. Go kill it.'

My name was announced just then. I put the phone in my back pocket and ran up to stage. 'Hello,' I said, facing a packed auditorium. 'How's everyone doing?'

'Great!' the crowd shouted back in unison.

Wow. An enthusiastic bunch.

'I'm doing great too. I have a girlfriend now. Been about six months, actually.'

The crowd cheered with claps and whistles.

'She's much younger than me though,' I said. 'Okay, not that young. She can vote. I think.'

A few scattered laughs.

'Dating a younger girl is mostly fun. She's a little crazy and wild sometimes. Once, when we were making out, she asked me to say, "Who's your daddy?"'

Stray giggles in the crowd.

'She said she'd read online that this who's-your-daddy line was a thing for some girls. What's up with that? Why do some girls like a guy to say that? Is it a Western thing? From Hollywood movies perhaps? Has to be. Because in India, we don't have this concept. If we did, we could use any of the terms we have for other male relationships here. I mean, we have chacha and mama … right?'

I switched to a seductive tone: 'Who's your chachu? Who's your mamu? Who's your fufa, baby?'

The crowd burst into wild laughter and applause.

'I can't believe you used that who's-your-daddy bit again,' Payal said, throwing a cushion at me. 'I only asked you to say it to me that one time. And I was very drunk then.'

We were lying in bed in my flat. For all practical purposes, it had become Payal's home as well. She stayed five nights a week at my place and spent the weekend either at her Parel apartment or with her parents in Ghatkopar.

'I'm sorry, baby,' I said, laughing. 'It's a stupid joke, but it always works. When I say "Who's your chachu?" in a low, husky voice, there are always laughs.'

'Seriously, mister. Stop using your girlfriend for material.'

'Real-life sources always lead to better writing,' I said, kissing her. 'But baby, tell me something.'

'What?'

'Who's your tauji?' I said in a soft, seductive voice.

'Eww. Seriously, double, triple eww. Yuck. Stop it.'

I laughed as she started slamming me with one of the pretty ethnic cushions she'd bought from Anokhi. Payal had redone the furnishings in the house. The bedspread, the cushions and the curtains in the bedroom now matched. She'd also decorated the window ledge, adding a string of fairy lights on the wall and some extra cushions for comfort. When a woman comes into a man's life, rather, when the right woman comes into a man's life, everything improves.

I snatched the cushion from her hands and threw it aside. I held her face and brought it closer to mine. 'I love you,' I whispered in her ear.

'You're very bad,' she said.

'I know,' I said. 'But then, who's your dadaji?'

'Stop it, Saket Khurana.'

'You did ask me to say who's your daddy. How is this any different? Just because it's in Hindi?'

'I was drunk. And super turned on. And we don't discuss things we said or did in bed when we were drunk and turned on.'

'Oh, really? Why not?'

'Okay, then let's talk about the time when you asked me to put my finger in—'

'Stop!' I said.

'See,' she said, laughing.

I looked at her with affection. She blushed. Did she love me just as much as I loved her?

'What are you thinking?' I said.

'We're out of Harpic,' she said.

'What? Now that's a romantic line that's never been said in bed before.'

She burst out laughing. 'No, really, we do need Harpic. Can you add that to the shopping list?'

'Baby, I was in such a romantic mood.'

'This is real romance. When you discuss the most mundane thing ever, and yet, it still feels special.'

'But, Harpic?'

She leaned forward and kissed me. 'I love you, Saket, so much.'

'I love you too.'

Grinning cheekily, she opened the drawer of the bedside table. She took out a pair of pink fluffy handcuffs and handed them to me.

'What the hell is this?' I asked.

'Ordered it on Amazon.'

'What for?'

'I want you to tie me up.'

'What?'

She looked at me and gave me a sheepish smile.

I placed the handcuffs around her wrists and snapped them shut. 'Payal Jain, you're one wild, naughty girl.'

'Only with you. You bring that out in me.'

I pulled her closer.

'Now, before we begin, don't you dare use the word "handcuffs" in your comedy material, ever,' she said.

∼

My comedy career on the rise. A beautiful, smart girlfriend taking care of me and my home. An insane sex life. Yes, for a few heady months, my life was perfect. Even though it was all about to come to a nasty, crashing end.

Before we get to that, however, let me tell you about my sex life during this phase. From someone who had never done anything physical when she first met me, Payal turned into an insatiable sexual beast, taking me along for the ride.

Once, she came backstage before my show to surprise me. With only a curtain separating us from the audience, we proceeded to do unspeakable things to each other. On my birthday, she decided to engage in some role-play. She wore an airline-stewardess uniform she'd ordered online. She brought me hot towels on a tray. Needless to say, hottest night ever.

Our role-play phase continued for a while after my birthday. We tried doctor–patient, professor–student, policewoman–criminal, call girl–customer (her idea, not mine). Each time, the sex got hotter, and our connection closer.

And it was more than just the sex. I was falling like never before. In love. Into the madness of love. Not a minute passed when I didn't think of Payal. I hated it when she had to go away and stay over at her parents' place. Speaking of her parents, I never interacted with them. In fact, for them, I didn't even exist. That's how Payal wanted it.

And then, just like that, the party was over.

One evening, Payal and I were sitting on the window ledge and working on our laptops. I was writing a new set about saas-bahu serials. She was reading a pitch from a cloud-kitchen company looking to raise money, when her mother called.

'Hi Mom. I'm busy,' Payal said, picking up the phone. 'I'll call you tomorrow morning on my way to work.'

Even though Payal had the phone to her ear, I could hear her mother's voice.

'Okay, fine. But definitely call me in the morning. It's important.'

'What happened?' Payal said.

'A rishta has come for you. And what an amazing one it is. Really, it is a kamaal ka rishta.'

'What? Mom, I don't want any rishtas right now.'

'Yes, you will. Once you hear the details. Your father and I are so excited.'

'I don't have time for this ...'

'Tomorrow morning. Call me.'

Payal cut the call and kept her phone aside. I looked at her, confused.

'Don't worry about it,' she said. 'It's all nonsense.'

'Kamaal ka rishta?'

'Whatever. She talks like that.'
'Has this happened before?'
'What?'
'Matches coming for you ...'
'Yeah, a few times.'
'You never told me.'
'Some were even before I knew you. Like Akanksha's husband's best friend.'
'And?'
'I dismissed it.'
'What about since we started dating?'
'There've been a couple of them. From within the Jain circle. Someone's parents saw me at the Jain temple and approached my parents. That sort of stuff.'

Payal got off the ledge and placed her laptop on the coffee table. Then she went into the kitchen to heat up dinner, which the part-time cook had made earlier in the day. A minute or so later, the microwave went 'ting' as it finished reheating the food. Payal brought the dinner out and set the table.

'Why didn't you tell me?' I said.
'Nothing worth telling. Come, let's eat.'
We ate in silence.
'Say something. Why are you so quiet?' Payal said, mopping up the chole with a roti.
'I can't lose you, Payal.'
'Huh? What are you even talking about?'
'Well, I don't know how kamaal ka this rishta is ...'
'It's kamaal ka for my mother. Not me,' she said. 'Can you pass me some more chole? I'm so damn hungry.'
'Payal, be serious.'

'About what?' she said, adding the chickpea curry to her plate with a serving spoon.

'Your parents are looking for rishtas for you. Sooner or later, they'll expect you to get married.'

'I won't agree to them.'

I put my spoon down and stopped eating. 'Tell your parents about us. You and me.'

Payal laughed.

'What's so funny?' I said.

'Are you crazy? I've told you about them, have I not?'

'It's the truth though. You and I are together.'

'My family isn't designed to handle the truth, Saket. We don't do truth.'

'So, I'll have to stay hidden all my life?'

'Come on. I didn't say that.'

'What is your plan then?'

'You tell me. Should there be a plan?'

I remained silent.

'Nothing to say? I thought so. Anyway, I'm done with dinner.' Payal stood up.

We cleared the table and took everything back to the kitchen. I put the remaining food in smaller containers and kept them in the fridge. Payal rinsed the plates and left them in the sink. I wiped the dining table with a damp cloth. She filled the water bottles to be kept on our bedside tables. Usually, this silence in which we performed these daily rituals would've been normal. Today, however, there was a heaviness in the air.

'It's not like I don't want to have a plan.' I finally broke the silence. We were in the bedroom, sitting on our respective sides of the bed.

'Don't worry about it,' Payal said, rubbing some moisturizer on her face. Girls have a hundred skincare rituals that guys have no idea about. She had, for example, a specific cream for her under-eye area, one for her face, another one for her arms and legs, and yet another one for her feet. Why are all these creams different? And what exactly do they do?

'I love you, Payal,' I said.

'But what does that mean finally?'

'As in?'

'Is there a future for us?'

When a woman uses the word 'future' in the context of a relationship, it's dangerous territory. One wrong utterance, and you could blow things up. Forever.

'When I say I can't live without you, I mean it. I want to be with you.'

'But you don't want to get married.'

'I didn't say that.'

'It's written all over your face. And you've told me this as well. The idea of marriage scares you.'

'I did say that, yes,' I said. 'Marriage does scare me.'

'But you don't want me to get married to anybody else either. In other words, you don't want me to get married at all.'

'You're twisting my words …' I said.

'I got it, Saket. There's no marriage-type future with you.'

'It's not like that, Payal.'

She turned sideways to face me. Even when angry, she looked … so cute, so beautiful, so mine. It was impossible for me to argue with her.

'I'm sorry,' I said. 'I just freaked out when I heard your mom get so excited about the rishta.'

'I'm not her.'

'I know.'

'You want me to tell them about us. They'll freak out, but eventually, and let's say hypothetically, I manage to convince them, and they come on board …'

'Go on,' I said, holding my breath.

'What do you think they'll expect us to do?'

'What?'

'Get married.'

'Oh.'

'And you're not ready for that.'

'Not right now. You know what I went through. It's been less than a year since my divorce.'

'They don't believe in dating, living-in and not getting married.'

'I know.'

'Now you see why I can't tell them about you? When we have a plan, I will.'

'Punjabi, older, divorced and a stand-up comedian. It'll be hard to tell them.'

'I'll deal with it, Saket,' Payal said.

'I love you.'

'Thank you.'

'No "I love you" back?'

'I'll tell you tomorrow.'

'Why tomorrow?'

'Let me see no what the kamaal ka rishta is,' she said.

I threw a cushion at her. She laughed as she caught it and threw it right back at me. I grabbed her. 'I'll show you something else kamaal ka right now,' I said, turning off the lights.

∼

'Can you talk?' I had a message from Payal.

I was in a meeting with Reliable Polymers, discussing the event flow for their upcoming annual retreats.

'In a meeting, baby. Call you back?' I messaged her.

'Soon, please,' she replied.

'I'll see you at home in the evening?'

'I can't come to Bandra tonight.'

'Why?'

'Call me. Will talk then.'

I finished my meeting and called Payal from the cab on my way back home.

'Hey, sweets, what's up?' I said.

'How was your meeting?'

'Good. Finalized everything. Flying to Goa for their first event next week. Then travelling for a week to the remaining conference venues.'

'Terrific.'

'Yeah. Anyway, what happened? Why am I not seeing you tonight?'

'I've to go to my parents' house.'

'On a Wednesday night?'

'Yeah. There's a tricky situation at home. But I'm handling it.'

'What situation?'

'Don't freak out, okay? But that kamaal ka rishta Mom was talking about?'

'What about it?'

'It's a bit complicated …'

'What do you mean?' I said.

'This rishta is from Jignesh uncle's side.'

'Who?'

'Jignesh Jain. Dad's longtime accountant.'

'So?'

'We're also close family friends. My parents have known Jignesh uncle and Supriya aunty for decades.'

The cab entered Pali Hill, and I reached my apartment building.

'Wait, I have to take the lift. Let me call once I reach upstairs.'

I look the elevator up to the fifth floor and called Payal again the minute I entered the flat. 'Go on,' I said.

'Yeah, so the complication is that it's Parimal.'

'Who's Parimal now?'

'Jignesh uncle's son. He's the rishta.'

'Kamaal ka rishta apparently.'

'There's nothing kamaal ka about him. However, my parents are damn excited, only because my mother and Supriya aunty are great friends. Jignesh uncle and my dad also meet each other socially once every week.'

'What does all this mean, Payal?'

'It means that I have to meet them tonight … Spend an evening with them. They're coming home. I can't not show up.'

'"They" as in Jignesh uncle and Supriya aunty?'

'Parimal also.'

'Oh. Okay, so the boy's side is coming over to see you. It's getting formal.'

'It's not like that, Saket.'

'What's it like then?'

'Just dinner with some guests at home.'
'What are you wearing tonight?'
'What?'
'Tell me what you are going to wear tonight.'
'How does it matter?'
'Just tell me.'
'Salwar kameez.'
'There you go. You're dressing traditionally. Like a good prospective bahu.'
'Relax, Saket. Mom wanted me to wear a saree, but I said salwar kameez is fine.'
'Wow, okay, there was a dress code that had been planned.'
'I'll handle it, Saket. It's. Under. Control,' Payal said, pausing after each word.
'Tell me more about this Parimal.'
'I don't know him so well.'
'I thought you guys were family friends.'
'Our parents are. I haven't been in touch with Parimal in years.'
'But you know him?'
'I knew him when I was a kid. As Parimal bhaiya. Can you imagine?'

The mention of the word 'bhaiya' triggered rakhi-brother memories. 'Yes, I can imagine it quite well actually,' I said in a serious tone.

'Oh, I'm sorry,' Payal said, as she understood the context. 'I didn't mean it like that at all. I barely interacted with him.'

'Fine. Let's hope you get to interact with him properly today.'

'Stop it! It's a formality. I need to get through a family dinner, that's all.'

'Fine.'

'I'll talk to Parimal personally. I'll tell him it's not going to work out. He'll understand and back out.'

'If you say so.'

'What's that supposed to mean?'

'Who in their right mind would back out of being with someone like you?'

'Aww. Is that a compliment? That's sweet. Miss me?'

'No, I don't. Bye, and have fun at your dinner.'

'Are you jealous?'

'No.'

'A little?' Payal said, sniggering.

'Bye, Payal.'

'I'll see you soon. I'm staying over at my parents' place tonight. But I'll come back to yours after work tomorrow.'

'Why? You won't go jewellery shopping?'

'What jewellery shopping?'

'For the wedding ceremonies? What comes first in Jain traditions? Roka?'

'Not funny.'

'He's a Jain too, right? That must help.'

'I don't care what or who he is. I only care about you.'

'What does Parimal do for a living?'

'He's a CA, like his dad. Why?'

'Cool, well-educated too. Parimal and Payal. Wow, your wedding card can have a "P weds P" thing on the opening page.'

'Stop it, Saket,' Payal said. 'And bye. I love you.'

I kept quiet.

'No "I love you" for me?' Payal said.

'Bye,' I said and hung up.

I opened my laptop and decided to write a new comedy set to distract myself. Maybe some chartered-accountant jokes.

∼

'Who is it?' I screamed from the bedroom as my doorbell rang five times in a row.

I rubbed my eyes and checked the time on my bedside clock: 2 a.m. Who would ring my doorbell at this hour? I dragged myself out of bed and walked to the main door. I looked through the peephole.

'Payal?' I said, quickly opening the door.

'Surprise!'

Payal wore a maroon-and-golden salwar kameez, with elaborate zari embroidery on the dupatta.

Was I dreaming?

'You ordered for me, sir?' she said coyly, stepping in and closing the door behind her.

'Huh? What?' I stared at her, still sleepy and confused.

'My madam told me to come see you,' Payal said. She ran a finger down my face. 'That you were lonely and needed some cheering up.'

'What's going on, Payal? Aren't you supposed to be at your parents' house?'

'Shh, I'm not Payal. I'm Shabnam. Payal is your girlfriend, right?'

'Huh?'

Okay, are we in a surprise role-play situation?

'Let's go inside,' she said, pushing my chest.

Brushing past me, she went to the kitchen and brought out a bottle of wine. She took a sip straight from the bottle and then offered it to me.

'Sir, would you like some wine?'

'I was sleeping,' I said.

'But sleeping alone no? Why? Why alone when Shabnam's here?'

She walked up to me seductively and pecked me on my lips.

Oh, screw it. I'll ask Payal about what happened at dinner later. Let me deal with Shabnam now.

'Thank you for coming, Shabnam,' I said.

'My pleasure. Sir, will you make the payment now or later?'

'And how much is the payment?'

'Up to you, sir ... It depends on the service you choose. Shall we go to the bedroom, sir?'

Before I could say something, she led me into the bedroom. Then she took out her phone and played a song from *Umrao Jaan*.

In aankhon ki masti ke
mastaane hazaaron hain ...

'What the—'

'Shh,' Payal, or rather Shabnam, said, shushing me and drawing her dupatta over our heads.

'Sir, I'm here to please you. I'm yours, whatever you want to do.'

'Whatever?'

'Yes, I know you're angry with your girlfriend. She's been bothering you, right? Making you feel jealous?'

'Yeah, a little.'

'Don't bottle up that anger. Take it out on Shabnam tonight, in whatever way you want to.'

She kissed my lips hard, almost biting me.

'You're strong,' she said, rubbing my arms. 'Let's see what you can do.'

My eyes met hers. I'd missed her all evening. I'd tormented myself by imagining all kinds of scenarios—Jains bonding over Jain tacos and Jain sushi and discussing how amazing it would be for Parimal Jain and Payal Jain to get married and create more no-onion-no-garlic Jain babies. I wasn't just a little bit jealous. I was insanely jealous. I was extremely possessive about my Payal.

'Rough sex or nothing,' she said.

'Rough?'

'Yes. I'd like you to tie me up, pull my hair, grab my neck. Do anything. Use me. I'm yours.'

'Payal but—'

'Shabnam, I'm Shabnam,' she said.

My eyes met hers. Something sizzled. And we proceeded to have our steamiest, hottest night ever.

When we were done, both of us plopped down in bed.

'Do I get my Payal back now?' I said after a while.

'Yes,' she said, smiling.

'What was *that*?'

'Tell me, how was it?' she said.

'Hot. Insanely, mind-numbingly hot.'

'It was amazing for me as well.'

'Now that we're back to our senses, well, sort of, what are you doing here at this time? Didn't you have dinner at your parents' place tonight?'

'I had dinner with them, and I was supposed to stay over. But I insisted on returning because I have to go to office early. The driver dropped me to Parel. After he left, I took a cab to Bandra.'

'Wow, you took an Uber this late?'

'What to do? Shabnam had to service a client.' She kissed me on the cheek.

'How was the dinner?'

'I'll tell you about it at breakfast. For now, I want to savour this moment, not talk about Jain dinners.'

'Okay. Anything I need to worry about?'

'Yeah, a lot.'

'What?' I said, concerned.

'That I'm not going anywhere. So, you better be worried about that,' she said, ruffling my hair and snuggling closer to me.

～

'No more Nutella, okay?' Payal said, spreading the chocolate-hazelnut spread on her toast. 'Just stop buying it. I can't resist it if it's in the house.'

We sat at the dining table. Payal wore a blue pinstripe suit, ready to leave for office. I was in workout clothes since I was planning to hit the gym after Payal left.

'But you love it,' I said, peeling my one dozen boiled eggs and separating the whites.

'Sometimes, what we love can be bad for us,' she said.

'Deep,' I said, eating the bland egg-whites one by one.

'How can you eat that? Do you even like it?' she said.

'Nothing to like. It's for my protein targets. Now, let's focus—how was the dinner?'

'Boring,' Payal said. 'Lots of feet touching and eating unhealthy carbs you would never approve of.'

'I didn't even approve of doing this dinner in the first place.'

'I spoke to Parimal privately.'

'What did you tell him?'

'I said I'm not ready for marriage right now. Our parents are obviously excited, but I'm too young. Also, that it's too early in my career, and I want to focus on that for a while.'

'What did he say?'

'He said, well, doesn't matter what he said.'

'I want to know.'

Payal let out a sigh before she spoke again. 'He said, "I won't stop you from having a career." And that "I can wait for marriage if you're not ready yet."'

'Wow.'

'What wow, Saket?'

'He's keen.'

'It doesn't matter. Because I'm not.'

'Okay, what happened then?'

'Nothing, Mom brought us pani puri. We ate it and discussed the best pani-puri spots in Mumbai.'

'You discussed pani-puri spots with him?'

'I had to make some small talk.'

'I don't know why, but discussing pani-puri spots sounds a bit intimate.'

'Intimate is what happened last night, in this house,' she said, deliberately licking a bit of Nutella off her finger in a suggestive manner.

Payal finished her breakfast. She stood up, placed her plate in the kitchen sink and washed her hands.

'And what did your and his parents say?' I said.

'They're all mad. Ignore them.'

'Still. Tell me.'

'Nothing, they kept saying nonsense stuff like "what a brilliant, amazing idea this is," and how "two best friends will become one family."'

'That's nothing?'

'They can keep dreaming. But nothing will happen. In fact, I figured out why my dad is so excited about Parimal.'

'Why?'

'Because Parimal is smart and hardworking and can help run Dad's business later. Vansh, on the other hand, is a lazy idiot. He won't know the difference between a cable and a shoelace. Anyway, my cab is here. Bye. See you tonight,' she said, kissing me.

'Parimal is smart, eh?' I said as she entered the elevator.

'It's so cute,' she said.

'What is?'

'When my hulk of a man in a sleeveless gym T-shirt gets jealous. Bye, cutie,' she said, blowing a kiss as the lift door shut in my face.

∼

A full week later, I was sitting on the window ledge and working when I heard the main door unlock. Payal entered the apartment and slammed the door shut.

'I hate her,' she said.

I looked up from my laptop. 'Who?' I said.

'My mother.'

'Now what?'

'She's lost the plot. Completely.'
'What happened exactly?'
'This Parimal thing.'
'That's still an issue?'
'I didn't think it was. But, unfortunately, it is.'
'What happened?'
'Parimal's parents called my mother. They told her that Payal has told Parimal she's not keen.'
'Okay, then what?'
'My mother then told them, "What does Payal know? She's never even spoken to a boy properly. She's just shy."'
'Are you?'
'Stop it, Saket.'
'I don't know why you've created this impression of being a naive, innocent girl at home.'
'What do I tell her? That their daughter does call-girl role-plays at night?'
'No, that may not go down well. What happened next?'
'Parimal's parents got encouraged again. They now want to take the next step.'
'Which is?'
'Do a roka? Formalize the rishta? I don't know. I'm telling you, my parents have gone bonkers.'
'Stop this, Payal.'
'I'm trying. I fought with my mother again today. I've literally blocked her on my phone.'
'How is that a good idea?'
'You have a better one?'
I remained quiet. I went to the kitchen and brought a glass of water for Payal.

'I need stronger stuff,' she said.

'Later. First drink this and calm down. Let's talk about what is to be done.'

'My dad's obsessed. It's not that he has found the perfect son-in-law. No. He's found the perfect heir to his business. Parimal and he share a passion.'

'What is that?'

'Cables.'

'They're passionate about wires and cables?'

'Well, yes. Parimal gave my dad some ideas about new PVC materials and told him how to cut costs and improve margins.'

'Then he should hire him as a business consultant no? Why does he have to get his daughter married to him?'

'Tell him that,' Payal said. She chugged the entire glass of water down in one go. 'Now, can you give this girl a real drink?'

Nodding, I went back to the kitchen and looked at the alcohol stock. 'We're out of wine. Gin and tonic okay with you?'

'Sure, anything that helps me not think of my mother.'

I made two drinks and came back to the living room.

'Thank you,' she said. 'Don't get upset. But after my mother's encouragement, Parimal's parents sent something home.'

'What?'

'Gold bangles. It's a tradition. Don't read too much into it. I just told you because I don't want to hide anything.'

'What the hell is going on, Payal?' I asked loudly.

'Please, don't raise your voice. I've already been in a shouting match with my mother. I asked her to return the bangles.'

'And?'

'She doesn't want to. She said, "What do you know about all this?" Plus, "Parimal's mother will feel bad."'

'Payal, seriously.'

'I'll put a stop to all this,' she said in a firm voice.

'How?'

'You were right.'

'What?'

'We have to tell them about us.'

'What do you think their reaction will be?'

'Chernobyl. Hiroshima. Nagasaki.'

'Huh?'

'Nuclear explosions. What else? However, it'll at least put an end to this Parimal nonsense.'

'Will it?'

'Yes, I'll tell them we're dating. I'm assuming they'll want to meet you. And once they meet you, they'll like you.'

'Big, big assumptions.'

'I'm optimistic. You're an IIT graduate. Parimal isn't.'

'Is that how these things are decided?'

'In my parents' eyes, yes.'

'What else?'

'You were working abroad. Even built your own company. You can also run a business.'

'I'll have to make cables?'

'Baby, men have fought wars for their women. You can't even make some cables to get the girl of your dreams?'

'But I do comedy—'

Payal interrupted me, 'I'll say that comedy is a hobby for you. You took a break after selling your business and working in the US for a few years.'

'It's not a hobby, Payal. It's who I am now. A stand-up comic.'

'Please, it's for them. Just for now.'

'And then what? I'm supposed to go to the factory in Thane and check accounts and extrude cables?'

'Listen, my dad runs the business just fine. In his head, he eventually wants a male heir, and his own son can't be one.'

'Male, eh?'

'Yes. That's how he is. His daughter may buy and sell big companies at Blackwater, but he doesn't think I can manage a two-acre plant.'

'I can't though. And this heir thing? So this means we're expected to get married?'

'Not immediately. I'll say we're in no hurry. I know your marriage phobia, relax.'

'It's not that …'

'It's okay. I can wait, or even do without it. As long as you and I are together.'

I looked into those beautiful eyes, so full of love and courage. 'I love you so much, Payal. I'll do anything for you.'

'Will you? Just one little thing?'

'Yes.'

'Cool, colour your hair.'

'What?' I said, shocked.

'Those grey sideburns. I love them and I find them hot. Not my parents though.'

'I should colour my hair black?'

'Yeah, I think it's a dark brown though. L'Oréal colour number two.'

'What?'

'Nothing, just go to the salon. They'll match it with the rest of your hair.'

'You'll tell your parents my age, right?'

'I'll keep it vague. You're fit. And with dark hair, they'll think you're in your late twenties.'

'I'm thirty-four.'

'I know, sweetie.'

'I feel objectified.'

'Do you?' she asked, tugging at my T-shirt. 'Wear a nice formal shirt too. None of these extra-tight, hot T-shirts that your arms pop out of.'

'Fine. You'll tell them about my divorce?'

'Not right now. Why give them more than they can handle at one time?'

'So you'll lie about my age and previous marriage? And when they eventually find out, what then?'

'I won't be lying. I just won't be revealing a few things yet.'

'Fine.' I thought about what else could go wrong. 'They'll know I'm Punjabi, right?'

'That, yes, they will. But it can be handled. Will you be okay pretending to be vegetarian?'

'What?'

'In front of them.'

'That will be a lie.'

'A small one. This much lying is allowed for the sake of love.'

'Fine, fine. When are we doing this?'

'Well, first, I have to unblock my mother.'

'Please do, Payal. She's your mom.'

'Fine,' Payal said reluctantly. She opened her phone and unblocked her mother's number.

'Good,' I said. 'Talk to your parents, and tell me what they say. Then we can plan things accordingly.'

I went to the kitchen to heat up dinner.

'I won't just tell you. I'll make you listen in,' she said.

'What?' I said, arranging all the dinner items on a tray.

'Yes, I'm going to keep you on call while I have this conversation.'

'How?'

'I'll ring you just before I go and I'll keep the phone in my handbag, which I'll keep next to me.'

'What will that achieve?'

'You'll know exactly what transpires. And what I'm dealing with. That way, you can't accuse me of not trying my best.'

'I'll never accuse you of that.'

'Still, I want you to listen. It'll help us plan the next step.'

'You sure you won't get caught?'

'No. Just put yourself on mute. Don't worry.'

~

'Hi,' I said as I picked up Payal's call.

'So, am at my parents' place. I'm going to talk to them. Where are you?'

'I'm at Starbucks, in Khar.'

'So late? It's 10 p.m.'

'What to do alone at home? It feels lonely without you.'

'Aww. I can't come tonight. I told my family that I need to talk to them post-dinner. It's a formal, scheduled meeting.'

'What did they say?'

'They seem worried. They asked what happened. Now I'll tell them.'

'Cool. All the best.'

'Thanks. Okay, quiet. I mean mute. Just listen. Going now.'

I heard her place the phone in her handbag. I could hear distant but clear voices as Payal entered a room.

'What on earth has happened? Why did you want to talk to us like this?' I heard a female voice. That would be Payal's mother, Yashodha Jain, I figured.

'Nothing, Mom. It's something I've wanted to talk about for a long time.'

'You lost your job?' a young male voice said, laughing. Vansh, her brother.

'No, I didn't,' Payal said. 'And before you comment on my job, tell me, do you even have a job?'

'I'm doing lots of things, sister,' Vansh said.

'Like what? Playing video games? Doing vodka shots in the afternoon with your loser friends?'

'Get lost,' Vansh said. 'You don't even have friends.'

'Stop it, you two,' I heard a firm adult male voice. Anand Jain, the father. 'Payal beta, what is it?' he said.

'It's nothing to worry about,' Payal said.

'Then?' Yashodha said.

'This Parimal thing …'

'You've already fought enough with me on this,' Yashodha said. 'You don't even understand these things, Payal.'

'What fight?' Anand said.

'She wants to return the bangles they sent.'

'Why?' Anand said. 'They sent it out of love. They treat you like their own daughter.'

'But I'm not their daughter.'

'You will be. Their daughter-in-law,' Anand said in a definitive voice.

Maybe I was the one who needed to worry here.

'I'm twenty-two, Dad. Too young to be someone's bahu.'

'How old is Akanksha? Same age as you no? She's been married two years already,' Anand said.

'Yes, exactly,' Yashodha said in an excited voice. 'Akanksha looks so happy. Did you see her Diwali photos on Facebook? She looks radiant in that onion-coloured zari lehenga.'

'I'm not Akanksha, Mom. I'm not into onion-coloured zari lehengas. I work at Blackwater. I'm not aspiring to be a stupid housewife,' Payal said in a loud, irritated voice.

'Your own mother is a stupid housewife,' Yashodha said.

'I'm sorry,' Payal said. 'I didn't mean it like that, Mom.'

'Black your company name, black your tongue. Is this how you talk to your mother?' Yashodha said.

I let out a sigh as I took a sip of my black coffee and continued to listen in.

'I don't think I'm needed here,' Vansh said.

'No, stay. I'm coming to what I really wanted to say,' Payal said.

'What?' Vansh said. 'Say it fast, sis.'

'I met someone,' Payal said.

'Met someone?' Yashodha said. 'What do you mean?'

'A person. Someone I like,' Payal said.

'Who?' Anand said in a suspicious voice.

'A boy. There's a man in my life. I like him.'

'What?' Yashodha screamed as if Payal had confessed to being a Pakistani spy.

'What man? Who is he?' Anand said.

'Sis, you have a boyfriend? Well done. Smashed him already?'

'Shut up, Vansh,' Payal said.

'Calm down, sis. I love this. For a change, I'm not the one disappointing our parents.'

'Maybe you should leave, Vansh. Get out,' Payal said.

'Nah, now I want to stay and watch. Maybe get some popcorn too. My sister isn't a little girl anymore. Mom, what are you going to do?' Vansh chuckled.

'Oh my God. What is happening?' Yashodha said. 'That's why I told you, ji, girls should get married soon.'

'When have I disagreed?' Anand said. 'God has already sent us the perfect son-in-law in Parimal. You're the one who's not making any progress.'

'Mom! Dad! Listen to me,' Payal said in an exasperated voice. 'I can't marry Parimal. Or anyone else other than Saket. Okay?'

'Saket?' Anand said. 'Now who's Saket?'

'I told you. I have a man in my life—Saket.'

'Saket what? What's his surname?'

'Saket graduated from IIT Bombay,' Payal said, hoping my degree would rescue the situation.

'What's his surname, Payal?' Anand said. All Indian parents care about religion, community and caste first, the CV later.

'He built his own tech company and sold it in the US. Then he worked at Yellowstone, another top private equity firm.'

'US? Where did you meet him?' Yashodha sounded like she was in pain, as if someone had died in the family. Or their cable factory had burnt down.

'He lives in Mumbai now.'

'What's his last name? This is the third time I'm asking,' Anand said impatiently.

'Saket Khurana. Yes, he's Punjabi. But he's a really decent guy. Mostly vegetarian too,' Payal said.

'Mostly?' Yashodha said.

'He's vegetarian,' Payal said quickly.

Okay, lie number one delivered.

'He's not Jain?' Anand said in a puzzled tone, as if Payal was not dating a human but a being from another species altogether, like a chimpanzee or a red-tailed monkey.

'No, but he's a good person. And since you asked, I first met him at a comedy club.'

'Yo, sis, you go to clubs? Since when?'

'Comedy club.'

'What is a comedy club?' Yashodha said. 'Like *Comedy Circus* on TV?'

'Not really, but yes, something like that. Mom, that's not important. What's important is that I like him, and he likes me.'

'Since when have you known him?' Anand said.

'Almost a year now,' Payal said.

'And you never told us anything?' Yashodha said.

'Is there an environment in this house which allows us to freely share things?' Payal said.

'Why? What's wrong with the environment here?'

'Leave it, Mom,' Payal said. 'I'm telling you about it now. And you can meet him as well.'

'I'm not meeting anyone,' Yashodha said. 'First, you do wrong things and then …'

'What wrong things have I done, Mom? I topped school. Went to Stanford. Work at a good job. What's so wrong about this thing that I've done? I can't like someone?'

'You can't just marry anyone you want to,' Yashodha said. 'Listen, ji,' she continued, addressing her husband, 'you also tell her. Why do I have to be the bad one?'

'This is not good, beta. We can't approve of this,' Anand said.

'I shouldn't need approval from anyone. It's my life,' Payal said.

'Look at her,' Yashodha said. 'Send girls abroad more, and this is what happens. All that Stanford-Stanford drama she did, and you melted. Mumbai doesn't have colleges or what? There's KC College, there's Jai Hind College. So many of them in the city …'

'Dad,' Payal said, 'he's a really nice guy. He's great at business too, by the way. In case that's important.'

'Why would that be important?' Anand said.

'As if I don't know … You like Parimal because he can take over the family business.'

'Ha ha. What about me, sis? I'll be the CEO,' Vansh said.

'Yeah, Dad, go ahead and make him CEO,' Payal said. 'How many months to bankruptcy, you think?'

'You're so mean, sis.'

'I … I don't know what to say,' Anand said. 'A Punjabi guy. Someone you hid for a year. I'm shocked. It's all wrong, beta.'

'Meet him once, Dad. Please, with an open mind.'

'We're not—' Yashodha said, but Payal interrupted her.

'Mom, please, I beg you. Just meet him. Think of him as my friend. Okay?'

I felt bad about Payal having to beg like this. She was fighting for me. For us. And it made me fall in love with her even more.

'Male friend?' Yashodha said.

'Meet him as a human being,' Payal said. 'Only once? Please?'

'What do you think, ji?'

'I can meet anyone, beta. But don't expect me to say yes. Also, you know Jignesh's family are our old friends. We can't just say no to them.'

'For now, one meeting,' Payal said. 'That's all I wanted to ask you tonight.'

'I'm going to bed,' Anand said.

'And I'm going to play *Fortnite*,' Vansh said.

'Good night, Dad,' Payal said. 'Bye, Vansh.'

I heard footsteps as Anand and Vansh left the room.

'Are you close to him?' Yashodha said, now alone with her daughter.

'Yes,' Payal said.

'How close?'

I guess she wanted to know if we'd had sex.

'Not close in that way,' Payal said. *Okay, lie number two delivered.*

'Are you sure?'

'Yeah, Mom.'

'What all has happened?'

'We've hugged,' Payal said.

Seriously, Payal? How can you lie with such a straight face?

'That's all?' Yashodha said sternly.

'We've kissed,' Payal said.

'Kissed?' Yashodha said, her voice tense and upset at the same time.

'Once, barely. Just once. Accidentally,' Payal said, back-pedalling immediately.

Ladies and gentlemen, the award for accidental kisser and best fibber of the year goes to—drum roll—Payal Jain!

∼

'It looks beautiful!' Payal said on a video call with me.

I sat in the outdoor section of the coffee shop at the Leela, Goa. The beach was right in front of me.

'I'm in Goa, baby,' I said. 'I could move here.'

'Please do. I'll come along,' Payal said. 'Anyway, when are you coming back?'

'In another week. I leave Goa after my show today and fly to Kochi. Then I go to Jaipur, then Siliguri and, finally, back to Mumbai.'

'Okay, what date is your return flight?'

'Let me check ... I land back in Mumbai on 11 November.'

'Oh, that's a Sunday. Let's meet my parents that day.'

'Really? That day itself?'

'Yes, I don't want to delay things. I'll tell them you'll come home for half an hour. We'll keep it casual, just a cup of tea.'

'What if they poison my tea?'

'No, they won't do that.'

'You sure?'

'We're Jains. We don't believe in killing life. We don't even kill insects or pests.'

'Reassuring,' I said.

∼

'Okay, one more time. Let's discuss the plan for tomorrow,' Payal said.

'We've discussed it a million times already,' I said as I packed my bags in my Siliguri hotel room. All the Reliable Polymers shows were done, and I was finally going back to Mumbai the next morning.

'Just once more. You land at 11 a.m., right? Then you come straight to my home in Ghatkopar? Or will you go to Bandra, keep your stuff, get ready and then come?'

'I thought we agreed that I'd go to Bandra first? You want me to come straight to your house?'

'Maybe. I just thought you could come directly,' Payal said in a playful voice.

'Why? I'll reach your place a little after noon then. You told me your parents won't even be back home until 1.30 p.m. What's that temple with the long name you said they go to on Sundays?'

'Babu Amichand Panalal Adishwarji Jain Temple in Walkeshwar. And yes, they'll only be home after 1.30 p.m.'

'Okay, so then why should I come to your place earlier?' I said, zipping up my suitcase.

'Are you dumb? "Why should I come earlier?" Seriously, bro. Does a girl have to spell it out for you?'

It took me a few seconds to figure out what Payal was talking about. 'Oh,' I said. 'Oh, okay. I get it now.'

'You do? Or should I send you an email explaining it in detail?'

I laughed. 'Baby, but how? At your parents' house?'

'I have my own room. And I'll be home alone. Vansh is in Bangkok with his friends, partying as usual.'

'What about the house help?'

'On Sundays, the help gets a day off.'

'Aha,' I said. 'Now you're talking. Oh, I've missed that. So much ...'

'That's all that you've missed, I know.'

'Hey, that's not true. You only—'

'I'm kidding,' Payal interrupted me. 'I've also missed my man for ten days.'

'Won't it be weird if your parents find me in the house when they arrive? Just with you?'

'I thought of that too—you spend an hour with me, then leave. Have a coffee somewhere in Ghatkopar, and come back after 1.30 p.m. Sounds doable?'

'Absolutely doable. Wow, great thinking, Payal. Can't wait to see you tomorrow.'

'Same here,' Payal said before ending the call.

How had I lucked out so much? How did I find a girl as amazing as Payal?

I switched off the lights and hit the bed, hoping to fall asleep fast so that the morning came sooner.

∽

'Landed! And early. It's only 10.35 a.m.!' I messaged Payal as soon as the aircraft touched the ground at Mumbai airport.

'Super! We get more time then. Come soon. I'm so nervous,' Payal replied.

'Why?'

'In case you forgot, you're going to meet my parents in less than four hours.'

'Oh yes. I almost did forget that. Okay, baby, let me come over and calm your nerves down.'

～

The cab pulled into the driveway of a posh and swanky building called Riddhi-Siddhi Niwas. A guard stood at the barrier gate. He asked me for my ID and other details.

'Whose house?' he said.

'Mr Jain,' I said.

'There are eight Jains in the building.'

'Anand Jain, fifth floor,' I said.

'Purpose of visit?' he said, typing on a touchscreen tablet.

'To have tea,' I said.

I couldn't tell him it was to have sex with Mr Anand Jain's daughter and then to talk to him about marrying her.

'What?'

'They invited me for tea.'

'I'll put "social visit". It's an option here. Thank you,' the guard said. He finished typing in his tablet and pressed a button, making the boom barrier go up.

～

'You wore a suit?' Payal said, looking me up and down.

She'd answered the door before I even had a chance to ring the doorbell.

'This is the same suit that I wore for the Reliable Polymers shows. It's the only formal clothing I have.'

'Thank you for making an effort to dress up. It's sweet,' Payal said.

She wore a cream-coloured salwar kameez with a red-and-yellow bandhini dupatta. Even in this simple outfit, she looked beautiful. What she wore didn't matter. Payal would've looked beautiful wrapped up in an IRCTC bedsheet.

'I have to impress the parents,' I said. 'May we hug? Is it safe?'

'Yes, I'm alone at home.'

'Gosh, I missed you,' I said, as we embraced each other for one long minute. Holding Payal after ten days felt like coming home. Even though I was at her psycho parents' home.

I looked around the living room. It was a giant space, the size of half a tennis court. The walls had framed pictures of various Jain saints and temples. There were brass and bronze statues of numerous gods as well. *Was I dating a priest's daughter?*

'What's this gigantic house, Payal? How big is it?'

Payal laughed. 'It's not that big. Five thousand square feet, I think.'

'My Bandra place is five hundred. You can fit ten of them in here.'

'That's Pali Hill, a more expensive neighbourhood.'

'Still, this building is so posh. Hi-tech security and all. The guard outside was tapping away on a tablet as he took my details. The only thing my building guard taps on is his gutka.'

Payal giggled. I leaned forward and kissed her. It felt weird to kiss her in her parents' living room, surrounded by all the images of gods and temples. It felt like the gods were watching us, and cursing me to hell. I suddenly became aware of a sound, a repeating chant rather.

'What's that sound?'

Payal pointed to a small device plugged into a socket near the door. It was playing the 'Om, Om' sound on a loop.

'Come, sit,' Payal said, waving towards a huge sofa set, which had a truckload of foam stuffed into it.

Payal and I sat facing each other, at least ten feet apart.

'Nervous?' Payal said.

'About meeting your parents? Yes,' I said.

'Just be yourself. And remember, we're just friends. Be cordial and matter-of-fact. More than anything, stay calm.'

'Yes. And I stay platonic too, right?'

'Of course,' Payal said. 'Don't even think about doing anything in front of them.'

'What about doing something now. Before they come back?'

'Patience, mister.'

'Is there another room we can go to?' I said. 'You have your own room here, right?'

'Someone's in a hurry,' Payal said and chuckled. She stood up and gestured for me to follow her to her bedroom.

'Welcome to my room,' she said, shutting the door behind us. 'I haven't really lived here since I left for Stanford. But still, this is my space.'

I looked around. The bed, covered with a pink bedcover, had a couple of stuffed toy animals kept on it. The walls had posters of Mariah Carey, Indra Nooyi and Kalpana Chawla. It still resembled the room of a school student, with a study table and a bookshelf filled with books on SAT preparation and US college-application guides. I also saw a framed picture of a naked old man sitting cross-legged.

'Who's this?'

'He's a revered Jain saint.'

'And he's wearing nothing because ...'

'Because he's a Digambar Jain saint,' Payal said. 'No irreverent comments on this, okay? My family believes in him.'

'I wouldn't dare,' I said, pretending to zip my mouth shut.

We sat on her bed.

'I'm so happy you're here. I have so many memories associated with this room,' Payal said.

'Want to make some more?' I said, bringing my face closer to hers.

She pushed me back gently. 'One-track mind,' she said. 'Here I am, feeling all sentimental about you seeing my childhood room. And all you want to do is make out.'

I laughed. 'No, I would love to see your childhood photo album, actually.'

'You would?' Payal said in an excited voice. 'Wait'—she stood up—'let me take it out of the closet.'

I pulled her back by her hand and made her sit down again. 'That was a joke,' I said. 'I can look at it later.'

'I knew it. One-tracker.'

'I've been away from you for too long.'

'It was only ten days.'

'That's 240 hours. Or 14,400 minutes, and I don't know so much math, but that's a hell lot of seconds. I'm going a bit crazy,' I said, pulling her closer.

'I can see that, Mr Man-in-a-Suit.' She brought her mouth to my ear. 'Today,' she whispered, 'you look like a corporate boss. Make me your secretary.'

'Payal, what are you saying?' I said, laughing. 'You and your role-plays!'

'Shh. Not Payal. I'm Rosie. Your secretary. Did you like the work I did, sir?'

'What work?'

'Tell me you didn't like the work I did. That you're furious with me.'

'What?'

'Play along, boss,' Payal whispered, and bit my ear.

I decided to play along. I went and sat on the study chair. I picked up a sheet of paper. 'Rosie,' I said in an irritated voice. 'What's this?'

Payal stood before me. 'What happened, sir?' she asked in a mock-innocent voice. 'You don't like what I did?'

'No,' I said, my voice angry. 'There are so many spelling mistakes. You can't even spell the company name right.'

'I'm so sorry, sir.'

'What will the client think? You've already emailed this to them?'

'Yes, sir, I did,' Payal said. 'I'm so sorry, sir.'

'This is horrible,' I said, throwing the paper aside.

'What can I do, sir?' Payal moved closer to me. 'I'm ready to be punished. Any way you want. Just don't be angry with me, sir.'

'Any way?' I asked. '*Any*?'

Payal threw away her dupatta. 'Any way you want, sir. I've been a really bad girl,' she said.

Okay, I must admit that for some reason, Payal's silly play-acting always really turned me on. I wanted to rip off her clothes. Thankfully, she undressed herself. I took off my clothes too.

I pushed Payal onto the pink bed, which creaked a little. I kissed her hard, biting her lip.

'I'm sorry, sir,' Payal said. 'I'll never do this again. Please, punish me.' Then she turned around, her bare bottom arched towards me. 'Spank me, sir.'

I lightly slapped her behind.

'Harder,' she said.

Even though I was the 'boss' in the scenario, I followed everything she said.

'Have I been a bad girl?' Payal said.

'Yeah, you're so bad,' I said as red marks appeared on her bottom.

'I'm so turned on, spank me harder,' she said. I was super turned on too, and about to enter her from behind.

The bedroom door pushed open. Payal's parents entered the room.

'Mom!' Payal turned her head and screamed, still naked and on all fours on her bed.

Initially, I didn't realize what had happened. I think I spanked Payal once even after her parents had entered the room. It took me a few seconds to register reality and understand that I was in a really messed-up situation. *What am I supposed to say? Hello, Uncle. Hello, Aunty. I would like to introduce myself. I'm Saket. I was just about to mount your daughter from behind, that too in your own house. Would you like me to be your son-in-law?*

'Payal!' her mother screamed, her mouth and eyes wide open.

To the men reading this: Guys, I hope you never, ever find yourselves in such a situation. However, just in case you do, let me tell you the first thing you should do. I didn't do this at that moment, but you should learn from my mistake. Anyway, the first thing to do in such a scenario is to cover your penis. I didn't because I was too shocked to see the Jains, possibly my prospective in-laws, randomly appear in the room like that. I froze, like a deer caught in a truck's headlights. Except that this deer was fully turned on. It took me several extra seconds to realize that I needed to find something to cover my intimate parts with. Meanwhile, in those several extra seconds, Payal's mom, my mother-in-law-to-be, the pious Yashodha Jain, had a good look at my manhood. As did her husband, the devout, returning-from-the-temple-with-the-long-name Mr Anand Jain. Making things worse was my penis itself—it did not realize that the entire game had changed. That we were no longer going to do the fun stuff we thought we were going to do. Blissfully unaware, my junior remained hard, staring right back at our surprise visitors.

I tried to look for a cushion to cover my bits with. I couldn't find one. However, I found a stuffed teddy bear. I picked it up and placed it in front of my private parts. It looked like I was trying to poke my stuff into a teddy bear, which, in a way, is even more wrong and perverted. However, I had to cover my modesty.

Payal, meanwhile, had been smart enough to cover herself in the pink bedsheet in a nanosecond.

Payal's parents stood there frozen, not saying a word after their initial screams and gasps. I wondered what I should do. Greet them? Shake their hand? Touch their feet? Do a namaste? I couldn't do any of that right now. My hands were busy holding the teddy bear to cover my dick.

'We'll come outside, Mom. Please, give us some privacy,' Payal said.

How could she speak in sensible sentences right now?

'Come,' Payal's mother said, dragging her husband out, who was as perplexed and shocked as I was.

I finally turned to look at Payal after her parents left.

'Damn, this is bad,' she said, letting out a huge sigh.

'Yeah? You think so?' I said, still trying to come back to my senses.

'But how the hell did this happen ...' Payal said, and checked the time on her phone. 'It's just 12.10 p.m. They were supposed to come home after 1.30 p.m.'

'You tell me,' I said.

'I don't know what happened,' Payal said, getting up and wearing her clothes.

'What do we do next?' I said, my brain still numb.

'Get dressed, what else? And Saket, what exactly are you doing with my teddy bear?'

~

'I just told you, Mom, Dad. Saket is my boyfriend.'

We sat on the humungous sofas in Payal's humungous living room. All the framed pictures and statues of all the gods in the room made me feel like I was in a religious morality court, on my way to getting condemned. Or maybe stoned to death. Or starved to death. Or fed Jain food to death.

'Boyfriend?' Payal's mother said. 'And what were you guys doing? Such an obscene thing.'

'We love each other, Mom,' Payal said.

The men in the room, that is, Payal's father and I, hadn't spoken at all. I think while men are obsessed with sex, when it comes to discussing it like this, they freeze up.

Om, om. The chanting machine continued to produce its sounds, making the awkward silence even more awkward.

'You said nothing had happened. Only hugs,' Yashodha said.

'I lied to you. Sorry.'

'You lied? And that's all you're sorry about?' Yashodha turned to her husband. 'Are you going to say anything at all?'

Payal's father cleared his throat to speak. 'I don't have to say anything. I've already messaged who I had to.'

'Who?' Yashodha said.

'My friend Patil. Senior police inspector at the Ghatkopar police station. He's sending some men.'

I felt the earth move under me.

Om, om.

'Police,' Payal said, throwing up her hands in exasperation. 'What? Why would you call the police?'

'Who the hell does he think he is?' Anand shouted. He turned to me and spoke in a menacing tone, 'Whoever you are, I'll make sure you rot in jail.'

Jail? Dude, what the hell was going on? I was supposed to have tea, talk and then leave. *Serve me tea, dhokla and khandvi. Not cops.* Okay, I had to speak now.

'Hello, Uncle, I'm Saket,' I said, standing up. I turned to Payal's mother, 'Hello, Aunty, nice to meet you.'

'You sit,' Anand shouted. 'Just sit in your place until Patil's men arrive. Good thing we got an SMS notification from the guardhouse. We turned around and came back. Didn't even go to the temple today.'

That explained it. It was the damn tablet with the guard. Fuck the security systems of these modern buildings, I tell you.

'Uncle, but ...' I said, wondering if I should make a dash for the exit while I still could.

'Sit,' he said in a firm voice.

'Sit down, Saket,' Payal said calmly.

I sank back into the sofa, which looked like it could swallow small children. Considering how messed up the situation was, it was ironic how comfortable the seating they had provided me was.

Payal broke down in tears. 'This is why I never share anything with you guys. Because you won't listen, and will overreact. Can't we just talk?' she said, wiping her tears.

I wanted to get up and give her a hug. However, I wasn't sure if Anand had a Ghatkopar-friendly gun he could shoot me with.

'Uncle, please,' I said. 'She's crying. Please, just listen to us. For five minutes. And can we please turn off this Om-Om machine for a while?'

'Why?' Anand shouted. 'It creates good vibrations in my house. Unlike you, who's brought in all the bad vibrations.'

'It's just distracting. Fine, we can leave it on.'

Om ... Om...

'I've never been more humiliated in my life,' Anand said.

Dude, that line applied to me.

'I understand, Uncle,' I said. 'I'm sorry. Payal and I met after a long time. We got carried away.'

'That's not getting carried away. That's depravity,' Anand said.

'It's not what you think,' I said.

'We don't have to think. We saw how you're using and exploiting our daughter,' Yashodha said.

'He's not!' Payal screamed.

'Look at her, she's a kid,' Payal's mother continued. 'How old are you?'

Damn, did she have to ask me this now? And what was I supposed to do? Lie and say twenty-eight? No, lying, on top of getting caught like this, would be a terrible idea. I chose to remain quiet instead.

'Answer her. How old are you?' Anand said.

'I'm thirty-four,' I said.

'What? Did you say thirty-four?'

'Yes, Uncle,' I said, my head lowered as if I'd admitted to something shameful. I wanted to add that I had fifteen per cent body fat and could bench 150 kilos. I don't think he'd care.

'She's twenty-two,' Anand said. 'Do you realize that?'

'I do, Uncle. But—'

'But what?' Anand said in a stern voice. 'Is this what you do? Trap young girls and use them?'

'No, Uncle. Not at all. I love your daughter. Too much. I've never loved anyone in my life as much as I love her,' I said.

From the corner of my eyes, I saw Payal secretly make a heart symbol by bringing her hands together and making the tips of her fingers touch. 'I love you,' she mouthed silently.

I don't know why, but I broke down in tears. How did this even happen? This was supposed to be the meeting where I impressed her parents. I had wanted to knock their socks off. Instead, they'd caught me wearing nothing *but* socks. I kicked myself for making this stupid, impulsive plan to sneak into Payal's house earlier.

'You don't love her. This is pure lust,' Anand said.

'He does,' Payal said, in tears herself.

Payal's mother gave her a tissue and held her hand. 'No, beta, don't cry,' she said. 'Young age is like that. We all make mistakes. That's why we get our children married at an early age.'

'It's not a mistake, Aunty,' I said. 'We've been in a relationship for a long time now.'

'How long?' Anand said.

'Almost a year,' I said. 'I'm self-sufficient and well-qualified. I'm from a good family. I can take care of your daughter well. This is not what you think. We were stupid today, yes. But this is not all there is to us.'

'What family? Where are you from?' Payal's mother said.

'My parents live in Chandigarh,' I said.

'And they didn't get you married?' Yashodha said. 'Why aren't you married till now?'

Payal and I looked at each other. I decided I couldn't lie anymore. 'I was married,' I said.

Payal's parents gasped.

'Meaning?' Payal's mother said.

'I'm divorced now. We separated four years ago.'

Payal's mother rolled her eyes at her husband, cueing him to react with appropriate disgust and anger.

'Divorcee? You're a divorcee,' Anand said, as if I'd carried an infectious disease into their house. He stood up and began pacing around the living room. Like all Indian husbands, he decided the best response was to blame his wife.

'Yashodha, this is all because of you. You've not been able to give good values to our children,' Anand said.

'And you? The one who said, "My daughter is so bright, she will go to Sheperd"?'

'Stanford,' Payal said.

'Whatever. Stanford. Send her to those white colleges in white countries. She'll come back with corrupted morals, isn't it?'

'But I'm the one who's saying speed up the process with Parimal. Imagine if Jignesh and Supriya find out.'

'Oh my God, no.' Yashodha looked horrified. 'We can't let that happen. Get rid of him. Payal, get rid of this fellow and never mention any of this to anyone.'

'Mom, I can't just—' Payal said but her father interrupted her.

'He'll be thrown into jail, I'll make sure of it.'

'A police case will make this come out in the open. People will talk about it. Please, Anandji, no police. Let's just deal with it here,' Yashodha said.

Anand thought about things for a few seconds. Thankfully, his wife's suggestion saved me some Ghatkopar Jail time.

'You, I'm talking to you,' Anand said, wagging a finger at me. 'I'm giving you one last chance. Get out of Payal's life and our life and this house. Now and forever.'

'Uncle, but—'

'I'm forty-five, you're thirty-four. What are you calling me uncle for?' Anand said.

Because you look like an uncle with your pot belly.

'Okay, I'm sorry, Mr Jain, but—'

He interrupted me again, 'My age difference with you is less than your age difference with Payal. In that case, Payal should also call you uncle, isn't it?'

I figured his question was rhetorical. I remained silent.

He continued, 'For the sake of my family name, and because Payal has a good rishta, we're letting you go. Else, you would be in jail.'

'In jail for what, Unc ... I mean, Mr Jain?'

'What do you mean?'

'What have I done wrong? Is it wrong for two consenting adults to have a relationship?' I said.

'This is entrapment,' he said. 'And I have contacts in the police and everywhere. I'll destroy you and your career.'

This was Jain rage going unchecked, dude. I looked at Payal. *Say something, girl.*

'Dad, you can't do this. I want you to meet him properly. Saket is important to me.'

'You're under his spell. He's too old for you. And he's divorced. What were you even thinking?'

'I was thinking that I'd finally found a real person who loved me for who I am. Unlike this family, where everyone pretends all the time and everything is fake,' Payal said.

Thwack! I heard a sound as Yashodha deposited a tight slap across Payal's face. 'Ungrateful girl! So much your father has done for you, and you call all this fake,' she said, her face red with anger.

Payal held her face in shock, unable to believe what had just happened.

'Get out,' Yashodha said to me.

'Patil's men will be here in five minutes,' Anand said.

I looked at everyone in the room, all of them as still as the bronze statues around me. I figured nothing good would come if I continued to stay there.

'Okay, fine. I'll leave, Unc … sorry, Mr Jain. Bye Mrs Jain. Thank you. I hope to see you again. Let's resolve this when we're all calmer.'

'Never … I'm warning you. Never approach Payal or our family again,' Anand said, his finger pointed towards the main door, showing me the exit.

Om, om, I heard the machine behind me as I left.

∼

'I feel so trapped,' Payal said, looking out at the sunset.

We sat in the café of the Oberoi Hotel at Nariman Point, near her office. She had finished work early and come to see me for half an hour before going back home. Ever since that crazy day at her house, things had changed dramatically. Payal's mother had moved into her Parel apartment. Yashodha Jain now dropped Payal off at work every morning and then picked her up in the evening. On top of that, Payal also had to spend the entire weekend at her parents' place in Ghatkopar. All of this made it impossible for her to come to my place or for me to go to hers. Even for this brief meeting, Payal had slipped out of office and walked over to the Oberoi before her mother came to pick her up.

'Beer?' I said.

'Mom will smell it instantly,' she said, shaking her head.

We sat across from each other in silence. That fateful day had hit us like an earthquake, turning our lives upside down.

'My window ledge misses you,' I said.

'That's *our* ledge,' Payal said. 'You have no idea how much I miss the Bandra apartment. I wanted to sneak out of work one day and come over.'

'No, don't. Let's not take any more chances. If your parents find out, it's over for us.'

'I miss you, Saket,' Payal said, holding my hand.

'I miss you too. How long does your mom plan to play the warden and guard you? She can't do this forever.'

'Presumably until they get me married. Which they now want to do at turbo speed.'

'Are you serious?'

'Yes.'

'With that Parimal?'

'Yeah. They're in love with him.'

'Payal, we can't just sit around. We must do something.'

'Like what?'

'I must meet them again. To convince them that I'm not some pervert.'

'How? They won't even let you into the building, forget the house. Security won't allow it.'

'Then somewhere outside? Tell me a place they visit frequently. I'll pretend to run into them. Where do they go the most?'

'Jain temples.'

'I could bump into them there.'

'They'll know it's a plan. Why else would you be at a Jain temple?'

'Any other temples they visit?'

Payal thought for a second before she spoke again. 'They go to Siddhivinayak once a month.'

'Okay, that's a famous temple. It's plausible for me to run into them there.'

'It's crowded.'

'I'll figure that out. But Payal, can you also come to the temple with them that day, please?'

'Baby, are you sure?'

I shushed her, placing my finger against her lips. 'I've been told that men have fought wars for love. I can visit a temple.'

~

Siddhivinayak, in Dadar, is one of Mumbai's most popular temples. Dedicated to Lord Ganesha, it draws huge crowds of devotees from morning to night. Payal's parents believed in doing an early-morning darshan, at 4 a.m.

The night before their intended visit—and my planned 'bumping into them'—I had a show until midnight. After the show, I hung around at the Crayon Club bar.

'What's up, bro? How was the show?' Mudit said as he came and sat next to me.

'The show was good,' I said.

'And how's life?'

'Life's complicated at the moment.'

'Really? What happened? And how's that schoolgirl you're dating? What's her name?'

'Payal. And she's not a schoolgirl. She's a private equity analyst. With Blackwater. And we're serious. You know all this. Not funny, Mudit.'

Mudit laughed.

I maintained a serious expression.

'Okay, tell me everything. What's going on? And by the way, why are you wearing a kurta today?' Mudit said.

'Yes, I'll tell you. I'm supposed to meet her parents in a couple of hours ...' I then went on to recount everything that had happened on that crazy day.

Mudit's mouth hung open as I finished.

'And now, I plan to run into her parents at 4 a.m., at Siddhivinayak, and make an elevator pitch. For our relationship. That's why the kurta.'

'Bro, wait,' Mudit said, letting out a long breath. 'Are you saying that Payal's parents saw your junior?'

'Stop it, dude, and yes,' I said.

Mudit burst out laughing. 'Bro, you have to do a comedy set about this. I'm telling you, it'll be a massive hit.'

'Mudit, this is my life. And I'm suffering,' I said and stood up to leave.

'The best jokes come out of life and suffering,' Mudit called after me, still laughing.

∼

'We left home ten minutes ago,' I received Payal's message.

It was 3.40 a.m. I was half a kilometre away from Siddhivinayak, having decided to walk from the comedy club to the temple.

'Great, I'm just about to reach,' I replied, crossing the last traffic signal before the temple.

The Siddhivinayak Temple is relatively small as compared to other famous temples in India. Mumbai's space constraints apply to everything, including places of worship. While the temple wasn't exactly crowded at this hour, it was still buzzing with activity. The bright temple lights and the sound of bells ringing, all set against the pitch-dark pre-dawn sky, made the experience of being there even more ethereal.

I'd reached the temple before the Jains arrived. I went into the sanctum sanctorum, where the saffron-coloured idol of Lord Ganesha is placed for darshan. Another name for Lord Ganesha is Vighnaharta, which means 'remover of obstacles'. As I bowed and prayed to him, I wondered if he would remove my obstacles. I apologized for what I'd done wrong, and prostrated myself before him, my face touching the floor. I got up, and the priest applied a saffron tilak on my forehead.

When I turned around, I saw Payal and her parents standing a few steps away. My heartbeat quickened. Payal noticed me, but she didn't react. I quickly moved aside to let her family complete their darshan. Like me, they bowed, they prayed and the priest applied tilak on their foreheads. As they stepped away from the idol, I approached them.

'Uncle, hi,' I said, and regretted it instantly. Why did I have to say 'uncle'? Fortunately, my voice was drowned out by the ringing of the temple bells.

'Namaste, Mr Jain, nice to see you here,' I said a little loudly, and folded my hands.

It took a few seconds for Anand Jain to register who I was. When he did, he recoiled like he'd spotted a venomous snake. He grabbed Payal's arm to ensure she remained with him.

'What are you doing here? I told you to get lost,' he said.

Okay, not the best start.

He turned to his daughter. 'What's he doing here, Payal?'

Payal didn't respond.

'I came to the temple,' I said. Technically, I wasn't lying. However, Ganpati knew the real story. I hoped he would forgive me for concealing the truth for the sake of love.

'Yashodha, let's go,' Anand said, still gripping Payal's arm. Without another word, they marched out of the temple, dragging Payal with them into the courtyard.

I ran up behind them. 'Mr Jain, Mrs Jain, please. Wait. I just need to talk to you once. Nothing else.'

'We're not interested in anything you have to say. Please, leave us alone,' Yashodha said.

'We're here in Ganpati's home. This is about Payal and my life. Please,' I said.

'You don't have to worry about Payal's life,' Yashodha said, pulling her daughter close to her.

'Mom, Dad, please, don't grab me.' Payal spoke for the first time. 'And what's the big deal about having a talk?'

'Stop talking back—' Yashodha said.

'I'm not,' Payal interrupted her. 'I'm asking you to consider his reasonable request. Let's just sit down and talk, like mature people. Not run away. We're all adults here.'

'What adult stuff you do, we know,' Yashodha said.

'I could've run away with Payal,' I said in a calm yet firm voice. 'But I didn't. Legally, you can't stop us.'

'Are you threatening us?' Anand said, sounding incredulous.

A few temple-goers noticed the altercation between us.

I lowered my voice and continued, 'I'm here out of respect for you both, sir. There's a tea shop outside the temple, near the mithai shops. It's open. Let's go there. I want to talk to you about something.'

'Talk about what?' Yashodha said. She looked at Payal with a worried expression, as if I was going to drop a bombshell about Payal being pregnant or something.

'Just a normal conversation. Over a cup of tea. Please ...' I said.

'Mom, Dad, it'll only take a few minutes,' Payal said.

Anand and Yashodha exchanged wary glances. Then Payal's father gave a brief nod.

Feeling a little relieved, I led them out of the temple complex to the tea stall.

'Four teas, please,' I said to the owner of the tea stall.

We sat down on the rickety wooden stools kept outside the shop.

'Without sugar for me,' Yashodha said. 'And none for him as well,' she added, pointing to her husband.

'Less sugar, not completely without sugar. Less milk, and really hot,' Anand said.

No matter how upset Indian parents are, they're still particular about their tea.

'Say whatever you want to say. Make it fast. We don't have time,' Anand said.

I'd been waiting for the tea to arrive, hoping it would calm the hot tempers. 'Yes,' I said, sitting up straight on my stool. 'Firstly, once again, I apologize for what happened that day ... when you walked into what we thought was our private moment.'

'What do you mean private moment?' Yashodha snapped, eating a sugar-filled modak from a box purchased from the mithai store next to the tea stall.

'Let's leave all that behind, ma'am. I've apologized multiple times for it. The Jains are known to be the most forgiving people. You have this beautiful concept of "michhami dukkadam", isn't it? It means to seek forgiveness. That's all I ask from you.'

Payal's parents looked at each other, surprised. For a moment, their anger seemed to subside, before Anand remembered the situation again and regained his stern expression.

I continued, 'Anyway, coming to the point, in the interest of time ...'

'There is no point,' Anand said, picking up a modak from the box his wife held out towards him. 'We're being forced to sit here.'

I wished they would offer me a modak too. I was hungry. I needed sugar to deal with the stress.

'Okay. I know about Parimal,' I said.

Payal looked at me, surprised.

'You told him?' Yashodha said to Payal, looking at her daughter with her default expression of disappointment.

Payal shrugged her shoulders.

'Yes, she told me,' I said. 'And I understand you think he's the right match for her. I can see why.'

Payal's parents looked at me, surprised again.

I continued, 'However, I don't think Payal will be happy with him, if that matters to you. Neither will Parimal be happy with her. Sometimes, it isn't only about what looks right on paper. It's also about chemistry and compatibility.'

'And you think you and Payal are compatible?' Yashodha said, smirking. 'There's a huge age difference between you two.'

'I understand that. But we are compatible—it isn't about biological age alone. Even if it were, I'm fitter than many twenty-year-olds. Also, I plan to remain healthy.'

'You're divorced. And not even a Jain. Do you see what that will do to us in society? And what work do you do now anyway?' Anand said.

'I'm a professional stand-up comic,' I said.

'Stand-up what?' Yashodha said, genuinely confused.

'I perform on stage and make people laugh. I get paid for it. Reasonably well now.'

'I'll tell all my relatives that Payal is marrying a stage artist?' Yashodha looked horrified.

'I'm doing this by choice. This is my passion. If need be, I can always get a tech job or start a business. In India or abroad. I still get offers,' I said.

'What's your name again?' Anand said.

'Saket, sir.'

'See, that's all fine, Saket. But we don't approve of this match.'

'Why not?'

'We just don't. You can't force us to.'

'Neither can you stop us,' I said.

Anand stood up with a disgusted expression. 'If you threaten us like this, I don't want to be here. Payal, Yashodha, let's leave.'

'Sit, Dad, please,' Payal said.

We stayed silent as Anand fumed for a few seconds. Then he sat down again.

'Let us do it the right way,' I said. 'You can speak to my parents. We can have a ceremony whenever you want. I would ideally like to wait some time before the actual marriage, as would Payal, that's all.'

'Ceremony?' Yashodha said.

'Roka or whatever traditions you follow before marriage. We would like to do it with your blessings.'

Anand and Yashodha looked at me blankly, as if I was a foreign tourist talking to them in Greek.

'Listen to me carefully, Mr Saket,' Anand said after a long pause. 'I'm not going to repeat this or meet you again. Payal is going to marry Parimal. We'll perform the ceremonies, but between Parimal and Payal. Clear?'

He set his empty teacup aside and popped another modak into his mouth. He spoke again only after finishing the sweet. 'This is the last time I want to see or hear from you. Otherwise, I'll have you arrested. And you'll never be able to live in Mumbai. Payal, Yashodha, get up.'

Yashodha stood up. But Payal didn't move.

'Get up. Now, Payal,' Anand shouted.

Payal stood up reflexively. And before I could respond, they were gone. I realized they'd left the mithai box behind, with four modaks inside. I popped all four into my mouth, hoping the sugar overdose would numb my pain. It did. A little bit.

I dropped my face into my hands, fighting back tears.

'You will pay for the tea?' the tea-stall owner said, tapping my back.

∼

Messages to Payal didn't get delivered. Calls wouldn't go through. Her WhatsApp display picture vanished. She'd blocked me. I checked her Instagram and Facebook profiles—I'd been blocked there as well.

I hadn't heard from her since the Siddhivinayak meeting a week ago. In desperation, I called the Blackwater landline number.

'Blackwater Capital, how may I help you?' a lady answered.

'May I speak to Payal Jain, please?'

'Who should I say is calling, please? And what is this regarding?'

'Tell her it's Saket. It's personal.'

'Please hold a moment,' the receptionist said.

I was kept on hold for two minutes, but it felt like two hours.

'I'm sorry, sir. Ms Payal is in a meeting. Can she call you back?' the receptionist said.

'Sure.'

I couldn't write a word for my new set. Comedy was the last thing on my mind. I hadn't been able to work, work out or work things out with Payal.

Why hadn't she called? How could she block me? Did I mean nothing to her?

Painful questions swirled around in my head like stones in a blender, pounding my brain.

Two hours later, my phone rang. It was the Blackwater landline number.

'Hi Saket,' Payal said, her voice subdued.

'Payal, finally!' I said. 'Where have you been? I've been trying to reach you for days. I even called your office earlier.'

'I know. I was in a board meeting. It just ended. Why did you call at work?'

'What am I supposed to do? You've blocked me everywhere.'

'Yes. Sorry about that.'

'Why?'

'Mom and Dad made me do it.'

'And you did it?'

'They took my phone and did it themselves. Things are really bad at home.'

'How bad?'

'It's awful, Saket. They've gone nuts. Anyway, this isn't the best place to talk. I'm at work.'

'Then meet me.'

'How? They keep an eye on me all the time.'

'Sneak out for a bit?'

'They track my location through some app on my phone.'

'Are you serious?'

'Yes. I'm on an electronic leash.'

'And you're putting up with all this?'

'Mom threatened to kill herself.'

'What?'

'Yeah, listen, I can't talk freely right now. I'll call you when I can.'

'You could've called or messaged earlier too. From another number, from this landline number. You could've somehow reached out …'

'I'm sorry, Saket. It's been rough, trust me. Speak soon, okay? Bye.'

~

'Another drink?' Mudit said.

'Don't ask me. Keep them coming,' I said.

Mudit and I were at Janata Bar at Pali Naka, within walking distance from my house. Every shop around Janata Bar had become posh and gentrified over the last few years due to rising real estate prices. Hardware stores had turned into chic cafés, utensil shops had become upmarket bakeries and rubber-tire shops had transformed into fusion restaurants. But Janata Bar, for whatever reason, had remained unchanged. It was still a place where drivers, labourers and demotivated, heartbroken comedians gathered to get the cheapest drinks in town.

Mudit ordered another round of Old Monk rum and Coke.

'Buy a bottle, it'll work out cheaper,' the waiter said, noticing the amount and the pace at which we were drinking.

Before I could shake my head and say no, Mudit had already made the decision. 'Fine, get us the bottle. And some starters. Tandoori chicken,' he told the busy waiter, speaking loudly to make himself heard in the heaving, crowded and noisy bar.

'That fat, evil Anand Jain. I'll smash his smug face, Mudit,' I said, or rather the Old Monk version of me said. I clenched my fists.

'No, you can't do that, bro,' Mudit said. 'We make people laugh. We make people happy. We don't hurt them.'

I took a big sip of my drink, finishing it, and slammed the glass hard on the table. 'What's the point of these biceps and delts if I never use this strength to teach the bad guys a lesson?' I said.

'He's not a bad guy. Just an overprotective father.'

'This isn't protection. This is imprisonment. He's keeping his daughter captive against her will—making her block me, tracking her location, her mother hovering around her like the world's most out-of-shape bodyguard. What the hell?'

'Did you ask Payal to move in with you?' Mudit said.

'No. I've done nothing. Just been a pussy, meeting them first in their home and then at the temple. Requesting them. Being reasonable.'

'That phase is over, bro. You tried. Now do what you have to do.'

'Yeah,' I said, my words slurring. 'And ... what would that be?'

'That you have to decide no, bro.'

The waiter arrived with a bottle of Old Monk, a two-litre plastic bottle of Coke and a steel jug with ice. Janata Bar was the opposite of pretentiousness. Sometimes, I wished the entire world was the same.

Mudit made us two more drinks. I was already feeling buzzed. My phone rang. I stared at the screen—the call was from some random landline number.

'Leave it,' Mudit said. 'It's probably spam. Just drink up.'

He handed me a glass and cut the call. A second later, the same number called again. Mudit disconnected it. 'The government needs to do something about these spam callers,' he said.

My phone rang again. It was the same number.

'Wait,' Mudit said, 'let me sort these idiots out. Calling again and again.'

He picked up the call. 'No, brother, we don't need mutual funds, property, insurance, an RO filter, shares or credit cards. Why are you spoiling our evening like this?' he said.

The person on the other end said something. Mudit's face dropped. 'Huh? Oh, Payal? It's you? Sorry, this is Mudit. Yes, he's here.'

Mudit handed me the phone, biting his tongue and pulling his ears in an apologetic gesture.

'Payal?' I grabbed my phone. 'Yes, it's me. What number is this? Yes, I'm in a noisy place. Wait, let me step out.'

I walked out to the main road. Noisy conversations were replaced by noisy traffic. I found a relatively quieter side lane. 'Better now?' I said.

'Yes, I can hear you,' Payal said. 'I'm at Rockin Scissors.'

'Where?'

'It's a salon in Ghatkopar. I came here so I could call you from their phone. Even if my parents see my location, it's okay.'

'Oh, okay. I came out with Mudit.'

'Where?'

'Janata Bar, in Bandra.'

'I miss Bandra so much.'

'Then come here. Better yet, move here.'

'What?'

'Just move into my apartment. I'll handle the rest,' I said.

This Old Monk confidence is something else, I tell you.

'How?'

'We have no choice, Payal. Run away and come to me. I miss you. I love you. I can't live without you.'

'And my parents said they'll kill themselves if I continue things with you.'

'Nobody does that, Payal. They'll come around.'

'They won't. Saket, I called to tell you something. Promise you won't get upset?'

'What?'

'They're coming today. That's why I came to the salon, to get my make-up and hair done.'

'Who's coming?'

'Parimal and his parents. Along with a few of his close relatives. Mine as well.'

'Why?'

'They wanted to do the roka ... I said no. Anyway, it's just a small family dinner with twenty people.'

'Payal!' I screamed so loudly that two passers-by turned to look at me. I lowered my voice, 'How could you?'

'Saket, don't assume I'm on board with any of this. But Mom and Dad gave up food—'

I cut her short, 'They manipulate you like this and—'

'They ate nothing for four days, Saket. Mom fainted once. The doctor said she could've died.'

'What are you even saying?'

'Jain Paryushan is eight days of fasting. Mom and Dad said that if they ever find out I'm in touch with you, they'll sit on an indefinite fast during the next Paryushan. They'll keep going until death.'

'What?'

'I'm serious, Saket. They're devout, practising Jains. They're trained to bear a lot of suffering.'

'And to manipulate you with it.'

'I don't know, Saket. But I can't just run away and move to Bandra like this.'

'Then convince them. Do something. You're just toeing their line.'

'No, I'm not. I'm calling you, aren't I? Even though they made me swear I wouldn't.'

'Thanks for the big favour,' I said, kicking an empty mineral-water bottle in frustration.

'Don't fight, please. I'm already stressed,' Payal said.

'Yeah, stress will spoil your make-up. You need to look good in front of your groom and your in-laws.'

'Stop it, Saket, please.' Payal started to weep.

'Payal, please don't cry,' I said.

'Then don't say such hurtful things.'

'Come see me. Now. Leave your phone at the parlour. Or I'll come there.'

'There's traffic. It won't work. I'll have to go back before either of us can reach.'

'Fine. Whatever.'

'I'm sorry, Saket. I'll try to see you soon.'

'It'll be even harder to convince your parents after this roka, you know that, right?'

'It's just a dinner. I won't let them call it a roka. Please be patient, Saket. Let me see what can be done.'

'If you say so ...'

'Okay, Mom's calling. I have to go. Bye,' she said, ending the call.

'Bye. I love you,' I said to a disconnected line.

∼

'Bro, where were you? I'm hanging out with plumbers here,' Mudit said as I walked back into Janata Bar.

'Sorry, Mudit. I had to speak to Payal. Where's my drink?'

'Here,' Mudit said, topping my glass up with a lot of rum and a little bit of Coke.

I chugged it all down in one go.

'Bro, easy,' Mudit said. 'This isn't one of those protein shakes you have after the gym.'

'One more,' I said.

Shaking his head, Mudit made me another drink. 'I'm guessing the call didn't go well,' he said.

'I took your suggestion. Asked her to move in. I said, come to Bandra right now. Move into my apartment, and don't leave, like ever. Told her I'll handle the rest.'

'Well done. That's my brave best friend. What did she say?'

I told him the entire story about her parents going into full-on Anna Hazare hunger-strike mode.

'Are they nuts?' Mudit said, stuffing his mouth with a fistful of spicy peanuts.

'Yeah. And tonight, Parimal and his extended family are visiting them. And some of Payal's relatives too.'

'What? It's her freaking roka? Tonight? And you're sitting here with carpenters and electricians, drinking Old Monk?'

'Fuck,' I said. 'It's a roka, right? That's exactly what I told her.'

I knocked back another drink. The rum inside the Old Monk bottle had receded to a dangerously low level. I picked up a piece of the tandoori chicken and tore the meat off with my teeth.

'Yeah, I'm not a Jain. So what? This is who I am. I drink rum and eat chicken. Make me another drink,' I said to Mudit.

'We can't just sit here and drink away, bro. We have to do something,' Mudit said.

'Like what?'

'I don't know. You're just going to let this roka happen? Because if it goes through, your game gets three levels harder.'

'Exactly what I told her.' I stared at my drink for a few seconds. Then I stood up.

'What?' Mudit said.

'You're right. We need to do something. Let's go.'

'Where?'

'Ghatkopar, baby. Let's take this party there,' I said, taking a sip of the rum directly from the bottle.

~

The Uber driver took us to Riddhi-Siddhi Niwas in forty minutes.

A security guard stopped us at the entrance. 'Who do you want to meet?'

Mudit rolled down his window. 'My friend is here to meet his father-in-law. Any problem?'

'What? Which apartment?' the security guard said, raising an eyebrow as he noticed we were both piss drunk.

'Anand Jain, fifth floor,' I managed to say despite my inebriated state.

'Your good name?' the guard said.

'Mudit and—' Mudit began but I placed my hand over his mouth.

'We're Parimal Jain's cousins. There's a family gathering,' I said.

'That may be so, but what's your name?' the guard said.

'We're from Parimal Jain's side. Tell them,' I said.

'I have to give one name.'

'Mudit,' Mudit said. 'Mudit Saxena.'

The guard dialled the intercom in Payal's apartment. A household help picked up the phone. The guard spoke to her for a few seconds. I thought our cover would be blown right there. Somehow, the maid fell for it. The guard ended the call and opened the gate.

We left the cab and took the elevator up to the fifth floor. Outside Payal's apartment, there were nearly two dozen pairs of slippers lined up on both sides of the door. I rang the doorbell.

'The door's open,' Anand Jain shouted from inside. A second later, he stood at the entrance. It took him a moment to recognize me.

'You?' he screamed, then instantly lowered his voice to avoid being overheard by the guests inside. 'You rascal, how did you even get in?'

He opened his phone and checked the automatic visitor notification.

'Mudit? You lied about your name,' Anand said as he read the notification. 'But what else can I expect …'

'Uncle, I'm Mudit,' Mudit said. 'Saket's friend.'

Anand ignored him completely and spoke to me. 'I don't want to see you. I'm calling security.'

'I don't want to see you either. I need to see Payal. Call her,' I said, full of Old Monk confidence.

'You're drunk?' Anand said, sniffing the air around me like a constipated mouse.

'Call her, or I'll go inside and find her myself,' I said.

'Security,' Anand spoke into the phone. 'Please come to the fifth floor. I'm in danger.'

'You're not in danger, Uncle, or Mr Jain or whatever. I'm just here to see my girlfriend, who's being kept here forcibly,' I said.

'Get lost,' Anand said.

'Who is it, ji?' Yashodha called out as she came to the door. She looked at Mudit and me, aghast. Both of us wore old T-shirts and shorts—Janata Bar couture. In contrast, the Jains looked like actors in a Tanishq Diwali ad. Anand wore a brocade silk kurta with a matching embellished waistcoat. Yashodha wore a purple saree with golden embroidery all over it. She also wore a massive diamond necklace, gleaming with more stones than South Africa's total annual production.

'Where did he come from? This curse?' she muttered.

Okay, she was referring to me.

'Aunty, please call Payal. I'll speak to her and leave,' I said.

'We have a family function going on,' Yashodha said.

'I'm coming in,' I said.

'No, you're not,' Anand said, blocking the door with his arm, as if that would stop me. I could snap his arm like a twig. And given my mood, I was about to.

Anand called the building security again. They told him the guards were on their way up. Fine. I could take them on too, if needed. Rage seethed in me. I wanted to see my girl. I couldn't let a weak, fat man who only ate carbs stop me.

'I'll call Payal,' I said, dialling her number from Mudit's phone. She didn't pick up.

What was she doing inside? Talking to that asshole Parimal? Hadn't she noticed the commotion at the door?

The lift doors opened in the corridor outside the Jains' apartment. Three puny but self-important-looking guards came running towards us, as if this were a hostage situation.

'Take them away,' Anand said.

'Let's go, Saket,' Mudit said, eyeing the guards. 'We can deal with this later.'

'I'm not going anywhere,' I said.

'Take them, I said!' Anand shouted.

One of the security guards came towards me. He seemed intimidated by my size and signalled another guard to come up behind me.

'Don't touch me,' I said, raising my hands as they tried to hold me. I clenched my fists, ready to punch.

One of the security guards pulled out a walkie-talkie. He asked for backup like he was Tom Cruise in *Mission: Impossible*.

'My girlfriend is inside. Payal Jain. I'm only here to meet her. This man is preventing me from going in. Take *him* away, not me,' I said.

The guards hesitated for a second, confused.

Anand was livid. 'This is my house. What are you waiting for? Take him away! I'm calling the police.' He dialled a number. 'Patil, send a few men, please. Yes, the same rascal. He's landed up at my daughter's engagement and is creating a ruckus.'

Engagement? What the fuck did he just say? This wasn't a family get-together or even a roka? It was a *freaking engagement*? Did Payal lie to me?

'The cops are coming,' Anand said. 'You won't leave otherwise.'

Mudit shook my shoulder, realizing things had escalated while the Old Monk was wearing off. 'Let's go, bro, he's called the cops.'

'Fuck the cops, man. They're getting Payal engaged,' I said.

The entrance door opened and Payal emerged. She was wearing a pink lehenga with delicate red flowers embroidered all over it, each flower centred with tiny gold and silver stones. Even drunk, I noticed the intricate details. She looked like the most beautiful bride in the world. And even though I had sworn off marriage for a while, I could've married her right then and there.

'Payal,' I said, my voice softening. 'I just need to talk to you.'

'Payal, go back inside, now!' Yashodha said.

'Saket? Mudit?' Payal looked at us, shocked.

'Two minutes, Payal. Please, Mr Jain, Mrs Jain ... I want to talk to her for two minutes, then I'll leave,' I said, my voice breaking. *No, I wouldn't cry. Staying angry was better.*

'Go inside, Payal,' Anand said firmly. 'We have guests. Yashodha, take her inside, and attend to the guests.'

'No, Dad, let me talk to him,' Payal said, her eyes locked on mine.

I could tell she still loved me. I couldn't bear to be away from her for even one more minute. No, I would take her away with me, right now.

'Go inside, Payal,' Anand said. 'The police will take care of him.'

'Two minutes, Dad?'

Before her father could respond, Payal ducked under his arm, which was still blocking the door, and stepped outside.

'This isn't the best time and place, Saket,' Payal said as she came towards me.

I swear I could've grabbed her face and kissed it right there. Somehow, I resisted.

'Payal.' Anand pulled his daughter back by her elbow. 'Have you gone mad?'

'Dad, leave me alone. You go inside. I'll talk to him and then come in. I promise.'

'No, I'm going to be right here,' Anand said, peeking inside his house to ensure his other guests hadn't seen us.

'I love you, Payal,' I blurted out.

'Get out of here!' Anand said. 'Guards, take him away. Right now.'

The three guards pounced on me immediately. I could've pried them away easily, but I didn't. My entire focus was on Payal.

'Come with me,' I said, even as the guards tried to pull me away. 'I don't have all the answers, but we'll figure it out together. Come with me, Payal, now.'

'Saket,' Payal said, 'what are you saying?'

'I'm saying leave your house and come with me.'

'I'll make sure you rot in jail,' Anand said, calling someone on his phone to see where the cops had reached.

'How can I do that?' Payal said. 'And now? I have guests at home.'

'You're getting engaged, Payal. You're fucking getting engaged! After living with me, sleeping in the same bed with me for a year.'

Anand came forward and slapped me hard across my face. He would've hit me more, but Mudit stopped him.

'Uncle, we're leaving. Saket, let's go,' he said.

'Payal, please. *Please*?'

Both she and I teared up.

'Please, Payal?' I said again. I hoped my pleading would remind her of my tiny apartment, the ledge we spent countless nights on and how much I loved her.

A few of the guests came to the door. A young man in his mid-twenties was among them. Was it Parimal?

'What happened, Uncle?' he said, hovering behind Anand.

'Nothing, Parimal. Guy's a mental patient,' Anand said. 'Lives around here, gets drunk often and bothers everyone.'

Full marks for improvisation, Anand Jain. Are Jains even allowed to lie?

'Oh, are you okay, Uncle?' Parimal said.

'Yes, yes. The guards are taking him away. His friend is also here,' Anand said and turned to Mudit. 'You'll take him to a good hospital, right?'

Mudit nodded. Anand signalled to his guests to go inside. They complied.

'I'm not mental, you're the one who's fu—' I started, but Mudit covered my mouth with his hand.

I looked at Payal. She made eye contact with me for a second. Her father tapped her shoulder, and she turned away and went back inside. I had asked her to come away with me. She hadn't answered me. No answer was also an answer.

'We'll take him, sir, don't worry,' one of the guards said.

'The cops are coming. Hand him over to them,' Anand said.

'Yes, sir. But, sir?'

'What?' Anand said.

'If there's an engagement function, is there any chai and mithai for the guards?'

~

'I told you, nothing happened. We just came to see Payal Jain, who's in a relationship with my friend,' Mudit said.

We sat in Inspector Patil's room, in the Ghatkopar police station, on wooden chairs that threatened to collapse under our weight. The alcohol had finally worn off.

Inspector Patil was in his forties, balding and clearly not interested in dealing with this stupid non-case. He wore a police uniform two sizes too small for his wide girth.

'Anand Jain alleges you were harassing him. Trespassing into his house,' Inspector Patil said, cracking his fingers.

'There was no harassment. We rang the bell and asked if we could speak to Payal,' Mudit said.

'I only wanted to see my girlfriend. And we never trespassed. We never entered their house,' I said.

'Did she want to see you?' Patil said.

'Yes,' I said. 'Her father's not letting her talk to me. She's an adult. She can do whatever she wants, isn't it?'

'Yes, and she's gotten engaged. To someone else. Look, they sent mithai.'

Patil took out a box of kaju katli from under his desk and offered it to us. I was hungry as hell, but I still had enough pride to not eat the mithai from Payal's engagement.

Mudit, however, took two pieces and stuffed his face. *Traitor*.

'Probably the first time the police have offered anyone mithai. Thank you, sir,' Mudit said.

I glared at Mudit. He looked at me, surprised. 'What?' he said, taking two more pieces of the sweet. 'Sir is offering it to us, bro.'

The inspector burst out laughing. 'Are you an idiot?' he said to me. 'Landing up drunk at her engagement. What did you expect? That she'll run away with you?'

'Yes,' I said, dead serious. 'She wants to, I know it.'

'Then why is she eating dinner with her fiancé right now while you're sitting in a police station?' Patil said, laughing again.

My face dropped. This crass inspector had delivered a truth I didn't want to hear. I began to cry—horrible, embarrassing, loud sobs.

'Abe chutiye,' the inspector said, 'stop it. And eat the mithai. I could've fed you lathis. But I'm giving you kaju katli instead. Eat.'

I obeyed him and took a piece. Damn, it tasted good.

The inspector continued speaking: 'You seem to be educated, and from a good family. What are you doing? You've built such a big body, but don't you have a little brain?'

I kept quiet.

'Sorry, sir,' Mudit said. 'He just heard about her parents planning a ceremony. We were drunk and didn't know what else to do. He loves her a lot.'

'This love business will destroy you,' Patil said.

Mudit and I remained silent.

'Now, Mr Jain is an important member of the society here. I must oblige him. I have to put you in the lockup tonight.'

'Sir, please,' Mudit said.

'Shh,' the inspector said. 'I'm not filing a report. That would complicate things and drag them out. But I have to tell him that you're in my lockup tonight.'

'Why the hell do I have to be in jail? I'll marry that girl. I'm ready to do a court marriage with her. Right now.'

'Is she though?' the inspector said. 'Is she ready to marry you?'

'Ignore my friend, sir,' Mudit said. 'Is there a way we can leave without having to stay in the lockup?'

'No. And if you want to leave tomorrow morning, you must promise me something.'

'What?' I said, as he was looking at me.

'You cannot contact her. Or go near her.'

'Is it illegal to do that?' I said.

'Don't teach me law. I can still file three cases against you. Keep defending yourself in court for years then.'

'No, sir. It's fine, sir. We can stay in here tonight,' Mudit said.

'Good. At least you have one sensible friend,' Patil said, signalling to the cops to take us to the lockup.

We were taken to an eight-foot-by-ten-foot cell that we shared with three other men who remained unbothered by the cramped and dank room. I didn't know what crimes they were in for. Hell, I didn't even know what crime I was in for. I used to live in a multi-million-dollar house in Silicon Valley. I had a job in private equity. What the hell was I doing in a jail cell in Ghatkopar?

Mudit fell asleep soon. The man next to me farted in his sleep. It was disgusting on one level, and funny on another. It felt like my own life had become one big dark comedy act.

My mental chatter continued even as I lay on the cold cell floor and tried to sleep: Was Inspector Patil right? Did Payal not want to be with me? How could that be possible? She loved me. She'd told me so a million times. Why didn't she walk away with me then? Because of her parents? Should I have said something else? Should I have said, 'Let's go get married in court right now?'

Well, we couldn't have gone to a court right away even if she'd agreed. The courts remain closed on weekends. But shouldn't they keep at least a few courts open so that marriages can be registered on weekends? That's usually when people decide to get married, isn't it? Anyway, why was I thinking about judicial reforms?

Payal had not come with me. End of story. She had gone right back inside. And her parents, they probably hated me now. At this point, they would rather their daughter was a lesbian than be with me. Are there Jain lesbians? There ought to be, right?

See, that's how my brain works. The most random nonsense mixed with some real emotions. Mudit woke up at one point and looked at me.

'Try to sleep, bro,' he said.

'Can't,' I replied.

He patted my shoulder and shut his eyes again.

'Payal will come back to me no, bro? She won't marry that stupid Parimal, right?' I said.

Mudit didn't answer. He only shrugged and went back to sleep.

∼

I thought Payal would call or message me.

Five days—120 hours—had passed since her engagement. I sat on my window ledge in agony, staring at my phone, waiting for her text.

'Hi baby,' she would say, followed by 'Are you okay?' and 'I'm so sorry about that day.' I'd be upset, but I would ultimately forgive her. She would somehow sneak out and come over to my place. We would make love and promise to never leave each other. I would then tell her that my fears about getting married a second time were overblown. I would drive to the family court in the Bandra Kurla Complex right then and make her my wife. That's it. No Parimal Jain, no Anand Jain or Anyone Jain could come in our way after that.

My phone rang. But it wasn't her. I picked up Mudit's call.

'How are you feeling?'

'Fucked.'

'She didn't message, I guess.'

'No.'

'Oh, well.'

'I have to meet her.'

'Bro, remember what the inspector said?'

'I don't care.'

'You're on your own trip. Anyway, how's the new act coming along?'

'What act?'

'Saket! We have an international comedy festival scheduled. White people are coming to perform at the club. You're the desi act, bro. We need to top them.'

'Oh, right. That. I have to get back to it,' I said. I hadn't even started.

'Please do. The performance is in a week. Next Saturday.'

'Yeah. I'll do it.'

After the call ended, I sat and stared at a blank Word document for over an hour. It's hard to write comedy when your life's turning into a tragedy. Why the hell hadn't Payal messaged?

I had to shift to Plan B: Get new SIM cards. I left my apartment and went to the Airtel shop on Linking Road in Bandra. After furnishing a dozen ID proofs and filling in even more KYC forms, I finally obtained three new SIM cards.

What's the deal with KYC—Know Your Customer—forms anyway? Do they really think having a copy of my Aadhaar card or electricity bill means they *know* me? They have no fucking clue. Do they *know* that my heart is in a million pieces right now? That my girlfriend, who used to sleep inches away from me, has now blocked me? That I need new SIM cards just to message her because I'm that desperate? If they don't, how can they claim to have done my KYC? You have no clue, dude—shove that Aadhaar-card copy wherever you want to.

I put the new SIM card in my phone and set up a new WhatsApp account. Then I messaged Payal: 'Hi, this is me. Can we speak?'

She read the message, but didn't respond.

One hour later, I sent another message: 'It's me, S. Please reply.'

I saw the blue ticks. Someone had clearly read the message.

'Payal, are you there? It's me,' I sent a third message.

Finally, I got a response.

'Me Sunita. Payal ki didi.'

What? Before I could respond, I got a call from Payal's number.

'Payal! Finally! Where have you been?' I said, quickly picking up the call.

'This no Payal. This Sunita. I working Payal house.'

'Oh. Where's Payal?'

'I don't know. Morning went to office.'

'How do you have her phone?'

'This my phone. She give her SIM card. Payal madam take new number.'

Not only had Payal's diabolical parents made her block me everywhere, but they'd also changed her number. They'd anticipated that I'd try to call from other numbers. Jains are smart. No wonder they're richer and more successful than most other communities.

'Who speaking?' Sunita said.

'Nothing, wrong number,' I said, which was a totally idiotic thing to say because literally half a second earlier, I had asked for Payal.

'Your good name, please?'

'Do you need a bank loan?' I said.

'No.'

'Car insurance? RO filter? Property in Panvel?'
'No, not needing anything.'
'That's a shame. I can give you good deals.'
'Who this? S for what?'
'S for Salman Khan. Okay, bye,' I said and disconnected the call.

~

'Payal,' I said. 'Hi.'

I stood in the Express Towers lift, which I'd been taking up and down for two hours. I'd arrived at 5.30 p.m. I couldn't wait in the lobby because her SWAT-team-like mother would come to pick her up. I couldn't show up directly at her office either. I didn't want her to feel embarrassed in front of her colleagues. So I decided to wait for her in the lifts. This meant going up and down non-stop until Payal left work and entered one of the lifts to go down to the lobby. There were two lifts serving her floor, and Payal could take either of them. In other words, this dumb approach of mine had a one-in-two chance of working. But I still did it. I took one lift up, then came out and went down in the other. Once on the ground floor, I switched back to the other lift and went up again. I was ready to keep doing this until I bumped into Payal. Does this sound ridiculous? Yes. But love makes men do ridiculous things. It makes them scale walls, climb mountains and, I've heard, even fight wars. I was only taking the elevator.

It took me two days to finally see her. On the second day, at 7.30 p.m., Payal entered the same lift that I was in. I had a minute, quite literally, to make my elevator pitch to save my love life. Apart from Payal and me, there was one other person already in the lift—a distinguished-looking man in his sixties.

Payal took a few seconds to spot me in the lift. 'Saket,' she said in a hushed voice. 'What are you doing here?'

'What do you think I'm doing here? Trying to meet you.'

'I can't. Mom's downstairs,' Payal said, fear on her face. 'She can't see you here. Please, Saket, understand my situation.'

'Are you serious? What about my situation? Do you have any idea what I'm going through?' I said, my voice loud enough for the other man to look up from his phone.

He looked at Payal and me in quick succession. I ignored him.

'Payal, I need ten minutes with you. Alone,' I said.

'Saket, if my mother sees us, she'll make me quit my job—the only semblance of sanity I have in my life.'

'She won't see us, don't worry. That's why I've been going up and down in these lifts the past two days.'

'What?'

'Nothing. Can we get off at the parking level? Or any other level? We can just stand somewhere and talk.'

'I already told Mom I'm coming down.'

I checked the display panel—we'd already reached the tenth floor.

'Can you tell her you forgot something in office?'

'Fine, I will. But where do we go?'

'The parking? We can stand and talk.'

'It's dark and smelly there,' Payal said, 'with drivers all around.'

'Do you think I care about all that at this point?' I said.

'Excuse me,' the old man said, startling both of us.

'Yes?' I said, somewhat irritated.

'I'm Lokesh Agrawal. I have a law firm, and our offices are on the tenth and third floors. If you need a private space to talk in, you can sit in one of our meeting rooms on the third floor ...'

Payal and I looked at each other.

'I'm going there now. Would you two like to come with me?' the man said.

The lift doors opened at the third floor. I looked at Payal. She nodded.

'Thank you so much, sir,' I said.

The man, Mr Agrawal, led us to the office of Agrawal and Bansal Legal Associates. The Agrawal–Bansal-powered law firm occupied the entire third floor and a part of the tenth floor. Young associates scurried around, printing documents and typing away at their computers. We passed an empty meeting room, and Mr Agrawal gestured that we could use it.

'Thanks again, sir. We'll only be ten minutes,' I said.

'Take your time, no rush,' Mr Agrawal said as he left us there.

Payal and I entered the meeting room which was filled with legal books. It reminded me of the meetings with my lawyers, where we'd haggled and argued over my divorce settlement for hours. Today, however, I was here to close a marriage deal. And I only had ten minutes do it.

Payal called her mother. 'Hi Mom. I forgot to get a printout. Yes ... Just ten minutes. I'll be down soon,' she said on the phone before turning to me. 'How have you been?' she said.

'You blocked me. Everywhere. You changed your number. Never tried to reach out. And now you ask how I'm doing?'

'Saket, you know what happened. That day, you landed up drunk and—'

'What choice did I have?' I interrupted her, my voice rising.

'Please don't shout,' Payal said, hands on her ears. 'Everyone only shouts at me these days.'

'I'm not shouting. I'm just in pain. I'm distressed. Lost. Empty. Purposeless. Depressed. That's how I've been. And I wish you'd reached out.'

'Have you thought even once about asking me how I've been? Or what I've been going through?' Payal said, her eyes welling up.

'What happened, Payal?' I said, my voice softening.

'It's too much, Saket. I can't. I can't put up with all this. They're tracking my location, and controlling my life. They stop eating if I protest. They threaten to jump off the roof.'

'Have you tried talking to them?'

'Yes. A million times. They think I have a mental problem. That I've been brainwashed. They've put me in therapy.'

'What?'

'They don't get it. After the two episodes at home, they don't understand why I want to be with you, not Parimal.'

'Do *you* understand it?'

Payal looked straight into my eyes for one long minute. She didn't answer my question.

'Do you miss me?'

'You have no idea how much,' Payal said as a tear ran down her cheek.

'You do?'

'I can't think, work or eat. But at the same time, I'm so scared about what my parents will do. I know I might be coming across as cold and uncaring right now, but it doesn't mean I'm not in pain.'

'I'll marry you,' I said.

'Stop,' Payal said.

I continued speaking. 'I said I wasn't sure about marrying again. But I'm sure of one thing—I can't be away from you, Payal. It's not possible. I can't function. I can't even do normal everyday things. And if marrying you is what it takes to be with you, then let's do it. In fact, we're in a law office right now. Can't we do it here? Or do we need to go to a court? Is there a night court?'

'We can't. Have you lost your mind, Saket?'

'Why? What's so crazy about wanting to marry the love of your life?'

'For one, my mom is waiting downstairs. And two, you're not ready to get married again, that too so soon. You're doing this just to somehow make things work.'

'I can't lose you, Payal.'

She looked at me, and yet more tears rolled down her cheeks. Gently, I wiped the tears with my hands. She shook her head.

'What?'

'It won't work.'

'What won't work?'

'This.' She gestured at the space between us. 'You and I need to accept it. Maybe they're right. We were just a phase for each other.'

'A phase?'

'The older-guy thing for me. The younger-girl thing for you. It was exciting. But ultimately, it wasn't meant to last.'

'Whose words are these? Yours? Your parents'? Or that friend of yours?'

'Akanksha.'

'Did she say all this?'

'She's not wrong, is she? The age difference matters. Twelve years, Saket. I was four when you went to college.'

'You can't put it like that.'

'Then there's my community. And the fact that you're divorced. And that you showed up drunk …'

'Can we just forget that day?'

'If only it were that simple, Saket. I can't completely go against my parents. They'll really do something to themselves if I choose you.'

'And yet, you were with me for a year.'

'I wasn't thinking ahead, about the consequences.'

'Where is that old Payal? I miss that Payal. The one who didn't overthink and lived in the moment.'

'That Payal is growing up. She had to.'

I looked at her and saw both love and sadness in her eyes. I hugged her. She didn't resist it, but she didn't hug me back either. I checked the time—we had three more minutes.

'It's quite simple now, Payal. I'm ready to get married. So is Parimal. It's your choice,' I said, letting go of her.

'It's not just my choice. I have to consider my family.'

'Yes, being with me means going against them for a while. But in the end, it's still your choice, Payal.'

When she didn't respond, I continued, 'We'll win them over, babe. I'm a comic. I'll eventually make them laugh, and this whole crazy phase will seem like a joke.'

'Saket, you don't get it,' Payal said firmly. 'This isn't a joke. My entire extended family, Parimal's extended family, they all think that Parimal and I are the perfect match. If I go against all of them, do you realize the shame my parents will face? Jains can be brutal. My parents will be ostracized.'

Okay, this isn't going well, Saket Khurana.

I looked at her. She looked away. 'Are you breaking up with me?' I said.

Payal stood up. 'I need to go. Mom will be waiting.'

'At least have the guts to answer me.'

'I told you. This isn't working. It's not meant to be.'

'So, you *are* breaking up with me.'

'I'm sorry, Saket. It's not me breaking up with you or you breaking up with me. Sometimes, things just don't work out.'

It felt like a huge heavy rock had just dropped on my head.

'Sorry, I have to go. Mom's given me two missed calls already,' Payal said.

'But …' I started. However, no words came out.

We walked out of the meeting room, me following her.

'Also, Saket, a request,' she said, turning as we reached the elevator.

'What?'

'Don't contact me. Don't reach out. Don't think of me. I'm also trying to do the same. It's hard. Let's not make it harder,' she said.

How do you not think of the person you love the most in the world? The elevator dinged. She looked at me and came forward to give me a hug. Before I realized what was happening, she waved a silent goodbye and disappeared into the lift.

As soon as the lift doors closed, I fell to my knees. I cried, I don't know for how long.

Mr Agrawal tapped my shoulder. 'Are you okay, young man? What's the problem?' he said.

'I'm not a young man,' I said, 'and that's the problem.'

~

'You know what I love? Spam messages on my phone,' I said.

A few people in the audience giggled.

'No, seriously, I do. They just make me feel less lonely. I may not have a girlfriend anymore, but at least someone wants to teach me how to make two crores a month by trading in stocks. Someone out there cares. I actually send a thank-you to all of them. Plots in Lonavala that'll double in price in three years? Thank you, sir, for sharing this amazing scheme with me.'

The audience laughed.

'Anyway, yes, so I have a life update. Turns out, I don't have a girlfriend anymore. She broke up with me.'

The audience went 'aww' and 'oh no'.

'Any guesses why she broke up with me?' I said to the entire audience.

'You cheated on her,' someone screamed.

'No,' I said. 'I didn't cheat on her, bro.'

'*She* cheated on you,' another audience member said.

'No, she didn't,' I said.

'That's what *you* think,' the same person said.

'Fuck you,' I said. The audience laughed—partly at me using a curse word and partly because I'd replied in an upset voice. Except, I hadn't made up that upset voice for the sake of the set. I was genuinely upset. Comics aren't supposed to take offence. We offend so many people, after all. However, that day, I've no idea what triggered me. Because I didn't stop there.

'Fuck you, man,' I said. 'She didn't cheat on me. I think *your* wife or girlfriend cheated on you, isn't it?'

Okay, this wasn't funny at all. Why did I just say that? We can pick on the audience a bit, but we aren't supposed to attack them. At that time, of course, none of this crossed my mind.

'You know why she broke up with me? Because I'm divorced. And too old. She's marrying a younger guy. I could beat the shit out of that younger guy, but anyway. Anybody who's divorced in the audience? Anyone too old? Come on, admit it, you losers.'

The audience looked at me, horrified. I hadn't called the entire audience losers. I was only calling old and divorced people losers. And in that, I was making a joke about me being the loser. You see, I'm old and divorced. So, I'm the loser. See the joke? No? Well, neither did the audience. A few people got up and walked out of the auditorium.

'Who are these guys who are walking out? The divorced ones or the old ones?' I said.

For the first time ever, Mudit came on stage in the middle of my act. He tapped my shoulder and whispered, 'Let's go, Saket.'

'What?' I was surprised to see him on stage.

He put his arms around my shoulders and tried to tug me. 'Come with me.'

'I'm okay,' I shouted. 'He's the boss, guys. But he's taking me away. Where? To Ghatkopar Jail?'

Another attempt at a joke that didn't land. Nobody knew the context, after all.

Mudit snatched the mic from me and spoke to the audience. 'I'm sorry, guys. Saket isn't feeling well today. But we have a replacement act coming up, so stayed seated. Big, big applause for Saket Khurana.'

A few in the audience clapped, looking confused even as Mudit dragged me backstage and took me to the bar outside.

~

'I told you I'm fine,' I said to Mudit.

We sat in the club bar. He didn't allow me to drink alcohol. Instead, he forced me to gulp down glasses of water. He had lectured me for half an hour. He still had more to say.

'You're not fine, bro. Come on, more water.'

'No more water, Mudit, please. I'll burst.'

'You went on stage drunk.'

'I just had a few beers before the act.'

'More than a few.'

'Cut me some slack. My girlfriend left me and is getting married to someone else.'

'Boohoo. Should we all cry? Rename this place the Crying Club instead of the Comedy Club?'

'I'm sorry the act didn't go well today. It happens sometimes.'

'Not just "didn't go well". You bombed. Big time.'

'Fine, I bombed. So, kill me.'

'You abused the audience.'

'They said Payal cheated on me.'

'They were fucking joking. Having fun. That's what people come here to do. What are you? A baby? And you called the audience losers.'

'That was a joke about me being old and divorced. It didn't land.'

'It crashed. And created a dumpster fire. We'll get terrible reviews on social media for sure.'

'I'm sorry.'

'It's not good for the club. We're trying to scale here, bro. Investors don't like a place that abuses and mocks the customers.'

'Is it all about money to you, Mudit? Really? That's it? You want to raise capital, and this upsets your plans? You don't care about what your best friend is going through?'

'Stop it. If money is all that mattered, I would've also joined investment banking and not been foolish enough to open a comedy club.'

I didn't respond.

'You think I don't care about you? Really?' Mudit said.

'You do. But you don't get it. You don't get what I'm going through.'

Mudit took a sip of water before speaking again. 'You're right, I don't get it. Why are you so into this girl anyway?'

'I love her, Mudit. I've never loved anyone like this.'

Mudit smirked.

'What?' I said. 'Tell me what you're thinking.'

'Okay, this will sound harsh. You asked for it. Hear me out. I think you found a hot young girl and felt super attracted to her. She liked you as well. The sex was insane. She was inexperienced. You taught her everything, which is super hot as well. She submitted to you for a year. You lived in this world of crazy sex with a babe. It became a drug. Now that she's gone, you miss your drug. This is the withdrawal phase. It's making you do insane things like day drinking, that too before your act, and insulting the audience.'

'I didn't insult them. I made a joke that didn't land.'

'Whatever. Point is, you're not in love. Every man has a mid life crisis in his thirties or forties. Nobody wants to be middle-aged and old. Payal came into your life and made you feel young. For a while, it was like being back in your wild twenties again.'

'I never had a wild twenties. I was always studying. Or busting my ass off for my start-up.'

'All the more reason why this is hitting you so hard. You never had your wild twenties. Or wild anything. This was the first time you did something crazy and exciting. This was nothing like the boring, occasional sex you had in Silicon Valley with a wife who never loved you.'

'Mudit,' I said, my voice loud.

'Sorry. But am I right or not?'

'Partly. Yes, Payal brought excitement. But it was more than that. We went grocery shopping. We sat on the ledge and worked in silence for hours. We cooked together. We went on walks …'

'Yes, you played house-house with her for a while. Which makes the withdrawal worse. It also makes you feel way more lonely. But you know what?'

'What?'

'It was all an illusion. She's twenty-one, Saket.'

'Twenty-two.'

'Fine. She's twenty-two. And she's beautiful, smart and comes from a rich, conservative Jain family. You knew these facts from day one. What did you think her parents would say, "Okay, beta, marry that middle-aged, divorced stand-up comic who lives in a rented one-bedroom flat in Bandra?"'

'I'm not middle-aged.'

'Getting there soon though.'

'So are you.'

'Yes, and that's fine. Bro, there's nothing wrong in getting old. Nothing wrong in having fun with a young girl either. Hell, a part of me was jealous. But where it starts going wrong is when you start assuming it's something else. A hot adventure is not a lifelong partnership, Saket.'

'It wasn't just a hot adventure for me.'

'Well, seems like it was one for her.'

'No.'

'Yeah? Why did she leave you then? Why did she not walk out with us that day when we went to her house? She had her fun, bro. And when it was time to get real, she wanted to marry someone more suited to her and her family.'

I stared at Mudit.

'I know it hurts. Reality often does,' Mudit continued. 'That's why humanity needs comedy clubs. To get away from it all.'

I stood up. 'I'm going home. Is it okay if I take a few weeks off?' I said.

'You have acts scheduled next weekend.'

'Cancel them. I don't want to bomb again.'

∼

The Home Diva account was public. I scrolled through Akanksha's previous posts, going back two years. She had turned every major life event into a piece of content. Her posts began around the time of her marriage. Every ceremony—roka, engagement, sangeet, haldi, jaimala, kanyadaan and pheras—had multiple posts. Each post featured a long caption explaining the significance of the ceremony, how emotional she'd felt when the haldi was applied to her face, or who had designed the dresses she'd worn. Each post ended with hashtags like #blissful #grateful #lovebeingatraditionalgirl.

Even after the wedding, she continued posting about her #blissful marriage. One post was about cooking a meal for her husband for the first time. In that, she demonstrated how to make heart-shaped rotis—you roll out the dough in a flat circle, use a steel katori to cut out some bits, to make it heart-shaped, before cooking the rotis. 'More than anything,' the caption read, 'a great meal for your husband must have the most important ingredient—love.'

I had to talk to Akanksha Chandak—my last hope.

I sent her a direct message:

Dear Akanksha,

This is Saket, Payal's friend. I would like to meet you to discuss a few things. There have been some misunderstandings between Payal's family and me, leading to a lot of distress. Since you're Payal's most trusted friend, I would like to explain my side to you. Then you can decide if you want to help resolve the issues between us.

With regards,
Saket Khurana

P.S. You have a wonderful Instagram account, and you're an amazing content creator.

I added the fake flattery at the end, hoping it would help my case.

She replied an hour later:

Hi Saket,

Thank you for your compliments. I'm shooting some content videos in Kala Ghoda this Wednesday. I can meet you for coffee at the Kala Ghoda Café at 4 p.m. Does that work?

Akanksha

I fist-pumped and replied immediately, confirming our meeting.

~

The Kala Ghoda Café, located near Colaba, is a quaint yet spacious coffee shop. Spread over two levels, it is housed in an old heritage building, typical of the Kala Ghoda area. Its stark white interiors, however, give it a modern warehouse feel.

I was already seated in the café with a cup of black coffee when Akanksha walked in. She wore a lime-green saree with a dark-blue blouse, and had accessorized the outfit with lots of silver jewellery. Another young girl, dressed in a white T-shirt and jeans, accompanied her. She seemed like Akanksha's assistant, carrying a selfie stick, a mic and two shopping bags full of clothes.

'Hi,' Akanksha said, extending her hand and taking off her sunglasses. 'Sorry, I'm a bit late. Shoot took long. Saket, right?'

'Yes, I'm Saket,' I said and stood up to shake her hand. 'And it's okay, you aren't that late. How was the shoot?'

'Good. It was a collab video with a new designer launching a traditional line. This is Garima, my manager.'

'Hi Garima,' I said.

'Garima, why don't you sit upstairs and download the videos onto your laptop?' Akanksha said.

Garima nodded and went to the upper level. Akanksha and I sat downstairs. She ordered a cappuccino and spent a few minutes taking ten photos and two videos of the coffee cup from different angles. Once she was done, she set her phone aside and turned to me.

'Sorry, I'm collecting food content,' she said. 'I might launch another food-influencer account.'

'Sounds great. Anyway, Akanksha, we never met, but I feel like I know you.'

'I feel that way too. Payal has spoken so much about you.'

'What did she say?'

'Everything. Trust me, I know every detail about you and Payal.'

'Really?' I raised an eyebrow.

'Girls talk.' Akanksha brushed back a strand of hair from her forehead.

'How's she doing?' I said.

'She's getting better every day. All this has been traumatic for her.'

'Separating from me?'

'Everything. The entire drama. Her parents walking in on you guys. Then that day, on her engagement, when you showed up drunk at her house.'

'You were there at her place that night too, right?'

'Yes. I was there. Right after you left, I had to handle her and make sure she was okay.'

'What happened after I left?'

'She was distraught. I took her to her room and she told me what had happened. What you did wasn't right—showing up like that and creating a scene.'

'And was it right for her parents to force an engagement with Parimal like that?'

'What's wrong with her parents wanting her to settle down well?'

I looked at Akanksha. 'Payal and I love each other,' I said.

Akanksha smiled in response.

'What?' I said.

'Nothing. How can I help you, Saket?'

'Can you talk to her parents?'

'About what?'

'About Payal and me. You know everything about us. You know how happy she was with me.'

'Happiness isn't everything, Saket.'

'What do you mean?'

'What is happiness anyway? And how can she be happy if she knows she's hurting her parents?'

'This is about her life, not theirs.'

'Even for the sake of her own life, is this the best choice for her?'

'What do you mean?'

'Sorry, Saket, I don't mean to be disrespectful. But you're a lot older. You were even married before.'

'Yes. But we fell in love. Does love even consider age?'

'I don't think it was love.'

'Then what was it?'

'Forget it,' Akanksha said, taking a sip of her coffee. She wiped the milk-foam moustache from her lips with a tissue.

'Say it,' I said.

'You know about her thing for older men. Maybe it stemmed from that, from trying to win her father's love and approval all her life.'

'This is *not* about any daddy issues that she may have had. I'm not her fetish. I love her, and I'll marry her. We'll be happy together.'

Akanksha shook her head.

'You don't agree?' I said.

'I don't think my friend will be happy. Sorry, Saket, but she can do better than you.'

'And Parimal is better?'

'Well, he fits into their family, and she fits into his. They've been family friends for years.'

'But will he be compatible with Payal? Will he make her laugh?'

'People find ways to laugh. They don't have to marry a comedian.'

Ouch, I don't know why, but that stung.

'Does she love me?' I said.

Akanksha didn't answer.

'Did she say she loved me or not?'

Akanksha took a deep breath before speaking again. 'Saket, I'm going to tell you something, but you have to promise me that you'll never bring it up with Payal or anyone else. You can't even acknowledge that you know this.'

'What is it?' I said, concerned.

'Promise me first.'

'I promise. I swear I won't tell anyone, including Payal.'

'Good. Just know that, for me, the most important thing is my friend's well-being.'

'Is she okay?'

'She's better. And yes, she did say that she loved you. She was obsessed with you. When she was forced to stay away from you, she had a nervous breakdown.'

'What? What do you mean? How? When?'

'After the temple incident. She stopped talking, sleeping and eating. Anand uncle found a therapist for her. She had daily sessions with him and was prescribed antidepressants. Someone had to be with her all the time. It was really difficult.'

'Why didn't she tell me all this?'

'How could she? That would mean staying in touch with you. How could she heal if she kept seeing you?'

'Heal from what?'

'This unhealthy attachment and ... sex addiction with a much-older man.'

'Sex addiction?'

'Yes. The first step in treating any addiction is separating the addict from the drug.'

'Who said this?'

'Her therapist. He's qualified. He knows what's really going on, even if we confuse it with love.'

'And who's this therapist?'

'Dr Mukesh Jain. He has decades of experience as a psychiatrist.'

'Let me guess—Jain ... He's either a friend or relative of Payal's father?'

'Yes, Anand uncle has known him for years.'

'And he's also traditional,' I said sarcastically.

'You make it sound like it's a bad thing, but yes, he's a traditional Jain.'

'So, he's probably just doing what Anand Jain wants—brainwashing Payal into believing her love is a perversion and an addiction.'

'It's not brainwashing. It's the truth.'

'Really?' I said. 'And how do you know that?'

'I got married young, just like my parents wanted. To a boy from my community, close to my age. I'm very happy.'

'Good for you. But Payal might want something different.'

'She's my best friend. We grew up together. We're the same.'

'No, you are not,' I said, frustrated. 'She works at Blackwater, cracking multi-million dollar deals on a daily basis. The high point of your day is posting about heart-shaped phulkas and dressing up for Karva Chauth.'

'I see. So that's what you think of me and my content.' Akanksha stood up. 'And here I was, coming to see you, like a fool.'

Okay, I had messed this one up. Big time. I stood too.

'Akanksha, I'm sorry,' I said. 'Please, sit down.'

'No, I have to go make dinner for my husband. My day's "high point", like you said ...'

'I didn't mean it that way, Akanksha.'

Akanksha smirked and shook her head. 'You should see a therapist too,' she said and walked away. She'd barely taken a few steps when she turned around and came back.

'What?'

'By the way, that heart-shaped-phulkas post had more than five thousand likes, including one from a celebrity chef, and we even had a semi-genuine collab query from an atta brand,' she said, before storming out of the café.

~

Mudit had called me for the ninth time. I finally took his call. 'Hi Mudit,' I said, my voice groggy. I lay on my sofa. The bright afternoon sun fell on my face, making me squint.

'Oh God, bro. Why aren't you picking your phone?' Mudit said.

'I dozed off,' I said. I saw the bottle of rum, the cans of Coke and an empty glass on my coffee table. Okay, I'd passed out drunk. Like I had almost every other day for the past one month.

Who cares, let me make another drink.

I stumbled into the kitchen, opened the fridge and took out some ice cubes from the freezer. I came back to the living room and made myself a drink.

'What are you doing? Did I hear ice cubes dropping into a glass?' Mudit said.

'Maybe. Anyway, what's up?'

'Are you drinking?'

'I'm having cold water, dude.'

'Bullshit, I can smell the whisky through the phone.'

'It's rum. But nice try.'

'It's two in the afternoon, bro.'

'How does it matter? Any particular reason you called me?'

'Two reasons. One, your mother called me. You haven't returned your parents' calls in a week. Can you just call them back and tell them you're alive?'

'You could've told them that.'

Mudit remained silent.

'Fine, I'll do it. What's the second thing?' I said.

'There's an enquiry for a corporate show.'

'No, can't do it.'

'Bangalore. Easy money. One of those tech conferences. You could even do a day trip.'

'I'll pass, Mudit. Give it to one of the other comics.'

'They asked for you specifically.'

'Really?'

'Yeah. They saw clips of your previous corporate shows.'

'I'm not the same guy anymore.'

'Come on, bro, you can't throw away your career like that. It's a great gig. Many tech-company CEOs will be there. You'll get more shows after this.'

I gulped down the rum.

'Okay, that's a disgusting sound,' Mudit said. He could hear the alcohol glugging down my throat. 'Why are you drinking rum like it's water?'

'Sorry,' I said, slamming the empty glass on the coffee table. 'Anything else?'

'So, I just decline it? Say no to a lakh you could earn in a few hours making jokes you already know?'

'Yeah. Whatever. I have to go. Anything else?'

'Yes. Just don't check Instagram for a while.'

'Why?'

'You follow that Payal's friend's account, right? That hot diva housewife or something?'

'Akanksha? And it's Home Diva.'

'Yes. Don't look at her feed, bro. You aren't in the right place.'

'Why can't I see it?' I said.

'Trust me. Don't,' Mudit said and hung up.

I immediately opened Instagram on my phone. I saw why Mudit had warned me. Akanksha had posted a congratulatory post about Payal and Parimal's upcoming wedding, with a professionally shot picture of the two.

For the first time, I got a proper look at Parimal—fair, reasonably slim (even if not super fit), clean-shaven except for a light moustache, and a few inches taller than Payal. He had a wide grin on his face as if he'd hit the jackpot. Well, he had.

Payal and Parimal both wore light-beige traditional outfits. Payal held Parimal's forearm and looked down with a shy smile on her face. I searched for some sadness in her eyes, any hint that she wasn't happy on the inside. I couldn't find it.

You know what's worse than a break-up? A break-up where you can see your ex is happy and has moved on.

Back in the pre-social-media days, it was hard to see that happen unless your ex was your neighbour or something. Today, social media has made it possible for you to watch your ex act coy with their new partners, even as you gulp your sixth rum and Coke in the middle of the afternoon. Did the inventors of social media ever realize this? Mark Zuckerberg, do you know your apps are causing pain to all the men and women who've been dumped?

I read the caption under the photograph: 'Big congratulations to my bestie Payal and her super handsome, super cool bae Parimal for getting engaged. They'll be having a full-on traditional Jain wedding soon, and I'm doing a poll here to ask you all, my followers, this question: Should I post regular updates and pictures from the wedding or not? This will be a deviation from the typical Home Diva content, but gosh, I'm so excited! Welcome to the married world, bestie—it's better out here!'

Even in my drunk state, I could tell that the caption was wrong, on multiple levels.

One, Parimal was not super handsome. Fine, he didn't look awful in this picture where the lighting, the make-up and the photographer were all on point. But super handsome? Come on. He could pass off as a doorman at one of those posh heritage hotels. If Parimal was super handsome, what would she call Hrithik Roshan?

Two, Parimal was definitely not super cool. He was a chartered accountant. How can a chartered accountant be super cool?

Three, what was with calling Parimal 'bae'? Parimal was an arranged match. The Jain seniors had worked out the whole deal. Like farmers arranging to buy goats at the village fair. He ain't no bae, babe.

Four, why the manipulative clickbait poll? Indians are obsessed with weddings. They'll never say no to seeing regular updates and pictures of any wedding.

Five, saying 'the married world is better' or whatever—no, sweetie, not in my case. Just ask my divorce lawyer.

I saw the poll results: Ninety-two per cent of the people wanted Akanksha to post the marriage pictures. I wondered who the other eight per cent were. Were they bitter, jilted lovers like me? Those who ran away from the word 'marriage'? Who the hell knows?

I poured myself another drink. Then another. The rum bottle got over soon. Never mind, I had plenty of alcohol in the house. I went to the kitchen and came back with a bottle of vodka. But there was no Coke or ice left. Who cares? I drank the vodka neat, straight from the bottle.

I put on an Arijit Singh playlist. Every song was about heartbreak. Somehow, it felt like all the lyrics had been custom-written for me. How does Arijit get it?

A song from *Aashiqui 2* filled my living room:

Sun raha hai na tu, ro raha hoon main …

'Are you listening? I am crying,' the song said.

But Payal wasn't listening. She was probably shopping or getting her mehndi done.

I took a swig of the room-temperature vodka. It went down my throat like fire. I liked it. I liked any pain that diverted my attention from the Payal pain.

'Fuck it. I don't need her. I don't need anyone,' I said, taking another big sip of the vodka. More fire in my belly.

I walked to the window ledge—Payal's spot. The exact place where she would sit every day, legs stretched out, laptop on her thighs, staring out the window in between work. I could see her—she was still sitting there.

'Saket, come sit next to me,' Payal said.

'Yes, baby,' I whispered, leaning forward to kiss the cold concrete wall.

That was the last thing I remembered.

∼

'Where am I?' I said, blinking.

I'd woken up on a narrow bed with a stiff white sheet under me and a brown blanket over me. I saw wires attached to my chest and an IV drip going into my hand. Okay, this looked like a hospital. Was I dreaming? Was I dead? Was this where the newly dead first arrive? After all, even on earth, newborns generally arrived in a hospital first.

'Patient woke up!' someone shouted.

Okay, this *was* a hospital. And I was the patient.

My mother came running into the room. What was my mother doing here? More importantly, what was *I* doing here?

'Saket,' my mother whispered, hugging me tight.

However distant you might feel from your parents, a mother's hug always feels nice.

'How are you feeling?' she said.

'Why? What happened to me?'

My father entered the room at that moment, his face more emotional than I'd ever seen. A nurse followed him in, and she helped me sit up, propping the pillows behind my back.

'Sorry, where am I? Which hospital is this?'

'Holy Family Hospital,' my mother said.

'When did you come to Mumbai?' I said, still puzzled.

'Five days back,' my father said. 'Mudit called us.'

'Where's Mudit?'

'He's on his way.'

My parents didn't tell me what had happened. They kept the conversation light, talking about how big the tomatoes had grown in their vegetable garden back in Chandigarh and how this winter was particularly cold.

Mudit arrived half an hour later.

'Doing okay, bro?' he said.

'Yeah. Do I really need to be here?'

'Yeah, bro,' Mudit said. 'You definitely did.'

My parents left the hospital to get some rest at my place, leaving just Mudit and me in the room. 'What happened to me, Mudit?'

He told me the whole story. I'd passed out drunk on the window ledge in my apartment, rolled over and fallen to the floor, hitting my head on the ground. Even though it was just a three-foot fall, I'd hurt myself badly. I remained unconscious for an entire day and night. It was Mudit who found me the next day. He'd come to check on me after I hadn't answered my phone. When I didn't respond to the doorbell, he called a locksmith to open the door. They found me lying on the floor, with a pool of blood around my head and a nasty gash on my forehead. He rushed me to the Holy Family Hospital in Bandra, where they admitted me immediately. I'd lost blood, was dehydrated and my system was full of alcohol. Mudit donated his own blood and watched over me until my parents got there. I remained in a near-coma-like state for five days, surviving on IV drips.

'Wow, so much happened. I'm sorry, Mudit. I'm an idiot.'

'This girl, man. And yeah, you really are an idiot.'

I stayed silent.

'If I hadn't come to check on you, I would've lost my best friend. Your parents would've lost their only son. But no, it's all about that chick. We mean nothing to you,' Mudit said.

I lowered my head.

'Career, family, friends, your health. Nothing matters. It's just Payal, Payal, Payal.'

'No, it's not like that,' I said weakly.

'It is. She's married to someone else now, by the way.'

'Is she?' I said, looking around my bed.

'What are you looking for?'

'My phone.'

'See? Now you want your phone. Just to check that dumb Akanksha's account and see if she's posted Payal's wedding pictures.'

'I need my phone for other things too,' I said.

Mudit took out my mobile phone from his pocket and handed it to me. 'It's out of charge,' he said. 'I'll give you a charger. But I swear, if you check Payal's wedding photos, I'll kill you myself.' He handed me the charger and helped me plug in my phone.

'When do *I* get unplugged?' I said, tugging at the wires on my chest.

'They'll do some tests first. But, hopefully, by tomorrow.'

'I can go home then?'

'Yes. But not to Bandra. You're going home to Chandigarh.'

'What? Mudit, why?'

'Stop it. Your parents are worried sick. They haven't slept properly in a week. They won't leave you alone in Mumbai, not when you're in this state.'

'I'll be fine here in Mumbai. Please, I don't need to go back to Chandigarh. I want my space.'

'You don't get to decide these things right now,' Mudit said.

On the flight from Mumbai to Chandigarh, my parents and I hardly spoke. In our family, like most other Indian families, we dealt with conflict by pretending that nothing had happened. If no one brings it up, it doesn't exist, right? So, the default mode is either silence or small talk. My parents chose small talk.

'These Indigo cashew nuts are good,' my mother said.

'I miss Jet Airways though. Their imli candy was amazing,' my father said.

Yes, their son had been found unconscious in his apartment, with his head split open, and had been in a near-comatose state for nearly a week. All this, after going through a horrible divorce less than a year ago. But none of that mattered.

'Vistara has good food as well,' I added. It's funny how comfortably we can take on the dysfunctional patterns of our family.

My parents lived in a small independent house in one of Chandigarh's better sectors. Built on two levels, the ground floor had a living room, a kitchen, a bedroom and a bathroom. There were two more bedrooms upstairs—one of them was mine. This was the room where I'd spent my childhood, prepared for IIT and returned to during college vacations. One of my wedding functions had even been held here. In fact, Raashi's parents lived just two kilometres away.

I remembered the first time my parents had gone to visit them about the prospective match, my mother had come back excited. She thought Raashi and I were a match made in heaven—just as Payal's parents now thought that she and Parimal were perfect for each other. According to Indian parents, if the match is within the same community, then it's a match made in heaven. Maybe God checks the community status before making such matches.

'Beta, come down,' my mother said, knocking on my door. 'Lunch is ready.'

'Coming, Mummy,' I said. I got up and hurriedly followed my mother downstairs. I'd been itching to check Akanksha's

Instagram account when my mother knocked on my door. I knew there would be wedding pictures with disgustingly cheesy captions. I don't know why, but I felt like I just had to see them. Thank God for the momentary escape that lunch provided.

My parents and I sat around the dining table—the one with a slightly creaky leg, present in every Indian middle-class household. My mother had made gobi aloo, rajma, raita and parathas. It was one of my favourite meals.

'Thank you, Mummy, this is so good,' I said.

'I know you like rajma,' my mother said. 'Should I make matar paneer tonight? Or do you want paneer pakodas with tea?'

Punjabis talk about their next meal while eating the current one. In my family, food talk also serves to avoid real conversations.

'Or we can go out,' my father said. 'Chawla's Chicken, in Sector 17.'

'Do you know what happened to me?' I said. My parents looked startled at my sudden change of topic.

'Yes, we do. You drank too much,' my father said after a pause.

'We're not upset, beta. You made a mistake. It happens,' my mother said.

'But it's okay if you're upset. Or worried. That's understandable. What's not okay is you guys pretending like there's nothing else on your minds apart from matar paneer and Chawla's Chicken.'

'I was just—' my mother said, but I cut her off.

'Mummy, the problem is that we never discuss our true feelings in this family. I'm guilty of it too. I don't tell you what I feel about you.'

'Like what?' my father said.

'Forget that. Did Mudit tell you why I ended up drinking so much?'

'He said there was some girl. She left you, and you took to alcohol, to cope,' my father said.

'What else did he tell you?'

'He didn't give us any details,' my father said. 'And he said it was over now, so it doesn't matter anyway.'

'Yes, you don't have to tell us,' my mother said. 'Girls these days are bad. They trap boys for timepass and then—'

'Her name was Payal. She didn't trap me. Neither did I trap her. It wasn't timepass either. We were in love. For a year. We spent a lot of time together. She practically lived with me.'

My mother looked at me, shocked.

'She did,' I said. 'Living in isn't that uncommon in Mumbai.'

My mother began to tear up.

'Why are you crying, Mummy?' I said.

'You should've never left Raashi. It's hard for you to be alone.'

'Mummy, please, this isn't about Raashi. We were totally incompatible.'

'I don't know these terms like "incompatible",' my mother said. Then, turning to my dad, she said, 'Listen, you and I, have we ever used words like incompatible?'

My father didn't respond, assuming the question was rhetorical. He just took another paratha and smeared it with extra ghee.

'Mummy, stop it. My divorce is done. Please, don't talk about Raashi ever again.'

'How much money did she take finally?' my father said.

I gave them the final figures.

'2.4 million dollars? That's like, what, twelve crore rupees?' My father gasped, his spoon almost slipping out of his fingers.

'She took twelve crores? That bitch,' my mother said.

'Yes,' I said in a calm voice. 'And I'm still relieved that it ended.'

My mother broke down in tears. 'She's taken all your money,' she said in between sobs. 'Then you left your job in the US. And now you're living in a one-bedroom rental, doing comedy-vomedy.'

'It's okay, Mummy. I live in Pali Hill. The rent I pay there will get me a whole house in Chandigarh. And stand-up comedy is my passion. I've finally decided to live my life on my own terms.'

'But you're not happy. Look at what happened,' my mother said.

'That's different. That's because Payal and I couldn't be together.'

'What was this Payal's last name?' my father said. Last names are Indian parents' two-factor security check: helps figure out the community, fast.

'Payal Jain,' I said. 'And it doesn't matter. She's married now. The wedding happened last week,' I said.

'What?' both my parents said in unison.

For the next half an hour, I gave my parents a summary of whatever had transpired between Payal and me, minus the super-intimate bits.

'When she left, I felt pain. I drank to ease the pain, until … you know what happened.' I finished my story. I waited for my parents to react. Nobody said or did anything for a minute.

Finally, my mother stood up. 'I made gajar ka halwa as well. I'll get it from the kitchen,' she said and left.

A Punjabi mother's best response to any crisis is an extremely high-calorie dessert.

My father remained silent until my mother returned from the kitchen. The beautiful aroma of ghee and caramelized sugar filled the room. I took a bowl full of the halwa and began eating. It tasted delicious. If there was a Nobel Prize for gajar ka halwa, my mother would get it, hands down.

'There's no shortage of girls for you. Even now,' my mother said.

'*Even now*, is it?' I said, blowing air on a spoonful of halwa to cool it.

'You're young, handsome, educated. An only child. No kids. I still get rishtas for you.'

'Please, Mummy. No more rishtas. I hate this rishta business.'

'If you're lonely, just accept it, beta. You're still young. You can marry again,' my father said.

'No, Dad. I don't want to get married. Don't worry, I'll get over Payal.'

'Saket, beta, don't drink so much,' my mother said, genuine concern in her voice.

'Yes, I'll be careful' I said. 'I promise you. But you must also promise not to pity me. Or go on a mission to find another girl for me. Payal happened I don't know how. I'll never let myself go emotionally like that again with any other girl.'

'You have a long life ahead of you. Don't think like that,' my father said.

'I tried marriage, and failed. Tried love, failed again. All this isn't for me.'

'What is for you then?' my mother said.

'My work. My workouts. My fitness. My friends. My parents. There's a lot more to life than having a partner or a wife or whatever,' I said and stood up.

'Where are you going?' my mother said.

'I'm going for a long run. I haven't exercised in a month.'

~

'Wow, look who's back in town,' Mudit said, giving me a long hug.

After spending two weeks in Chandigarh, I took an evening flight back to Mumbai, and came straight to the club from the airport.

'Thank you for saving my life,' I said.

'You think I would've let you get away so easy?'

'I love you,' I said.

'How are you, bro?' Mudit said.

'Surviving,' I said.

'You'll be fine. My suggestion is that you sink yourself in work. Let's line up an act for you. How about the coming weekend?'

'Give me some time. Before doing stand-up again, I just want to get back to a normal life in Mumbai. I want to hit the gym hard.'

'Take all the time you want,' Mudit said, smiling.

~

Strange, dark thoughts ran through my mind on the cab ride from the club to Bandra. I wanted to end it all. I passed by the Bandra–Worli Sea Link.

Mumbai is a vibrant city full of options. However, it offers limited choices when it comes to committing suicide. You can do the usual—slit your wrists, hang from a ceiling fan or pop a handful of sleeping pills—but none of these have the essence of Mumbai in them. These options are also somewhat lame. Nobody would even notice. She wouldn't notice. And neither would her parents.

I wanted to go out with a bang, literally. I wanted her to see how she had wrecked, shredded, ground and crushed my heart when she left.

Maybe the Bandra–Worli Sea Link? That's dramatic enough to make the headlines: 'Saket Khurana, thirty-four-year-old wannabe stand-up comedian jumps off the Bandra–Worli Sea Link after getting dumped.'

She'll care then, wouldn't she?

Except that the stupid Sea Link isn't high enough. What if I don't die? What if I fall those fifty-odd feet into the sea, and the Koli fishermen who live nearby rescue me? Then they would become the heroes of the story instead: 'Koli fishermen save failed stand-up comedian, unsuccessful in his marriage, career, love and suicide attempt.'

No, that wouldn't work. She'd probably become even more convinced that dumping me was the right decision.

Fortunately, the cab crossed the Sea Link and entered Bandra before I could contemplate further on my diabolical plans to make the headlines.

~

When I unlocked my Bandra apartment, the house felt like my own, even though it was a bit dusty and cold. I kept my luggage in the bedroom and came back to the living room.

I went to the window ledge. Pain shot through my chest. Images of Payal sitting there flashed through my mind. They felt so real that I even lifted my hand in reflex, to touch her imaginary hair.

I went to the bathroom to wash my face. The sight of her little plastic toothbrush still in the toothbrush stand was enough to bring back another flood of memories. We would brush in the bathroom together. She would tell me that she had better teeth because she followed a cleaner vegetarian diet. I would argue that eating all that meat made my teeth stronger. I missed that morning banter. I missed talking to her. You can brush away at your teeth, but how do you brush away the longing to talk to someone?

This will get better, right? It has to.

People get over other people. Especially now that she was married.

She's gone. The Payal chapter is closed. Accept it, Saket.

I brushed my teeth hard in frustration, hoping it would wipe away all thoughts of her from my mind. My gums began to hurt and bleed. I washed my brush for two minutes, listening to the water gurgling down the pipe. What else was there for me to do anyway? My life had become one of those slow Bengali art movies that win awards.

I went back to my bedroom and stretched out on the bed. I had zero motivation to do anything. It was a miracle I was even breathing and managing to keep my heart beating. Thank God for the involuntary respiratory and circulatory systems. Were it not for them, every heartbroken person would fall dead just from the lack of motivation that follows a break-up.

You have to lift yourself up. You have to get over this.

A niggling voice in my head continued to talk sense, even though it spoke in whispers.

Maybe I should look at Akanksha's Instagram account after all. I'd resisted it so far, but perhaps it would show me, in stark and clear images, that Payal was now married to Parimal. It would help my brain register that she was well and truly gone.

I pulled out my phone and opened Akanksha's account. She'd shared several new posts since I'd last checked her page. One post was about designing the best picnic for your family with healthy vegetarian Indian snacks.

'*Theplas instead of sandwiches,*' she wrote in the caption. '*Far more nutritious, healthy and tasty, and in line with Indian culture and food habits. We don't need to copy the West for everything.*'

I wasn't sure if theplas were actually healthier than sandwiches, but who cares? The comments praised her for upholding Indian traditions. One person wrote that her post proved how much smarter Indians were as compared to westerners, since we'd invented the thepla. He didn't mention how westerners invented Instagram and the Indians hadn't, but I guess that wasn't the point.

Then I found the posts about Payal's big fat Jain wedding.

The first couple of posts were pictures from Payal's sangeet ceremony. It seemed to have been a grand affair held in the banquet hall of one of the city's top five-star hotels. Payal wore a saffron lehenga and looked prettier than many Bollywood starlets.

There was a picture of Parimal posing on a bent knee, handing Payal a red rose. I thought it was corny, but that's Ghatkopar chic for you. Another picture showed Payal touching her in-laws' feet, while her mother-in-law tried to stop her from doing so. The mother-in-law had perfected the I-love-that-you're-doing-it-and-you-better-be-doing-it-but-please-don't-do-it pose. One more picture showed all the guests dancing, and Payal dancing with them.

If she's dancing, she's happy, right?

The next two posts were about the actual wedding. Payal wore a red zardozi lehenga, which, according to the caption, belonged to her grandmother. Parimal wore a bandhgala. I swear, if Payal wasn't standing right next to him, I would've thought that he was a scrawny waiter who'd photobombed all the pictures.

I saw a picture of the jaimala ceremony, where Parimal and Payal exchanged garlands. Another picture showed them doing the pheras. In the kanyadaan picture, Payal sat in her father's, or rather, in my life's villain's lap.

Every time I moved to the next picture, it felt like I was stabbing my own heart. I felt numb at first, but then an excruciating pain shot through me.

All of this didn't actually happen. These people just got dressed up for a photoshoot for Akanksha's Instagram account.

A drone shot showed the expansive wedding arrangements. For all the austerity, simplicity and minimalism that Jains generally display in their daily life, some Jain weddings can be lavish, over-the-top affairs. There were more than fifty food stalls, possibly serving every dish imaginable—in a Jain variant, of course. There were statues, fountains, lights and flowers, all arranged in a kitschy mismatch throughout the venue. Again, a bit tacky in my opinion, but definitely Ghatkopar chic.

The wedding post caption read: *'Blessings to #PaPa, my favourite new couple in the world. May God bless you on this amazing journey together, and may you achieve all the happiness and success in life. Congratulations, Payal and Parimal!'*

Wow. They had a hashtag now. #PaPa.

Akanksha had posted one more update about Payal and Parimal. It was a picture of #PaPa in Paris. Both Payal and Parimal were carrying a ton of shopping bags from designer stores like Louis Vuitton, Hermès and Burberry, to name just a few. They wore matching white puffy jackets and stood in front of the Arc de Triomphe.

The post caption read: *'So, #PaPa sent me this picture after I told them my followers are begging for an update. Looks like they're having a great time on their honeymoon in Paris. P.S. Coordinated white jackets are a win-win. #PaPa are truly couple goals.'*

Dozens of comments had poured in, expressing their best wishes for the newlyweds. One comment, however, did have this to say: *'Where's the mangalsutra? It's not good for a newlywed bride to not display her mangalsutra.'*

What would India do without our tradition enforcers? Thank God for them.

I spent the next two hours going through the pictures. I zoomed in on each one of them. If I had a compound microscope, I would've put them under it. I noted down every single detail possible—the earrings, the necklaces, the outfits, the hand-holding, the food, the facial expressions—whatever I could see before the pixelation kicked in.

The wedding pictures, the matching jackets and the word 'honeymoon' kept swirling around inside my head even as I switched off the lights and hit the bed. Of course, I couldn't sleep. Here's how the dumb chain of thoughts in my head went:

Is she on her honeymoon now? What time is it in Paris? They must be out for dinner. Is she eating with him right now? Will they even find Jain food in Paris? Will she be drinking with him? Does Parimal know she drinks? Maybe they already had dinner and have gone back to their room. They could be having sex right now. It's their honeymoon, after all. But ... Payal ... having sex? With someone else? How's that possible? That's not someone else, Saket. That's her husband. But how can Parimal touch her? I'll kill that Parimal. I'll run that bastard over with a car. What would she be wearing to bed in Paris? Some new honeymoon lingerie? Some tacky Ghatkopar-chic night suit that her parents gave her? Will she be missing my T-shirts? Should I send one of my T-shirts as a gift to her? That'll make her melt, right? That'll make her run away from Parimal. Isn't it? No, she won't. She's married to him now. He's buying her Louis Vuitton and Hermès ...

'Stop!' I screamed at my neurotic mind. I sat up in bed and took deep breaths.

'Saket Khurana, get a grip. You have to stop this,' I spoke out loud.

But I didn't get a grip. For it was the same story every night. I would open Akanksha's Instagram, look at Payal's wedding and honeymoon pictures, and let my brain go into overdrive.

I couldn't work either. Without Payal, I felt zero desire to be funny or create new material. Nothing had made me happier than having Payal laugh at my jokes. Payal was definitely an essential ingredient in the joke-generation factory inside my head. What do they call them? Muse?

'Working on a new set?' Mudit messaged me one day.
'Can't do this. I'm quitting comedy,' I responded.
'What? What will you do then?' he replied.
'Have to figure that out. Let's meet and talk.'

Mudit and I met at the Yoga House café in Bandra. Located inside a yoga studio, the pure vegetarian café offered a variety of salads, porridge, soups and all things organic and good. We sat on floor cushions, facing a balcony, with a low wooden table in front of us.

'Could you have picked a healthier place?' Mudit said sarcastically as he scanned through the menu.

I ordered a porridge and a superfood salad for the both of us.

'Thanks for coming,' I said.

'No worries. How are you?'

'Better. But not fully there yet ...'

'Still thinking of her?' Mudit said.

I kept quiet.

'You do, right? How often do you think of her?'

I let out a huge sigh. 'Let me put it this way—I never not think of her.'

'Wow,' Mudit said. 'Like, even now?'

'Yeah. When I was going through the menu, I tried to look for dishes Payal would like. You know, Jain-friendly stuff.'

'Everything here is Jain-friendly,' Mudit said, and began reading out from the menu. 'There's the Ayurvedic Oats Porridge. Or the Yoga House Khichdi. Or the Tofu Brown Rice. Wow, this place is Jain heaven.'

'Yeah, well. Anyway, I do think of her all the time. But the thing is, now I'm at least aware that it's a problem. I want to think of her less. I want to move on.'

'And how are you going to do that?'

'Avoiding alcohol. Spending time at the gym.'

'Okay, all that's good. How about work?'

'That's the thing, Mudit. Something has died in me. Comedy won't happen anymore. Payal was the fuel, the life force, you know ... She propelled me to write, to create.'

'Oh, stop it, man. You were already on stage when you met Payal.'

'Yeah, but later on, it all became linked to her. She was my—'

'Muse?' Mudit interrupted me. 'Seriously? We're comics, bro. Not M.F. Husain or Picasso.'

'Whatever. Without her, it seems difficult.'

'You need to properly get over her, bro. Really, this isn't good. I don't like what she did to you.'

'Am working on it. I called you here for that. I'm going to take some big steps just to get over Payal.'

'What big steps?'

'I'll tell you, but promise not to freak out.'

'Are you turning gay? Bro, I like gay people, and I love you and all, but you and I can't be that—'

'No,' I said, interrupting him. 'What? It's nothing like that. Stop it.'

Mudit laughed. I smiled as well.

'See, you *can* smile. All it takes is a half-assed joke,' Mudit said.

'I know I'll be okay. But right now, just like alcohol, I have to avoid something else.'

'What?'

'Mumbai.'

'Huh? What do you mean?'

'I can't be here, Mudit. There are too many places here that remind me of her. The dozens of cafés we went to, the lanes of Bandra that we walked, the grocery stores we shopped at. Marine Drive, Bandstand, Carter Road, Nariman Point, Colaba—it's like every corner of Mumbai is stamped with her memory.'

'Don't forget Ghatkopar,' Mudit said, grinning.

'Fuck, that too. Though I'll never go to Ghatkopar. But it's true. And she still lives in this city. With her husband.'

'That she does.'

'I'm afraid of being here.'

'Why?'

'Am afraid I'll have one of those weak moments and end up doing something stupid. Land up at her place, or her parents' place, or her office, or her dad's factory …'

'Bro, no. Not her dad's cable factory. Her parents' home was bad enough. In the factory, they'll probably tie us up with electrical cables and electrocute us.'

'Us?'

'Bro, if you're doing something that stupid, I'm obviously not going to let you go alone,' Mudit said.

'I love you, Mudit,' I said.

'I love you too,' he said as he blew on a spoonful of hot porridge. 'But no gay stuff between us, okay?'

I laughed.

'You're meant to laugh, man. When life screws you over like this, we comics are supposed to make material out of it. Not sit and cry.'

'I'm not crying. I'm doing this rationally. I need to leave Mumbai.'

'For a break?'

'No. For good. I can't be here, Mudit. I'll end up doing something ridiculous ...'

'You'll run away?'

'Call it whatever. If it helps my sanity, so be it.'

'What about me?' Mudit said.

'That's going to be the hardest part about leaving this city. You're here.'

'Then don't go.'

'You could visit me. Or better yet, just move with me.'

'How can I? I have the club and everything else here.'

'I know.'

'Where are you planning to go anyway?'

'I want to work again and make some good money. My best bet is something related to my previous job. Start-up investing.'

'Venture cap? Private equity?'

'Yeah. I want to work for a few years. Re-establish my contacts. Then I want to set up my own start-up. Something that has the potential to scale and grow big. I want to make solid money this time. No selling out early to buy a stupid suburban house in the Bay Area.'

'Money, eh?'

'What?'

'Nothing. I thought you never cared about money. You left money and came to Mumbai. To follow your heart.'

'And where did following my heart lead me to? Doom. It's better to bring back the cold, rational and, hopefully, rich Saket.'

'I prefer the warm, emotional one,' Mudit said, 'who cares about feelings more than numbers.'

'Feelings suck, man. They lead you nowhere. I'm done. I need to find the highest-paying job that I can get.'

'Where? You going back to the US? So far away?'

'No. The US has Raashi. Mumbai has Payal. None of these places. Plus, the taxes in the US are too high.'

'You of all people are talking about taxes now?'

'Cold and rational. Told you.'

'Where, then?'

'Dubai. A few months ago, a firm called Pantheon Fund approached me with an offer. I declined it then, but I think I can make it happen again.'

'Oh. You have it all figured out already.'

'Dubai is also closer to Mumbai. You can visit me, easily.'

'I'm so bummed you're leaving Mumbai. How will I manage without you?'

'Then come with me. To Dubai.'

'What will I do there?' Mudit said.

'We'll figure something out. We can work together to build something.'

'Bro, it's going to be hard to leave the club right now. Maybe one day ... Tell you what, though, once you open your own start-up, and it's going somewhere, I'll come join you. How about that?'

'Done. Whatever my next venture is, you'll be the co-founder,' I said.

'Wow, that does sound cool. Plus, I'll get rich too.'
'Most start-ups fail. You know that, right?'
'Yeah. But I think you'll make it work.'
'What makes you so confident?'
'Nobody can be that unlucky—in love and in work,' Mudit said as we both burst into laughter.

PART II
DUBAI

'You're the most hard-working guy we have. And you're quitting?' Advik, my boss, said, leaning back in his swivel chair as he waited for me to respond.

'I'm sad to leave as well,' I said.

I sat in Advik's office at Pantheon Fund, my employer for the last two years. Advik had started Pantheon seven years ago, and it had already grown into a two-billion-dollar fund.

'Why are you leaving? Joining one of our competitors?' Advik said, getting up and walking to the bay window that overlooked the Burj Khalifa.

'No.'

'We can match any offer. You know that.'

'I'm not joining another firm. Pantheon's a great place.'

'Then?' Advik said, still looking outside.

'I'm going to build my own start-up.'

'Oh.' Advik turned around to look at me. 'When did this happen? I didn't know you had the start-up bug.'

'It was always the plan. A long time ago, I had a start-up that I sold.'

'Oh yes. I remember you telling me about that during your interview.'

'Yeah. I think I'm ready to build something again. I'm sorry to leave the Pantheon team though. Also, I must apologize to you, because you gave me a chance to work here.'

'Well,' Advik said. 'You got to do what you got to do. I built Pantheon to help entrepreneurs achieve their dreams. How can I hold back my own people from doing the same?'

'Thank you.'

'I hired you because I loved your profile. You had experience. Plus, you had the ability to make bold moves. Like that comedy career you tried.'

I winced.

'That was so cool. Do you still do stand-up gigs?'

'No,' I said. 'That died a few years back.'

'Why?'

'Long story,' I said.

'Hmm. Anyway, what's the start-up?'

'Well, I'm calling it SecurityNet. It's a cybersecurity company, particularly for cloud-based platforms.'

'Okay, sounds interesting. I like ideas that can be described in one line.'

'Thank you.'

'Tell me more. I'm curious. How does it work?'

Over the next fifteen minutes, I gave him an outline of what SecurityNet was going to be, and its use case in the fast-growing cloud-server space.

Advik came back to his desk, sat down, opened a drawer and took out a cheque book. In true *Wall Street* Gordon Gekko style, he slid it towards me. 'I want in,' Advik said. 'On whatever you're doing. I like what I heard.'

'Really? Advik, it's brand-new. I need to build it up from scratch.'

'That's okay. The sooner I get in, the bigger the upside.'

'Pantheon invests in companies that have achieved a certain size. SecurityNet hasn't even begun.'

'I'm not investing as Pantheon. I'm investing in a personal capacity. How much do you need to get started?'

'Half a million US dollars.'

'And who's funding it right now?'

'I have some savings. My best friend, Mudit, is putting in some money. That'll cover half of it. For the rest, I was going to approach some VC firms.'

'No need,' Advik said. He wrote a cheque for two hundred and fifty thousand dollars and handed it to me. 'Works?'

'Wow. I came here to resign. I thought you'd be mad. I'm getting a cheque instead.'

'That's how life works sometimes. Am I in then?'

'What percentage do you want for this?'

'I'm putting up half the investment. So, fifty per cent?'

'I'm doing all the work. I keep fifty per cent for that. The remaining fifty, you, Mudit and I divide on the basis of our investment ratios. You're putting in half the money, so half of fifty. Twenty-five per cent.'

'Can I get more?'

'Take it or leave it,' I said.

He laughed. 'You're smart. And a tough negotiator.'

'Don't you want your founder to be that? Cold, rational and tough?'

'I do. Done. We have a deal,' Advik said as I shook hands with my new investor.

~

'Fifty million. Did you say fifty million dollars?'

'We are not getting fifty million. That's just the valuation for SecurityNet,' I said.

I was on the phone with Mudit, sitting in my office in Dubai. It was a small room with glass windows facing the main road. It had been two years since the launch of SecurityNet. Our team had grown to thirty people, and we had a modest two-thousand-square-feet office space in Media City.

We had just closed a Series B, or a second round of funding. Two private equity firms had invested five million dollars each, receiving a ten per cent stake in return. With this ten-million-dollar raise, we could expand our operations by hiring more people and growing our server infrastructure.

'Fifty million. Say, seventy rupees to a dollar. Wow, that's like three hundred and fifty crore rupees,' Mudit said.

'It's only the valuation. On paper. Relax, we have a long way to go, Mudit.'

'Still. You created this company. From zero to fifty million, in two years.'

'Well, you helped. You gave me the seed money.'

'How much is my stake worth now?' Mudit said.

'Mudit, there's no point in doing all these calculations. You can't get this money. Every cent coming into the company is for growth.'

'I want to feel rich, bro. Even if it's only on paper.'

'Okay, fine. So, you had a twelve and a half per cent stake. Now, we all get diluted to accommodate the new investors. Meaning, you now own ten per cent.'

'Ten per cent of fifty million. I'm worth five million dollars? Seriously?'

'On paper, yes.'

'Fuck me. Really? Why am I still running a comedy club?'

'Because this is a paper stake. And it'll remain so until we have an exit—either the company gets acquired or we do an IPO.'

'We will, though, right? One day?'

'As they say here in Dubai, inshallah. God willing, we will. Lots of hard work ahead.'

'I'm coming.'

'What?'

'I'm coming to Dubai.'

'To visit?'

'No, I'm moving there. I'm joining SecurityNet. Helping you grow it. And growing the value of my stake as well.'

'Really? You aren't kidding, are you?'

'You have a role for me?'

'Yeah. Marketing, branding, business development. We need a head for all that.'

'I'll do it.'

'What about the club?'

'I have people here. There's a manager who can handle things. I'll keep kicking his ass virtually from Dubai.'

'Cool. When can you join?'

'When is the next flight out?'

I laughed.

'I've missed you,' I said.

'I've missed you too, bro. And it's nice to hear you laugh.'

'You come here. Maybe I'll smile more after all. It does get lonely here.'

'Still no girlfriend?'

'Nope.'

'It's been, what, four or five years, bro? Start dating. You're not still hung up on that girl in Mumbai, right?'

Yes, I still was. And he'd just reminded me of her.

'Leave all that. Let's talk about your move. We need to start your immigration paperwork,' I said.

How could I tell Mudit about the PTs, or the Payal Triggers, that I still lived with? Under normal circumstances, four to five years is more than enough time for people to recover from a break-up. But here I was, thirty-nine years old now, a fully grown, mature man with grey hair. How could I still get so affected by anything even remotely related to her?

I walked out of my office and went up to Alok, the CTO of the company. 'I'm leaving,' I told him. 'I'll just work from home for the rest of the day.'

Alok looked at me in surprise. It was only one in the afternoon. I rarely left the office before midnight.

'Everything okay, Saket?'

'A bit unwell. I'll be fine.'

~

In Dubai, I lived in a one-bedroom flat in a building called Princess Towers, around four kilometres away from the office. Despite the brutal summer weather, I decided to walk back home. I hoped the heat and the sweat would wash away all thoughts of Payal.

'She probably has a kid by now. Maybe two,' I mumbled to myself.

It was forty-five degrees centigrade outside, which meant that nobody was foolish enough to be walking on the pavement—except for me, of course. I felt I deserved this punishment for being unable to fix my brain even after so much time had passed. I could move countries, create a company from the ground up and raise funding. I could not, however, figure out a way to stop thinking about Payal. Anything could trigger them—the damn PTs were everywhere. I see a girl in a corporate suit—boom, I'm back in Express Towers. *Is Payal still going to office there? What would she be doing all day? Stop it, Saket, she's married. She's gone.* I'd bring myself back to reality, only to be hit by another PT a few hours later.

'Any dietary restrictions, sir?' a server would ask me at a random restaurant. That's a PT. Guess who has dietary restrictions? Jains. And who's the Jain who continues to haunt me? Bingo. A glass of white wine was a PT. As was the word 'chartered accountant'. Wedding scenes in a random movie, couples holding hands, songs Payal and I had heard together … the world was a minefield of PTs, and there was no way I could avoid them.

I pulled out my phone. It was hard to see the screen under the scorching sun. I increased the brightness and opened WhatsApp. I sent a message to Neha: 'Hi. Sorry for the late reply. Let's catch up soon?'

'Hey, no problem,' Neha replied immediately.

Neha and I had met at Alok's birthday party at the Barasti Beach club some two weeks ago. She was working in Dubai, and her brother was Alok's best friend. That's how she'd landed up at the birthday celebrations. We spoke briefly at the party. She worked in a consulting company and wanted to open her own online bakery business.

Maybe I'm an idiot when it comes to reading signals from women. I really thought she wanted my business advice. I gave her tips about making a business plan. She listened intently, smiling frequently as I spoke.

'See, a business plan's like a recipe. Or a movie script. If you have a good plan, a solid script, your dish, or the movie, will turn out well.'

'I love how you explain things. Thank you,' she said.

'You're welcome,' I said.

'I'd love to get more of your guidance. If you want to hang out sometime, for drinks or dinner or whatever …'

'I keep pretty busy,' I said, 'with my own start-up.'

'Oh, okay. Only if you want to,' she said, looking somewhat taken aback.

I finally realized she had something else in mind. She wanted a date, not a business-advice session.

'I hardly socialize,' I said.

'I understand,' Neha said. 'Shall we exchange numbers anyway?'

A few days after that party, she messaged me saying how nice it was to talk to me and that if I ever wanted to take a break from work, I could message her.

I wasn't interested. However, perhaps meeting other people would help me move on. Maybe meeting Neha would help me deal with the PTs. Even Mudit kept telling me to go on dates.

'What are you doing this evening?' I messaged Neha.

～

'An inside table, of course,' I said to the waiter. I had done my hot sauna walk for the day.

Neha and I arrived within minutes of each other at Attiko, the rooftop bar and restaurant at the W Hotel in Mina Seyahi. The waiter led us to a table in the air-conditioned section indoors. Attiko has a stunning view of the Palm Jumeirah, a man-made island in the shape of a palm tree. Its fronds are lined with villas that have their own private beaches. From the thirty-second floor, however, the multi-million-dollar Palm villas looked like toy homes arranged along the water.

'What an incredible view!' I said.

'I'm glad you like it,' Neha said. She was the one who'd suggested we meet here.

Neha was wearing a short, fitted orange dress. Heads had turned when she entered Attiko with me. Despite her attractiveness, Neha stirred nothing in me.

'Where are you originally from?' I said.

'Lucknow,' she said.

'Ah, okay,' I said. Possibly, the dullest response a man could give, ever. I could've at least asked her something about Lucknow. Like if she fancied tunde kebabs or chikankari suits or something.

We ordered two tequila sodas.

'How about you?' she said. 'Where were you before you came to Dubai?'

'Mumbai. Although I'm originally from Chandigarh.'

'Chandigarh ... Nice city,' she said.

Chandigarh is the quintessential 'nice city'. Maybe it's the planned roads that make people believe the place is nice. But nice also means boring, which is where this date was going anyway.

'Yeah, Rock Garden and all,' I said.

'What?'

'The Rock Garden? It's this famous place in Chandigarh. Been there too many times. Every time someone visited us from out of town, we had to take them to the Rock Garden. Traumatic memories.'

'Why traumatic?' she said, sounding concerned.

'I mean, not really traumatic. But I just went there way too many times. I was trying to make a joke.'

'Oh.'

'That landed flat.'

'Who landed?'

'The joke. Sorry, that's comic lingo. I used to be a stand-up comic, a long time back.'

'Stand up?' she said.

'Stand-up comic? Like people who make jokes on stage?'

'Oh, interesting,' Neha said in a disinterested tone.

I remembered a time when the conversation would flow and the jokes would land effortlessly. My mind went flying back to one of those random nights in that tiny Pali Hill flat.

Payal and I were lying in bed, chatting.

'Good show today?' Payal said.

'Yes, the audience loved it. They were hooting and whistling.'

'That's great. Listen, do you still do the push-up-bra bit?'

'Yep. It always works. I always get the loudest laughs for the dhakka-maar bra.'

'I actually have an objection to file on that,' Payal said, sitting up and turning towards me.

'What?' I said, looking at her twinkly eyes.

'You say that push-up bras are technically a fraud.'

'Yeah …'

'How is it a fraud? They advertise it as that.'

'Well, the men don't know.'

'I use push-up bras sometimes. I'm not that big.'

'I know. It's okay.'

'It's okay? Excuse me?'

'Yes, it's okay, baby. I love you anyway, whatever your size.'

'Ouch,' she said.

'What?'

'Nothing. It's okay, Saket. I love you too anyway, whatever your size.'

'Huh?' I sat up. 'What do you mean?'

Payal smiled.

'Is it small?' I said.

'Well ...' Payal trailed off, a grin on her face. She fluffed a pillow and leaned back against the headrest.

'What?'

'I've seen bigger,' Payal said.

'Ouch. Double, triple ouch. Where have you seen them?'

'In porn.'

'Oh, of course. Porn actors are the outliers in size. The top one per cent. It's like they've cleared the porn-JEE.'

'Well, you certainly wouldn't clear that JEE. Good thing you took the other JEE.'

'Ow!' I said. 'That hurts. You're brutal, Payal Jain.'

'It's okay, baby,' Payal said, patting my shoulder. 'I still love you.'

'You're so bad,' I said, grabbing Payal as she burst out laughing.

'What happened?' Neha said as she caught me smiling.

'Huh? What? Nothing,' I said, coming back to the present. 'Anyway, when do you want to open your online bakery business? What's the timeline?' I said.

'We'll see. I'm quite happy with my job too,' she said.

Okay, she never really wanted to open a business.

'Tell me something. When you asked to meet me, was it to discuss business plans or something else?' I said.

'Like what?'

'Like us dating potentially.'

She smiled. 'Maybe,' she said. 'You're single, right?'

'Yes,' I said.

'How come?' she said, tilting her head a little to the side.

'As in how am I single even at this age? What's wrong with me?' I said.

'No, nothing like that. Sorry.'

'It's okay. I'm thirty-nine. So, yes, I shouldn't be single, but I am. I was married a long time ago. Got divorced about six years back.'

'Any relationships since then?'

'Yes, one. It ended a while ago.'

'What happened?'

'I …' I hesitated. 'I'd rather not talk about it, if that's okay?'

'Sure. Did it end recently?'

'No, around five years ago.'

'Oh,' she said, probably thinking I was a weirdo who found it difficult to talk about five-year-old break-ups. She wasn't wrong though. I was that weirdo.

'And have you dated anyone since then?' she said.

I shook my head.

'Oh,' she said again.

'I had to focus on my job and then my company. How about you? What makes you single?'

'It's not by choice,' Neha said, smiling ruefully. She brushed her hair back from her forehead. She had some make-up on. The dark-red lipstick she was wearing made her lips look even thicker. Or maybe she'd had her lips filled—that seemed to be an extremely popular trend in Dubai. She looked like a heroine in one of those Abbas–Mustan murder-mystery movies—a little tacky, but sexy nonetheless.

'I came to Dubai five years ago. I've met quite a few guys on dates. However, all they want to do is party and then sleep with me. Nobody wants anything serious.'

I nodded.

'That's why I'm still single. Even though my friends say, "You're a catch, how are you not taken yet?"'

'I agree with them,' I said, more out of courtesy than anything else.

'Yeah, so that's that,' she said, smiling. I smiled back.

Two minutes of awkward silence followed. It felt like two hours. She twirled the straw in her glass. I took a sip of my drink. What are you supposed to do on dates that fizzle out even before the first drink is over? Someone needs to write a bad-date protocol manual, seriously.

Maybe I should talk, I thought. What do I say? I don't even know her. Dating and meeting new people is so stressful. I decided to ask the lamest first-date question ever: 'What are your hobbies?'

Seriously, Saket, that's how boring you've become?

'I like playing musical instruments.'

'Oh, which ones?' I faked interest.

'In school, I used to play the piano and the violin. Now, I have a keyboard at home.'

'Ah, okay. I have a keyboard too. Only, it doesn't make music, it makes code.'

'What do you mean?' she said.

'It was a joke. Like when you say "keyboard", you mean the synthesizer, a digital piano, yes?'

'Yeah.'

'And I use the keyboard on the computer to write code. Anyway, forget it. Didn't land again.'

'What didn't land?'

'Nothing. Should we ask for the cheque?' I said.

Or a gun, so we could shoot ourselves out of this misery?

'How did this happen?' I said, biting my lip to prevent myself from bursting out in anger. Hands on my waist, I stood in front of the four stacked computer monitors in Alok's cubicle. Our website and our server both had crashed. Our helpline number was choked with calls, most of them with complaints from irate customers.

'Our own cloud server crashed,' Alok said, furiously moving his mouse around, trying to figure out what had happened.

Others in the office gathered around us. Mudit came out of his office as well. He had moved to Dubai and worked for SecurityNet now. We'd set his office up in the room right next to mine.

'Did someone hack us?' I said.

'No, there's just too much load on the server,' Alok said.

'This looks terrible as far as all our clients are concerned. Like we're a fly-by-night company that can't even keep its server running.'

'I'm sorry, Saket.' Alok stood up, looking downcast.

'But in a way, this much load on the server is a good thing, isn't it?' Mudit said. 'Our services are in demand ...'

'In a way, yes,' I said in a loud voice. 'But we can't have our server crash. This is just sloppy. Increase our server capacity. When have I ever stopped you from spending on infrastructure, Alok?'

Alok looked visibly shaken at my rare outburst of anger.

'Fix it,' I said.

'Yes, Saket,' he said meekly.

'Now!' I yelled.

'Calm down, Saket,' Mudit said, grabbing me by my shoulder. 'Come, let's go to your office.' Mudit took me back to my office and shut the door.

'What's the matter with you? Had too much of your pre-workout supplement today?' he said, sitting on one end of my office table.

I sank into my chair and let out a sigh of frustration. 'Our server and website crashed. Do you even realize what that means?' I said.

'Yeah, I do,' Mudit said, rubbing the back of his neck.

I checked the site functionality on my own desktop. We were still down. In anger, I banged my fist on the table.

'Control, bro. What's with all this aggression?'

'This stupid Alok,' I said. 'Should I fire him? Maybe I should. It'll send a strong message.' I stood up to go out.

'Stop it,' Mudit said, physically restraining me. 'He's a kid. Sit down.'

I paused for a second and sat down again.

'Alok is just a geek you hired from Bangalore. He made a mistake. It happens. We're growing gangbusters, bro. Nobody could've anticipated this demand. The team will fix it by tomorrow.'

I nodded and took several deep breaths.

'What's going on with you?' Mudit said.

'What do you mean?'

'You don't sound okay. This is not you. Chill a bit.'

'You don't build a unicorn by chilling. You have to work hard.'

'You've always worked hard. But you have these anger issues now. You've become hard.'

'Hard?'

'We used to do comedy. You made people laugh. This is not the Saket I knew. That Saket would've made three jokes by now about me using the word "hard".'

I smirked. 'Comedy. What an idiotic phase that was.'

'It wasn't idiotic. It was you being authentic and following your heart.'

'If you want to fuck your life up properly, follow your heart.'

'So, what do you want to follow now?'

'Money,' I said, and turned to my desktop again.

'When did Saket become all about the money?' Mudit said. 'The same Saket who gave almost everything to his ex-wife just to be free and come to Mumbai …'

'When Saket realized that without money, a man is nothing,' I said, clicking through the process logs from right before the site's failure.

Mudit leaned forward and switched off my monitor.

'What the …?' I looked up at him, irritated.

'Let's get out of here. Our site is down. It's a forced day off.'

Mudit took me to Topgolf. Located in the Emirates Golf Club, it's a snazzy, hi-tech golf driving range plus bar and restaurant. We hired one of the many bays from where you can hit golf balls into the large ground in front. Mudit also ordered two large pints of beer and burgers for both of us.

'My diet, Mudit,' I said.

'Uff, what are you? A Miss Universe model?'

I sneered.

'You're too stuck up,' Mudit said. 'Loosen up. To misquote a little, "Pardon my French, but Saket is so tight that if you stuck a lump of coal up his ass, in two weeks you'd have a diamond …"'

'That's from *Ferris Bueller's Day Off*. Great movie,' I said.

'Thank God, you still remember some fun things,' Mudit said. 'Come, hit some balls with me.'

Mudit stood up and collected a ball from the automatic ball dispenser. He took a driver and hit a hard shot. The geotagged ball flew, and the screen in the bay trajectory showed it landing 140 yards away.

'Not bad.'

'Your turn, mister.'

I hit a shot.

'110 yards?' Mudit smirked. 'So much for the pumping-iron man. You're weak, bro.'

'Dude, I've never played golf in my entire life. This is the first time I ever lifted a club,' I said.

'Maybe you should take it up then. Have some fun, Mr CEO,' Mudit said, taking another shot.

'I'm going to bust your ass,' I said, 'eventually.'

'In your dreams.'

We played for an hour. Mudit's best shot was 170 yards. I couldn't go beyond 140. We finished the game and sat down on the couches in the bay.

'I have to come and practise,' I said. 'This isn't acceptable.'

'Ouch, someone is hurt,' Mudit said, grinning. 'This ain't deadlifting, bro. This requires skill and coordination.'

'Deadlifting does too.'

'Yeah, right, so much skill,' Mudit said. He stood up and did a mock deadlift with a golf driver, pretending to struggle and making a grunting sound.

I laughed.

'Good to see you laugh, bro,' Mudit said. He lifted his beer glass to clink with mine.

'Thanks for bringing me here,' I said. 'I needed this.'

'What has got you so wound up anyway?'

'Nothing. Work. The company.'

'Do you know the buzz about our next funding round? A three-hundred-million-dollar-plus valuation! You're travelling to New York next month to meet the investors. Things are looking good.'

'I don't know. It doesn't feel as good though.'

'Why? What else is bothering you?'

I took a sip of my beer. 'Nothing really, just that ... nothing interests me in life now. I work, and that's it. If I'm not working, I feel weird.'

'Weird? As in ... lonely?'

'Maybe. Don't get me wrong. I have you. The people in the company. And we're growing, doing amazing. But sometimes, it all feels meh. Like, what's it for?'

'Okay, bro, I know what your problem is.'

'What?'

'You need love in your life.'

I recoiled. 'No, thanks.'

'Okay, fine. That was just a nice way of saying it. What I meant is, you need to get laid.'

'What?'

'When was the last time you got some action?' Mudit said, gesturing with his hand to make things clearer.

'I don't know,' I said. 'Why is that important? And do we order some more food?'

'Don't change the topic. You haven't even touched your burger. Tell me, when was the last time you did it?'

I shook my head.

'Bro, don't tell me that you haven't since …' he paused mid-sentence.

'I haven't. You know I haven't dated anyone.'

'Yes. So, wait, nobody since Payal? Wow,' Mudit said.

Oh, why did he mention her name? It's going to ruin my first happy evening in months.

'You need to go on dates, bro. At least try,' Mudit said.

'I tried. A while ago.'

'Oh?' Mudit raised an eyebrow. 'And you didn't tell me?'

'It was lousy. No reason to talk about it.'

'Why was it lousy? Who did you go out with?'

'This girl, Neha. Met her at that office party.'

'Oh, that hot chick? Alok's best friend's sister, right? She and her brother came to pick Alok up after work one day and I saw her.'

'Yes. That's her.'

Mudit mock-punched my shoulder. 'Not bad, bro. What happened?'

I recounted my awkward date at Attiko. 'And that's it. We didn't really communicate after that,' I said.

'From what you tell me, she was DTF, bro,' Mudit said.

'DTF?'

'Down to fuck. Get it?'

'I'm seriously getting old. I don't know these new-gen acronyms.'

'Not the point. She wanted you. You should've just done it.'

'But I didn't see the fit. We weren't compatible long-term.'

'First, do it. Then figure out all this performance-review type compatible-long-term stuff.'

'How?' I said. 'I'm not like that. Anyway, since that day, I gave up on dating.'

'Why, Saket?' Mudit said.

'It's me. Raashi and Payal, in their own ways, burned me badly. Sometimes I think I'll never have a proper relationship with anyone again. And that's a bit …' I trailed off, searching for the right word.

'Sad? Depressing? Pathetic?' Mudit said.

'Yeah, a bit of all of that. Is there a word that combines all three?'

'Let's make one—sadepathetic,' Mudit said.

I laughed.

'I still think you need to get laid.'

'I don't think that's the answer.'

'Sadepathetic again. Listen, I have a solution for you.'

'What?'

'Have you heard of SBs?'

'Sorry, but no. Gosh, I'm so outdated.'

'Sugar babies.'

'What? Sounds like a girl band.'

Mudit smiled. 'Nah, it's something else. You take care of a girl—give her an allowance every month, and in return, she becomes your girlfriend.'

'What do you mean?'

'She gives you the benefits of a girlfriend, you understand?' Mudit winked at me.

'You mean she has sex with you?'

'Come on. She makes love to you. Let's be gentlemen about it.'

'And I pay her?'

'To support her, yes. Another gentlemanly thing to do.'

'Dude, this sounds like hiring a hooker.'

'Not really. She's steady and exclusive with you.'

'A hooker on a subscription plan?' I said, raising one eyebrow.

'Come on, bro. So harsh. Okay, fine. It's SaaS. Only, it's not "software as a service". It's "sex as a service". With some friendship and love thrown in, maybe,' Mudit said and grinned.

I remained silent and looked at Mudit, shaking my head.

'Don't be so judgemental. For centuries, women and men have had this arrangement. They meet each other's needs,' Mudit said.

'But I pay her?'

'Which real-life girlfriend comes for free?' Mudit said.

'Come on, Mudit. We both know what this is. And I don't want it.'

'What *do* you want then? You can't date because you won't let anyone get close. You won't do this because of some morality or principles. Are you going to be alone and celibate all your life?'

'Maybe.'

'You're kidding me,' Mudit said, his voice tinged with irritation. 'Pooja was five years ago, bro.'

'Payal, not Pooja.'

'See, I even get confused about her name sometimes. But man, you're still hung up on her.'

'I honestly want to move on and date someone. It's just not happening.'

'Then try my approach. Sugar it.'

'Sugar is bad for you,' I said, lifting my burger with both hands and taking a bite.

~

Dubai is part of the Arabian Desert, one of the driest places in the world. A desert, by definition, is an area where it barely rains. And yet, on that fateful day, it didn't just rain in Dubai, it poured. It was almost as if the rain gods had decided to compensate for all the years of drought in a single day.

Because of the downpour, it took me thirty minutes just to find a cab to the airport. Then, somewhere along Sheikh Zayed Road, the rain turned torrential. Water beat against the windshield as traffic on the usually superfast highway came to a standstill.

'I'll miss my flight,' I said.

'Inshallah, you'll make it,' the cab driver said.

It took the cab three hours to finally reach the airport. I ran to the check-in counter, dragging my large suitcase behind me.

'Relax, sir,' the airline personnel manning the check-in counter said. 'The flight is delayed.'

'Oh. By how long?' I said.

'We don't know that yet, sir. There's a huge backlog of flights waiting for take-off. But we're looking at a couple of hours, at the very least.'

'What?'

'We'll keep you updated,' she said, attaching baggage tags to my suitcase. 'For now, you can proceed to the business-class lounge. Please wait for further announcements.'

~

The Emirates Business Class Lounge at Terminal 3 in Dubai is the size of a football field. It stretches across the entire terminal, a level above the boarding gates, with more than a dozen seating areas and multiple dining options.

Under normal circumstances, the lounge is a quiet, peaceful haven for travellers. But these were not normal circumstances. The whole place was in chaos. Passengers scurried around, trying to get flight updates from overwhelmed airlines staff, who, in turn, were busy working the phones. The flight-status display board showed most flights as either terribly delayed or cancelled. My own flight was delayed by five hours.

Thankfully, though, I found a sofa in a quiet corner of the lounge to relax and maybe take a nap in. But just as I was about to shut my eyes, I saw her.

Wow, I must be exhausted. I'm hallucinating.

She was sitting across from me, furiously typing on a laptop. I shut my eyes for a second.

Wait, did I actually see her?

I opened my eyes again. She was wearing glasses, the laptop hiding half her face. And she was mumbling softly as she typed.

Okay, it has to be her.

My eyes popped wide open. *Payal?*

She was dressed in a grey tracksuit, her hair tied in a long ponytail. Her face looked slightly fuller than when I had last seen her five years ago.

What do I do? Should I leave? Sit somewhere else? Should I go up to her and say hi? What if she's with her husband?

I observed her for a while. It didn't look like she had any company.

I walked up to her.

'Payal?'

She stopped typing and looked up at me. It took a few seconds for recognition to set in.

'Saket?' She stood up.

'I saw you from across the lounge. Sorry, I know you're busy. But I thought I'd say hi.'

'No,' Payal said as she regained her composure. 'It's absolutely fine. Saket Khurana! God! How long has it been? Five years?'

Five years, eight months, thirteen days.

'Has it?' I said.

'Yes, it has been that long,' Payal said, exhaling deeply.

For a moment, we both hesitated, unsure whether to hug or not. I settled the confusion by holding my hand out towards her.

'Hi,' she said, shaking it.

The touch of her hand still felt familiar.

'Good to see you,' I said.

'Same here. Where are you sitting?' Payal said.

'Right there,' I said, turning and pointing to my luggage on the couch across the room. 'We're all stuck today.'

'Yeah. Have you eaten dinner yet?' she said.

'No.'

'I was about to go eat. Want to come with me to the buffet?'

We walked over to the dining area. We took a plate each and did a round of the buffet. I loaded my plate with kebabs. We came back with our food and sat across each other at one of the many small dining tables.

'Dal chawal? That's it?' I said.

'Yellow dal and some chawal, that's heaven for me. What more could I want?' Payal said.

I smiled.

'You're still hitting your protein targets, I see,' she said.

'Trying to,' I said, eating one of the chicken kebabs.

'You look good. Fit, as always.'

'Thanks.'

'What about me?' Payal said. 'How do I look, compared to five years ago?'

'You look fine as well,' I said.

To me, you're still the most beautiful woman I've ever met.

'I have to wear these glasses now,' Payal said, removing them and keeping them on the table. 'Especially when I'm working on the laptop. Otherwise, I get a headache. I'm getting old.'

'You're not old. I'm the one getting old,' I said. 'Forty next year, can you believe it?'

'You don't look like it,' she said.

'Thank you,' I said. 'Anyway, travelling alone?'

'Yeah, am on my way back to Mumbai from New York. Finished a work trip. How about you?'

'I'm on my way to New York, for work.'

'Ah. I don't even know if my flight will leave today,' Payal said, looking at the flight-status board. 'It says there's a four-hour delay.'

'Mine's delayed by five hours. Took me three hours to reach the airport from home, instead of the usual thirty minutes.'

'Home? You don't live in Mumbai?'

'I moved to Dubai many years ago. Started my own company here.'

'Oh. How come?'

To get over you.

'Better opportunities here,' I said.

'What about stand-up?'

'I left all that.'

'Really? You left stand-up comedy?'

'It's not like I was that great.'

'You were,' she said.

Our eyes met properly for the first time.

'How's Parimal?' I said, switching topics and looking away.

'Parimal is fine. Busy with the business. He's doing well.'

'That's great,' I said.

'How about you?' Payal said.

'What about me?'

'Are you married?'

I shook my head.

'Oh, okay. And are you ...' She fell silent.

'Am I what? Dating someone? No.'

'Okay,' she said.

'It's by choice,' I said. 'I like being single.'

'Is it? Having fun in Dubai?'

'Yeah,' I said. 'I am. We're building a good company.' I proceeded to tell her about SecurityNet and the company's journey so far.

'That's incredible,' she said after I finished. 'Already going for a third round of funding. Saket, that's truly amazing.'

'Thank you.'

'No wonder you don't date. You're married to your company.'

'True,' I said, even though that wasn't the reason.

You, you are the reason.

'Well, I'm glad you're in a good place,' she said.

'How about you? How's life? Work? Any kids?'

'Kids? No, not yet,' Payal said and laughed. 'I'm only twenty-seven. I want to focus on my career.'

'How's that going?'

She opened her bag and gave me her business card.

Payal Jain

Vice President

Blackwater Capital

'Now that's impressive,' I said. 'VP at twenty-seven.'

'Youngest vice president in the Mumbai office. It's okay if I have kids a bit later, isn't it?'

'Of course. Congratulations on doing so well.'

'Thank you.'

'But things are good otherwise as well, right? You and Parimal?' I said.

Please, please say things are not that good. I don't know why, but I need to hear that.

'Yeah, things are good,' she said, and then, after a pause, added, 'They are fine, yes.'

'Okay, I'm happy to hear that,' I said.

'I'm happy to hear that you're doing well too.'

'Yeah, whatever happens, happens for the good,' I said.

Okay, that wasn't necessary. Why did I even say it?

'Hmm. True, I suppose,' Payal said.

'More food?' I said.

'No, I'm full.'

What do we do now? The dining is done. There were still hours to kill before our flights. Should we just go our own ways? Say goodbye here?

'I have to do some shopping,' she said. 'From the shops downstairs.'

Ah, she found the perfect exit plan. Girls always do it better. No awkward goodbyes—just a natural parting of ways.

'Okay, sure,' I said. 'Was nice to see you.'

We stood up to leave.

'What are you going to do?' she said.

'Sit and wait for flight updates. What else?'

She laughed. 'Want to come with me? Walk around the airport a little? We're stuck here for hours anyway.'

Okay, so she wasn't trying to escape.

'You sure?'

'Yes, come. It'll be fun.'

'All right,' I said.

'I have to buy some shirts for Parimal and his dad. Maybe you can help me choose.'

How was this fun? What was I supposed to say? 'Yay, let's go buy shirts for your husband and your father-in-law?'

'Sure, let's go,' I said.

∼

'Which blue is better?' Payal said, holding up two shirts, each a different shade of light blue.

'I can't tell. Both are nice,' I said.

We had come to Brooks Brothers, a posh store selling men's clothing.

'The problem with guys is, there are only three colours that you can buy for them—black, white or blue. So difficult to choose,' she said, sifting through the shelves.

'What about the ones with stripes? Or checks? That lavender one is nice,' I said, pointing to another rack.

In the end, she picked up all the eight shirts I had pointed to.

'I need another suitcase to carry these,' she said, smiling, as she looked at the two huge shopping bags in our hands. 'Good excuse to get a new trolley bag. I've been wanting one.'

After Brooks Brothers, we went to Tumi, a high-end luggage store. She bought a trolley bag, which cost more than the shirts had. Of course, for a VP at Blackwater, a sixty-thousand-rupee cabin bag was no big deal. We packed the shirts in the new trolley—I had to press down on the trolley while she zipped it shut.

As we walked around the stores, we passed a perfume shop.

'May I? Last store, I promise,' she said, pointing at it.

'Sure,' I said.

We walked in, and she began browsing the perfume racks.

'Saket, come here for a second,' she said, calling me from across the aisle.

I walked up to her and she held both her wrists up towards my face.

'What?' I looked at her, confused.

'Tell me which one is better?'

Tell me why you are doing this to me? Making me smell your scent, mixed with perfume. It'll take me weeks, months—maybe even years—to get over it.

I held her wrists lightly, one at a time, bringing them close to my nose and inhaling.

'This one, the right wrist,' I said.

'Okay, so that's Gucci's Guilty,' she said.

'No, wait,' I said, and did another round of sniffing.

Did I do it because I wanted to hold her hand again?

'Maybe the left one,' I said, still holding her wrists.

'That's Obsession,' she said.

I dropped her wrists instantly. 'What?'

'The perfume. It's called Obsession, by Calvin Klein.'

'Oh.'

'So, tell me, which one should I take? Guilty or Obsession?'

I am guilty of obsession.

'Take both,' I said. 'They smell nice on you.'

She looked at me and smiled. She asked the cashier to pack both the perfumes.

We walked back to the lounge. She returned to her original seat, and I was about to go back to mine when she said, 'Bring your bag and sit here.'

'But aren't you working?' I said.

'No, not anymore.'

Nodding, I moved to the couch adjacent to her.

Her phone rang just then. 'It's Parimal,' she said, checking the caller ID. 'Video call.'

'Oh, okay,' I said, standing up to leave.

'You don't have to go. I'll just sit sideways, so you're out of the frame.'

Were we doing something wrong? I couldn't say.

She wore her AirPods and answered the call. I couldn't see or hear Parimal.

'Still no flight updates. It keeps showing delayed,' Payal told Parimal.

A few moments of silence followed as she nodded at the screen.

'I'm in the lounge. Waiting. What else to do? I did shop though. Bought some shirts for you and your dad,' she said.

Parimal said something on the other end.

'Yeah, I'll show you. I bought eight. Had to buy a trolley bag to keep them.' Payal rested her phone against a glass on the table in front of her. Then she picked up the Tumi bag and kept it on her lap. She opened the bag and lifted the shirts out one by one.

'Forget about the bag and focus on the shirts,' Payal said to Parimal. 'I needed the bag anyway.'

After a pause, she spoke again, 'I know Tumi is expensive. It's okay. I can afford it … The price is for the brand, Parimal. You can't compare it to American Tourister … Can we not argue over this? Please, just look at the shirts. I can still exchange them if you don't like any particular one.'

She showed all the eight shirts to him again.

'You're being picky for no reason. And just forget about the price no?' she said at some point during the conversation.

'Yes, I'll update you about my flight status. Yes, I'll return these three shirts. Bye,' she said, ending the call.

She let out a big sigh and, keeping her phone aside, turned back to me. 'Sorry, that took a while,' she said.

'Everything okay?' I said.

'Yeah. Turns out, I bought too many shirts. He doesn't need so many. I'll just go return a few,' she said, standing up.

'I can come with you,' I said.

'No, it's okay. I don't want to bother you.'

Before I could respond, a female Emirates staff member approached us, holding an iPad in her hands.

'Hello. What flight are you on?' she said.

'EK203. To New York,' I said.

'Okay,' she said, tapping a few times on her iPad. 'Sir, ma'am, I'm sorry, but your flight to New York is cancelled due to bad weather.'

'I'm not on the same flight actually,' Payal said.

'Oh?' The woman looked at both of us, surprised.

'We're not together,' Payal said.

Thanks for that, Payal. I needed the reminder.

'Which flight are you on, ma'am?' the staffer said.

'EK500 to Mumbai.'

'Okay, give me a minute,' the staffer said, checking her iPad. 'Sir, for New York, you'll be booked on the same flight tomorrow night. You'll receive a message confirming this. Meanwhile, we've arranged a hotel room for you near the airport.'

'I won't be needing that,' I said. 'I live in Dubai. I'll just go home.'

'Oh, okay. In that case, I can help you exit the airport.'

'Thanks,' I said.

'And for you, ma'am, you've been shifted to EK506 to Mumbai, scheduled for tomorrow morning at 9 a.m. A room has been booked for you at the airport transit hotel, which is in the terminal building itself.'

'Okay, thanks,' Payal said.

'Take the lift down and turn left. You'll find the transit hotel. Show them your boarding pass and they'll assign you a room.'

'Sure,' Payal said.

'Sir, you can come with me now. I'll help you exit immigration and leave the airport.'

'Yes, sure,' I said.

Was this it? Was this goodbye? I knew this meeting would end, but did it have to be this abrupt?

I collected my bag. Payal hoisted her laptop bag onto her new trolley bag. Was she going to say anything? Should I?

'That's it then. Time to say bye,' I said.

'Huh?' she said, surprised. 'Is it?'

'Yes. We both go our own way now,' I said.

In this airport. And in life.

'It was nice to see you again,' Payal said.

'Same here,' I said. 'It's good to know that you're doing well, and that you're happy.'

'I'm glad that you've achieved so much as well. And that you're happy.'

Who said I was happy? Where did you get that idea?

'Yes, indeed. I've a lot to be grateful for,' I said.

She nodded.

I would've said 'stay in touch' or 'see you soon', but I knew that wasn't an option.

'I'm still blocked, by the way,' I said.

'What?' Payal looked puzzled. 'Where?'

'Everywhere. Facebook. Instagram. Even WhatsApp. Though I think you changed your number long back, right?'

'What number of mine do you have?' she said.

I opened my phone and showed her the number I had. Her name was still saved as Payal, with a heart emoji next to it. Damn, why did I still have that emoji?

'Oh, this number is old. Sunita didi has it now,' she said.

'Yes, I know that,' I said.

She looked at me, somewhat confused. 'Anyway, here's my new number.'

I saved the number she gave me this time as 'Payal New'—no emoji.

'I just unblocked you on Instagram and Facebook as well.'

'You did?'

'It's just silly now. We've all moved on, haven't we?'

'Yeah, true,' I said.

Liar, liar, liar.

'I don't post much though,' she said.

The airline staffer became impatient. 'Sir, if you could come with me now, I'll escort you through immigration. There are other customers who need assistance.'

'Sure, coming,' I said to her and then turned to Payal. 'Bye, Payal.'

'Bye, Saket,' she said.

'Best of luck. Have a good life,' I said.

Who the fuck says 'have a good life?' That was dumb.

'Yeah. You too,' she said.

I walked away, feeling the distance between us grow with every step. Every cell in my body ached, as if someone had ripped off my skin. Why did I have to run into her? I had learned to live with my successful career and my low-key depression. I had learned to manage my PTs. And now this?

Why, God? Why?

~

On the cab ride home, I opened my phone and checked Payal's WhatsApp profile. The display picture was of her and Parimal, dressed in matching black ethnic wear. His arm was around her waist. I needed to see this—it was a slap, reminding me that she was with someone else now. I zoomed in. Payal was laughing, covering her mouth with her hand. Three and a half billion women on this planet, and yet, hers was the only display picture I blew up to stare at.

Before I could check Payal's Instagram feed, Mudit called.

'What's up, bro? You must be at the airport. Your flight's on time?' he said.

'No, it's been cancelled due to bad weather. I fly out tomorrow now,' I said. I left out the bit about meeting Payal.

'Oh. That's fine, a one-day delay doesn't matter,' Mudit said. 'Let me know if you need my help to reschedule any meetings.'

'I can do it,' I said.

'You okay, bro? You sound low,' Mudit said.

It's scary when your best friend knows you so well.

'Yeah, just tired,' I said. 'Spent so many hours in the airport. And then no flight. But am headed back home now.'

'Whatever happens, happens for the good. There must be something good in this as well.'

'I doubt it.'

'You're safe. That's what matters.'

'Love you, man.'

'Love you too, bro. You want me to come over?'

'Not in this weather. I'm tired too. Let me just sleep.'

'Fine. But do sleep. Don't check your phone or do work stuff.'

'Okay. Good night, bro,' I said, and ended the call.

I put my phone back in my pocket. I didn't have to check Payal's Instagram right away. Nothing good would come of it. It would just be pictures of her happy married life with Parimal. Each post would be like a nail hammering into my heart. I didn't need to torture myself any further.

'Right there. The building on the left,' I said to the cab driver as we reached my apartment complex.

~

'This isn't just a Series C investment. This is a vote of confidence in all of us. This is our investors saying whatever we're doing is valuable. That we, at SecurityNet, have built something they want to be a part of.'

Everyone in the room applauded as I finished my brief speech to the entire SecurityNet team. My New York trip a month ago had been incredibly successful. Four different private equity investors had pledged a hundred million dollars in new investment at a much-higher-than-expected valuation of half a billion dollars. Mudit felt it deserved a small celebration—the team needed a pat on the back. He organized a dinner at Gazebo, an Indian restaurant in Jumeirah Lake Towers.

As people began to mingle over chilled beers and starters, Mudit came up to me holding two Budweiser bottles.

'To half a billion,' he said, handing one of the bottles to me.

'Like I always say—' I started, but Mudit interrupted me.

'It's on paper. I know, sir.' He laughed, clinking his bottle against mine.

We were still chatting when one of our employees came looking for Mudit and took him away. Left alone, I made my way to the terrace, unlocked my phone and checked Payal's Instagram account—for the fifth time that day. I'd been doing this compulsively for the past month—while on the way to New York, in New York, in between investor meetings, on the way back to Dubai and then every day since I'd been back.

The posts were exactly what I'd expected: Payal documenting her life in bits and pieces, especially during vacations and festivals. She didn't post often, averaging just two posts a month. But I had five years' worth of pictures to look through, which meant over a hundred posts—an entire photo album of the love of my life living her life, loving another man.

Oh Instagram, the things you show!

I could see the places where Payal had gone on holiday in the first year of her marriage—Paris, Amsterdam and some Jain temple in Gujarat. In the second year, they went to Phuket and Shimla. The third year, it was a trip to Sydney. In each place, they always took one particular shot—Parimal standing straight with one arm around Payal, who stood next to him, her arms wrapped around his waist, her head on his chest.

Some of her posts included photographs of both sets of parents and the extended family. Payal never wrote much in the captions, just simple heart or blessing emojis, or the occasional 'Happy Diwali to all' message.

Swiping through each picture of Payal and Parimal felt like taking a knife and stabbing myself. Yet, I couldn't stop. I noticed every detail, from the handbag Payal carried to the dress and the earrings she wore.

'What are you doing?' Mudit's voice startled me from behind.

'Huh?' I quickly locked my phone and turned around. 'Nothing.'

'Is that Payal?' Mudit said.

'What? No,' I said.

'You were looking at Payal's pictures, weren't you?'

'No,' I said firmly.

'Didn't she block you everywhere?'

'Yeah,' I said. 'It wasn't Payal.'

'Show me your phone. I'm damn sure it's her.'

'It's another girl.'

'Then I'm even more interested to see this new girl you're stalking. Show me.'

Mudit extended his hand. From the look on his face, I knew he wasn't going to take no for an answer. I unlocked my phone and placed it in his palm.

'It *is* her. I knew it,' he said, scrolling through my Instagram feed. 'How did you get unblocked? Did you hack into her account or something?'

'Dude, no.'

'Then?'

I remained silent.

'Are you in touch with her?' Mudit asked.

I shook my head.

'Then explain this.'

I let out a huge sigh. I told him the entire story about meeting Payal at the airport lounge that night.

'Wow. You met Payal ...'

'By accident,' I said. 'I didn't plan it.'

'And you didn't tell me?' Mudit said.

I shrugged.

'Should I be worried, bro?' Mudit said, looking closely at my face.

'No. I swear, we just ran into each other at the Emirates Lounge. Made some small talk, ate together, and that's it. We went our separate ways after that.'

'She did. You haven't.'

'I have too. I'm not in touch with her. Nothing since that day.'

'So why are you still checking her Instagram account one month later?'

'I don't know.'

Mudit scrolled and saw some of Payal's posts. 'Every picture is with her husband,' he said.

'Yes. She's happily married.'

'Maybe it's good you saw this. Should help you close the chapter,' Mudit said, shaking his head.

'Yes, maybe.'

'Now do you agree with me?'

'About what?'

'That you need to move on. Date other people.'

'I have moved on.'

'Okay, then let me set you up on a date? There's this girl I'm sort of seeing right now. She has a cousin who seems nice. Shall I introduce you to her?'

'No, Mudit! Not right now.'

Mudit pursed his lips. 'See?'

'It's the company. We need to grow it, take it to the next level. That means ten times the work. Where is the time to date?'

'Really? Nobody in our company dates?'

I stayed silent and turned sideways, looking towards the buffet counter where employees loaded their plates with dal makhani and paneer tikka masala.

'Saket, look at these pictures,' Mudit continued. 'She has her arms around her husband. She lives with him, travels the world with him, sleeps with him. You ran into her by accident, but otherwise, she's never bothered to check where you were or how you were doing. Do you realize all that or not?'

I looked at Mudit.

'Here's the reality, bro. She threw you out of her life. Like one throws garbage out of their house. So, should you still be investing so much emotion into this?' he said.

'No, I shouldn't,' I said, sighing. 'That's why I'm wary of dating. I end up investing too much. It happened with Raashi and then with Payal too. I get into a relationship, and it just takes over my life. Eventually, I get fucked emotionally. It's not worth it.'

'Who's telling you to get emotional? You think I'm emotional about Nadia?'

'Who's Nadia?'

'This girl I'm dating. Whose cousin I want you to meet.'

'Nadia?'

'Yeah. Nadia and Amelia. They're from Ukraine.'

'Ukraine? What? How did you even meet them?'

'At a bar.'

'You're dating a Ukrainian girl?'

'I like to know more about other cultures. Besides, I like helping people.'

'Helping?'

'Well, I support her. Financially. A little bit.'

'What? Mudit. What the hell are you up to?'

Mudit laughed. 'Whatever it is, it's better than this emotional drama you've carried in your heart for years. We're men. We don't have to get so emotionally invested to have fun with women.'

'So, you …'

'I what? Have a sugar baby? Yes, I do. It helps her and me.'

'Mudit, that's weird.'

'Weirder than compulsively looking at pictures of your ex and her husband? Almost six years after your break-up?'

I didn't answer. I put out my hand, and Mudit placed my phone back in my palm.

'What do you think? Meet Amelia?'

I looked at Payal's Instagram account. A recent post showed Parimal and her in the Maldives, eating breakfast in their private pool villa. I showed the picture to Mudit. He just smirked.

'You're right, Mudit. I'm almost forty. This shit isn't funny anymore,' I said, deleting the Instagram app from my phone. 'I have to truly move on.'

'Good job, bro,' Mudit said. 'So, double date? Nadia, Amelia, you and me?'

'Nothing else has worked so far. Let's try it your way.'

'Great.'

'Is it really a date though? It almost sounds like a deal.'

'What's the difference anyway?' Mudit said, laughing.

A DJ played the latest hit song, 'Bom Diggy Diggy' from the movie *Sonu Ke Titu Ki Sweety*, as the SecurityNet team hit the dance floor.

Michelle, from the design team, ran up to us. 'Come on, Mudit sir, Saket sir. Join us. We all have to dance!'

'Let's go,' Mudit said, and dragged me with him to the dance floor. 'Learn to let go, bro,' he said. 'And don't just stand—dance, bro,' he said.

~

Six years later ...

'Ladies and gentlemen, may I have your attention, please?' Wajid, the lead singer of the Dubai-based band The Seen, spoke into the mic. His drummer and bassist kept a soft beat going in the background.

The guests at my forty-fifth birthday party paused their conversations and turned towards the stage.

'What a fantastic evening. What a setting, isn't it guys?' Mohsin said. The guests all cheered in response.

We were at Cloud 22, an exclusive poolside club on the twenty-second floor of Atlantis The Royal, the top hotel in Dubai. Mudit had organized the entire evening, from booking the space to managing the hundred-plus guest list. He'd invited the whole SecurityNet team, along with our investors, vendors and friends.

'How much did this whole thing cost again?' I said to Mudit, standing next to him as he refilled our glasses with Dom Pérignon champagne.

'I'm afraid if I tell you, you might faint. We don't want that to happen to the birthday boy, do we?'

'How much, Mudit?' I said, concerned.

'Too much, but it's my personal money. Not company funds. Don't worry, our investors won't think we're partying at their expense.'

'Bro, why did you have to do all this?'

'Two reasons. One, it's you, my best friend.'

'Thank you. And two?'

'Two is that you're the one who helped me make all this money anyway.'

Mudit and I laughed.

'Look around, bro. Look how far we've come,' Mudit said, pointing at the club space and at the setting sun. The sky was a surreal pink and gold. 'We must celebrate ourselves now and then.'

'True. Where's Tania though?' I said, referring to my girlfriend.

'She's sorting out the cake. She wanted to roll it in for you,' Mudit said.

'Roll it in?'

'Well, it's huge. Five feet. Needs to be brought out on a trolley.'

'Mudit, dude. Why?'

'It's okay, bro. It's your birthday. Anyway, how are things with you and Tania?'

'Hot. Exciting. Fun.'

'But?'

'But what?'

'I know you too well. There is a "but" somewhere in there.'

I laughed. 'Yes, well ... *but* I think I may be ready for a change in a few months.'

'Bro, you're brutal. How times change though,' Mudit said, 'Remember how reluctantly you agreed to meet Amelia five or six years ago? And look at you go now.'

'You're the one who taught me all this. Only keep the fun. None of the emotional load. So, I change them frequently to avoid all that load.'

'Yeah, but Tania seems nice.'

'She is. But you know, every now and then, it's best to refresh the cache.'

'Savage,' Mudit said.

'Sir,' bass guitarist Mohsin's voice boomed from the speakers. 'Where are you, Saket sir? We need you on stage to cut the cake. Mudit sir, you too.'

Mudit and I walked up to the stage.

Tania emerged from the wings, pushing a trolley with a massive five-tier cake on it. The cake, dressed in an off-white and blue fondant, had an elaborate floral design running all across it. It looked so beautiful that it seemed sinful to even consider cutting it. The only thing more beautiful than the cake was Tania. Did I tell you about her?

Tania and I had started dating six months ago. It began when Sophia, the girl I was dating before Tania, had to go back to Romania. Before Sophia, there was Juliette, and I may be getting the order wrong, but before her, I was with Ruby, Katherine, Krisha and a couple of other girls whose names I forget. It all started with Amelia, of course, who Mudit introduced me to six years ago. A deal, an arrangement or simply two people meeting each other's needs—call it what you want, but the system worked for me. All the fun, and none of the drama.

'Cut the cake, sweetie,' Tania said in her thick Ukrainian accent.

See, she even calls me 'sweetie'. Who said this was only about sex? There's love and caring involved as well, even if it's part of an understanding.

I took the knife from Tania and cut the gorgeous cake, slicing across one of the tiers. The entire crowd applauded and sang 'Happy Birthday' in unison. Many of the men, particularly the married ones, were busy checking out Tania, while their wives cast disapproving looks in her direction. I could sense they were all burning with envy. Tania was their worst nightmare.

My beautiful twenty-four-year-old Tania had a perfect hourglass figure. And she knew what to wear to highlight it. For instance, the silver-grey Prada dress that she'd worn for the party ended at her upper thighs and clung to her like second skin. I know it was from Prada because I'd bought it for her. Her eyes matched the dress. Her golden hair reached all the way down to her hips.

'Happy birthday, my darling,' she whispered in my ear as she fed me a slice of cake and hugged me. 'We celebrate our way later.'

Wow, I still couldn't believe that I'd been against this system until a few years ago. Mudit had found me heaven on earth, and idiot me had resisted it.

This, however, wasn't the only major change in my life. The last year had been an eventful one. In Mudit's words, we finally went from being paper rich to real-bank-account rich. The company moved to a large new office in a modern building in Downtown Dubai. We did a secondary placement, which meant the founders got a chance to sell some of their own shares for cash. Mudit used some of the money he received to buy a boat and a fancy racing car, confirming my suspicions about his massive midlife crisis. I kept most of my money in the bank, but I did splurge on a new villa on the Palm. I liked the water view, and the beach was right outside my house.

I got off the stage and mingled with the guests as the waiters went around serving the cake to everyone.

'Happy birthday, Saket. What an amazing party,' Richard Morris, the managing director at one of the private equity firms that had invested in us, came up to me.

'Thank you, Richard,' I said.

'I should thank *you*. SecurityNet has been our most successful investment,' he said.

'Glad to hear that, man.'

'I'm here in Dubai for a few days. Let's discuss the IPO strategy? Next year, right?'

'As they say here, inshallah,' I said.

'Five,' Richard said, holding up his hand, with his fingers all open.

'What?' I said, smiling.

'You know exactly what five means,' Richard said, laughing as we clinked our glasses.

I did actually: A five-billion-dollar IPO valuation was already being discussed amongst our investor group.

'The only thing that personally matters to me is that our customers love SecurityNet. Valuations and money shall follow,' I said.

'That's why I love doing business with you. It's never just about the money or the deal. It's always something personal,' Richard said.

'Yeah, I'm learning though. To separate the personal from the deal,' I said.

~

Riyaz, my driver, pulled into the driveway of my villa. I gently shook Tania to wake her up. She'd nodded off in the backseat, with her head on my shoulder.

'We're home,' I said softly.

'Hmm? Oh,' Tania said sleepily, lifting her head. 'Too much champagne, baby.'

'I know. You even drooled on me,' I said, pulling her cheek lightly.

'I'm sorry, sweetie,' she said, giving me a peck on my cheek.

Riyaz stopped the car at the porch, right near the koi pond, and opened the door for us. Tania and I got out and walked into the house. The high ceiling inside made my foyer feel like the lobby of a chic contemporary hotel. I still found it hard to believe that this was my house. That I owned it. That's the thing about suddenly coming into a lot of money. In reality, you're wealthy. Psychologically, however, you're poor. Sometimes, I feared that the people I'd hired to take care of things around the house would come and ask me what I was doing here.

My ten-thousand-square-feet villa with its five bedrooms had come at a price of fifteen million dollars, that's around a hundred and five crore rupees. It was a huge amount. However, the secondary share sale had netted me fifty million dollars. The house was less than a third of that. And my current SecurityNet stake, if the IPO-valuation rumours came true, would be close to a billion dollars. Yes, I could afford this, I reminded myself.

I stood in the middle of the living room, in awe of the art and the lights and everything else in my own house.

'Sir, you're back,' Shanti didi, my housekeeper, said, walking into the foyer from the kitchen. 'Is there anything I can get for you or madam?'

'No,' I said. 'We've already eaten, thank you. You can leave for the day.'

As she left, Tania leaned in and said, 'Let's go up. The celebrations aren't over yet.'

'Baby, I'm genuinely tired,' I said.

But Tania paid no attention to my protests as she pulled me up the steps. She pushed me into the bedroom and shut the door behind us.

'Tired, is it?' she said, running a finger down my nose and lips.

I took a deep breath as her touch sent a shiver down my spine.

'Yeah, we did drink a lot. You even dozed off on the drive back,' I said.

Tania went up to the bay windows and drew the sheer curtains. We could still see the twinkling lights of the other Palm villas and the beach outside.

'I'm fresh after my nap now.' She came back to me and kissed me. 'How about you? You want to nap now?' she whispered in my ear.

'Baby, if you do all this, which man will not wake up?' I said.

'Good. Because even if it's your forty-fifth birthday, you're not that old,' she said.

'I am old, babe. Forty and then five more.'

Shaking her head, she unbuttoned my shirt and slid her hands inside. 'Tell me, how many forty-five-year-olds have a chest like this?' she said, running her hands over my pecs.

'Thank you,' I said, and kissed her cheek.

'I realize I haven't given you a birthday present yet,' Tania said.

'It's all right, baby. You don't have to. I have everything.'

'No, it's not all right. I'll get you one soon. Meanwhile, can I be your present for tonight?'

'You always are.'

'Would you like to unwrap your present?' she said, making a cute, kiddish expression.

Before I could respond, she pushed me back into the bed and climbed on top of me. 'Happy birthday, baby.'

Half an hour later, our hot-and-heavy session ended, leaving us both exhausted and sweaty. Tania lay down next to me, scrolling through the Louis Vuitton website on her phone. I wanted her to leave, as I always did when the sex was over. I had rented an apartment for her in the Marina. I checked the time. We'd finished some seven minutes ago. Would it be rude of me to suggest she leave?

'Riyaz will drop you home, baby? He has to finish duty and go home,' I said.

'Oh,' Tania looked up at me, somewhat surprised. 'Of course. I wasn't sure if you wanted me to stay over tonight.' She picked up her dress from the floor. Her naked body glistened in the dim light as she slid into the dress.

'When have I ever?' I said.

'It's your birthday today ... in case you didn't want to sleep alone.'

'That's okay, sweetie. I'm used to it.'

I walked back into the house after saying bye to Tania on the porch. The villa felt larger than before. I went to the entertainment area adjacent to the living room, where there was a hundred-inch flat-screen TV. I switched it on and scrolled through all the entertainment options in the world—Netflix, Prime, YouTube ... and a bunch of other platforms. But I didn't feel like watching anything. I switched on my PS5 game console to play *Elden Ring*. Five minutes, and I got bored. I turned off the TV and thought about going to the games room on the first floor. I had fitted it with a snooker table, foosball, darts, a pinball table and a retro video-games console, similar to the ones we had in childhood, where one had to put in a coin to play a game. I didn't feel like playing anything. That's the thing about having nice things. They're fun only when you have someone to enjoy them with.

I made my way up to the master bedroom, where Tania and I had just made love or, to be accurate, had sex. I made the bed, which had become messy after our session, changed into my nightclothes and sat down with a book—*The Courage to be Disliked*. I'd barely read two pages when my phone rang.

'What a party, bro,' Mudit said. 'Well done.'

'What well done?' I said. 'You're the one who organized it.'

'Yeah, that's true. I was praising myself,' Mudit said, laughing. 'Your best friend is pretty cool, isn't he?'

'He's the best.'

'What are you doing?'

'Reading, in my bedroom.'

'On your birthday?'

'We already had a party. I drank too much anyway.'

'Where is Tania?'

'Must be reaching home.'

'You sent her back? Really?'

'Yeah. I need to sleep.'

'You guys still did it, right? Don't tell me you didn't get laid on your birthday.'

'Mudit?'

'What?'

'Do you and I have any semblance of privacy between us?'

'No. So, does that mean yes? You did it, didn't you?'

'Bye, Mudit.'

'Oh, wait, no. I called for a reason.'

'What?'

'There are murmurs. Strong murmurs.'

'About what?'

'A buyout offer. Someone out there wants to buy SecurityNet.'

'Like a stake?'

'No. The whole thing. An acquisition.'

'What?'

'Yeah. Someone from Goldman Sachs called me.'

'The investment bank?'

'Yeah, bro. A senior guy from their Mergers and Acquisitions division.'

'What did he say?'

'He said he has a client who owns a company that wants to acquire SecurityNet.'

'What about the IPO? Don't we have plans to do that?'

'We do. But if this buyer gives us a good offer, then who knows? We should talk to them.'

'Okay, find out more. Who's this client?'

'He won't say. He wants to have a meeting with us first. He said if we show real interest, he'll bring the client in at the next meeting.'

'All this is in Dubai?'

'Yes. Don't worry, you won't have to go anywhere. I'll call him in next week then?'

'Sure, whenever,' I said.

'Cool. Good night, bro. And happy birthday. Glad you got laid.'

'Stop it, Mudit.'

Mudit burst into laughter before ending the call.

~

'Give us one minute, Max,' Mudit said. 'Let me talk to Saket in private.'

'Sure,' said Max Glenfell, the managing director of Goldman Sachs's Mergers and Acquisitions division, getting up from his chair. Alan Smith, his junior associate, followed suit. Max and Alan were British and had flown in from the Goldman Sachs London office. Their formal suits and crisp British accents reminded me of the BBC news presenters.

'No, no, you guys stay here,' Mudit said, gesturing for Max and Alan to remain seated. 'Saket and I will go to his office for a minute.'

We were all sitting in the swanky twenty-seater conference room, in the new SecurityNet office in Downtown Dubai. Max and Alan had just finished giving us a short presentation on the proposed buyout.

Mudit and I left the room and hurried to my office.

'Bro, it's real,' Mudit said, closing the office door behind him. 'Someone wants to buy the whole company. In cash. The cleanest exit ever.'

'We exit? Like completely?'

'Yes. Can you believe it? None of the IPO hassle. No need for roadshows, compliance, regulations and investor relations. No risk of being at the mercy of market conditions.'

'True,' I said. 'But it also means we're out. What will *we* do? What will *I* do? I'll have no job.'

'Bro, you won't *need* a job. You'll have close to a billion dollars in the bank. Not just paper wealth either.'

I looked out of my window. In the distance, the Burj Khalifa soared into the clear blue sky, much like how SecurityNet had soared over the years.

'I already have everything I want. What will I do with so much money? And all the free time?'

'Come on, bro. We'll find something productive to do. Maybe build another start-up. Or do fun stuff. Go back to running a comedy club, only this time, we go to work in a Rolls-Royce.'

I smiled, still unconvinced.

'Okay, listen. I can talk to them. We'll sell the company to them, but not the whole thing. Say, ninety per cent? We keep the remaining ten per cent. And you stay on as the CEO, if that's what you want.'

'I don't know what I want,' I said.

'Take your time to figure it out. Point is, we should stay engaged with them. Discuss whatever terms we want. I'm sure they'll be happy to let you run it anyway. For now, let's meet the mystery client.'

'Okay. We can do that. I'm curious about who the client is anyway.'

'We have to sign a non-disclosure agreement. Once we do, Max will get his client in.'

'Fine, let's do it,' I said.

We went back to the conference room. Max and Alan looked up at us questioningly.

'Guys,' I said, 'we're interested. But we have some conditions.'

'Sure,' Max said. 'What conditions?'

'I'll discuss them with the buyer. When can I see them?'

'There's an NDA that needs to be signed first …' Max said.

'Send it to me. I'll e-sign it,' Mudit said.

'I'll fix the meeting for next week,' Max said, grinning from ear to ear.

∼

I hadn't met Tania in a week because work had been insane. Finally, on a Saturday evening, we decided to meet for drinks at Li'Brasil, a stunning sea-facing Lebanese-Brazilian fusion restaurant at the Address Beach Resort.

'You don't have time for me,' Tania said, pouting. 'Don't you like to see me now?'

'That's not true, baby,' I said. 'There's just too much going on at work. Now, what would you like to drink?'

'Aperol spritz,' she said. I decided to have the same drink.

'I wanted to talk to you about something,' Tania said after we'd placed our order.

'Oh? What happened?'

'I have a cousin, Paulina. She's just finished her graduation in Kyiv.'

'Okay ... What about her?'

'She wants to move to Dubai.'

'To work here?'

'Yes, maybe. I thought I'll ask you, for help ...'

'To help her get a job?'

'No. To make her your girlfriend.'

'What?' I sat up, startled.

'For a little while, baby. Until she figures out what she wants to do.'

'Tania, what are you even talking about?'

'You know, like you gave me an apartment and an allowance because I'm your girlfriend? Like that. It's out of love only, right?'

'Well, yeah ...' I said, trailing off mid-sentence.

'If you can do that for Paulina too ...'

'But I already have you.'

'You can have both of us.'

I looked at Tania, absolutely gobsmacked. Even as my brain scrambled to find something to say, the waiter arrived with our order, two beautiful orange-coloured cocktails.

'What do you think?' Tania said, picking up her glass and taking a sip.

'You want me to be in a relationship with you *and* your cousin?'

'Okay, she's not really my cousin. We grew up in the same village. That's what we call each other there. Don't worry, we're not actually related.'

'That's not the point. You're okay with me having two girlfriends?'

'One of them is me, right? Plus, I'm older and I was here before her. So, I'll be the main girl.'

'Main girl?'

'You haven't heard of this concept? Main girl, side girl?'

'No.' *What was even going on in this world?*

'Anyway, doesn't matter. You don't have to give her an apartment. She can live with me. Just give her an allowance. A bit of shopping now and then, like you do for me. It would mean a lot.'

Nothing in life had prepared me for this situation. I remained silent, confused about what to say next.

'Would you like to see her picture?' Tania said.

'Well, it's not about that …' I said. Before I could finish my sentence, Tania turned her phone screen towards me. A beautiful young brunette sat on a beach, wearing a red bikini.

'Trust me, you'll love her,' Tania said.

Is it wrong to have two girlfriends? What if it's the first girlfriend who encourages you to get a second girlfriend? Or wait, were they even my girlfriends?

I took a sip of my drink.

'I don't know what to say, Tania. I've never done this before. Date two people at the same time.'

'It won't be the two of us together. Some days you see me, other days you see her. That's it.'

'It's not about the scheduling.'

'Or if you want, on some days, we can both come over and the three of us can have fun together.'

'What?'

'I don't mind it, baby. Paulina won't either. Would you like that? The three of us together?'

I burst out laughing.

'What?' Tania said. 'I'm serious.'

'Tania, babe, I'm extremely busy at work right now. Lots of things need my attention. I have some big investors visiting us next week. I really can't decide if I want another girlfriend, apart from the gorgeous one I already have.'

'Every man enjoys multiple girls.'

'Is it?'

'Threesome is every man's fantasy.'

'Yeah, but it's a fantasy. I never thought I'll ever have the option to make it real.'

'You do now. Think about it.'

'Yes, I will.'

'If you want, I can have Paulina visit. You try her for a few days.'

'Tania, no!'

'Really, I don't mind. Don't give her anything for those days.'

Okay, was she my old girlfriend or my new pimp? I couldn't tell.

'Give me some time. Right now, I'm happy with you. You're amazing. Okay?'

'Fine. Thank you,' Tania said and smiled, though with a somewhat disappointed look.

'Now, do you want to have the next drink here or back at my place?' I said.

~

'Why the hell are they being so secretive? We signed the NDA, and they still haven't told us who the buyer is,' I said to Mudit as we walked towards the office conference room.

Max and Alan had already arrived, along with two of the buyer's representatives. On entering the conference room, I noted that one of them was Caucasian and the other of Indian origin. Both were dressed in crisp formal suits and looked like they were in their forties.

'Hello, everyone,' Max said as we all sat down. 'I'm happy to finally introduce our client today. This is Philip Stevens and Neeraj Gupta from Blackwater. Philip, Neeraj, meet Saket and Mudit, co-founders of SecurityNet. Philip handles all of Blackwater's Asian and European business while Neeraj heads their India operations.'

'Blackwater?' I blurted out. Mudit and I looked at each other, shocked.

'Yes, is that surprising?' Philip said, smiling and extending his hand towards us.

'Yeah,' I said, shaking his hand. 'We weren't expecting a private equity firm.'

'Why?' Neeraj said.

'We thought we were talking about a full buyout. Not a stake sale.'

'We do want to fully buy out SecurityNet, on behalf of one of our portfolio companies. If this deal goes through, we'll merge SecurityNet with the company in question.'

'Which portfolio company?' I said.

Neeraj leaned forward. 'This cannot leave the room. It's a listed company. Any merger discussions are sensitive news. This must be kept private,' he said.

'We signed a ten-page non-disclosure agreement. What else can we do? Write down another promise in blood?' I said.

'No,' Max stepped in quickly. 'Our client trusts you. They're just re-emphasizing the need for discretion.'

'Okay,' I said. 'Whatever we discuss, it stays in this room.'

'It's CloudX.'

'The cloud-server company?' I said.

'Yes. It's Bangalore-based,' Philip said. 'A billion-dollar-plus revenue, and a twenty-billion-valuation. Started—'

'I know CloudX,' I interrupted him. 'It started about fifteen years ago. Recently received fresh investments from AWS, which is Amazon Web Services, right?'

'Correct,' Neeraj said. 'And Blackwater was one of the earliest investors in CloudX. It's been one of our most successful investments. Over 100x return.'

'Congratulations,' I said.

'Thank you. So, AWS wants CloudX to have a cybersecurity business. If CloudX does it on its own, it'll take time. We feel it's better to acquire an existing cybersecurity company that's doing great work,' Neeraj said.

'Like SecurityNet,' Philip added.

'Thank you. But I don't see the point of selling, honestly,' I said. 'We were going to do an IPO soon and get listed. We get to keep our equity.'

'CloudX is already listed,' Neeraj said. 'If it buys you, you become part of the merged listed entity. Also, we can pay you in equity as well.'

'I thought this was a cash-buyout conversation?' Mudit said.

'Well, we would prefer to pay in cash,' Philip said. 'However, if you want some of the consideration as equity in the merged entity, we're open to it.'

'What about SecurityNet's existing management and team?' I said.

'What about it?' Philip said. 'We would like them to continue.'

Mudit and I looked at each other. Whatever concerns we had, they had addressed them already.

'Give us two minutes to discuss this,' I said to Philip and Neeraj.

Mudit and I hurried out of the conference room and walked up to the coffee machine in the pantry. Nobody else was around to overhear us.

'Can you believe it? The buyer is Blackwater?' I said.

'Yeah, I know. Solid guys, right? At least now we know it's a real party with money. Not some random firm,' Mudit said.

'Not that, Mudit. Don't you understand?'

'What?'

'It's Payal's firm. Payal works there.'

'That was like centuries ago.'

'She was still there when I ran into her six years ago.'

'Bro, can we not bring your ex-ex-ex-ex into the picture now? Aren't you with Tania at the moment? Or is it Paulina? Or wait, both of them?'

'Still with Tania. Considering Paulina's free-trial-before-subscription offer. Anyway, not the point. Payal probably still works there. She was doing really well the last time we met.'

'Let her. How does it matter? It's a huge firm. One of the biggest private equity investors in the world.'

'That's true.'

'And they have literally addressed every concern you had. You stay CEO, and get equity.'

'Yeah.'

'Our investors will love it too if we do the deal. They'll make money and get a chance to exit,' Mudit said.

'True,' I said.

I stayed silent for a few seconds, evaluating the buyout proposal in my head.

Mudit leaned against the wall, his legs crossed at the ankles. 'So? Moment of truth. What do we do?'

'You're right. It's time to make serious money. Let's do it,' I said.

Mudit grinned and high-fived me. We walked back to the conference room.

'Let me negotiate with them first, and you can then join in to help us get the best price,' Mudit said to me at the door of the conference room.

'We discussed your proposal,' Mudit said as we took our seats.

'And?' Philip said.

'We can consider it. What valuation will CloudX give us?' Mudit said.

'Ah.' Philip smiled. 'Finally, the question that matters.'

Mudit and I sat on the edge of our chairs.

'Your last valuation,' Max said, as his analyst put up a slide on the conference-room projector, 'was at two billion.'

'That was two years ago.'

'Yes,' Max said. 'Our client is aware of that. So, we propose to buy SecurityNet at 2.5 billion dollars.'

Mudit and I stood up, almost in sync.

'Guys, I think we're all wasting our time,' I said. 'Nice to have met you though.'

'Wait, Saket, please. Sit,' Max said. 'Mudit, please, have a seat. We can discuss this.'

'There's nothing to discuss. Word on the street is that we could have a hot IPO and get listed at a five-billion valuation, and you want to buy us at a distress price,' Mudit said.

Mudit and I took two steps each towards the conference-room door.

'Let's make it three billion, if that helps,' Philip said.

Wow, two confident steps, and half a billion dollars gained. If we played this game right, we and our investors could end up richer by thousands of crores.

Mudit and I turned towards Neeraj and Philip.

'Let's discuss our mutual expectations? Much better if we all sit down,' Neeraj said.

Nodding, Mudit and I walked back to our seats and sat down again.

'Five billion,' Mudit said. 'Half in cash. Half in equity.'

'Mudit,' Philip said, clearing his throat, 'I understand that you both feel your company has a lot of value, and it probably does.'

'It does have a lot of value. And a lot of future potential too,' I said. 'We haven't even entered that many markets yet. We're also developing so many new technologies.'

'You may be right. However, we don't know all that. To give you a proper bid, we'll have to conduct a thorough due diligence,' Philip said.

'You've worked in private equity, Saket,' Neeraj said. 'You know how this works.'

'Fine,' I said. 'Do the due diligence. Whatever it takes.'

'But I'm afraid, even with that, five billion is too much. That is the best-case, market-risk-dependent IPO price in a year's time. We're giving you certainty, and we're giving it now. You'll both agree we deserve a discount for that,' Philip said.

Mudit and I looked at each for a second, then I gave him a slight nod.

'Four and a half,' Mudit said.

'Three and a half,' Philip said, 'subject to due diligence and with no unexpected concerns coming up during that process.'

'Where do you think you are to be bargaining like this? Mumbai's Fashion Street?' I said.

'What's your final number?' Neeraj said.

'4.25,' I said.

'3.75,' Philip said.

Max and his analyst kept moving their gaze from Philip to me, like they were watching a tennis match.

'Four billion,' I said, 'if we shake hands now.'

'Subject to proper due diligence?' Neeraj said.

'Of course,' I said.

Philip extended his hand. 'I think we have a deal,' he said.

'We certainly do,' I said and shook his hand.

'Superb, I'll send a draft conditional term sheet,' Max said, unable to contain his excitement as he mentally calculated his investment-banking commission. 'The due-diligence team will work from your office. When can we start?' he said.

'As soon as possible,' I said.

'How many people will be conducting the due diligence? We'll need to make seating arrangements and access cards for the team,' Mudit said.

'It'll be a mix of people from Goldman Sachs, Blackwater, CloudX and our auditors from EY. Around eight of us, I think.'

'Eight people?' I said, a little surprised.

'Yes,' Max said. 'It's a multi-billion-dollar deal, Mr Khurana. The team will go through everything with a fine-toothed comb.'

'And how long will they take?'

'A couple of weeks. Maybe a month.'

'A month?'

'Let's try to wrap up the due diligence as soon as possible, Max,' Philip said, rubbing his hands.

'Max, just let me know when the team's expected to start, and I'll get everything ready,' Mudit said.

'Sure. I'll email the details across to you. Along with the term sheet,' Max said. 'We're closing at a price of four billion. Correct?'

'Yes. Four it is. Four big ones,' Philip said as we all shook hands and concluded the meeting.

~

'What are you doing?' Mudit said when I picked up his call.

'Reading on my Kindle,' I said.

'The most boring rich guy in Dubai. Where's Tania?'

'She's gone to pick up Paulina at the airport.'

'Ah. I stand corrected. Someone's life is going to become quite interesting.'

'I don't even know what's happening there. Anyway, what's up? It's midnight. Everything okay?'

'Yes, everything is okay. Well, sort of.'

'Sort of?'

'Yeah. I mean, something amusing happened.'

'Amusing?'

'I found it amusing.'

'You've called me at midnight. It can't just be for something amusing.'

'I hope you take it that way as well.'

'Okay, now cut the suspense and tell me.'

'I got the list of people who're coming to do the due diligence. Had to arrange their access cards and cubicles, right?'

'Yeah? So?'

'There are two of Max's analysts. Two people from CloudX's finance team. Two directors from EY. And there's one MD and one VP from Blackwater.'

'Okay, that's quite an army, but it's fine. What's so amusing here?'

'That MD from Blackwater …' Mudit trailed off.
'Yeah?'
'It's someone we know. Rather, someone we used to know.'
'Who?' I said, a little concerned now. 'Wait, no way. Are you messing with me?'
'I wish I was, but I'm not. It's our madam, Payal Jain. Now MD at Blackwater India.'
'Holy fuck,' I said. The phone almost slipped out of my hand.
'You there, bro?'
I gripped the phone tighter. 'Yes, yes,' I said. 'Did you say Payal is part of the due-diligence team? She'll be working out of our office?'
'Yes,' Mudit said. 'Isn't it funny though?'
'No,' I said in a serious voice. 'What the hell, Mudit. You got me into this.'
'Relax, bro. Let's meet up and discuss how to handle it.'
'Now?'
'Yes. Let's go to BDP. I'll pick you up.'

∾

The whole world may be asleep at midnight, but not Dubai. And definitely not the people at Bar Du Port, or BDP. Located at the Dubai Harbour, the buzzing nightclub and restaurant originally hails from Lebanon. We had come on a Wednesday, BDP's famous ladies' night. The entire outdoor terrace was jam-packed with beautiful women and rich men.

Mudit ordered a bottle of champagne to celebrate signing the term sheet and poured me a glass.

'Now, tell me, how did *I* get you into this, bro?' Mudit said.

'I never wanted to sell in the first place. I even raised concerns about Payal working at Blackwater right after we heard about them.'

'Okay, fine. But should we say no to a four-billion-dollar buyout offer because your ex-girlfriend from ten or twelve years ago works there?'

I remained silent.

'Bro, you know markets can turn bad, and we may not even be able to do an IPO next year. And here we have a one-shot confirmed deal.'

'It's a good deal, yes,' I said.

'So, it's the deal that matters, not one little member of the due-diligence team that will be in our office for the next three weeks.'

'Three weeks?'

'Maybe four or five, or even six. Doesn't matter, bro. At the end of it, we get our deal done. That's it. Focus on that. Don't worry about Payal. She may be an MD or whatever, but in this deal, she's just small fry. We're the big guys now.'

'I don't feel comfortable with her being around,' I said. 'Can we remove her from the team?'

'How? What do I tell them?' Mudit said. 'That we don't want her on the team because you dated her in the past?'

'Obviously not that. Find another reason?'

'Bro, she's the one from Blackwater who made the original investment in CloudX. She's definitely going to be involved in such a huge acquisition.'

I kept quiet and stared at the bubbles in my champagne glass.

'Saket, you and her, that was twelve years ago,' Mudit said. 'You're over her now, right? Or does this girl still have a hold on you?'

'No hold, of course,' I said. 'She has zero hold. I'm over her.'

'Why is there an issue then?'

'It's just annoying and an irritation.'

'We can all be professionals, right?'

'I suppose so.'

'Cool. Let Payal and her team come and do their work. Let them go through whatever information they need to. After that, we sign the final deal and collect our money. That's it.'

'Hmm ... When do they start the due diligence?'

'Tomorrow,' Mudit said.

'What? She's going to be in office *tomorrow*?'

'Technically, today,' Mudit said, glancing at his Rolex. 'It's past midnight.'

The DJ increased the volume as he played an Arabic-English fusion track. The crowd at BDP went wild on the dance floor. Mudit left to join them.

I stayed behind at the bar and checked my phone.

'Miss you, baby. Paulina wants to see you soon,' Tania had messaged me.

~

'That's Jensen and Gloria from EY. That's Rishabh and Sandeep from the CloudX team and, of course, you already know Max and Alan,' Neeraj said, introducing us to the due-diligence team.

We had all assembled in the office conference room to kick things off.

'The Blackwater team members are on their way. They should be here in two minutes. Sorry about that,' Neeraj said.

'That's okay,' Mudit said, handing out the new ID and access cards to the due-diligence team members present.

I sat next to Mudit, debating if I should leave the room. Mudit could easily handle things.

'And here they are,' Neeraj's voice interrupted my thoughts even as the conference-room door opened. 'That's Anirudh and Payal from the Blackwater team.'

I turned my head to look at her. She looked the same as the last time I'd seen her. She wore a formal charcoal-grey business suit with pinstripes. The frame of her spectacles had changed—it was a sleek rimless pair now.

I checked my breath. I was still calm. It was interesting to see her, that's it. No emotions stirred within me, unlike the last time around. Time does heal a lot of things.

'Hello,' Payal greeted everyone in the room. Our eyes met for a nanosecond and we gave each other the perfect friendly-yet-professional half-smile.

'Treat this office as your own,' Mudit said to the due-diligence team. 'And let us know how we can help with the process.'

'To start off, this is a list of documents we'll need,' Jensen said. He handed a document to Mudit, who passed it to Farhan from our finance team.

'No problem,' Farhan said, 'we'll start preparing them right away.'

'I think the teams can take it from here,' I said and stood up. 'I'm not really needed here anymore.'

Payal looked up at me.

Neeraj stood up as well. 'That's right. We should let our more capable colleagues take over,' he said. 'But Saket, I'm here in Dubai tonight. Are you free for dinner? Just you and me?'

I hated schmoozing with clients. I would rather Mudit did it. Besides, I'd been planning to meet Tania and, finally, Paulina.

Mudit gestured with his eyes for me to accept. He was right—I could sit through one boring dinner for the sake of four billion dollars.

'Sure, Neeraj,' I said. 'Let's meet at the Arts Club. Eight o' clock.'

~

The Arts Club in Dubai is in the Dubai International Financial Centre (DIFC), near downtown. The posh members-only club originated in London, but the Dubai branch is even swankier and trendier. Set over five floors, which are all connected by a glass elevator that runs along a four-storey-tall chandelier, it's one of the most beautiful dining and drinking spots in Dubai. Every evening, the club is full of beautiful and rich people.

I had booked a table at Rōhen, the fine-dining Japanese restaurant at the club.

'I'm vegetarian, actually,' Neeraj said as he flipped through the menu, which read like a list of marine life.

'Oh,' I said. 'I'm so sorry. I should've checked before making the reservation.'

'It's okay. I should've told you. Never mind, there are some vegetarian dishes,' he said.

I ordered vegetable tempura and an avocado roll for Neeraj.

'This is like our bajji or pakodas,' Neeraj said when the tempura was served.

'Exactly,' I said, and I wondered if I should've taken him to Bikanervala in Karama instead.

I had ordered codfish for myself. I was in the middle of a cut, which meant no rice at dinner. Going out is no fun while one's in calorie-deficit mode, particularly with a boring client.

'Looks like the due-diligence team has hit the ground running,' Neeraj said.

'Yes, everyone came prepared. Impressive,' I said.

'May I make a request?' Neeraj said. 'Something that'll make the due diligence go smoother and faster.'

'Anything for that,' I said. 'I'd really like us to conclude it soon.'

'The person who's finally going to sign off on the due diligence is Payal Jain. Our MD, and the principal on CloudX.'

'Is that right?' I said, my ears perking up at the mention of her name.

'You know her?'

I took a few moments to respond. 'She was there at the meeting today, right? On her laptop.'

'Yes. She's smart and dedicated. If she feels confident that they've done all their checks, we can wrap this up faster.'

'Okay, what I can do to help?'

'Could you give her some time? Maybe meet her for lunch? Explain your vision for SecurityNet and where you think the growth areas are. She needs to hear it from you to justify the high valuation.'

'I have to do it?'

'You created the company. You run it. It must come from you.'

I kept quiet. My phone buzzed.

'Where are you, baby? Drinks later tonight?' Tania had messaged.

'I'm at the Arts Club,' I replied while Neeraj waited for me to finish typing.

'Oh, Paulina and I are nearby, at Clap. In DIFC itself. Can we come by?' Tania responded.

'Okay. Come to Rōhen. I'm wrapping up a work dinner,' I replied and kept my phone aside. I turned to Neeraj. 'I'm so sorry,' I said.

'Work stuff?' Neeraj said.

'No, some close friends. They'll join me later. What were you saying?'

'If you could have lunch with Payal …'

'Lunch?'

'It's better if it's kept casual. Just share your vision for the combined entity. You can do that, right?'

'I can but …'

'Let me check with her as well,' Neeraj said, and before I could react, he'd already sent Payal a message.

'She's free tomorrow. Is that okay?' Neeraj said as he kept his eyes on the phone.

'Yes.'

'Any place you'd suggest?' he said. 'Somewhere near your office?'

'Sure. Let's do Bosporus. It's around the corner from the office.'

'Cool,' Neeraj said, typing on his phone. 'Fixed it for 12:30 p.m. Thank you for doing this. Trust me, this will move things along faster.'

I nodded and fake-half-smiled.

A couple of minutes later, two young girls came up to our table. One of them was Tania. She wore a short red dress.

'Tania,' I said, standing up and giving her a hug.

'That's Paulina,' Tania said, introducing me to the gorgeous six-feet-tall girl, who could easily pass off as a ramp model in her long emerald-green dress.

'I'll see you girls at the bar, okay?' I said to Tania and Paulina. They both nodded and left.

I turned to Neeraj.

'All right, Neeraj,' I said. 'I have to go. I'll do the lunch with Payal.'

'Okay, bye,' Neeraj said, still looking a bit dazed after seeing my "close friends".

∽

I stepped into Bosporus, which, with its walls of beautiful peacock blue and white mosaic tiles, was a gorgeous dining spot. Bosporus has several branches across Dubai and is famous for its delicious Turkish food and shisha.

'Your friend is already here,' the hostess said when I told her about my reservation.

She's not my friend.

On the way over, I'd repeated the four rules of engagement with Payal: One, keep it professional. Two, don't discuss anything personal. Three, don't make too much eye contact. Four, stick to the deal. That's it.

Payal sat at one of the corner tables in the outdoor patio. She was furiously typing on her phone, probably replying to a work email. As always, she was mouthing the words as she typed. Strange, how some things never change.

'Hi Payal,' I said, stepping in front of her.

'Oh hi,' Payal said as she looked up at me. She kept her phone aside and stood up.

Rule one: Keep it professional. No hugs, not even side ones.

We shook hands.

'Please, sit,' I said.

Both of us sat down, facing each other.

'How are you doing?' Payal said.

'We're doing great. Last quarter-on-quarter was eighteen per cent growth.'

'Huh?' Payal said, somewhat surprised.

'SecurityNet, right? We're doing great,' I said.

'Oh yes. That's good to know,' Payal said.

'How about you? How's the due diligence going?'

'Early days still ... but your team is quite competent. They understand our needs and are preparing the information for us.'

'That's good,' I said. 'I'm glad you're getting what you need.'

Awkward silence. Twenty seconds, which felt like twenty minutes. She looked at me. I looked away, staring down at the menu to follow rule number three: Avoid eye contact.

'Should we order?' I said.

'Sure,' Payal said, picking up a menu.

'Are you vegetarian?' I said.

Payal looked at me with an amused expression.

'What?'

'You know that already,' she said. 'Don't you?'

'People change,' I said.

She looked at me again. 'Do they?' she said.

I shrugged.

'Well, I'm still vegetarian. I'm a Jain, after all,' she said.

'Okay. No onion and garlic too?'

'No, that's fine. I'm not so rigid now, especially when travelling abroad.'

'I suggest we order the appetizer platter. It has all these mezze dips along with freshly baked Turkish bread. Everything is vegetarian.'

'Perfect,' Payal said.

'Cool.' I signalled for a waiter to come take our order.

'You can order your chicken though,' Payal said. 'You need your protein, right?'

I looked at her.

'You need your protein, right?' she said again.

Okay, this is a business meeting, I wanted to remind her but didn't.

'An appetizer platter and a chicken shish taouk,' I told the waiter.

After he left, Payal said, 'When I asked how are you doing, I didn't mean SecurityNet. I meant *you*. How are *you*? I'm meeting you after, what, like five years?'

No. Six.

'Yes, something like that.'

'Six years, actually ...' Payal said.

'Do you want me to go through what could be the key growth areas for SecurityNet over the next few years?' I said.

'What?' Payal said, somewhat taken aback by my abruptness. 'Sure, I guess ... I mean, that would be helpful, yes.'

'All right. Let's begin with the cross-selling potential,' I said.

For the next fifteen minutes, I went on about our future business plans. Payal listened with full concentration, taking copious notes on her notepad. I stopped when the waiter arrived with our food. The appetizer platter was a crescent-moon-shaped silver platter with ten different mezze items. The Turkish bread was freshly baked, all fluffed up and huge, the size of a rugby ball.

'This looks amazing,' Payal said.

I poked a hole in the bread with a fork to let the steam out.

'Is it okay if we just eat for a few minutes?' Payal said. 'I want to take notes when you talk about the projections, and I can't do that while eating.'

'Of course,' I said.

'This is delicious,' Payal said as she took a bite of the bread dipped in hummus.

'Yes, it's nice,' I said.

We ate in silence for a minute.

'You didn't answer me,' Payal said. 'How are you doing?'

'I'm doing great,' I said. 'The company has scaled new heights. You know that. I never imagined that we'd reach this point.'

'It's fantastic. And I see you continue to maintain your health.'

'I try. It's harder to maintain muscle strength as you get older though,' I said.

'Hence the protein,' Payal said as the waiter arrived with my shish taouk.

I smiled.

'How's life been otherwise? How's Dubai treating you?' Payal said.

'It's been good,' I said. 'Mudit is here. I've made some new friends too. This is home now.'

'I'm glad to hear that,' Payal said.

Another round of awkward silence followed. Should I also ask her about how she was doing? I didn't want to. But would it be rude if I didn't?

'How are you doing, Payal?' I said finally, more out of courtesy than curiosity.

Before Payal could respond, my phone began to vibrate. I'd kept it face up on the table, and Tania's picture flashed on the screen. Payal noticed the picture for a second and looked away.

'Sorry,' I said, cutting the call.

'It's fine, you can take it,' Payal said.

'No, I don't usually take personal calls during a work meeting.'

Payal nodded. Her girl brain probably connected Tania's picture with the word 'personal' and figured out what was going on here.

A second later, a text message from Tania flashed on my phone screen: 'Call me back when you can, baby.' A cartload of hearts and kiss emojis followed the text. I don't think Payal read the message, but she certainly noticed the emojis.

I picked up my phone and typed a quick response: 'Sure, baby. In a work meeting. Talk later.'

I put the phone on Do Not Disturb mode and kept it aside.

'Nice food here,' I said, taking another bite of my shish taouk.

'Yeah,' Payal said. 'So, do you really want to know?'

'Know what?' I said.

'You asked me how I was doing, before that call came? In case you still wanted to know my answer to that …'

Payal Jain's elegant yet brutal sarcasm. Still in place after so many years.

'Of course, I do. How's everything? Work, health, life?'

'Work is good. Still with Blackwater, as you can see.'

'MD now, as I can also see.'

She laughed. 'Thank you. I got lucky. Some of my investments did well. Like CloudX.'

'Pretty young for an MD at Blackwater.'

'Maybe. Not young otherwise. I'm thirty-three, can you imagine?'

'Wow,' I said. 'Hard to imagine *you* being this age.'

'That's how old you were when we first met,' she said.

Ah, you remember all that? I thought you got those memories erased for good, with Jain metal scrubbers.

'True,' I said.

'Healthwise, I'm good, I think. God's grace. I don't get enough sleep though. This job! You know private equity.'

'Yeah … But sleep is important.'

'I know. You used to tell me all the time. The three pillars of fitness—diet, exercise and sleep.'

You remember that too? Okay.

I smiled in response.

'Life ...' she said, and sighed. 'Well, a lot has happened in life.'

'Oh, okay. How's your family? Parents? Parimal?' I said. 'That's your husband's name, right?'

'Parents are fine. Parimal, I don't know. He should be fine, I think.'

What do you mean, I wanted to ask but didn't.

'Okay. Good,' I said. 'Anyway, I also wanted to tell you about SecurityNet's AI strategy. On the AI—'

'Parimal and I are not together anymore.'

I looked at Payal, shocked. 'Oh ...'

'We got divorced two years ago.'

Okay, I want to know more. But what about my rules? The AI strategy discussion also awaits us. But damn, I want to know what the hell happened.

'Really?' I said.

'Yeah. Anyhow, you wanted to discuss SecurityNet's AI strategy?' she said.

'I did, yes.'

'Let's do that now. Let work meetings be work meetings. If you want, we can meet separately after work someday, in a personal capacity.'

I looked at her. 'Right,' I said. I went over our AI strategy as we finished our lunch.

'Thanks for lunch,' Payal said.

'You're welcome.'

'And let me know if you want to meet after work someday to talk about the other stuff,' Payal said, adding, 'only if you want to.'

'Oh, yeah, sure,' I said. 'I'll let you know.'

No, you may not. Just turn around, go back to work and forget about her. And her personal life.

~

Mudit and I sat in my office. We had just finished going over a report on SecurityNet's progress in Europe.

'We'll need to open a European office at some point,' Mudit said.

'Frankfurt?' I said.

'Possibly.'

Someone knocked on my office door. I looked through the glass wall and saw Payal standing outside.

'Hi Payal, come in,' Mudit said, opening the door to let her in. 'How's it going?'

'Hey Mudit. Sorry to disturb you guys.'

'Hey, no worries,' I said. 'How can we help?'

'I needed Mudit for a minute.'

'Me?' Mudit said.

'We need some data on customer-wise revenues. It's all classified. The IT head needs you to sign off on this. The file won't open until you enable access,' Payal said.

'Oh, okay, of course. I'll come do it in a few minutes? Let me wrap up this meeting with Saket first?'

'Oh, yes, of course. No problem,' Payal said and left.

Mudit looked at me. 'It's going fine with Payal, right? It's all quite professional?'

'Yeah, I guess,' I said.

'I guess, as in?'

'Did you know she got divorced? Two years ago?'

'What?' Mudit said in a high decibel.

'Shh, keep it down. I just found out about it. I had lunch with her the other day, to discuss our future strategy.'

'*Our* future?'

'Very funny. SecurityNet and CloudX's future strategy. Neeraj set up the meeting, remember?'

'Yeah. But how did her divorce pop up in that discussion?' Mudit said, raising an eyebrow.

I recounted my entire lunchtime conversation with Payal for Mudit's benefit. 'That's it. She asked me how I was doing. I felt obligated to ask her the same. That's when she told me she got divorced.'

'And she also said she wants to meet you separately to discuss personal stuff? Wow.'

'"Let work meetings be work meetings." That's what she said.'

'Bro, she clearly wants to hang out with you.'

'No, she doesn't.'

'She's the one asking all the personal questions. Sharing stuff about herself. Suggesting you meet outside of work.'

'She's here in Dubai. She doesn't know anyone. Maybe that's why ... Maybe she just wants to meet me as an old friend.'

'Perhaps. Suits her now to make you "an old friend".'

'What do you mean?'

'Be careful, that's all. Don't get affected or involved, bro. And did you say Tania called you during lunch?'

'Yeah, but I didn't take the call.'

'And you said Payal saw her name, and her picture?'

'I think so.'

'Excellent. She should know times have changed. You have options. Great, hot, upgraded options.'

'There's nothing like that happening with Payal anyway, Mudit.'

'That's even better then. You'll meet her outside of work?'

'She pretty much asked me to. Besides pure curiosity and nothing else, I do want to know what happened between her and Parimal.'

'Oh, that was the loser's name, right? Parimal Jain,' Mudit said.

'Yeah.'

'Here's the thing about some of these Jain marriages. It is often a last-name Jain marrying another last-name Jain. You don't even know when they get married or divorced. The last name remains the same. I could've never guessed Payal is divorced.'

I laughed. 'That's a good one. Comedy-set-worthy. I would've included it in my set back in the day.

'Where are you guys going to go?' Mudit said.

'Not sure. After work means drinks? Or dinner? Or both?'

'Too much. Just do tea.'

'Tea?'

'Yes. That's what old friends do. Just meet for a quick cup of tea. Get all the dope on her divorce and run.'

'Cool. Will do that. I'll fix a time and date to meet her for a quick cup of tea. That's it.'

'Excellent. Now, let me go unlock all our secrets for these capitalist moneybags,' Mudit said, hurrying out of my office.

∽

L'ETO Caffe became extra famous after actor Alia Bhatt's Instagram reel went viral. In the reel, she talks about her superstar husband, Ranbir Kapoor, flying in the famed milk cake from L'ETO London all the way to Bulgaria, where they were shooting a movie together. I, however, simply chose this café in the Mall of the Emirates since it fell midway between Payal's hotel and my house.

We'd decided to meet on a Saturday afternoon, and Payal reached the café before me. From her knee-length floral dress to her handbag and open-toe platform shoes, she was all in white.

'Sorry, this mall is huge,' I said. 'Took me a while to walk here from the parking.'

'That's fine,' she said.

No hugs. No handshakes. Only smiles as we sat down across from each other.

I ordered a jug of hot ginger and spice tea and a slice of the famous milk cake. The waiter returned quickly with our order. I slid the cake towards Payal.

'The Alia Bhatt cake. Tell me if it's worth the hype,' I said.

Payal took a bite of the cake, spooning up some of the creamy milk it was dipped in. 'Wow,' she said. 'This is so good. But ...' she paused mid-sentence.

'But what?'

'Tastes like rasmalai,' she said.

I took a spoonful too. 'Come to think of it now, it does,' I said and both of us laughed.

We sat in silence for a couple of minutes. Then I said, 'Okay, so Parimal and you ...'

'Yes, we got divorced.'

'That's strange,' I said.

'What makes you say that?' Payal said.

'I remember seeing your Instagram account long back. There were so many pictures of you and him. On trips around the world. You guys seemed happy and content.'

'Isn't Instagram amazing? It makes everyone else other than you look happy,' Payal said, taking a sip of her tea.

'You were not?' I said.

Payal looked away. She turned to me after a few seconds. 'I was trying to be,' she said. 'I thought I could make our marriage work. I was wrong.'

'What happened?'

'It wasn't one specific thing. It was a lot of things. Right from the start, the foundation of it all. You remember all the drama at that time, right?'

I looked into Payal's eyes. I didn't just remember all that drama. I had it etched in every neuron in my brain. And it wasn't just drama for me. It was trauma.

'I do,' I said, keeping my cup down. 'Which is what makes it more surprising.'

'Meaning?'

'The way it all happened ... I thought you were really into the guy, I mean, eventually ...'

'The way what happened?' Payal said.

'Forget it, it was a long time ago. Why bring up old stuff?'

'No, tell me. Why did you think I was "really into the guy"?'

'Well, you completely cut me off. Got married so fast. Never bothered to get in touch. I figured you must've come to like the guy a lot.'

'That's what you thought?'

'Yes. Plus, your family loved him. He was Jain and age-appropriate and had never been married before. That's why it's even more shocking that you and Parimal got divorced. Are Jains even allowed to get a divorce?'

'Is that supposed to be funny?'

'Sorry, that was insensitive.'

Payal nodded. 'It's okay,' she said in a subdued tone.

'How are you doing now?' I said.

'I'm much better. I'm grateful for work. It keeps me busy.'

'Okay ...'

'I didn't cut you off by choice,' Payal continued.

'Leave it, Payal. It's old stuff. You have your version, I have mine.'

'And what's your version? I cut you off because I met Parimal?'

'Didn't you? You blocked me everywhere, so I couldn't reach you either. Then, within a couple of weeks, I hear that you're married. Then followed years of smiling pictures of both of you, holding each other in different exotic locations. What else was I to conclude?'

Payal kept quiet. She seemed overcome with emotion.

'This was a bad idea,' I said, trying to keep my voice calm. 'This is why I wanted to keep our conversations about business only.'

Payal took a deep breath, as if composing herself. 'You're right,' she said. 'I did do all that. But maybe you don't have the full picture.'

'How can I have the full picture if you never told me anything?'

'I can tell you now. Will you listen?'

'Of course,' I said.

'You wanted to know what led to my divorce, right?'

'Yes.'

'Like I said, it wasn't one incident. It's important I tell you everything that happened, right from around that time.'

'What time?'

'When my parents found out about you and me twelve years ago.'

PAYAL SPEAKS...

'I'm not in touch with him, Dad. I made a promise to you that day, and I haven't broken it,' I said.

Dad lay on the sofa in the living room, one hand massaging his chest. He held the other hand out towards me, asking for my phone.

'Please focus on your health, Dad. Are you okay?'

'Just give it to him,' Mom said.

'Why?'

'I want to make sure you've blocked him,' Dad said, his eyes shut. He seemed to be in pain.

'I did block him. On WhatsApp and Instagram,' I said. Not from my heart, I wanted to say but didn't.

'Show me,' Dad said, opening his eyes.

I couldn't believe that I was being made to go through this humiliation and being treated like a child. I handed him my phone.

Dad fumbled through the apps on my phone. 'How do you check this, Yashodha?' he said.

'How would I know?' Mom said. 'You please don't stress yourself right now. Dr Verma is on his way.'

'I will be stressed until I know that haramzada is out of our lives,' Dad said.

'There's no need to abuse anyone, Dad.'

He ignored me. He went through my contacts list. No Saket. He opened Instagram.

'How do I check whether he's blocked here or not?' he said.

'See my list of blocked people,' I said. I opened the blocked list for him. Saket was the only one in it.

'Good,' he said. 'Can you block him everywhere else too? Like your email and Facebook?'

'Who blocks anybody on email?' I said.

'I just want to make sure. What's your phone's password?' Dad said.

'Why?'

'Just tell me.'

'That's personal, Dad. Besides, I have my work emails on this phone. It's all confidential stuff.'

'I'm not going to check your work emails or anything.'

'Why do you need the password then?'

'To make sure I can check anytime that you've not unblocked him.'

'Dad, I'm not a child. You cannot control me like this.'

'Ah.' He winced in pain.

'Are you going to give him the password, or will you make sure he has a heart attack?' Mom said.

I gave him my four-digit password. He noted it down on his phone. For someone in cardiac pain, he seemed quite alert.

The doorbell rang a minute later—Dr Verma had arrived.

'What happened, Anandji?' Dr Verma said.

'Chest pain since last night,' Dad said.

Dr Verma put on his stethoscope and checked Dad's heartbeat. 'There is some arrhythmia,' he said after a while. 'If you want, we can admit him in the hospital for a night or two and run some tests. Maybe run a continuous ECG,' Dr Verma said.

'Hospital?' Mom said, looking concerned. 'What happened to him?'

'Relax, Yashodhaji. Just being cautious. We don't want to take chest pain lightly.'

~

I took the stairs at Kokilaben Hospital, each step heavy and tired. I had come straight from work, braving two hours of Mumbai traffic to reach the hospital in Andheri. It was close to 11 p.m. when I entered Dad's room. He was watching Sudarshan News on the television.

'Sorry, I'm late,' I said. 'Work and traffic. Both too much.'

'Come, sit. Did you have dinner?' Dad said.

'I did,' I lied. I hadn't had dinner, lunch or breakfast. Not for the past two days. I just couldn't eat. Akanksha had told me that Saket had reached out to her. He'd even met her. She'd also said that Saket seemed desperate and obsessive, and that I should stay away from him. Of course, he would be desperate and obsessive, just as I was to see and talk to him. I so wanted to call Saket. Ask him to meet me. To hold me once and tell me everything was going to be okay.

'How are you today? What did the doctors say?' I said.

'By God's grace, I'm lucky,' Dad said.

'What had happened?'

'They discovered a blockage in one artery. Over ninety per cent.'

'Oh no.'

'Don't worry. They'll do an angio and put in a stent tomorrow. I'll be okay after that. All God's blessings.'

'I'm glad, Dad,' I said.

'Thank you. Call Parimal, beta. He's a good boy. Ever since the engagement, you haven't spoken to him.'

'That wasn't supposed to be an engagement, Dad. You tricked me.'

'I did what is good for you. Have you even spent some quality time with Parimal? Gone out for a meal with him? Spoken to him about the future?'

'Why should I? Stop trying to control me so much, Dad.'

Dad looked away from me. He began taking short, fast breaths. I immediately called the nurse on night duty. She took his pulse.

'Why are you up so late? Exerting yourself like this. Sleep now,' the nurse said to him. She turned to me. 'Madam, don't visit so late. Exertion isn't good for heart patient.'

'Sorry, nurse. I'll leave now,' I said, getting up. 'Bye, Dad.'

Dad held me by my wrist. 'It's your father's wish, beta ... I could die anytime. Please marry Parimal. He's good for you.'

I took several long breaths to keep my composure. Then I extracted my hand from my father's grip and left the room.

As I walked towards the hospital exit, my head began to spin. Everything turned dark and I collapsed and fell on the floor.

~

'Ah, you're up,' Akanksha said. She was in the middle of recording her own video on her phone, which was attached to a selfie stick.

I looked around. I saw that there was an IV drip attached to my left hand. Clearly, I was in a hospital room, and Akanksha was making a reel about being in a hospital. Okay, was this all real or was it a weird dream?

'You fainted. Good thing it happened in a hospital,' Akanksha said. 'They admitted you immediately.'

'Which hospital?' I said, still disoriented.

'Kokilaben, where else?' Akanksha said. 'Your dad is on the same floor, five rooms away. You slept through the night. They took him for his angio early in the morning. The procedure went well.'

I nodded. She panned her phone to take a close-up shot of the IV bag.

'What are you even doing?' I said.

'I've never done a hospital video. I thought, let me record something since I'm here anyway. I'll figure out how to use it later.'

I sat up on the bed.

'Relax, you're okay,' Akanksha said. 'The doctor said you haven't been eating. Your blood sugar dropped too low, hypoglycaemia.'

'What time is it? I have to go to work. There's a live deal I'm working on,' I said.

'Can you calm down? It's the perfect excuse to take a day off. The hospital will give you a certificate,' Akanksha said.

'Still. I don't want to be here.'

'They'll discharge you today. But next time, don't diet so much. This exact thing happened to me when I skipped meals. To lose weight before my marriage.'

'What?'

'Yeah. Suraj said we'd go to the Maldives for our honeymoon. He wanted a relaxing place. Instead, it made me extra stressed. How would I look in a bikini? I cut down to one meal a day. One week later, I fainted. I told Suraj, no Maldives. That's why we shifted our honeymoon to Switzerland.'

'Good solution,' I said, my voice too weak to make the sarcasm obvious.

'You're also doing this for Parimal, right?'

I shook my head.

'Then? What happened?'

I remained silent.

Her eyes widened. 'What? Oh, that guy, Saket? Payal, you have to forget him. Parimal is your man now.'

'I love Saket. Every cell of my body does. I can't just switch off, Akanksha.'

'You can switch off. It's all in the mind, babe. You haven't met or spoken to Parimal. You haven't spent any time with him. You haven't given him a chance.'

'No. I don't want to,' I said, looking out of the window.

'Why?'

'I can't think of a life without Saket,' I said. 'And I'd rather die than marry Parimal.'

'That's what you feel right now. You're not thinking straight. Let it go, Payal. Spend time with Parimal. Think about the future. You can have a nice family with him. Your parents will also be happy.'

I felt shaky and woolly-headed. Was she right? Was I unable to think?

'Anyway, I have to go now. I promised my mother-in-law we'll make dhokla together today,' Akanksha said.

∼

'Are you sure you can take on more?' Nimit said. 'You're already working on two deals.'

I sat in my boss Nimit's office. I had requested him to give me more work.

'I can. There's an interesting company called CloudX. I want to see if we can invest there,' I said.

'You'll be overstretched. You're already working past nine every night.'

'I have the capacity, Nimit. It's okay.'

My phone buzzed. A text message from Mom popped up on my screen: 'Sunday. R City Mall, Ghatkopar. Urban Tadka, 1 p.m. Lunch with Parimal.'

I turned my phone face down.

'Sorry about that, Nimit. As I was saying, I can look at CloudX too.'

'If you insist,' Nimit said. 'But what about your work–life balance?'

'Right now, I am actively looking for work–life imbalance,' I said. Because my life is hell, I wanted to add but didn't.

By the time I got back to my desk, my mother had sent another message: 'Be on time. And wear the pink salwar kameez I got you on your last birthday.'

∼

Parimal wore a shirt with blue and black paisleys printed all over it, the kind of shirt that only certain types of Gujaratis and Jains find cool. It was also three sizes too large for his skinny frame. He had a box of Ferrero Rocher chocolates with him.

'For you,' he said, handing me the box.

'Thank you.'

'You look very beautiful,' he said.

'Thank you,' I said again.

Urban Tadka, a Punjabi-dhaba-themed restaurant, was packed with families with loud kids. We managed to get a table for two and sat facing each other.

'Lot of non-veg items here,' Parimal said, opening the menu.

'Yes …'

'Do you want to drink something?'

'Like what?' I said. I wondered how he would react if I ordered an extra-large tequila?

'Like mocktails?' he said. 'They have jamun lemonade. Virgin mojito as well.'

'Too much sugar,' I said. 'You can order one though.'

'Actually, it's a rip-off. Two hundred rupees for jamun lemonade. Not worth it.'

'Right.'

'What about food?' Parimal said.

'You should order whatever you want. I'll share with you.'

'They have parathas with chole. I wonder if they can make it Jain-style.'

'I'm okay with onion and garlic occasionally. Especially when I go out to eat and if they have nothing else on the menu. Too hard otherwise.'

'I keep it Jain as much as possible. They have khichdi too. That should be okay.'

'Fine,' I said.

A waiter came to take our order. Parimal spoke to him. 'Paneer parathas but without onion and garlic. Can you make the chole without onion and garlic too?'

'Paratha, yes. Not the chole. They are already made,' the waiter said.

'Okay, then one plate paneer parathas. No chole. And dal khichdi. Make everything Jain, okay?'

'Yes, sir,' the waiter said.

Parimal and I sat in silence after the waiter left, wondering what to talk about. I felt zero chemistry with him. I don't think people like Parimal can even be associated with a subject like chemistry. There's only one subject they know and understand—accounts.

'They have a combo deal too,' Parimal said suddenly, flipping through the menu again. 'Oh, the mocktail comes free in the combo deal. We could've ordered from here, better value.'

'You can call the waiter and amend your order,' I said, keeping a straight face.

Parimal gestured to the waiter to come back and changed our order.

'That was a good idea,' Parimal said, smiling for the first time since we'd sat down.

'Glad you found a good deal,' I said.

'Yes, it saved four hundred rupees straight. We would've had to pay for the jamun lemonade otherwise,' he said, my sarcasm flying well above his head like a badly aimed frisbee.

'Parimal, you know why this lunch has been arranged, right?' I said.

'Yes. So that we get to know each other better.'

'Correct. I don't know what you want out of a marriage or a partner. And whether I'm the right person for you or not.'

'Of course you are. Everything fits—age, family, religion.'

'There's more to marriage.'

'Like?'

'Like compatibility. Emotional connection. Passion. Matching interests. Chemistry.'

'Chemistry?'

'Yes. How you feel with the other person. Do you have a certain chemistry with them or not. Either it's there or it's not.'

'Do you feel we have it?'

We have as much chemistry as two inert rocks kept together, I wanted to tell him but didn't.

'I don't know. But our families are rushing us to get married. Possibly, in the next few weeks or perhaps a month.'

'I'm okay with an early date. The things you're talking about, all that can come later,' Parimal said.

'What can come later?'

'The closeness.'

'I don't think I'm ready to get married,' I said.

'Who is ready ever? The point is, if we're a good match, and if our parents want us to get married, then why not?'

But you and I are not a good match, I wanted to say.

'I don't know,' I said.

'Anand uncle is like a father to me,' he said.

'I know.'

'I heard he almost had a heart attack.'

'Yeah ...'

'I pray that nothing happens to him. But God forbid, if something does happen, don't you want him around and happy on your wedding day?'

~

'Stop crying, babe. It's spoiling your make-up,' Akanksha said. 'Oh dear, that mascara is ruined. Where's the make-up lady?'

The tears wouldn't stop. Within a month after that lunch with Parimal at Urban Tadka, I sat facing a mirror in a suite at the Four Seasons Hotel in Worli. The hotel's banquet hall and the garden right outside it made up the venue for my marriage with Parimal. Ironically, on our first date, Saket and I had come to Aer, the rooftop bar in the same hotel.

The hairdresser turned on the hair dryer, the noise helping to drown out the sound of my sobbing.

'I don't want to do this, Akanksha. I can't do this,' I said.

'You can, Payal. You're just nervous,' Akanksha said. She turned to the hairdresser and instructed her, 'Give more volume here no? And don't cover her forehead so much.'

'I don't want to get dressed, Akanksha. I don't even want this marriage.' I was panicking by now.

'Shh ...' Akanksha said, 'don't talk like that.'

I broke down completely. The hairdresser had to stop doing my hair as my whole body was shaking.

Akanksha held me by my shoulders. 'Calm down, babe. What's the matter with you?'

'I want to call Saket.'

'Why?'

'He was right. He said we aren't dealing with rational people. That we should run away. I want to run away.'

'Payal,' Akanksha said. 'Come to your senses. This is about your future, my love. You can't ruin your life over some stupid thing that you had with an older guy.'

'I just want to talk to him once. May I?'

'No.'

'Why?'

'Because I'm your best friend and I can't let you do what is bad for you.'

She handed me some tissues. It took me a few minutes to compose myself. The make-up lady came in and began fixing my make-up again.

'It's normal for girls to cry at their wedding, madam,' the woman said to me, reapplying some eye shadow. 'Every bride does. It's okay to have doubts. You'll be fine. Try your best not to cry now. I'll also give you extra-absorbent tissues. Use them to dab the tears immediately.'

There, the solution to my misery—extra-absorbent tissues to wipe off my tears the moment they spilled out. After dolling me up, they took me downstairs. My red zardozi lehenga weighed more than twenty kilos. It forced me to enter the banquet hall in slow motion. The Punjabi folk song 'Din Shagna Da' played in the background, making my entry look extra graceful and romantic. Guests threw rose petals at me as I walked to the stage. Now, even if I cried, it would look like happy tears. In any case, I had the extra-absorbent tissues clutched in my hand.

∽

The day after my wedding, I arrived at my in-laws' house, also located in Ghatkopar, for the Sva Graha Aagamana ceremony. This is a Jain tradition, where the new bride is formally welcomed by the groom's family into her new home. I hadn't slept the previous night due to the pheras taking forever to complete. Even at Parimal's house, the ceremonies continued all day. Underprepared, tired and sleep-deprived, I was led to a bedroom in the house, to spend my first night there with Parimal.

One of Parimal's older married cousin sisters said to me, 'Take it slow, okay? Tell him to be soft and gentle.'

I couldn't tell her that Saket and I liked it hard and rough. I simply looked at the floor to act like the perfect shy bahu. 'Okay, Didi,' I said.

'But don't forget to have fun,' she said and winked at me as she left me in the bedroom.

I looked around myself. Like they show in the suhaag-raat scenes in Hindi movies from the eighties, the entire bedroom was decked up with flowers.

What was I supposed to do now? Sit like a coy bride, with the ghoonghat over my head?

I sat on the bed. Normally, in the movies, there's a glass of milk kept on the side table. The man drinks it to gather energy before the action. Doesn't the woman need energy too? Shouldn't there be two glasses of milk? I thought of random things to keep myself distracted from the reality: that I was expected to have sex with Parimal within the next twenty minutes.

I waited for Parimal to arrive. Was it okay if a bride scrolled through Instagram while waiting for her husband to arrive for the suhaag raat?

I checked my phone. It had run out of battery. They really should give power banks to brides. How was she supposed to charge her phone otherwise, that too in a new place?

Okay, there you go, girl, your mind's all over the place. Again. Focus on Parimal. This is your special night, I said to myself.

I needed rest. I hadn't slept more than four hours in the last two nights. The barrage of relatives and friends who'd come for the wedding didn't stop, not even at Parimal's house. I must've touched a thousand feet. I was probably the highest collector of ashirwaads and blessings in Mumbai in the last forty-eight hours. Like my phone, I needed to be recharged.

The door creaked open. My heart began to beat fast. What did Parimal expect? A long, passionate night? I was his wife now. He had the right to expect that. However, the idea of him touching me was repulsive.

'Hey,' Parimal said as he came in and shut the door. 'Nice decorations no?'

'Hi,' I said.

He came and sat next to me. Then, without another word, he leaned forward and kissed me. I froze. It felt like something cold and metallic had touched my lips. He kept his hand on my breast.

'Can you remove this?' he said, tugging at my blouse.

It wasn't romantic. It wasn't even pleasant. But it wasn't threatening either. It felt like a child asking his mother to be breastfed. And what was I to do anyway? I was his wife now. Maybe this would help me get closer to Parimal.

I complied.

'And this,' he said, pointing to my bra.

I didn't want to. But I had to. I removed my clothes one by one, as instructed by Parimal. He quickly did the same.

Where Saket was a beast, Parimal was a toothpick.

Do not compare bodies, I reminded myself.

Parimal pushed me down on the bed, got on top and entered me. All this, without exchanging a single word or touching me anywhere else. It hurt. I wasn't turned on at all. I winced in pain. He started to move back and forth. Half a minute later, he grunted and then stopped. His body slumped on me, and the weight of it felt heavy.

'I'm done. I came,' he said, rolling over to his side of the bed. 'That was good.'

'Oh, okay,' I said.

'Did you come?'

'No.'

∽

'Relax, everyone is tired on the first night,' Akanksha said.

I had set up an emergency meeting with her at Prithvi Café, attached to Prithvi Theatre in Juhu. The outdoor café was filled with a bohemian crowd, consisting of theatre lovers, aspiring actors, artists and young people. Akanksha paid attention to me only after recording three videos of the famous Sulaimani chai, a lemon black tea, which we had ordered.

'It wasn't just that night. We tried again. Twice,' I said.

'And? How was it?'

'Hopeless. Akanksha, it feels like a punishment. I never imagined that sex could be *this* bad. Actually, it isn't just bad. It's awful. Like worse than getting your teeth pulled out at the dentist's.'

'What are you even talking about? Intimacy between husband and wife is the purest form of love.'

'There's nothing like that,' I said. 'Gosh, is this going to be my sex life?'

'Don't say sex. Say intimacy,' Akanksha said, taking a sip of the chai.

'What? Why?'

'Intimacy sounds better.'

'There's nothing intimate about it at all. It's like a trip to an incompetent gynaec. And you know the worst part?'

'What?'

'He always asks, "Did you come?" Like, seriously, bro.'

'What do you tell him? Just say yes. Always. That's what I do.'

'No. I said no.'

'Why did you do that?'

'Because that's the truth.'

Akanksha shook her head. 'You'll hurt his feelings like this,' she said.

'What about my feelings? We're going on our honeymoon in two days. What will happen then?'

'Is it just him, or is it also you?'

'What do you mean?'

'You say he's bad, fine. But what about you? Have *you* made an effort to want him?'

'How? I don't feel any desire for him.'

'Okay, I would never advise this under normal circumstances. But try this—get drunk.'

'What?'

'You're too wound up. I never advise alcohol. I don't even drink. But a few times, Suraj and I had wine before being intimate. It really helped.'

'I don't know if wine can fix this. Plus, Parimal doesn't drink.'

'You're going to Paris, the land of good wines. Tell Parimal to have some, like a tourist experience.'

∽

Paris is beautiful. When you see it for the first time, it feels like you're in a dream. I might've come to Paris with Parimal, but wherever I went, my thoughts drifted to one person—Saket.

We would've walked down the Seine, hand in hand. And stopped at that cute bakery, the boulangerie, as they called them here. I would've stared at the chocolate croissants greedily. Saket would've fussed, arguing and explaining to me just how much sugar, butter, carbs and calories each croissant had. I would've told him that Parisian calories don't count, and then gone ahead and stuffed myself with pastries and croissants. I smiled as I imagined Saket's shocked face watching me eat.

'What are you smiling about?' Parimal said as we made our way to the Eiffel Tower.

'Nothing,' I said. 'Can we go to that boulangerie on the corner of the street?'

'Sure,' he said. 'What is that place? A bakery?'

'Yes.'

Parimal and I picked up four chocolate croissants. He ate one. I ate the remaining three as we walked in silence towards the Eiffel Tower. In between, Parimal held my hand, as he often liked to do. When we reached the Eiffel Tower, there was a massive queue to go up.

'Not worth it,' Parimal said. 'Thirty-six euros per person just to go to the top. Plus, you have to stand in line.'

'I agree. Let's do a nice dinner instead,' I said.

'Okay. Where do you want to go? There's Rasoi. It's Indian, so it'll have Jain options.'

'We didn't come to Paris to eat at Rasoi, Parimal.'

'Oh. What then? Pizza? Pasta?'

Those are the few safe choices that Jains have when they travel abroad. It's either Indian food, pizza or pasta. Or packed theplas your parents forced you to take on the trip.

'Let's have a bottle of wine and a cheese platter for dinner,' I said.

'Wine?' Parimal looked shocked, as if I'd suggested we snort cocaine.

'Yes. We're in France, the land of wines. We must try it here. Like a tourist experience.'

'But it's alcohol.'

'It's okay, Parimal. God will forgive us this one time.'

'But ...'

'I need it. Okay? I feel like it'll help me open up to you better.'

Parimal thought about it for a few seconds. 'Okay, fine,' he said finally. 'Please don't tell our parents at home.'

'Are you crazy? Never.'

We walked away from the Eiffel Tower towards a street with several eating establishments.

'I'll start easy. Maybe mix my wine with some water first,' Parimal said as we entered one of the cafés.

~

'Careful,' Parimal said as I stumbled into a chair upon entering our hotel room in Paris.

We had finished a full bottle of red wine. I'd drunk most of it.

'I'm high,' I said, collapsing on the bed.

Parimal sat on the chair next to the study table in the room. He held a bunch of receipts in his hand and began typing something on his phone.

'What are you doing?' I said.

'Accounts for the day.'

'What?' I said, taking off my shoes.

'Checking how much we spent in Paris today. I always like to keep track of daily expenses.'

'Even on your honeymoon?' I said in a muted voice.

'What?'

'Never mind. Come here,' I said, patting the bed next to me.

He looked at me, surprised. 'Now?'

'Yeah, I'm nice and high. Why not?'

'I thought we do that at night. There's still light outside.'

'Is it illegal to do it if there is daylight outside?' I said.

'No. Actually, it gets dark late in Paris. At ten. It's because the geographic location—'

'Don't teach me latitudes and longitudes. Just come here,' I said, interrupting him.

He left the receipts and his phone on the table and walked up to stand in front of me.

'Remove my dress,' I said, 'slowly. And kiss my neck and shoulders while doing it.'

Parimal followed my instructions. 'Is this good? Am I doing it right?' he said as he pecked the back of my neck, like a woodpecker attacking the bark of a tree.

'Don't ask questions. Remove your clothes as well,' I said.

He undressed and reached for the bedside table to pick up a condom.

'Wait,' I said. 'There is no need to rush to that part.'

I pulled him into the bed. I kissed him, slower and longer.

'Slowly, use your fingers and lips to touch me all over,' I said. 'Nothing else is allowed.'

'How do I—' he started, but I shushed him.

He kissed my clavicle and then the top of my chest. Maybe it was the wine, but for a change, it felt somewhat nice. I held his head and pushed him down.

'Yes. Kiss me everywhere. Touch me and kiss me. Yes, Saket …'

My body froze. Even in my drunken state, I realized I'd made a blunder.

Parimal stopped and shifted up, coming face to face with me.

'What did you just say?' he said.

'*Suck it*. I said *yes, suck it*,' I said and pushed his head down again.

Lucky save, Payal, I said to myself. I can't have this happen again. And I won't be able to give this marriage a chance if I keep thinking of Saket. It's okay. I'll drink all the wine I need to, but I'll make it work with my husband. Make it work, Payal, come on, make it work.

'Does this feel good?' Parimal said after a few minutes, still working on my breast diligently, like a rabbit nibbling on a carrot.

'I told Neeraj I don't like to travel much. Yet he's put me in this investor conference in New York. I have to go next week.'

'Hmm,' Parimal said.

'He said it'll be good for my career. Networking with the senior partners in New York is important. In a way, he's not wrong,' I said.

Parimal looked up from his phone and stared at me for a second. 'New York? What?'

'Yes, I'm going there next week. I just told you. Our new India head, Neeraj, he's asked me to.'

Parimal looked at me blankly and then went back to his phone.

'I don't need the networking though. My deals are the best-performing ones in the Mumbai office. I cracked CloudX, and it's already up four times the initial investment that we made five years ago.' I said.

'Really?' he said without looking at me.

'Yeah. I think I should make MD in two or three years. I just need a few IPOs and exits to happen.'

'Sorry, I need to make a call,' Parimal said, walking off to the terrace.

'You promised the PVC material would reach Thane last Wednesday. What are all these sorry-for-delay emails then?' I heard Parimal speaking on the phone outside.

I went to the terrace and stood in front of him. He ended his call a few minutes later.

'What?' he said. 'Why are you standing here like this?'

'What do I do?'

'For what?'

'To get my husband's attention? To talk to him for a few minutes after work?'

'I'm here only.'

'But are you listening to me?'

'I heard you. You're going to New York next week.'

'Forget it,' I said and stormed back into the bedroom.

If this were a one-off thing, it would've been okay. But this was the norm. In fact, even as I was telling him about work, I already knew that Parimal wouldn't listen to me, and that he wouldn't ever admit to it. That's the thing about marriage. Five years of being with someone is enough time to let you predict their annoying behavioural patterns.

Parimal followed me in. 'You get upset over little things. I just had to make a short work call,' he said.

'Never mind. Let's get ready. We have to go to your parents' for dinner.'

~

'I know Dr Aditi Jain personally,' said Parimal's father. 'Just meet her. She'll sort out whatever issue there is.'

Parimal and I sat around the dining table with his parents. Over dal baati churma, we discussed IVF and what else we could do to get me pregnant and provide the family with a much-needed son.

'I've already gone to two doctors. My tests came back fine,' I said. 'And I tried IVF once. It was painful and it didn't work.'

'There's nothing wrong with me either,' Parimal said.

'If Aditi does the IVF, pregnancy chance is hundred per cent,' said Parimal's mother.

'Fine. I'll meet her,' I said with a resigned air. 'Though I don't think we need to have a child so soon. I'm only twenty-seven.'

'What do you mean soon?' Parimal's mother looked shocked. 'More than five years since your marriage. Everyone in society asks me, "What happened? Why no good news yet? Any problem?" What do I tell them?'

How about telling them that your son is a lousy lover? That he neither knows how to get his wife in the mood nor what to do with her in bed? Or that he isn't even interested in sex. And that neither am I now.

'You're trying naturally also, right?' she said.

I guess it was a civilized way of asking if we were having sex. But no, we weren't. And since I couldn't tell her that, I did what a bahu is supposed to do—pretend to be shy and look down at the food.

'Mom, please stop,' Parimal said.

'What is there to feel shy? This is important—'

'Payal will go to Aditi. Leave it, Supriya. Payal beta, did you try the churma?' Parimal's father said, interrupting his wife and saving us all from further humiliation.

~

'Parimal, I want to talk to you,' I said.

'About what?' Parimal said, hands on the steering wheel. We were in the car, driving back home from his parents' place. 'And before I forget, can you get me some formal shirts from New York?'

'Fine, I will. But I need to talk to you—'

'Actually, get them from duty-free. That'll be cheaper. No VAT, you see,' he said, interrupting me again.

'Parimal, I'll get you your shirts from New York and save you the VAT. Now, can we talk? About us?' I said.

'What about us?' he said, surprised.

'How is our marriage, you think?'

'It's normal. Why?'

'Normal? We don't talk heart-to-heart. We hardly do anything physical anymore. There is no connection between us. You have your factory. I have my career.'

'Both of which are doing well.'

'Yes. But what about us? Don't you want more out of this relationship?'

'More? Like what?' Parimal looked genuinely confused.

'You tell me.'

'A child? You're going to meet Dr Aditi ...'

'No, Parimal. You and me. What do you want between us?'

Parimal shrugged and continued to drive in silence. We had reached the entrance of our building when he spoke up: 'You know, VAT is called GST in India.'

~

'What happened?' I said to the airline staff manning the Emirates Lounge reception at the Dubai airport.

'Unprecedented rainfall in Dubai, ma'am. A lot of flights have been delayed or stand cancelled. Please be patient. We're doing our best.'

I nodded and walked into the lounge. It was unusually crowded, but I managed to find a quiet area and sat down to get some work done. I was in the middle of writing an email when I sensed someone come and stand in front of me.

'Payal?' a man's voice said. That voice. I knew that voice.

I looked up from my laptop.

'Saket?' I said, standing up in a daze.

'And that's the night I ran into you, Saket. At the Emirates Lounge,' Payal said. She took a sip of her ginger and spice tea and looked around. Every table in L'ETO Caffe was now occupied.

'I remember that night,' I said. I put down my cup and smiled.

'What?'

'Your marriage had problems even then?'

'Yes.'

'You never mentioned it. I recall buying those shirts with you. It made me think that you and Parimal are one team. Like one unit.'

Payal smirked and shook her head. 'For the record, he hated the shirts,' she said.

'How can you hate plain white and blue shirts?'

'He found them too expensive.'

'Doesn't he make good money in the factory?'

'He does. But more than making and spending money, he likes saving it. Getting value. He said he could've gotten similar shirts in India at a cheaper price.'

'To each their own. What happened after that?' I said.

'I still hoped my marriage would survive. I tried to make it work for three more years after that. Ultimately, though, it didn't.'

'Who initiated the divorce?'

'I did,' Payal said. 'Parimal thought there wasn't even a real problem. That it was all just me, overreacting to things.'

'How did your parents take it?'

'You know them. They're older now, but things are still the same. For them, divorce is ...' She stopped mid-sentence.

'Divorce is what?'

'Divorce is shameful.'

'Yeah, that's the reason why they considered me shameful. Well, one of the many reasons anyway.'

'It's not like that, Saket.'

'Leave it, Payal. It's in the past. So, one day you said, "I want a divorce," and that's it?'

'No,' Payal said, sighing deeply. 'It wasn't that simple. Lots of drama. Lots of family meetings.'

PAYAL SPEAKS ...

'I don't even understand what the problem is,' Parimal's father said. 'I see you guys. You live like any other normal couple.'

Parimal's parents, my parents, Parimal and I had gathered in my parents' living room. I had moved back home a month ago after telling Parimal I couldn't take it anymore. We had lived parallel but separate lives for far too long. It had become normal for an entire week to go by without either one of us exchanging a word. I didn't see the point of this marriage. Everyone else in the room couldn't see the point of what I was doing.

'Papa,' I said to my father-in-law, 'there needs to be a connection between husband and wife.'

'Meaning?' Parimal's father said. 'What does that mean? Connection?'

My mother spoke up. 'I know why this is happening. There's no child. If they had one, everything would be solved.'

'We sent them to the best of doctors,' Parimal's father said. 'Even Dr Aditi is shocked. This shouldn't have happened. The IVF should've worked by now.'

'I tried it three times. Each time, it was traumatic for me. For Parimal it's easy—he just masturbates into a cup and is done,' I said.

'Payal,' Mom said angrily. 'Is this the way to talk in front of your elders?'

'I'm simply telling you about the procedure. That's how it works, in case you want that grandchild,' I said.

'Payal beta, Parimal is a good boy. I work with him every day in the factory. Trust me, I haven't seen a more hard-working person. You've seen how the business has grown since he joined us. Our margins have doubled too.'

'I'm not hiring an employee, Dad. I want a husband, not someone who can improve the EBITDA or profit margin. I would rather he didn't work as hard and gave some time to the relationship.'

'Like how?' Parimal's mother said. 'Even Jigneshji doesn't give me time. Neither does Anandji sit and chat with Yashodha for hours. They are husbands. They don't do connection and heart-to-heart talk.'

'Yes, Anandji never has time. If I want to talk to someone, I have my kitty group,' Mom said.

'I'm sorry if I want more from my husband,' I said sharply. 'Am I allowed to do that?'

'More what?' Mom said. 'What more do you want him to be?'

'I want someone who listens to me. Soothes me with words when I've had a stressful day at work.'

'Why do you even work if it's stressful? Parimal makes good money now,' Parimal's father said.

'Because I want to work, Papa. Even if it's stressful sometimes. I just want my partner to support me. Talk to me. Make plans with me, for us. Care about meeting me. And ...'

'And?' Dad said.

'And is intimate with me. We aren't intimate. It's been two years. Nothing. Parimal is not interested in sex.'

'This is how she talks to me also, see,' Parimal said to the parents. Like those kids in school who go complain to the teacher, 'Look, ma'am, she's being so mean.'

'Payal beta, these things may be true. But life is above all that,' Parimal's mother said.

'What do you mean?'

'All this need for attachment, it's there because you're not close to God.'

'What?' I said.

'Yes. Attach yourself to God. Rise above all these worldly pleasures. At this age, these physical pleasures are anyway bad for you,' she said.

'I agree, do a fast. Paryushan is coming, it'll help,' Mom added.

'She can also have some cold methi water every morning. It'll curtail her impure thoughts,' Parimal's mother said.

I looked at all of them. Their great solution was to surrender myself to God, fast and drink methi water every morning?

'We've had too many meetings like this. You've all tried to help. I appreciate that. But I've made my decision. I met a lawyer,' I said.

'What?' everyone gasped in unison, as if I'd hired a professional assassin.

'I want a divorce,' I said. 'And I say this with great sadness, because Parimal knows I've tried to make things work for years.'

'You cannot divorce him,' Dad said, his voice faint.

'I can. It's my right,' I said.

'He's part of our family business. I can't stop him from coming to the factory,' Dad said.

'Then don't,' I said. 'He can continue working with you.'

'Anand, this can't happen,' Parimal's father said. 'We'll have no face left in society.'

'This will be too shameful,' Parimal's mother said. 'Yashodha, you know we'll be ostracized in the community. We'll become the gossip around town.'

'Are you going to say anything?' Parimal's father turned to him in agitation.

'She won't listen. I've tried enough times,' Parimal said.

If only he'd actually tried to talk to me ... I took out a big brown envelope from my laptop bag and kept it on the coffee table in front of us. 'This is a divorce settlement agreement.'

'What settlement? I'm not going to give you anything. You want this, not me,' Parimal said.

'I want nothing. No alimony. Not even a share in the factory, which technically belongs to me because it's my father's factory. But I don't care. I just want out. This is your chance to save, Parimal. If you sign this, I'll walk away with nothing,' I said.

Mom slapped me hard across my face. 'Don't think you can come and live here if you leave him,' she said.

'Oh, that's what it has come to now?' I said. 'Fine. I won't.'

Mom turned to my in-laws and folded her hands. 'I'm sorry for her behaviour. I don't know where we went wrong in her upbringing. Maybe we educated her too much.'

Parimal's parents didn't care about my mother's apology or explanation. They stood up to leave.

'I gave you my only son. He came into your family, and your business flourished. And this is how you reward me, Anand? With shame and badnaami in society?' Parimal's father said angrily before stomping out, his wife and son following him.

Nobody cared about our marriage. The only issue—the big shame.

'I'm sorry, Mom, Dad,' I said once the three of us were alone. 'I let you down.'

'Get out,' Dad said, barely controlling himself.

'Now?'

'Yes.'

I turned to my mother. She looked away.

Without another word, I went to my room, packed a few clothes and left.

Tears rolled down Payal's face. She looked at me and smiled. 'I'm sorry, Saket,' she said. 'I didn't realize I would get emotional talking about it.'

'It's understandable,' I said. 'You've been through a lot.'

'Yes. Things are better now though,' Payal said.

'They are?'

'Much better. Two years have passed since our divorce. Parimal has accepted it.'

'What about your parents?'

'Things improved between us. It took another crisis. You remember Vansh?'

'Your brother?'

'Yes. He had a drug problem. Had to go into rehab.'

'Oh no!'

'Yeah, and for my parents, more than the drug problem itself, it was the social shaming that they feared. What would people say if they found out that their son has a drug problem? They didn't keep him in rehab for too long.'

'He's okay now?'

'Sort of. They brought him home. Then six months ago, they reached out to me, asking if I wanted to move back to their house. Mainly to help take care of Vansh.'

'You agreed?'

'Yes, I live with my parents now.'

'What about your friend Akanksha? How is she?'

Payal looked up at me and gave me a wry smile.

'What?'

'She and I aren't friends anymore.'

'Why?'

'Her husband, Suraj ...' Payal said and stopped mid-sentence.

'What about him?'

'He hit on me once at a party. Made a move. I told Akanksha.'

'Oh. And?'

'Akanksha withdrew from me after that day. Eventually, she cut off completely,' Payal said, pursing her lips.

I nodded, unable to figure out an appropriate response. I checked the time on my watch.

'Oh, it's already seven. Almost dinnertime,' I said, changing the topic.

'We spent four hours here?' Payal looked surprised.

'Yes. And I'm kind of hungry. For real food. Do you have dinner plans?' I said.

Payal shook her head.

'We can eat together then. Come, let's go,' I said, standing up.

'Where are we going?' she said.

'Might as well show you some of Dubai. Let's go to Sushisamba.'

~

Sushisamba, located on the fifty-first floor of the St. Regis Hotel in the Palm, has one of the most spectacular views in

Dubai, if not the world. Towering high on the only skyscraper on Palm Island, the restaurant offers a 360-degree view of Dubai. On a clear day, one can see as far as the Burj Khalifa and Burj Al Arab to the north and the Ain Dubai, or the Dubai Eye, to the south. Apart from this, the entire Palm Islands, shaped like a palm tree, lie below.

We arrived just as the sun had set, and the sky, streaked with orange and pink all over, made the already stunning views even more dramatic.

'What is this place?' Payal said, her mouth wide open. 'People actually eat here?'

'Yes.' I laughed.

'What kind of food?'

'Japanese-Peruvian. And before you say it, don't worry. They have good veg options. I checked.'

'You checked?' she said, smiling, her eyes coming alive.

'The menu is online.'

We sat at a table by a window, facing the Dubai Eye. Payal ordered a couple of vegetarian dishes, and I added a chicken dish for myself. The food came quickly. The eggplant skewers and the Peruvian corn salad were delicious.

'You heard my story. What about you?' Payal said in between eating.

'What about me?'

'Are you happy?'

I took a moment to respond. 'Yes,' I said. 'Can't complain. Life's good.'

'Okay, how about ...' Payal trailed off.

'How about what?'

'Okay, don't answer if you don't want to. But are you dating anyone?'

I looked at Payal. She gave me a sheepish grin.

'You saw my phone that day, didn't you?' I said.

'I didn't mean to,' Payal said. 'Sorry.'

'It's okay. Yeah, I'm seeing someone. Her name is Tania.'

'Tania … Nice name.'

'Yeah. Ukrainian. She's from Kyiv.'

'Oh,' Payal said. 'How did you meet her?'

'Mudit arranged it.'

'Arranged it?' Payal's eyebrows went up.

'Yes. She moved to Dubai and was looking for friends. We've been together for almost a year.'

'Okay. What does she do in Dubai?'

'There's so much to do here. Shop, visit places.'

'I meant for work.'

'She's looking. Although she wants to become an influencer.'

'Okay …'

'Meanwhile, I support her.'

'That's nice. A guy must support his girlfriend and be there for her.'

I smiled. 'I don't mean emotional support. I meant actual financial support. I help her out with her living expenses in Dubai. She's young, so she needs that,' I said.

'How old is she? If you don't mind my asking.'

'Twenty-four.'

Payal looked into my eyes, trying her best not to be judgemental.

'We do like each other,' I said.

'Okay.'

'Want to see her picture?'

'Sure.'

I took out my phone and showed Payal a picture of Tania. In the picture, Tania wore a tight and sexy short black dress. Maybe I'd chosen the wrong picture.

'That's Tania?' Payal said.

'Yeah. And there's Paulina too.'

'What?'

I swiped through my phone gallery and pulled up Paulina's picture.

'Who's she?' Payal said.

'She's also ... I support her as well. We're close too.'

'Close, as in? You're dating her also?' Payal looked shocked.

'Yeah,' I said. 'But it's not what you think. I'm not cheating on Tania. She knows about this. In fact, Tania introduced me to Paulina.'

Payal shook her head in disbelief. 'Wait, Tania and Paulina both are your girlfriends? And you support both of them? Financially?'

'Yes, why are you asking in that way?'

'What way?'

'A judgy way.'

'I'm not. I'm just a bit confused and surprised. I've never heard of something like this before.'

'Times have changed, Payal.'

'And you like this ... relationship ... system ... arrangement?'

'I love it,' I said. 'Which guy wouldn't? Two perfect tens, dating you at the same time. Meeting your every need.'

'Every need?'

'I mean the needs I have now. They meet them. That's all I want now—no emotional drama, no obsessive attachments. Just have fun and keep things easy. I feel free.'

'Great,' Payal said.

'Now, you cannot leave Sushisamba without trying their dessert. Mochi ice cream. You'll love it,' I said.

∼

After dropping Payal back at her hotel, I came back home and lay in bed. I opened my phone and checked Payal's display picture on WhatsApp. I saw the typing prompt under her display picture, and then it disappeared. This happened a few times.

Meanwhile, Tania messaged me: 'Free to meet, baby?'

'Sorry, baby, have work tomorrow. Some other time,' I replied.

I was about to keep my phone aside when Payal's message finally popped up: 'Thank you so much for a fabulous tea and dinner. And thank you for listening to me.'

'Welcome,' I typed back and kept my phone aside, switching off the lights to go to bed.

∼

'We'll easily attain an eighteen per cent average growth in the next three years. What are you even talking about?' I said, my voice tense.

'Eighteen per cent is too aggressive. I would trim it down to a fifteen,' Payal said.

The due-diligence team had just presented its findings to me and SecurityNet's upper management.

'I disagree,' I said.

'It's what the due-diligence team believes. There are new markets that haven't been tested. To think business will boom there isn't realistic,' Payal said.

'It is correct,' I said.

'In my opinion, it's not,' Payal said.

Our eyes locked. In contrast to our heart-to-heart on Saturday, this was a heated professional argument.

'And what impact does your opinion have?' I said.

'I'll recommend to the CloudX team that they revise their offer. Four billion is too much. Maybe three and a half is better,' Payal said.

'What? A half a billion dollars less because *you* think so? No, *I* don't think so,' I said.

'It's not just my thinking. It's based on data. This would've come up even in the IPO due diligence.'

'We have a term sheet for four billion,' I said.

'Subject to due diligence and any material findings that might cause us to revise the bid. It's written in that same term sheet. Clause 3.1,' Payal said.

Damn, she was good. I remained quiet. I looked at her angelic face and delicate fingers, both of which camouflaged the tigress inside. The tigress who was going to cut down my company's price by over four thousand crore rupees.

'Would you like to see the clause in the term sheet?' Payal said calmly.

'No, I know the term sheet,' I said.

'Good. Three and a half is still a good price,' Payal said before standing up to leave the room.

~

I was on my way out when I ran into Payal in the office lift lobby.

'Done for the day?' I said.

'No, I still have work to do. Just going down to the café to get some lunch,' Payal said.

'At 5 p.m.?'

'Yeah. I lost track of time. How about you? Done with work?'

'Yes. Leaving early today,' I said. 'It's the first day of Navratri. I usually go to the temple today.'

'Oh nice. There's a temple in Dubai?'

'Yeah, in Jebel Ali. I'll go home first, change and then go.'

The lift arrived and we got in.

'That was a tough meeting,' I said.

'Yeah. Sorry if I was too firm.'

'No, I understand. You were doing your job. I would do the same if I were in your place,' I said.

'Really? You're not upset with me?'

'No. I appreciate you doing your work professionally.'

'Thank you. You sure you're okay? It's half a billion dollars.'

'It does sting, but you made sense. Anyway, it's just business. Forget upset, I'm proud of you,' I said, and corrected myself immediately, 'sorry, I mean, you should be proud of yourself.'

She looked at me and smiled. 'Means a lot coming from you,' she said.

What did she mean by that? Nobody can decode girls, I tell you.

The lift reached the ground floor.

'Have a nice evening,' Payal said as we exited the lift. 'Say a prayer on my behalf, please.'

'Sure,' I said. 'And you have a nice evening too.' I was almost at the entrance when I stopped and called after her. 'Payal.'

She turned around. 'Yes?'

'Do you want to come to the temple with me?'

'When? Now?' she said.

'No. Have your lunch. Finish your work. I'm going home first anyway. The temple is open until nine. We can go a little later. Say, around eight?'

'Okay,' Payal said. 'But I'd like to go change too. I'm wearing a corporate suit.'

'So what? God isn't going to judge you for that.'

Payal laughed. She still had that same beautiful laugh, the one I remembered from when I'd seen her at the comedy club twelve years ago. 'I'll still go to my hotel room and change into something more traditional.'

'Sure. I'll send you the location pin for the temple. See you later.'

~

I stood outside the pristine white Hindu Temple in Jebel Ali, waiting for Payal to arrive. The main temple room, with its intricately designed central dome, housed several beautiful idols of Hindu gods and goddesses. The impeccably clean temple had a serene and peaceful vibe, and it was popular amongst the large expat Hindu population living in Dubai.

My phone buzzed—it was Tania.

'Hey, baby,' I said, picking up the call.

'All set, sweetie? We're meeting at Ling Ling at nine, okay?'

Damn. Ling Ling. I'd made plans with Tania and some of her friends to bring in her birthday at midnight. How could I forget about it?

'Oh,' I said, 'is that right?'

'What? You know what's tonight, right?' Tania said.

'Yes, it's my baby's birthday,' I said.

'Yeah, Ling Ling. In the new Atlantis. Near your place, in the Palm itself.'

'I'm not in the Palm right now though.'

'Oh, where are you?'

'Jebel Ali. Came to the temple here. It's Navratri.'

'Navi what?'

'It's a special religious day for us. I can't drink or eat much. But I'll come. I don't have my car today, so I'll take a cab.'

'What happened to Riyaz?'

'Riyaz is fine. The car's gone for servicing.'

'Oh, I can pick you up, baby. I have a car today.'

'You do?'

'Well, my friend Sofia does. Her boyfriend gave her a Porsche, you know.'

'Wow.'

'Hint, hint. Birthday-gift ideas,' Tania said, giggling.

I remained quiet.

'I'm kidding,' Tania said. 'You give me lot. Anyway, Sofia is letting me drive her Porsche since it's my birthday tomorrow. Let me come pick you up.'

'No, Tania, it's okay. I can easily take a cab.'

'Why? I want to come pick you up. Gives me an excuse to drive.'

'Fine,' I said and checked the time. It was 8 p.m. 'Come by 8.45 p.m.,' I said. 'I'll send you the location pin. Bye.'

A little distance away, I saw Payal get off from a taxi. She wore a white salwar kameez with a red border, along with a matching dupatta. As she walked closer towards me, I also noticed the tiny red bindi and the dangly gold earrings she was wearing. A mere change of outfit had transformed her from a feisty capitalist banker to a traditional and demure-looking Indian girl. She had showered, and her hair was still wet. I couldn't take my eyes off her.

I have two stunning Ukrainian models in my life. Why am I looking at Payal like this then?

'Hi,' Payal said. 'Am I late? Sorry, took a while to finish up at work and then get ready.'

'No, you're perfect ...' I said. 'I mean, you're perfectly on time.'

Damn, what happens to me when I'm with her?

'Shall we go in?' she said.

I nodded and led her into the main temple hall. Given that it was the first day of Navratri, the temple was busier than usual. We went to pray at the Vaishno Devi idol, both of us with our hands folded. I smiled as I watched her mumbling some silent prayers. Her mumbling was the same as when she typed out emails. I was still staring at her and smiling when she suddenly opened her eyes and caught me looking at her.

'What?' she said.

'Nothing,' I said.

We bowed in front of the idol, foreheads touching the floor. We went up to the other idols and prayed there as well. Finally, we went up to the priest, who put a tilak on both of us. We sat down on the temple floor for a few minutes.

'Thank you for bringing me here. I feel so peaceful,' Payal said.

'I'm glad you came.'

'Anytime you want to come to the temple while I'm here, I'll be happy to join you,' she said.

We stood up to leave.

'Listen, Payal,' I said as we came outside the temple. 'I didn't realize this before, but I had dinner plans tonight. Someone's birthday.'

'Oh, okay,' Payal said.

'Tania's birthday, actually. I can't get out of that. I won't be able to join you for dinner.'

'Oh, that's absolutely fine. I didn't assume we were going to eat dinner together.'

'Yeah, but it's late and …'

'Relax. I eat alone daily. I'll go back to the hotel and just order room service.'

I checked the time. It was 8.15 p.m. 'I do have an idea though,' I said.

'What?'

'I have about half an hour before Tania picks me up. You see the building next door? That's a gurdwara.'

'Okay … and?'

'They have a langar. In case you're interested, you could eat there. I'm fasting, but I can give you company.'

'Langar?' Payal sounded excited. 'I love gurdwara food. Come, let's go.'

We went inside the gurdwara. I placed a headscarf on my head and Payal covered her head with her dupatta. We bowed and paid our respects to the holy book, and sat down for a few minutes, listening to the kirtan together.

'This is amazing,' she said.

We left the darbar and came to the langar area. We sat on the floor and volunteers served Payal with some dal, aloo sabzi, phulkas and raita.

'Best idea ever,' Payal said as she ate the sabzi with the phulka.

When we came out, I spotted the silver Porsche convertible with red interiors instantly. My phone rang. It was Tania.

'I can see you. Wait, walking towards you,' I said to Tania and cut the call.

I pointed towards the Porsche. 'I need to go there,' I said.

'Okay, I'll stay here only. You go ahead. I'll order a cab.'

'No, it's fine. Come,' I said.

We walked up to the Porsche.

'Hi Tania,' I said.

'Hey, you,' Tania blew me a kiss. She was wearing a short red-wine-coloured dress, which matched the interiors of the car.

'Payal, this is Tania. Tania, meet Payal. Payal is a colleague at work. We came to the temple together,' I said.

I saw the surprise on Payal's face at my introduction of her.

'Oh, nice,' Tania said. 'Sweetie, you ready to go?'

'Yes,' I said. 'Bye, Payal, I'll see you in office,' I said before walking around the car and getting in.

Payal nodded and waved me goodbye.

Tania looked up at Payal. 'Nice meeting you,' she said, smiling. 'And nice outfit, by the way.' Then she turned to me. 'Let's go, baby.'

Even as I fastened my seatbelt, the car zoomed off with a loud roar.

~

'Easy, baby, I'm tired,' I said to Tania as she pushed me towards the bed.

'I want you,' Tania said sexily. 'The birthday girl wants you.'

We had partied until 2 a.m. at Ling Ling with six of Tania's friends. Afterwards, she'd insisted on coming back to my place.

She removed my shirt and pulled off her dress in one quick move. Her slim and curvy body glistened in the moonlight streaming in through my window. Hovering over me, in her itsy-bitsy lace lingerie, she looked like she was made of fresh cream and honey.

'Take it off, baby,' she said, guiding my hand to her bra strap. When I didn't do anything, she removed the bra herself. Her perfect breasts dangled above my face. I placed my hands on them—they felt soft but cold. I removed my hands. What was happening to me? I had a gorgeous woman in my bed, on top of me, waiting for me to have sex with her. Yet, I didn't want to. I closed my eyes.

Payal. In the white salwar kameez. Praying. Eating at the langar. Walking. Smiling.

'Tania?' I said.

'Hmm?' she said, busy kissing my neck. 'What is it, baby?'

'Is it okay if we stop?'

'What do you mean?'

'I'm just tired,' I said.

'Really, baby?' she said. 'We haven't met in a while …'

'I want to. But, at the same time, I can't seem to, tonight.'

'Let me work on you for a few minutes, baby, and you'll be ready. Trust me,' she said, unzipping my pants.

'It's okay, baby, just stop,' I said, pulling myself away.

'Something's wrong, isn't it?' Tania said.

'No, I'm fine. Is it okay if we call it a night? Let's meet another time?' I said.

Tania sat back up on the bed. 'You don't find me attractive anymore?' she said.

'Are you kidding me? You were the most gorgeous girl at Ling Ling tonight.'

'Really?'

'Yes,' I said. 'Every guy was checking you out, baby.'

'But you don't want me.'

'It's just tonight. I'm tired.'

'Is it my lips? I need to get more fillers.'

'You get fillers?'

'Of course, all my friends do. There's this Botox place in the Marina.'

'Your lips are fine. And you're so young. Why do you need Botox?'

'Is it my boobs? You don't like them anymore?'

'Come on, Tania. You're perfect. You have a model-like figure.'

'I can get them changed. Any way you want. You want them bigger?'

'What? No. Please, Tania, relax. I'm just not in the mood today. Must be all the work stress. I'll see you soon though. Okay?'

Before she could suggest other cosmetology treatments, I said, 'Your Porsche is in the driveway, right? Come, I will drop you to the porch.'

Once alone in my bedroom, I lay in bed, unable to sleep. I picked up my phone. There was a message from Payal, sent several hours ago.

'Thanks again for taking me to the temple and the gurdwara. Felt wonderful. Have a great evening.'

I noticed she was still online. What was she doing up so late?

'You're welcome, Payal. Am glad you came,' I replied.

'Hi, up so late?' she texted back instantly.

'Yeah. Just came back home from the birthday dinner. What are you doing up so late? It's almost three,' I messaged her.

'I was asleep. Woke up and then I couldn't go back to sleep.'

'Why, what happened?'

'No idea. Also, I felt a bit hungry. Maybe I didn't eat enough at the langar.'

'Oh no. You should've.'

'Or maybe I'm just being greedy, but am craving something.'

'Craving what?'

'A snack. Something unhealthy. I don't care what it is, as long as it's unhealthy.'

I replied with three crying-with-laughter emojis, and then added, 'Order something from room service.'

How was this simple chat with Payal more fun than having Tania naked in my bed? Was I losing my mind? Was I not a man anymore? Or was I just too old?

'This hotel only has fancy things. All nicely plated with napkins and cutlery. I don't want that,' Payal replied.

'What do you want?'

'Something tasty, unhealthy and unpretentious. Is that a thing?'

I replied with another string of laughter emojis.

'Or maybe I should just try and sleep again ...'

'Where's the fun in that?' I replied. 'Let's go unhealthy-snack hunting.'

'What?'

'I know a place where you'll get what you want. Tasty, unhealthy, unpretentious.'

'Where?'

'I'll pick you up. Let's go.'

'Now?'

'Yeah, right now. Pick you up in twenty minutes.'

'We're doing this? Really? Going out to satisfy a pointless snack craving at three in the morning?'

'Yep. Because sometimes, the whole point of life is to do pointless things.'

~

'Good morning,' I said as Payal got into the cab. She was dressed in a Hello Kitty T-shirt and matching track pants.

'Good morning,' she replied. 'I can't believe we're actually doing this.'

The taxi left her hotel lobby and took the road towards Jumeirah.

'Where are we going?' she said.

'Kite Beach,' I said. 'They have a tea shop there that's open all night.'

'I'm in my nightclothes!'

'Don't worry, this place is, like you wanted, "unpretentious".'

Kite Beach, in Jumeirah, runs along the coastline of Dubai. Famous for kitesurfing, from which it gets its name, the beach is always full of families and young people. Open at night as well, it offers night swims and night kitesurfing, which are particularly popular in the hot summer months.

The cab driver dropped us where I told him to, near my secret tea shop. It was a small rectangular kiosk, built inside a shipping container, with an Indian guy manning the shop.

'What do you have right now?' I said to the guy.

'Karak masala chai. Biscuits, samosas and Maggi,' he said.

Payal's eyes lit up at the mention of Maggi. I smiled. 'We'll have two cups of tea and a Maggi.'

'I also want biscuits and a samosa,' Payal said.

'That's literally everything on the menu,' I said. 'Anyway, I'm fasting. I'll only have tea.'

Within minutes, our order was ready. I collected the food and told Payal to follow me towards the beach. I had carried a backpack from home. Once we found a nice place to sit, I took out a picnic mat from inside the backpack. Payal and I held it on either side, spread it on the sand below us, and sat down facing the waves. They made a soothing sound every time they touched the shore.

'This is perfect,' Payal said, dipping a biscuit in the tea and biting into it.

I looked at her and smiled.

'I haven't had a night out like this in ages,' she said.

'Me neither,' I said. 'Somehow, I just couldn't sleep tonight.'

Payal nodded. Then, after a brief pause, she said, 'Are you happy, Saket?'

'Yeah. I told you I am,' I said, looking at the waves. 'Happy with my work and the company we've built. And now, thanks to you, I'm about to get a truckload of money as well. Even though you've lowered the bid.' I smiled.

'I didn't mean happy in terms of work and money.'

'What else then?' I said, turning to look at her.

'May I ask something personal?'

'Yeah, sure.'

'Are you happy with this Tania-type situation?'

'She's not a situation. She's my girlfriend.'

'Is she?' Payal said.

'What do you mean? We hang out all the time. We care for each other. We have a good physical relationship.'

'Sure ...' she said. She took out the container with the Maggi in it from the brown paper bag.

'You don't approve of it, is it? You're judging Tania,' I said.

'Who am I to judge her?' Payal said, scooping up some Maggi with a wooden fork.

'What is it then? Why did you even ask me that question?' I said.

'I shouldn't have. Sorry.'

'No, tell me.'

'Is it real, Saket? Is what you have with Tania ... is it something deep and meaningful to you?'

I remained quiet. We sat in silence as she continued to eat her noodles.

'It's not real,' I said after a while. 'Yes, it's an arrangement. Friends with benefits, situationship, whatever you want to call it. But I don't want real now. I have trust issues.'

'Trust issues?'

'Yeah ... I got married. That broke down, and it was hard. But that hard was nothing compared to when my next relationship ended.'

'You mean you and I?'

'Yes. I went through hell. Not for days, weeks or months. But for years. Even today, I can't trust anyone to get that close to me. Or be that vulnerable. I don't know how I allowed it to happen back then.'

Payal stared at me for one long moment. I clenched my lips and looked away.

'Years, Saket? To get over us?' she said.

'Almost a decade,' I said. 'And a part of me has changed forever. Like, I can't imagine how I ever did stand-up comedy. How did I feel so free to do that?'

'I wish you were still doing stand-up though. You were good.'

'That me is gone. Like that me who fell in love so hard, it broke him when it ended. So yes, you're absolutely right. Tania, Paulina, and their kinds—whatever I have with them is superficial, like the Botox fillers they get done. Yet, it keeps the surface beautiful. It's not deep, sure, but it also means that I can't get hurt. Sometimes, you need to swim in a shallow pool so that you don't drown.'

'I'm sorry I couldn't stand up for you, Saket,' Payal said, looking into my eyes. She reached out and clutched my hand. I gently extracted it.

'It's okay,' I said. 'You were under intense family pressure. That's a real thing in Indian families. You tried your best.'

We sat in silence for quite a while before Payal spoke up. 'I can relate to your trust issues,' she said. 'I have them too.'

I looked at her.

'My marriage scarred me as well. I can't even imagine being with anyone now ...'

'Do you also want to try the Tania-type system? Do you want me to ask her if she has a brother? Back home in Kyiv?'

Payal laughed out loud. 'No, thanks. That's not my scene at all.'

'I can at least ask her to send some pictures,' I said. 'A Ukrainian toyboy. At least look at some photos?'

'Stop it,' Payal said, and punched my arm. For a moment, it felt like the same fooling around we used to do twelve years ago.

Our banter was interrupted by a young man who rode up on a unicycle on the cycling track that runs along the beach. He was dressed in a striped shirt and pants, resembling a circus clown.

'Excuse me, lovely couple,' he said, struggling to balance his unicycle.

'We're not a couple,' I said.

'Oh, okay, sorry about that,' the unicyclist said. 'I'm Jamal, a professional juggler. May I request you for a little help?'

'Sure,' I said.

'I've been practising a new act for a while now. But before I launch it in front of a bigger audience, I wanted to show it to a few people and get their feedback. May I show you the act and get your genuine opinions?'

Payal and I looked at each other.

'Don't worry. You don't have to pay me anything,' Jamal said.

'Sure,' Payal said. 'Let's see it.'

Jamal bowed to us. He got off the cycling track and dug the wheel of his unicycle into the sand to stabilize it. Then he put on some music with a peppy beat on his Bluetooth speaker. Jamal sat on top of the cycle and took out six balls from his pocket. He started juggling them, beginning with three balls and increasing to all six.

Payal's eyes remained transfixed on Jamal's hands, the balls in the air, and his focused-yet-smiling face. I alternated my gaze between the juggler and Payal. I found more happiness in Payal's delight from watching the act than in the act itself. Maybe that's what I liked about being with Payal. Her happiness automatically created my happiness.

'Bravo, superb!' Payal clapped as Jamal finished the act. He bowed, and I applauded as well.

Payal took out a 100-dirham note from her purse. Jamal vigorously shook his hands.

'Astaghfirullah! No, no,' Jamal said. 'I can't accept that. You're my test audience. Just give me feedback.'

'What feedback?' Payal said. 'You're fantastic. Just do it with a little more flamboyance and be proud. You're too good.'

'You're too kind,' Jamal said.

'Allow us to at least buy you a cup of tea,' I said.

'Sure,' Jamal said.

I went to the tea stall and returned with three fresh cups of tea.

'Thank you,' Jamal said as he took a cup from me. 'You guys live in Dubai?'

'I do. She's visiting,' I said.

'Okay. What are you doing out on the beach so late at night? Or rather, so early in the morning?' Jamal said.

'We couldn't sleep,' Payal said, 'and I was craving a snack.'

'An unhealthy and unpretentious snack, to be precise,' I said. Everyone laughed.

'Was it hard to become a juggler? What you did seems incredibly difficult,' Payal said.

'You know the hardest part?' Jamal said. 'It's not juggling the balls. It's juggling all the family pressure.'

'What do you mean?' I said.

'We can all agree that juggling is not in the list of the top-ten lucrative careers in the world,' Jamal said.

Payal and I smiled.

'What do you guys do?' Jamal said.

'Private equity,' Payal said.

'I have my own cybersecurity company,' I said.

'See, now these are jobs my parents would be proud of,' he said. 'Desi parents don't like jugglers. Not as their kids.'

'You're from India?'

'No, Pakistan. Lahore. But janaab, it's the same thing there. Desi parents want to control their kids until their kids are sixty. Maybe seventy, actually. After that, it's difficult, because then the parents are usually dead,' Jamal said.

Payal and I laughed.

'So that was the hardest part. Being nearly disowned by my parents. Having to survive on my own. Doing little gigs at kids' birthday parties and beach clubs, just to be able to eat. Fortunately, I managed to come here to Dubai. I can make a living now. I even have social media, with more than twenty thousand followers. I post reels of my acts. Helps me get more business. May I give you my Insta?'

We took out our phones as Jamal pointed us to his Insta account.

'That's impressive. How are things with your parents now?' Payal said.

'Not great,' Jamal said. 'They're both lawyers. As were their parents and grandparents. My family runs one of Lahore's most prominent law firms. I'm the first black sheep in generations.'

'Don't say that,' Payal said.

'My parents don't understand. I love my job. It makes me happy. That's all that matters. Hopefully, they'll understand that someday. If they don't, oh well. That's just too bad,' Jamal said and shrugged.

'Your job doesn't just make you happy. It makes people happy—kids, grown-ups, everyone. It's beautiful,' Payal said, her voice emotional.

'Thank you,' Jamal said and bowed to her. 'Anyway, I better leave. I'm impinging on your couple time. Oh wait, you're not a couple, right?'

'No, we're not,' Payal said and smiled.

Jamal waved us goodbye and vanished on his unicycle.

After he left, Payal sat quietly and stared at the horizon for a long while. As the first streaks of daylight spread across the sky, her face glistened in the blush of dawn. I saw a tear escape her eye.

'Payal? Are you okay?' I said.

Payal nodded, keeping her eyes fixed on the water. It looked like the sea was on fire, with the light from the rising sun falling over it. Payal's body began to tremble.

'You sure?' I said again.

She nodded vigorously, but her face told a different story. Within seconds, she broke down completely. She sobbed uncontrollably.

'What happened, Payal?' I said, gently placing my hand on hers.

'I couldn't juggle,' she said in between her tears. 'I failed to juggle.'

'What?' I looked at her, confused.

But Payal didn't respond. Instead, she continued to cry her heart out for the next five minutes. It was as if a dam buried deep inside her had burst open, and the tears wouldn't stop.

'What is the matter, Payal?'

She struggled to compose herself. I gave her some tissue that had come with the food package to wipe her tears. Eventually, she stopped crying.

'Look at Jamal,' she said, her voice catching. 'He fought with everyone close to him. Why? For the sake of what he loves. And what did he say finally? "I love my job. It makes me happy. That's all that matters. Hopefully, though, my parents understand that someday. And if they don't, that's just too bad."'

'I know, that was quite something.'

'He's doing gigs at birthday parties. Making a living somehow. But he's still doing what he loves, and he does it so well too. His family should support him. But forget that, they disowned him. Still, he smiles and does it. It's so ...' Payal paused, searching for the right word. 'So brave ...'

'It is,' I said. 'But I can't believe he's had such an impact on you.'

'Because he held up the mirror, Saket.'

'Mirror?'

'Yes, he showed me that even in the most difficult of circumstances, it's possible to stand up for yourself. You go toss balls at kids' birthdays, but you don't compromise on what's important to you. Now compare that to what I did. I had a high-paying job, but I still couldn't stand up for myself.'

'It's not easy to go against one's family,' I said.

'But it's not impossible either,' Payal said. 'And I failed to do it. I married the wrong guy, even when I knew he wasn't right for me. I made myself suffer. I made you suffer ….' She teared up again.

I put my arm around her shoulder. Holding her delicate body like that felt familiar, even after so many years.

'I doubted myself,' Payal continued. 'I believed some of their nonsense.'

'What nonsense?'

'All that stuff about you and me. That it wasn't love. It was just lust. The age difference. Sex addiction and blah blah …' Payal burst into tears again.

'Don't cry, please. It wasn't your fault.'

'How was it not?' she said. 'I didn't fight enough. I didn't believe in myself enough.'

'You were too young, Payal. What do we know at twenty-two?'

Payal looked at me tearfully.

'It's okay,' I said. 'Really. You were a twenty-two-year-old girl! It's hard to go against everyone at that age. It's difficult to not get influenced. I get it.'

She turned to look at me. She hugged me, nestling her head against my shoulders. Exactly how she used to twelve years ago.

'Still, I'm sorry, Saket,' she whispered.

I realized that we'd been holding each other for a few seconds longer than necessary. 'Be careful,' Mudit's words rang in my head.

'It's fine,' I said, withdrawing myself.

I checked the time. It was 6.30 a.m.

'Should we head back?' I said.

∼

It took six weeks for the due-diligence team to give their final sign-off. They had checked every file, document, receipt, invoice and data inside SecurityNet.

'Here, three and a half billion dollars, ready to go,' Neeraj said as he slid the final binding offer document towards me.

I flipped through the fifty-page document, pausing briefly at the page detailing my payout. At this point, I owned twenty per cent of SecurityNet, implying my stake was valued at seven hundred million dollars, or nearly six thousand crore rupees.

Mudit gave me a brief nod. 'We did it,' he mouthed silently.

I could almost hear 'The Money Chant', from the movie *The Wolf of Wall Street,* play somewhere in the background. I closed the offer document and set it aside.

'The legal teams on both sides have checked this, right?' I said.

'Thoroughly,' Max said.

I turned to Shailesh, the head of legal for SecurityNet.

'Yes, we have,' he said. 'It's good to go. Once all the parties sign, the transaction will close within thirty days.'

'In that case,' I said, 'all we need now is a pen. Anyone?'

Payal took out a pen from her laptop bag and handed it to me.

'Thank you, Payal,' I said.

'Before you sign, we have one request though,' Neeraj said.

'What?' I said.

'We'll complete the signing here. However, we want to host a party next month, to celebrate the deal. We'd like you, Mudit and other senior members from SecurityNet to attend it,' Neeraj said.

'Oh, okay, sure. We can survive one party with you guys,' I said, smiling. 'When and where?'

'Next month, after the transaction is fully complete. We'll do it in Mumbai.'

'In Mumbai?' I said, blinking at Neeraj.

'Well, yes. This is a big transaction for us. The event will help Blackwater and CloudX get great publicity. We also want to do some strategic media and PR meets.'

'I haven't been to Mumbai in years,' I said.

'We should go, bro,' Mudit said. 'It all began there. Let's go back and see how far we've come.'

I looked at everyone in the room. My eyes stopped at Payal.

'Don't worry, we'll throw a good party,' she said with a smile.

'Okay,' Mudit said, raising his hand. 'I just had an idea.'

'What is it?' Neeraj said.

'We'll do the event in Mumbai, but not at a boring hotel. I have the perfect venue for it—one connected to SecurityNet's founders,' Mudit said.

I turned to Mudit, raising an eyebrow.

'I used to run a comedy club in Mumbai. I sold it to the club's CEO a few years back, but it's still around,' Mudit said. 'Let's do it there.'

'A deal-closing party at a comedy club?' Neeraj said.

'That place means a lot to us. And it's not just a comedy club. It has a great bar and lounge. We can use that space,' Mudit said.

'Mudit, come on,' I started, but he raised his hand to silence me.

'And you know the wildest thing about that club? Saket used to perform there. As a stand-up comic,' Mudit added.

'What?' Neeraj said. 'That's it then. We must do the event there. Maybe Saket could even perform for us?'

'Ah, another superb suggestion,' Mudit said, clapping his hands.

'That sounds like a lot of fun,' Max said.

'It'll be awesome. The origin story. The humble beginnings of SecurityNet's founder at a comedy club,' Philip said. 'We'll get amazing media coverage for that.'

'Not to mention, the founder will also perform a stand-up set,' Neeraj said.

'Stop it, guys,' I said. 'Now, if you're all done with your crazy party ideas, may I sign this multi-billion-dollar deal?'

'Sure, yes,' Neeraj said and laughed. 'But I'm confirming your attendance at the Mumbai event. Whether you perform or not is up to you.'

'I'll come to Mumbai, yes. I'm not sure about doing the act,' I said.

'He'll do it,' Mudit said, winking at Neeraj.

'Guys, let's focus on the task at hand,' I said.

I signed the offer document. The room burst into applause.

'See you in Mumbai, Saket,' Neeraj said, shaking my hand.

~

I walked up to Payal's makeshift office at SecurityNet. She stood beside her desk, packing some documents into brown boxes.

'Excuse me, may I come in?' I said, gently knocking on the glass door.

Payal looked up.

'Oh, Saket. Yes, please come in.'

'Last-day packing?'

'Yes,' she said. 'And congratulations again on signing the deal.'

'To you as well,' I said. 'When do you leave Dubai?'

'Day after. My flight is on Sunday evening.'

'Okay. Any weekend plans?'

'Nothing. Just packing. Maybe some last-minute shopping—though I hate shopping. But I'll drag myself to Dubai Mall.'

'Ah okay. I asked because I'm going to the temple tomorrow. Ever since the deal closed, I've been meaning to go. Would you like to join me?'

'Oh yes. I would love to. I can meet you there directly?'

'No, I'll pick you up this time. Seven o'clock?'

'Sure. That works.'

'Also, this time, I don't have any dinner plans after. Would you like to have dinner together?'

'You sure? I'm happy to eat at the gurdwara again, or somewhere else by myself.'

'No, let's have dinner together. Tomorrow is your last night in Dubai, right?'

'Yes.'

'Cool. I'll figure out a nice place,' I said. 'See you.'

'Looking forward to it,' she said with a happy smile.

I tapped one of the brown boxes on my way out. 'Same here. Happy packing.'

~

'I look like Mahira Khan in this, don't I?' Payal said to me, pointing at the sky-blue salwar kameez she'd worn for the temple visit. It had delicate white embroidery all over it.

'Who?' I said.

'I bought this suit from a Pakistani boutique. Don't I look like one of those actresses from Pakistani serials?'

'I haven't seen any,' I said. 'But you look nice.'

'Thank you,' she said, smiling and blushing a little. 'Where are we going for dinner?' she said a second later.

'Tagine,' I said. We were in the backseat of my car. 'It's a Moroccan place at the One&Only Royal Mirage.'

'Fancy,' she said.

'It's your last evening in Dubai, after all.'

She smiled, but her expression wasn't enthusiastic.

'We don't have to go there,' I said. 'Would you rather we go somewhere else?'

'No, I'm sure this will be nice,' she said.

Why do girls say one thing when their face clearly says something else?

The car zipped along on Sheikh Zayed Road.

'Okay, Payal? Look at me,' I said.

She turned towards me. 'Yes?'

'Do you want to go somewhere else? Eat something unhealthy, unpretentious, fried and greasy from some hole-in-the-wall place? We can do that.'

'No, not today. That was a rare and crazy 3 a.m. craving.'

'It's your last night, Payal. I want you to be happy. I know all kinds of places, so tell me.'

'May I say what I really feel like eating?' she said, excited.

'Yes.'

'I want hot dal chawal. Like simple ghar ka khana. It's not fancy or exotic, but it'll hit the spot.'

'There are some Indian restaurants that can do that,' I said. 'But they are all still restaurants at the end of the day. Proper home-style food you'll only get in one place.'

'Where?'

'My house. I have a cook, Shanti didi. She'll make the kind of dal chawal you want.'

'Like yellow dal?'

'Whichever dal you want.'

'With pickle and curd?'

'We should have that at home, yes.'

'With papad and ghee?'

'Yes,' I said, smiling. 'I'm sure all that can be arranged as well.'

'Done,' Payal said excitedly. 'Let's go to your place then. I'll get to see your home as well.'

I looked at Payal. 'You sure?' I said.

'Yes.'

I turned to my driver. 'We'll go home instead, Riyaz,' I said.

~

'This is where you live?' Payal stood in my living room, staring at its double-height ceiling.

'This is home, yes,' I said.

Shaking her head, Payal walked to one of the sofas and sank in. I went to the kitchen and asked Shanti didi to make some dal chawal for us and serve it with all the accompaniments Payal had asked for. Then I returned to the living room.

'It'll take about an hour to prepare the meal,' I told Payal. 'Do you want to sit outside in the garden?'

'Sure,' Payal said.

The manicured garden outside had an adjoining beach with a view of the waterfront and the villas on the next frond.

'Wow,' Payal said. 'I knew you lived in a villa on the Palm, but this is just beautiful. And massive.'

'Yes, a bit roomier than the Bandra place no?' I said.

'A bit?' She laughed. 'This is, what, ten times larger?'

'More like twenty,' I said.

'I loved that Bandra place though. That ledge,' Payal said. She looked out at the water, wearing the same contemplative expression that she used to have when staring out from the window ledge of my Bandra apartment.

'You've come so far, Saket. You should feel proud of yourself,' she said after a moment.

'Thank you,' I said. 'God's grace. I'm still the same person though. Sometimes, even I can't believe this is my house. I feel like an imposter.'

'You deserve every bit of the success you've worked so hard for,' Payal said.

'Thanks. Listen, I'm such an idiot—I didn't offer you anything to drink. What would you like? Tea? Soda? Juice? Wine?'

'I would love a glass of wine. Look at this view. How lovely it would be to sip some wine and sit here in the evenings ...'

I went back inside, opened a bottle of white wine, put on some music over the Bluetooth speakers in the garden, and returned with the wine and two wine glasses.

'Cheers,' I said, pouring the wine for both of us.

'White wine,' she said. 'You remember.'

I smiled. We sat in silence for a while.

'Looking forward to going back to Mumbai?' I said.

'Mentally prepared to go back would be the right term,' she said. 'I knew the day was coming. I enjoyed my time in Dubai ...'

'I liked spending time with you, whatever little time we did,' I said.

'Yes, same here,' she said. 'And I'm glad we're spending my last evening here together.'

'I don't know when I'll see you next,' I said.

'You'll be coming to Mumbai, right? For the deal-closing dinner?'

'Oh gosh, yes. I don't know how I got pulled into that,' I said.

'Come on, it'll be fun. Mudit's idea of doing it at the Crayon Club is great. Otherwise, Blackwater events are either at the Oberoi or the Taj. Luxurious and perfect, but boring.'

I laughed.

'You'll do a small stand-up set, right?' Payal said, pouring herself another glass of wine. I'd barely had two sips of mine.

'No, no,' I said, waving my hand. 'I can't do that. I haven't performed on stage in years. And you know it doesn't work like that. One must prepare.'

'So, prepare. You have almost a month to write and practise.'

'I don't know if I'll be able to.'

'Of course, you will.'

I shook my head.

'It'll be such a blast, Saket. Imagine, a unicorn founder who doesn't take himself so seriously. Does a stand-up set at his deal-closing dinner. It'll become the talk of the town. It'll go viral.'

I smiled. 'I don't know, Payal. I could also end up making a total ass of myself.'

'No, you won't. Plus, that's what's special about you. You don't take yourself so seriously. You take risks. And when you focus on something, you just go get it.'

I realized why I had fallen so hard for this girl. When she spoke like this, it cast a kind of magic on me. Tania, Paulina and a dozen other Ukrainian models with their perfect bodies couldn't cast an inch of that magic spell. Payal didn't look like those girls. She had a wrinkle or two at the corners of her eyes now. A few strands of grey hair too. Her face was fuller, and her body was slightly less slim than before. And yet, when she spoke like this, she did something to me that could only be described in one word—magic.

'Are you even listening to me, Mr Saket Khurana?' Payal snapped her fingers in front of my face.

'Sorry, what?'

'I said you should totally do a set at the dinner. Not just that, you should also get back to doing stand-up more regularly,' she said.

'Get back to stand-up?' I smirked. 'No way. That was the old me. That's all gone.'

'Didn't you just say that you're still the same person?' she said. Our eyes locked.

'Just because I'm drinking doesn't mean I'm not listening,' Payal said and poured herself a third glass of wine.

What's happening to this girl tonight?

'Why would I go back to comedy?' I said.

'Well, I saw you when you were doing comedy. How absorbed you were while writing your set. How in the moment you were when you got on stage. How exhilarated you felt when you killed it with the audience. You do important work now, I know. But back then you just seemed ... more alive.'

'I was younger. And carefree ... unaware of the realities of life.'

'Well, maybe it's better to remain unaware then,' Payal said, the wine giving her extra courage to speak her mind. 'And anyway, what do you have to worry about now? I know how much money you got paid. A gazillion billion dollars.'

'Not that much, but, yes, a lot,' I said.

'Then? What's stopping you now? You need to bring that passionate Saket back.'

I looked at her and sighed. 'Let me check if the food's ready,' I said and stood up.

'There we go again. Practical Saket again, deflecting topics at important moments,' Payal said, slamming her glass on the table.

'First of all, no more wine for you,' I said. 'And second, let me come right back from the kitchen.'

I went back into the house. Shanti didi had finished preparing the dinner.

'Please serve it to us in the garden,' I told her.

When I went back to the garden, Payal smiled at me a little sheepishly. She picked up the wine bottle and waved it. 'You were right. There is literally no more wine for Payal.'

'Payal,' I said, taking the empty wine bottle from her. 'What did you do? Do you realize you drank almost the whole bottle?'

'Did I? Weren't we sharing?' she said, slurring.

I shook my head.

Shanti didi came out with the food at that moment. She'd arranged everything on a large tray, and she left it on the rattan table.

'Let's eat,' I said to Payal.

'No,' she said. 'Can you get me some more wine first?'

'Absolutely not,' I said. 'Come, eat.' I took a spoonful of the dal chawal and held it close to her mouth. She leaned forward and ate the food.

'Now eat the rest of your food yourself,' I said.

'No.'

'Are you drunk?'

'Not drunk-drunk. Just happy high.'

'So, you can eat the dal chawal yourself. Here, have it,' I said, handing her the plate and picking up my own dinner.

We finished our meal in a few minutes, and Shanti didi came back to clear the table. The food helped Payal sober up somewhat.

'Thank you, that was the most wonderful dinner,' she said, coming and sitting next to me.

'It was just dal chawal,' I said.

'I loved it. I had homemade food after such a long time,' she said. Then she gently held my arm and rested her head on my shoulder. 'Is this okay?' she whispered.

I nodded, even though I was unsure.

'Do you want me to show you the rest of my house?' I said.

'Oh, sure,' Payal said.

We walked back into the house and took the stairs to the floor above. I showed her the rooms one by one.

'You live in such a huge house all by yourself,' she said. 'Doesn't it ever get lonely?'

'It's okay. I'm used to it.'

'Does Tania stay over sometimes?' she said.

I looked at her, surprised by her mention of Tania. 'Sometimes. Mostly not though,' I said. 'I prefer it that way.'

'How are things with her? Where is she tonight?'

'We haven't really been in touch for the last few days.'

'Oh, what happened?'

'Nothing. I just wanted a break,' I said as we reached the master bedroom.

'This is your room, I assume?'

'Yes,' I said and walked to the window to draw open the curtains.

'It's beautiful. You can see the beach and the water from here as well,' she said, walking up to me.

'Thank you,' I said.

She stepped closer and placed her hands on my shoulders.

'We can have sex,' she said.

'What?'

'You heard me. We can, if you want.'

'No, Payal,' I said, gently removing her hands. I turned away from her and looked out of the window.

She placed her palm on my back.

'What happened?' she said. 'You don't want to?'

'Why, Payal?' I said. 'You don't have to do this. Why did you even say it like that?'

'I want to make you happy. I feel like ...' she said and paused mid-sentence.

'Feel like what?'

'I feel like I let you down. Caused you pain. After I got married, I posted all those pictures on Instagram only to make my marriage appear normal. I never knew it would cause you to suffer even more. I feel terrible, Saket. You used to be this vibrant, fun, full-of-life guy. Now you're rich and successful, yes. But that original Saket, the Saket I loved, the one that everyone loved, is gone. And I feel guilty and responsible for it.'

'And having sex with me tonight will be some sort of compensation for all that? Is that why you drank all that wine? Like you did with Parimal? To make it happen?'

'No, not like that, Saket,' she said, her eyes welling up. 'I just wanted to make you happy. Even if for a night. To tell you I still care for you. Even if I made the biggest mistake of my life.'

I didn't respond. I went and sat on the bed. She came up to me, bent down and held my face in her hands.

'Like you said that day, I was only twenty-two. Forgive me, Saket,' she said.

'I do,' I said. 'I do forgive you, Payal. You don't have to have sex with me.'

'I want to. I want to do anything you want me to do tonight. Please.'

I remained quiet.

'Tell me what you want. Anything. Don't hold back,' she said. 'No judging. You want one of those old wild nights. Just tell me.'

'I don't.'

'Okay,' Payal said. 'That's fine. In that case, I should make my way back ...'

'I'll tell you what I want,' I said, interrupting her.

'Yes, please.'

'I don't want to have sex. I want you to sleep here tonight, though, next to me, holding me.'

She looked at me, surprised.

'That's all I want. One night with you. No sex ... just to sleep holding each other.'

'Okay,' she said after a pause. 'Sure.'

'Come, I'll give you some clothes to sleep in.'

She went to the bathroom to change, and came out wearing my oversized T-shirt.

I tucked her into bed, drew the curtains close and turned off the lights. I came and lay down next to her. I kissed her forehead. We held each other like we used to in my Bandra home twelve years ago. Within minutes, we fell asleep.

That night, for the first time ever, my ten-thousand-square-feet designer Palm Villa house felt like what it had never felt like before—home.

~

'Good morning,' I said when Payal walked down the stairs, rubbing her eyes, looking silly and cute in my oversized T-shirt.

I sat at the dining table, drinking a cup of black coffee and eating an egg-white omelette.

She yawned. 'What time is it?'

'Ten,' I said. 'Come, have some breakfast.'

'Ten? I've never slept in this late. Wait, I have a flight this evening, right?'

'Yes, it's at 7 p.m. Relax, you have time. Come.'

'I haven't even packed,' she said, sitting down across from me. 'I'm so hungover,' she said. She poured herself some coffee.

'Something to eat?' I said.

She shook her head, cupping the coffee mug with both her hands.

'Anything at all? Pancakes? Nutella toast? Poha?'

'Don't tempt me. I've already eaten so much on this trip,' she said, sipping her coffee.

'Shanti didi can make something for you.'

'Maybe later,' she said. 'You're the same, aren't you?'

'Same, as in?'

'Caring. Keen to feed me. Providing a million choices for breakfast.'

I smiled.

'Thank you though. It's sweet,' she said.

My phone rang. I had kept it on the dining table. Tania's face flashed on the screen. Payal glanced at my mobile for a second and looked away.

Damn, why do iPhones have this stupid feature?

I contemplated what to do with the call.

'What happened? It's okay. Take it,' Payal said.

I picked up the phone.

'Hi,' Tania said.

'Hi Tania. I'm in a meeting. Let me call you back, yeah? Thanks. Anyway, I'll be a lot more free after today, so let's speak then. Bye.'

I kept the phone down on the table.

'You didn't have to do this,' Payal said.

'Do what?'

'Telling me you're on a break with her or whatever,' Payal said.

'I am.'

She shrugged and took a sip of her coffee.

'Nothing to eat?' I said again.

'No. Also, I better get going soon.'

'I'll drop you to your hotel,' I said.

'I can order a cab, Saket. Please, stop doing this,' she said, her voice irritated.

'Doing what exactly?'

'Nothing,' she said and looked away.

'What's the matter, Payal?'

She took a few deep breaths. 'Why did you do this whole thing?' she said.

'What thing?'

'Making me spend the night. Sleeping together, holding each other.'

'You offered. You said you would do anything I ask you to.'

'Why couldn't we just have sex, Saket?'

'What's the issue?'

'This messes me up,' Payal said. 'I don't ever want to get in that zone again.'

'What zone?'

'That whole emotional, getting-the-feelings zone. I'm happy alone now. And you're happy in your world. We didn't have to do all this.'

'But having sex would've been okay?'

'Yes. Would've been easier to deal with than this.'

Could someone in the world please write a book on girl logic? I'd be the first buyer.

'How so?' I said, puzzled.

'I can't explain it. It would've been like this meaningless, crazy, one-night thing you did with your ex. But this spending the night cuddling, eating breakfast together, dropping me back ...' she said and shook her head. 'It's a good thing Tania called. Jolted me back to reality. Yes, you'll be a lot more free after today, after I'm gone.'

'Is that what all of this is about? Listen, I was just ... Forget about Tania, please. She's not important.'

'I'll finish my coffee and leave,' Payal said, taking a bigger sip.

'We cool?'

She nodded.

'I didn't have sex with you because I was afraid,' I said.

'Afraid of what?' she said, squinting her eyes.

'I was afraid that if we did it, I would get super attached to you again. That whole emotional, catching-feelings bit ... You have that power over me ...'

'Power?'

'I can't explain it. I don't want to get trapped again ...'

'Trapped?'

'I can't find the right words. But see, whatever it is, I'm functioning decently in my life now. I have a system that works. I don't want to get trapped in another decade of pain for a few moments of pleasure. It's like I fell into a ditch. And it took me ten years to crawl out of it. I've barely just managed to stand up, so ...'

'So, you're worried I'll push you back into the ditch again? Or wait, am *I* the ditch?'

'No, not like that ...'

'And this "trap" you're referring to, that's me, isn't it? The recently divorced woman who obviously has nothing better to do in life now than to cling on to you,' she said.

'No, not like that, Payal. What are you even saying?'

'Exactly like that. You need to be careful, after all. Anyway,' she said, 'why did you ask me to stay over then?'

'Because I still care for you. You had a rough divorce. You dealt with it all alone. You've been through a lot. I wanted to be there for you.'

'Oh?' Payal smirked. 'So, you took *pity* on me? Thank you so much, Saket. Thank you for being there for this lonely divorced girl, while also carefully navigating the situation and not having sex with her to make sure that you don't get trapped. Or fall into a ditch. I'm so grateful.'

Ah, the sarcasm queen was back.

'Look, I'm saying this all wrong. I wanted to feel close to you too—'

'But within limits.'

'I don't know what is with you. Taking everything the wrong way. Eat something. You're hungover and cranky.'

'Yes, the problem is me—lonely, divorced, hungover, cranky, a trap, a ditch. Anything else to add to that list?'

'Payal, stop it. What happened to you? Was it Tania's call?'

'I finally woke up and came to my senses, I guess,' Payal said. 'Anyway, thanks for all the support on the deal. And for showing me around Dubai. But now the assignment is over. I'll go change and order myself a cab. You're free to return to your calls and your decently functioning lifestyle or whatever.'

Before I could try to stop her, Payal ran up the stairs. She came back down in ten minutes, having changed into her clothes. The Uber she'd booked had already arrived at the porch.

'Take care, Saket. It was nice working with you,' she said, getting into the cab.

'We'll be in touch, right?' I said.

'What for?' she said as the car drove away.

~

'Hi, reached Mumbai okay?' I sent Payal a message.

She didn't reply for a day.

'How are you doing, Payal? How is Mumbai treating you?' I sent another one.

No reply for two days. The same fate awaited the next three messages that I sent to her over the week. I saw her online on WhatsApp several times. But she never responded to me. Ghosting—the new-age equivalent of 'I am not interested'—is silent, but it stings.

I figured she wanted to be left alone. I also knew why. Instead of breakfast, I'd put both my feet in my mouth that day.

I decided to let things be for a while, hoping that the remaining paperwork for the deal would give me a legitimate reason to speak to Payal. The opportunity came one week later.

My legal team wanted a document from Blackwater: a list of authorized signatories from Blackwater who could sign off on the CloudX deal. It was a small technical requirement. I could've asked someone in my office to get it. However, I offered to call Blackwater instead. I said it would make them send it across faster.

'Hi, free to talk on a call? It's work-related,' I messaged Payal.

'Hi, sure,' she replied immediately.

Okay, so she can be prompt in her replies.

'Hi,' Payal said as she picked up my video call, looking surprised.

'Hi,' I said and smiled as our eyes met on the screen.

'Video call?' she said.

'Yeah, I thought a face-to-face chat is always better. Is that okay?' I said.

'Yeah, sure. Am in office though. Let me wear my AirPods,' she said. She put the earplugs on. 'Okay, we can talk now. What's up?'

'My legal team needs a Blackwater-authorized signatories document.'

'Oh? Okay. I'm sure our legal team could've sent that request to your legal team. Anyway, I'll arrange it.' She typed something on her laptop.

'Thanks, no rush ...' I said.

'Okay.'

'How are you?' I said.

'I'm good. Busy with work. All this deal-closing stuff.'

'I didn't mean in terms of work. I meant how are you otherwise, in life?'

Payal looked at me in silence.

'You didn't reply to my messages,' I said.

'I did, just now, before you called. For any work-related stuff, I'm here.'

'Payal, you're behaving exactly like I did during that Bosporus lunch.'

Payal let out a loud sigh.

'Really, how are you? How's life?' I said.

'Am a bit stressed out, dealing with some stuff.'

'Like what?'

She pondered over whether she should share more with me. She spoke after a pause, 'Dad just got dragged into a case.'

'What case?'

'Parimal and Dad. Parimal is contesting in court, for his stake in Dad's business.'

'It is your dad's business.'

'Yes, but Dad trusted him a lot. He'd assigned him the power of attorney in the past. Anyway, it's all a mess. I'm helping Dad get good legal advice, prepare the necessary documents, etc.'

'Sorry to hear that,' I said. 'May I help in any way?'

'No, Saket,' she said, her voice firm. 'It's being handled.'

'Okay. I was just trying to—'

'I can handle my stuff. As a divorced, vulnerable woman, I do pretty okay. Decently functional.'

'Ouch, someone hasn't forgotten. Payal, about tha—'

'If I can close a three-and-a-half-billion-dollar deal for my company, I can handle my life on my own. I don't need to cling to anyone.'

'I know, Payal. Can we forget about that day now?'

'I have. Anything else?'

'Yes. I think of you sometimes. About the time we spent in Dubai.'

'I thought this was a work call?'

'All right, fine. Speaking of work, I'm looking forward to coming to Mumbai, for the closing dinner.'

'Yes, it's in two weeks, right?'

'Yeah. And as you wanted, I might just do the comedy act. I've started preparing for it.'

'I didn't *want* you to do it. It was just a suggestion. It's up to you. You don't have to. The closing dinner will happen either way.'

'Why are you being so curt?'

'Curt? No. I'm in office, working, that's all.'

'Right. Also, I told Tania I definitely need a break. I need to figure out what I want.'

'Cool. Yeah, am sure you'll figure things out. Maybe get someone even younger and prettier. A famous model perhaps?'

'Why are you talking to me like this?'

'Like what? It's true. You can afford anything now, isn't it? If something doesn't work for you, you can simply change it.'

'That's not what I meant.'

'Do whatever makes you happy, really. Anyway, I'll have the authorized signatory list sent today,' she said before ending the call.

PART III
MUMBAI

'You didn't have to come to the airport yourself, Neeraj,' I said, 'that too so late.'

Mudit and I were in Neeraj's BMW on our way from the Mumbai airport to the St. Regis Hotel in Lower Parel.

'That's not a problem, guys,' Neeraj said. 'We're all so excited for the closing night. The Crayon Club idea was a real winner. Everyone loved it.'

'I just felt it would be different,' Mudit said.

'Yes, in fact, we've merged our annual Blackwater Family Day with the event,' Neeraj said.

'Family day?' I said, watching the road outside as the car zipped through the Western Express Highway in the middle of the night.

'Yes, we have an annual bring-your-family-to-work day at Blackwater. CloudX has it as well. We just combined it with this event.'

'Okay,' I said. 'So?'

'So, we thought why not have some people from Blackwater and CloudX bring their families to this dinner? They'll have fun and also see what a deal closing looks like.'

'Families? At a deal closing?' Mudit said.

'Only a few select senior people from Blackwater and CloudX can bring them. You see, it'll help with the press,' Neeraj said.

'How?' I said. 'And why do you even need the press?'

'Blackwater and other private equity firms have this negative, cold, capitalist image. We don't want that when the public, media or the government thinks of us. We want to show everyone that the people who work in firms like ours are humans too.'

'Are you though?' Mudit said.

Neeraj laughed. The car turned onto the Bandra–Worli Sea Link.

'What about confidential information?' I said.

'There's none. The deal is public. We're mainly inviting business media. As I told you earlier, it's a PR event,' Neeraj said. 'But you sound concerned. All okay?'

'Yeah, am fine,' I said. 'I just thought I'll do a little stand-up act. Now with families coming in, I don't know …'

'Why? Please do it,' Neeraj said. 'It'll be a hit. We also have a music band performing later. It'll be a chill evening, trust me. Just come and have fun.'

'Let me think about it,' I said, looking out of the window. 'Wow, Mumbai has changed. What's that bridge?'

'That's the new connector to the coastal road. It can take you to South Mumbai in minutes,' Neeraj said.

~

'Why were you getting so hassled, bro?' Mudit said to me in the lift as he and I went up to our rooms at the St. Regis.

'About what?'

'About the dinner.'

'What's with this family-day business they've combined the event with?'

'It's okay. Our deal is the most high-profile one they've ever done. They want to flex a little. Anyway, so what if some families are there? We're just here to have fun, right?'

'I'd finally decided to do a small comedy set. Prepared for it also.'

'So? Do it. Who cares?'

'You do know who'll be there, right?'

'Who?' Mudit said.

'Payal's parents.'

Mudit looked at me and burst out laughing. Even after the lift door opened on the thirtieth floor and both of us walked down the corridor towards our adjacent rooms, he continued to laugh.

'What's so funny, Mudit?'

'That you still care about those uptight Ghatkopar people. Gosh, what a night that was no? Ending at the police station. Anyway, so what? Say whatever you want to. Make the most inappropriate jokes.'

'I can't. It's a formal deal-closing dinner anyway.'

'Dude, you're the hero of the dinner. You did a multi-billion-dollar deal. They're just there as guests. Stop getting intimidated by them.'

I sighed.

'It's three in the morning,' Mudit said as we reached our rooms. 'I'm going to crash. How about you?'

'I'll stay up a bit. May have to modify my act.'

'At this hour?'

'Yes.'

'Seriously? For those old fogeys? Why? And who knows, maybe Payal won't even bring them. You should just sleep, and take it easy.'

'I can't. You're the one who got me into this in the first place.'

'Watching you nervous is the best comedy. Good night, bro,' Mudit chuckled as he closed the door on my face.

~

'Cake? What's this? A birthday party?' I said to Mudit.

'Everything is to create visuals for the media. Helps with PR, you see,' Mudit said.

We stood in the Crayon Club bar area, which had been transformed for the dinner. The bar stools and chairs had all been removed, creating a large, open space. A small stage had been set up for the cake-cutting ceremony. Around fifty guests had already arrived, and more were trickling in.

The mini stage had a backdrop of the Blackwater, CloudX and SecurityNet logos. The cake itself was in the shape of the CloudX and SecurityNet logos, fused into one.

'Congratulations again,' Neeraj said, walking up to us.

Waiters carried trays with glasses filled with champagne. Neeraj passed a glass to Mudit and me.

One of the auditorium doors connected to the bar was open. I could see the seats and the performance stage inside. I would be performing here after more than a decade. My heart began to beat fast.

'Money reached the bank?' Neeraj said, clinking his glass against mine.

'It did,' I said. 'Three days ago. Thank you.'

'My pleasure,' Neeraj said.

We were still talking when I noticed Payal arrive. She wore a navy-blue fitted dress with a white-gold necklace and matching earrings. She looked feminine yet formal at the same time. She stopped at the entrance and looked back, as if waiting for someone. A second later, her parents joined her as well. They looked considerably older, although just as uptight. I watched as they refused the various snacks the waiters offered them. Nothing Jain-friendly, you see.

Good, let them go home hungry.

I shifted a little, wanting to avoid making eye contact with Payal, and particularly her parents. Keeping my back towards the Jains, I forced myself to engage in a boring conversation with Neeraj about India's expected GDP growth rate and its impact on cloud server space demand.

'Hi Saket,' Payal said, startling me as she came up behind me.

'Oh hey, hi,' I said, turning around.

'Mom, Dad, this is Saket. He founded SecurityNet, the company CloudX just bought,' Payal said, reintroducing me to her parents.

Her parents looked dumbfounded.

Okay, she hadn't told them I would be here. Otherwise, they wouldn't have come.

'Hello,' Payal's father said in a meek, mouse-like voice.

Payal's mother just did a namaste.

'That's Mudit. And you've met Neeraj, my boss, before,' Payal said to her parents.

'The way Payal is cracking deals, Mr Jain, she'll soon be my boss,' Neeraj said and laughed at his own joke.

Payal's parents didn't react. They seemed to be in complete shock, wondering what to do next. Neither the food, nor the people, were to their liking. Yet, it was their daughter's workplace event.

'Remember me, Uncle? We met once, at your house. Outside your house, rather,' Mudit said, with the sole intention of needling Payal's father.

'Hello, Mudit,' Payal's father said, his voice subdued.

'You guys know each other?' Neeraj said.

'Not really,' I said quickly to ride over the awkwardness.

'Well, Mr and Mrs Jain, Saket Khurana is the man of the night. He's the founder of the company we just bought, for three and a half billion dollars.'

I hate showing off. However, that flabbergasted look on Payal's parents' faces made my day. It made all the hard work that had gone into creating SecurityNet worth it.

'Congratulations,' Anand said, coughing a little.

'Did you eat anything?' Neeraj said to Payal's parents.

'They are Jain. We'll need some special snacks for them,' I said.

Payal's father looked at me, surprised.

'I'll go arrange that,' Neeraj said. 'Meanwhile, Mudit and Saket, can you guys make your way to the stage, please? Let's cut the cake.'

∼

'Relax, bro,' Mudit said. 'You're palpitating over a seven-minute act? You just sold a multi-billion-dollar company.'

I took deep breaths. Mudit and I were backstage, in the tiny area where I'd waited a hundred times during my stand-up days. I peeped out. The small auditorium was filling up with people.

We had finished all the formalities. We had cut the cake, made a toast, done a few media interviews and taken group photographs with the senior management of Blackwater, CloudX and SecurityNet. After that, Neeraj had asked everyone to move to the auditorium for 'the founder of SecurityNet to showcase his other hidden talent—stand-up comedy'. Except that my 'hidden talent' had rusted.

'Bro, now it's just for fun. It's not your career anymore,' Mudit said. 'It's a flex. A unicorn founder doing stand-up comedy. The media will love it. You'll get famous.'

'I don't want to be famous.'

'Too late for that,' Mudit said. 'All the business papers will carry your picture tomorrow.'

'Oh dear.' I exhaled.

'Kill it,' said Mudit.

~

As I walked onto the stage, the crowd burst into applause. The spotlight shone in my eyes. A flood of memories came rushing back. My stand-up days, the nervousness before my first act and the noise my heart made. For a moment, it felt like another Saturday night from twelve years ago.

I scanned the crowd. Blackwater employees sat with their families, mostly their spouses or parents, and some teenage kids. A few people from CloudX and SecurityNet were there as well. I spotted Payal sitting in the fourth row, along with her parents.

'Hello everyone, how's it going?' I said.

'Great,' two young people said in unison from the front row.

'I'm doing great too. Thanks to you guys at Blackwater and CloudX. You guys sent me so much money, I don't have to do any real work anymore. That's why am here, doing comedy,' I said.

A few people sniggered in the audience.

'But seriously, my friend Mudit here, he told me, we're rich now. We must do some rich-people things. I have no idea what rich people do. I asked him, what can we do? And he's like, let's go to the spa. So, this morning, the two of us went to the spa, in the St. Regis Hotel, where we're staying, to get a Kerala Ayurvedic massage. Anybody here who's done that?'

A few people in the audience raised their hands.

'I'd never done it before,' I said. 'I went there. They made me lie down on this narrow bed, and then they poured oil all over me. Like, they soak you in a drum of oil. And I'm like, what's this? Are they going to deep-fry me? Give me a tadka?'

A few people laughed. Sitting in the first row, Mudit smiled when I looked at him.

I continued, 'It's nice to be rich though. My partner, Mudit, and I can finally travel business class. Even though we don't really have a business anymore,' I said, pointing at Mudit. He waved sheepishly as people laughed.

'No, seriously. I remember the early days of the company. If Mudit and I had to fly somewhere for work, we would opt for the lowest, cheapest seats available. Like, we wanted a class *lower* than economy. There should be one for people like us, isn't it? Those who want to save, no matter the flying conditions. Maybe call it survival class? Okay wait, that exists. It's called Indigo, isn't it?'

People clapped and laughed in the audience. Lot of Indigo pain points, I guess.

'Okay, guys, that was just a joke, no offence to Indigo. Anyway, when SecurityNet started to do better, Mudit and I said, "We're senior management. We should fly better." But we couldn't afford business class, not just yet. So, we flew this new class—premium economy. Wait, what? What does *premium economy* mean? Is it premium? Or is it economy? Make up your mind, guys. Who the hell got paid to come up with this name? Premium or economy? How can you be both?'

The crowd laughed. Mudit gave me a thumbs-up.

'Anyway, our company is called SecurityNet. Well, it's no longer our company, technically. You guys bought it, it's your problem now,' I said.

Neeraj laughed, though I could see a hint of worry on his face.

'Anyway, we do cybersecurity. Nobody understands what that is, right? We're like the guys who make the annoying pick-all-the-traffic-lights-in-the-picture tests. Sometimes, we ask that question even when there are no traffic lights in the picture. Yeah, we like to mess with people like that.'

The CloudX and SecurityNet teams laughed the most at this joke.

'Honestly, though, I've never understood those CAPTCHA things. You go to buy a train ticket. And the website goes, "Prove you're not a robot." Dude, what is that supposed to mean? Why would a robot want to buy a train ticket in the first place? It can just go for free, as baggage, right?'

Everyone in the audience laughed, except for one elderly couple: Mr and Mrs Grumpy Jain, who remained as glum as ever.

'Business class and all is fine, but speaking of train tickets, I miss Indian trains. As a child, I used to travel on trains with my family. India's train culture is unique. There are some products that only exist for trains. Like chains, to tie up your luggage to the berth. Yes, my mother used to love chaining up her suitcases. Someone might steal her nighties, you see.'

People laughed uncontrollably at this joke. I could see Payal laughing as well.

'But I remember this one time, when she'd chained and locked everything, all the suitcases, and then she lost the keys, and when Chandigarh station came …' I paused strategically. The audience, imagining the rest, spilled into laughter.

'Yes, we had seven minutes to break two locks and get out at Chandigarh,' I said. 'Anyway, I could go on with this comedy act,' I said, 'but who needs comedy, when your own life has been the biggest joke.'

A few in the audience laughed, expecting another routine.

'I just want to share something with you guys, something I've never shared in public …' I said, my tone serious.

The audience sat up straighter and looked at each other, wondering what was going on.

'This venue,' I said, 'has a lot of meaning for me. Twelve years ago, I left my job in the US and came here to Mumbai. My marriage had also ended. I decided to have a fresh start. Mudit, my best friend, gave me a chance to do stand-up comedy here. Right on this stage. And here I am today, twelve long years later, celebrating something else. With him.'

The audience clapped.

'There's been a lot of career growth in the last twelve years. And thanks to you guys, now I have a ton of money I don't even know what to do with. But I think the biggest growth for me isn't all that. It's the fact that I finally have the courage to be myself at forty-five, something I didn't have at thirty-three. Which is why I can stand here and say what I want to today.'

The entire audience listened with full attention.

'You see, twelve years ago, when I did my first-ever act here—which was terrible, by the way—I met someone. Right here, in the audience. She was twenty-one, I was thirty-three ...'

I looked at Payal. Even in the dim lighting, I could see that her face had turned white. She looked terrified of what I was going to say next.

'Yes, I know some of you will judge me. Cradle snatcher, too much age difference, whatever. At some level, even I did. I had just come off a divorce. People around me advised me this was not going to work long-term. That I was just living out some younger-girl fantasy. That this was just a rebound. It was lust, not love.'

I saw Payal's parents shift in their seats. They wanted to leave. Payal gestured to them to stay seated.

'Our communities didn't match either. And I met her parents in the most awkward way possible. Yeah, I was naked. I had to use a teddy bear to cover my most important bits.'

The audience gasped. Some laughed.

'I told you, my life itself is a comedy. Then again, in retrospect, everything is, isn't it?' I said.

Payal's father stood up.

'Sit down, Uncle, I'll only be two more minutes. I promise,' I said.

The audience laughed, unaware of who the man was. Payal's father hesitated, but then he sat down.

'Anyway, things didn't work out between her and me,' I said. 'I tried to fight for it. But it still didn't work out. She married someone else.'

The audience sighed collectively.

'And I thought, okay, it's just a break-up. I'll get over it. That's what they say on Instagram, isn't it? All those reels that say yes, you will heal. You'll move on. You need to focus on yourself. Get busy. I did all that. I moved. Countries, not cities. I got busy. And that's how SecurityNet was born.'

A few in the audience nodded.

'But no matter how busy I kept myself, I couldn't forget her. It was like she'd made some permanent grooves in my head. Whatever I did, wherever I went, forget a day, not even a few hours passed without me thinking of her.'

Pindrop silence in the audience.

'In all this, I thought, at least she's happy. As it turned out, she wasn't. It didn't work out for her either. Which is when I finally realized that maybe we were meant to be. Twelve years' age difference or whatever. Sometimes, people are just meant to be.'

The audience remained quiet. Payal looked emotional.

'One question has always puzzled me. When do you know it's love? How do you know it's not just an intense attraction,

12 Years: My Messed-Up Love Story

an infatuation? How does one figure out that this person is "The One"? The problem is, there is no easy way, no test to take to find out. You can't summarize it in an Instagram reel. Sometimes, only time will tell you. When you cannot live without them. Or even if you do, it's not the same life. When nobody else comes even close to making you feel the way you do when you're around them. For a year, then another year and, in my case, twelve years ...'

A few audience members nodded.

'But I'll tell you how I finally figured this out. Three days ago, you guys sent me the biggest bank transfer I'd ever seen in my life. That single amount had more zeros than a phone number. Yes, the moment that money-has-been-credited message popped up on my phone was quite something. It made me feel happy, sure. For about half an hour. After that, it was just back to normal life. Then at night, I thought about the other moments of my life that have made me happy. When was I the happiest? Most of those moments didn't involve major sums of money.

'Those moments were about taking a walk at night in Bandstand, sitting on the window ledge of my tiny Bandra apartment. It was having tea and Maggi at four in the morning on the beach. It was clearing up the dining table after dinner, visiting the temple. All normal, regular things, right? But they were the most special moments of my life. Because they all had one thing in common—she was with me, in every single one of them.

'And that's when I realized that she is The One. She's the one without whom I'm incomplete. The person without whom there is a life, but it's a life without joy. She's the one who can make even grocery shopping fun. I'd rather have cheap Maggi on the beach with her than dine without her in a fancy Michelin-star restaurant. Her mere presence gives me joy like no amount of money could. Yes, she's the one. Because, ultimately, her happiness automatically creates my happiness.'

I stopped for a second because I was choking up.

'I should've fought for her more,' I continued. 'I should've believed in myself and trusted my feelings. I shouldn't have given up. I gave up because I felt that maybe all the others around us were right. I gave up because I was afraid. Of marriage, commitment, society, everything.'

I cleared my throat. The audience waited before I spoke again.

'But I'll tell you the real comedy. It just so happened that life reconnected us. She came back into my life. After twelve years. She wasn't married anymore. Neither am I. Talk about God giving you a second chance. But you know what I did? I blew it this time too. I said mean things. I didn't understand her feelings. I was stupid. I didn't know what I wanted. I messed it up, again! I don't know why, when it comes to me and my love story, it always gets messed up.'

The crowd was hanging on to my every word. I paused and smirked before I spoke again.

'So, yes, that's it, guys. The biggest joke in my stand-up act is me.'

The audience sat in their seats in silence, stunned and confused by what I had said.

Payal stood up. Our eyes met.

It took a few seconds for the audience to make the connection. They figured out Payal was the girl I was talking about. Everyone shifted in their seats, turning at various angles to get a good look at her. Payal's father tugged at her elbow to make her sit back down. She shrugged his hand off.

The audience's eyes remained glued to Payal, wondering what she would do next.

She walked sideways, even as people in her row folded their legs in to enable her to come out to the aisle. She walked up to the stage.

We stood facing each other. The crowd made no sound.

Payal held the microphone in front of me and fumbled to find the switch. She turned it off. Only she and I could hear each other now. The audience could only see us.

She shook her head and smiled. We talked to each other in whispers.

'What?'

'Saket, if this is somehow a part of your act, and if all this ends in a prank or a joke, I'll kill you,' she said.

'No, obviously not,' I said and smiled, even as I teared up. 'I did all this preparation for weeks.'

'Okay, fine then,' she said.

'I'm sorry. I messed it up again.'

'No, you didn't mess it up,' Payal said, her eyes filling with tears.

'Be mine, forever? Will you?'

'I always was,' she said, not missing a beat.

We looked at the audience. They watched us in silence, with full concentration, as if watching a suspense movie, on mute.

'What do we do next?' she said.

'I don't know. Maybe we should kiss?'

'In front of everyone? My parents are here. My colleagues are here.'

'That's true.'

'I don't really care though,' Payal said.

'Okay, then,' I said, and took a step closer to her.

She stepped forward as well.

'But wait, the media is also here,' I said. 'This will be in the papers tomorrow.'

'That's also true.'

'You know what? I don't really care either,' I said.

'The audience is waiting, Saket,' Payal said. 'Either we leave the stage or—'

Before she could finish, I bent forward and planted a big kiss on her.

Whistles. Hoots. Cheers. The crowd went into a frenzy as we continued to kiss. Everyone apart from two people, of course—Mr and Mrs Grumpy Jain. The two Jains were upset and wanted to leave. However, the crowd got to its feet and started to clap, making it difficult for them to exit.

I switched on the mic and spoke to the audience.

'Sorry to have cut the sound, guys, but as you must've already figured, she said yes.'

Another round of laughter, applause, cheers and whistles followed.

Payal hugged me. She whispered, 'You didn't have to be this dramatic.'

'We've had a messed-up love story. Let us at least have a spectacular ending,' I whispered back.

EPILOGUE

Six years later ...

Payal, Kabir and I sat in the office of Rachel McDougal, the admissions officer at Dubai World School, Emirates Hills. Reading glasses perched on her nose, she went through the forms we had submitted for Kabir's admission.

'All right, I have all the documents in place here. Hopefully, Kabir can join us soon.'

'Thank you, ma'am,' I said.

'Your son is three years old?' Rachel said.

'I'm almost four,' Kabir said.

'That's nice,' Rachel said. 'You're going to be a big boy soon.'

'Yes, my birthday is in two months,' Kabir said.

'Mr and Mrs Khurana, you have a confident child,' Rachel said.

'Thank you,' Payal said.

'He gets that from his mother,' I said.

Payal and I smiled at each other.

Rachel noticed us looking at each other and seemed amused. She turned to Kabir.

'Kabir, what do you like to do? Sing? Dance? Play sports?' she said.

'I like to tell jokes,' Kabir said.

'What?' Rachel looked a little amused and surprised.

'Would you like to hear a joke?' Kabir said.

'Sure,' Rachel said and smiled.

'Why did the math book look so sad?' Kabir said.

'Why?' Rachel said, in a curious tone.

'Because it had so many problems,' Kabir said with a cheeky grin.

Everyone laughed.

'One more?' Kabir said.

'All right,' Rachel said.

'What did the ocean say to the beach?'

'What?' Rachel said.

'Nothing, it just waved.'

Rachel burst out laughing. 'You're very funny, Kabir,' she said.

'That, he gets from his dad,' said Payal, squeezing my hand.

ACKNOWLEDGEMENTS

Every book is a journey, and no journey is possible without companions.

My gratitude to Shinie Antony—my editor, friend and first reader for over two decades. She has stood by me through every draft and every doubt, with wisdom and unwavering faith. Her guidance has been nothing short of a blessing.

To my wonderful group of early readers—Bhakti Bhat, Jatin Jain, Virali Jain, Monil Kotak, Palak Panchamia and others—thank you for lending your sharp eyes and generous hearts to this manuscript. Your suggestions made the book stronger. Your encouragement made me stronger.

To the incredible team at HarperCollins—the editors who believed in *12 Years*, and the tireless marketing, sales, social media and production teams who worked with such passion. My gratitude also extends to the unsung heroes—the delivery partners who carry books to readers' homes, and the salespeople in bookstores, airports and train stations who put my stories into people's hands. You are all a part of this journey.

To my readers and followers across Facebook, Instagram, Twitter, Threads and YouTube—thank you for listening, for questioning, for cheering and for even scolding sometimes. In your voices, I find my motivation to keep writing.

Finally, to my family, my constant pillars of strength: my mother, Rekha Bhagat; my wife, Anusha Bhagat; my children, Shyam and Ishaan; my brother, Ketan, and nephew, Rian; my in-laws, Suryanarayan Annaswamy and Kalpana Suryanarayan; my brother-in-law, Anand, my sister-in-law, Poornima, and their children, Ananya and Karan. Thank you all for being there, always. This book carries a part of each one of you.

ABOUT THE AUTHOR

Chetan Bhagat is one of India's most acclaimed contemporary authors, with fourteen bestselling books to his credit. He is the author of ten blockbuster novels—*Five Point Someone, One Night @ the Call Center, The 3 Mistakes of My Life, 2 States, Revolution 2020, Half Girlfriend, One Indian Girl, The Girl in Room 105, One Arranged Murder* and *400 Days*—and four successful non-fiction titles—*What Young India Wants, Making India Awesome, India Positive* and *11 Rules for Life*. Chetan's books have remained bestsellers since their release. Many of his novels have been adapted into successful Bollywood films such as *3 Idiots, 2 States, Kai Po Che* and *Half Girlfriend*.

The New York Times called him the 'the biggest-selling English-language novelist in India's history'. *Time* magazine recognized him amongst the '100 most influential people in the world', while Fast Company, USA, listed him as one of the world's '100 most creative people in business'. Chetan writes columns for leading English and Hindi newspapers, focusing on youth and national development issues. He is also a motivational speaker, screenplay writer, YouTuber and podcaster.

Chetan quit his international investment-banking career in 2009 to dedicate his time entirely to writing and driving positive change in the country.

Chetan studied at IIT Delhi and IIM Ahmedabad. He is married to Anusha, an ex-classmate from IIMA, and they have twin boys, Shyam and Ishaan.

BESTSELLERS BY CHETAN BHAGAT

FICTION

400 Days

Twelve-year-old Siya has been missing for nine months. It's a cold case, but Keshav wants to help his mother, Alia, who refuses to give up.

'My daughter Siya was kidnapped. Nine months ago,' Alia said. The police had given up. They called it a cold case. Even the rest of her family had stopped searching. Alia wouldn't stop looking, though. She wanted to know if I could help her.

Hi, I am Keshav Rajpurohit and I am a disappointment to everyone around me. I live with my parents, who keep telling me how I should:

a) get married,
b) focus on my IPS exams,
c) meet more people and
d) close my detective agency.

But Alia Arora, neighbour and ex-model, wanted my help. And I couldn't take my eyes off her face ... I mean ... her case.

Welcome to *400 Days*. A mystery and romance story like no other. An unputdownable tale of suspense, human relationships, love, friendship, the crazy world we live in and, above all, a mother's determination to never give up.

From India's highest-selling author comes a page-turner that will not only keep you glued to the story but also touch you deeply.

One Arranged Murder

'Ever since you found Prerna, I lost my best friend' is what I told Saurabh.

Hi, this is Keshav, and Saurabh, my best friend, flatmate, colleague and business partner, won't talk to me. Because I made fun of him and his fiancé.

Saurabh and Prerna will be getting married soon. It is an arranged marriage. However, there is more cheesy romance between them than any love-marriage couple.

On Karva Chauth, she fasted for him. She didn't eat all day. In the evening, she called him and waited on the terrace for the moon and for Saurabh to break her fast. Excited, Saurabh ran up the steps of her three-storey house. But when he reached …

Welcome to *One Arranged Murder*, an unputdownable thriller from India's highest-selling author. A story about love, friendship, family and crime. It will keep you entertained and hooked right till the end.

The Girl in Room 105: An Unlove Story

Hi, I'm Keshav, and my life is screwed. I hate my job and my girlfriend left me.

Ah, the beautiful Zara. Zara is from Kashmir. She is a Muslim. And did I tell you my family is a bit, well, traditional? Anyway, leave that.

Zara and I broke up four years ago. She moved on in life. I didn't. I drank every night to forget her. I called, messaged, and stalked her on social media. She just ignored me.

However, that night, on the eve of her birthday, Zara messaged me. She called me over, like old times, to her hostel room 105. I shouldn't have gone, but I did … and my life changed forever.

This is not a love story. It is an unlove story.

From the author of *Five Point Someone* and *2 States*, comes a fast-paced, funny and unputdownable thriller about obsessive love and finding purpose in life against the backdrop of contemporary India.

NON-FICTION

India Positive: Simple Takes on India's Burning Issues

Does it make any difference to the ordinary citizen which party is in power? Whether it's a majority or a coalition?

What can we do to better job prospects for India's youth?

How can we create a more equal society?

How do we create more world-class educational institutes?

What can we do about social media warriors and trolls?

In *India Positive*, bestselling author and columnist Chetan Bhagat brings together essays that work as a manifesto for change. Examining a gamut of subjects—from education to employment, from GST to infrastructure, from corruption to casteism—Bhagat reflects on what we can do right in order to move forward and become a truly modern, progressive country. He expresses in these pages his belief that, if we want to see reform, we—as citizens—need to be the solution. If our country is to shine, Bhagat says, we need to stand up and be 'India Positive Citizens'.

In a world ridden with negativity, these simply written, perceptive and solution-driven essays are a must-read for anyone invested in the present and future of India.

11 Rules for Life: Secrets to Level Up

MANDATORY READING FOR ALL INDIANS.

One summer afternoon, Viraj, a food delivery guy, brings lunch for an author named Chetan. He is late and appears to be in distress. When Chetan asks him what the matter is, Viraj breaks down.

'I hate my life. My career is going nowhere. My girlfriend left me. I have no future,' he says.

The author offers Viraj a deal. 'I can fix this for you. Come back every day, when I order lunch. Each day, I will tell you one secret I've learnt about life.'

Welcome to *11 Rules for Life*, a no-holds-barred book that will transform your life.

In his most personal book yet, Chetan draws on his failures and triumphs, his many conversations with high achievers from all walks of life and over two decades as a celebrated motivational speaker.

Written in the inimitable style that has made Chetan one of India's top-selling writers, this inspiring, easy-to-read and straight-talking guide will help you rewire your brain for success in today's ultra-competitive and unfair world.

Ready to live your best life? If one book can change your life, this is it.

All these titles are also available in Hindi.

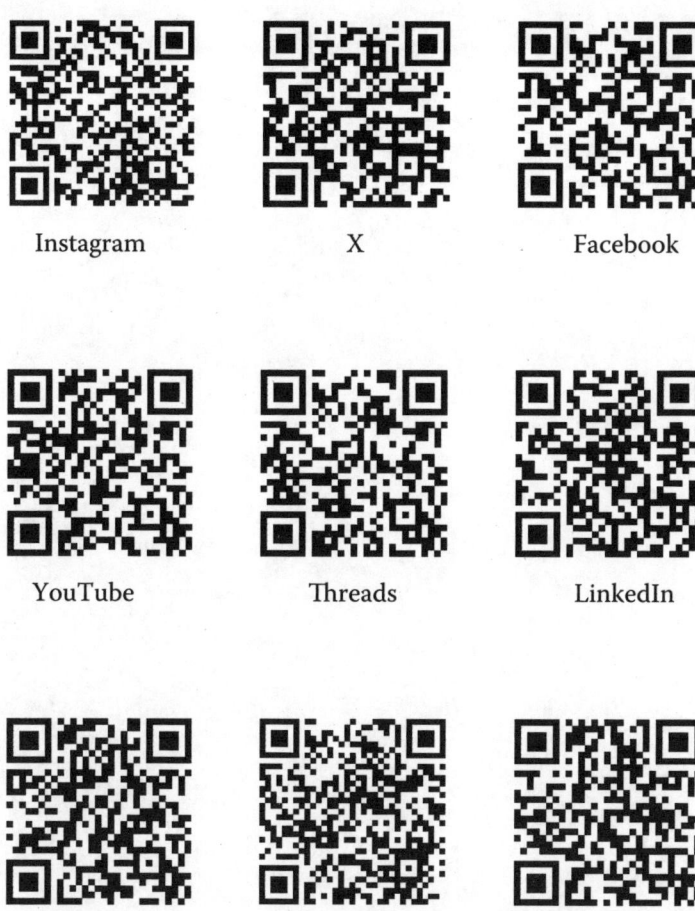

HarperCollins *Publishers* India

At HarperCollins India, we believe in telling the best stories and finding the widest readership for our books in every format possible. We started publishing in 1992; a great deal has changed since then, but what has remained constant is the passion with which our authors write their books, the love with which readers receive them, and the sheer joy and excitement that we as publishers feel in being a part of the publishing process.

Over the years, we've had the pleasure of publishing some of the finest writing from the subcontinent and around the world, including several award-winning titles and some of the biggest bestsellers in India's publishing history. But nothing has meant more to us than the fact that millions of people have read the books we published, and that somewhere, a book of ours might have made a difference.

As we look to the future, we go back to that one word— a word which has been a driving force for us all these years.

Read.